Eliza Cruger

Regina, and other Poems

Eliza Cruger

Regina, and other Poems

ISBN/EAN: 9783743300972

Manufactured in Europe, USA, Canada, Australia, Japa

Cover: Foto ©Raphael Reischuk / pixelio.de

Manufactured and distributed by brebook publishing software
(www.brebook.com)

Eliza Cruger

Regina, and other Poems

REGINA,

AND OTHER POEMS.

BY

ELIZA CRUGER.

As some far-flowing river glideth free
With censeless motion to the sounding sea,
While thousand lesser streams their tribute pay,
Swelling the volume of that mighty wave;
So move, O Song, upon thy devious way,
Till thou, like all things earthly, endest in the grave.

NEW YORK:

G. W. CARLETON, PUBLISHER.

LONDON: S. LOW, SON, & CO.

MDCCCLXVIII.

Entered, according to Act of Congress, in the year 1868, by
G. W. CARLETON,
In the Clerk's Office of the District Court for the Southern District of
New York.

CONTENTS

3

REGINA.

THE days had come when time should be no more:
And Earth, pale Empress, saw her crumbling throne
Tottering on the dark and lurid verge
Of fell Destruction's fearful precipice.
Sun, moon, and stars were blotted from the sky;
And darkness visible was over all
A dim and ghastly shroud.   All sounds were hushed.
All living things, save one, had vanished
In that dark night of Death.   One only thought
Rose dominant o'er a racked and dying world.

'Twas the last day of Earth, — upon whose breast
The dead lay heavy; but not yet had come
The hour that lit the fatal funeral pyre;
For Life yet lingered where Death's steed had passed,
And left the earth a vast uncharnelled grave.
One only, fearless and confiding, braved
The universal doom; — one, only, met
The pale Steed and its Rider, dying not; —
One only passion mocked Destruction's art.
'Twas Love, the ever trustful and the true, —
The star that leads to Heaven!
        Amid the dead,
Who peopled all that mighty sepulchre,
A pallid woman sat, watching above
A soulless form of clay that lay beside.
She heeded not the darkness that had made
All Earth a Silence and a Dread; — saw nought
Beyond the narrow circle where she sat.
Her all of life was there!
        A ray of light
Streamed sudden from on high; marking the spot
Where that pale woman sat, and watched, and prayed.
Borne downwards on the ray, a stately shape,
A wingëd angel came, and lightly stood

Beside the watcher's form; with keen regard
Eying the sunken cheek and wasted brow.
There was an earnest questioning in his gaze,
That seemed to say, "Why lingerest thou here,
Amid the dead the only living thing?"
"Because I love," came solemnly and slow
From the pale watcher's lips. — "Thou lovest, then,
And what?" — "Look there! it lieth at thy feet!" —
"The dead?" — "Thou sayest it, and wherefore not?
'Tis all that is left me now.   Ay, all! all!
And even that will pass away, ere long,
And meet mine eyes no more!   And then — and then —
I, too, may fold my weary hands and die." —
"It needs not wait till then," the angel said.
"Look round, O loving one, upon thy Earth.
See thou that nations have gone down to dust —
That War, and Plague, and Famine have held rule,
And with their thousand pangs dispeopled Earth.
The lamps that lighted worlds have all died out;
And in this voiceless darkness feel thy doom!" —
"I hear thee, and resign me.   Yet, once more,
Could I but pour upon the wingèd winds
The record of my life!" — "Thou hast thy wish," —
Outspoke the pitying angel, and he said
"Earth's hours are swiftly flying; but their tale
Is not yet told; so, watcher, tell thou thine." —

Regina.

There was a silent valley, where the sun
Was wont to linger; on its pleasant haunts
And joyous-flowing streams, pouring the light
That made them beautiful!   There the flowers grew
Hemming earth's robe of ever-living green
With rainbow-spangles, and a wealth of hues
That mocked the flashings of an autumn-eve.
There rose the fountains from the golden sands
To fling their cooing spray-showers on the grass
That grew so green beside.   The slender blades
Loved well the diamond drops that crowned them.
And oh! the sunny, the rejoicing river,
Whose waves sped on so merrily in their flow,
Singing a glad song ever; while my heart
Kept measure to its chiming melody;
And marvelled not why earth, and stream, and air,

Sang but one song, and changéd not the strain!
Who hath not heard the chorus to that song?
When from their leafy covert carol forth
The forest-minstrels, warbling out their glee
In changeful music; while, from every field,
Rings out the gay Cicada's chirping shout;
And each fair blossom, from its leafy cup,
Sends up a softened peal of bells, that seem
To mortal ears the sighing breath of flowers.
For, all unconscious still our earth-born race,
That ever, from the fairy throats of flowers,
There goeth up a hymn of daily praise
Unto the Life-Giver, ceasing not,   -
But flowing forth forever, and the same!

I was a child of nature. Never yet
Upon my heart had breathed the blasting wind
That bears the deadly coldness of the world,
The blasting wind, Sirocco, to man's soul.
And in this pleasant valley, I had learnt
To read the language of the stars and flowers.
And full of love, and all life's highest thoughts
Were the pure lessons that my teachers taught.
And well I learned them, graving on my heart
Each simple precept, and each holy law;
Till all mine acts had but one guiding rule,
And that was tracéd by a mighty Hand
Whose writing erreth not! And they who taught
My spirit such deep lore were only two, —
My father and my mother. They are gone;
And years have held their long and trying sway
Since they departed from me; yet my soul
Bears all the record of my early years;
No thought erased — no holy lesson lost!

My mother! O my mother! thou who wert
Mine earthly angel — look thou down, and smile
Upon thy dying child; for she hath kept
The lofty hopes thou gavest her, all undimmed
Through bitter struggles, and a weight of woe
That might have borne an angel down to Earth!
O true heart and loving! Earth had not
Home fitting thee, and so the Holy One
Called thee to share a blesséd rest on high;
And thou didst turn, resigned, but sadly slow,
From husband and from child: with meekest bow,
Laying thy fair head in the lap of Death,
And — as from a troubled sleep awaking

To find the real worse than fantasy —
We woke — O mother! thou hadst gone from us;
And with pale cheeks, and tightly claspéd hands,
We bore thee to thy rest; and then — and then —
Went back to life again. A changéd life,
Since thou, the loved and loving, wert not there.

And time crept on. My father's hair grew white
Beneath the mournful shadow that had fallen
Upon our lovely valley; and the strength,
The stately grace of manhood, had gone by
As a flower flung on the autumn gale,
Leaving but the phantom of his former self
To mock the old man's eye. But little cared
Or grieved my father for departed strength.
And when my gaze would rest all sadly on
The pallid brow, wan cheek, and dulléd eye,
Slow tracing there the tokens of decay;
His earnest voice would fall upon mine ear,
And bid me " mourn not o'er his fading prime;
For dear to him the signs that told of death.
A signal each of swift deliverance
From earthly bonds of clay; a herald, sent
To bear him onwards to that happy land
Where she, who had gone from us, waited still
To greet his entrance into that pure rest
Whence grief and death forever banished are."

One eve — it left its record on my heart —
The breath of tempests had been over earth,
But ceased their strife at noon, though yet the wind
Wailed moaningly, as struggling to be free;
And in the darkened east the storm-swept clouds
Hung lowering, like a pall; while the lightning's glare
Flashed pale and lurid o'er the heavy shroud
That veiled the sky beyond. Far in the west,
Along the mountain's distant horizon,
A sickly gleam at intervals was seen,
As though the shadow of the parted storm
Yet lingered there. The flowers — I only knew
Where they had been by the soiled petals lying
In the defiling dust. The storm had swept
Too surely on its fearful errand for the Earth
To wear its jewels still; and so its breast
Lay bare and open to the spoiler's touch.
And from the swollen river came a roar
Of senseless terror as it foamed and tossed
Convulsive in its dark and rock-strewn bed.

Save for the restless heaving of the wave,
Silence had held terrific revel there.

I heeded not the raving of the storm,
Nor marked its progress. I was a watcher
Beside a dying father, and I knew
That, ere the morrow dawned, my work of love
Would all be ended, and myself alone!
Through that long day of terror and of storm
Slumber had sealëd up the weary lids
Of the death-stricken; and the gasping breath
Was all that told me life yet lingered there.
So the long day went by, and evening came:
And as I looked upon my father's face
His gaze met mine. and with a sudden strength
He spoke to me. I hear him speaking now.

The Father.

"My child — Regina — there will soon be light
Upon an angel's brow, for I depart.
Yet ere I leave thee, mine own blessëd one,
There is a passing tale of other days
That thou must learn from me. I have not been
Alway a dweller in this mountain vale.
I was a lowly tenant of the earth,
And in my careless youth but little recked
Of country or of king. Content was mine:
And in my quiet home, true, honest hearts
Smiled ever on my boyhood; and my rest
Was calm and dreamless. Sorrow came, at last,
And death soon followed, till my happy home
Was only eloquent of the silent grave.
And then the quenchless thirst for parted peace
Came sudden to my soul; and so I left
My native valley for the stirring strife
Of earth's vast cities. Better I had died
E'en in mine hour of lonely sorrowing
Than lived to learn the falsehood of my race.

" With eager pace, and fleet, I crossed the hills
That formed the boundary of my native vale;
And ever, while my steps were onward bent,
Slow thought retraced the record of the Past;
And all the fading memories of youth
Passed freshly by me, as an odor borne
On winds that lately swept o'er Araby.
As in the sliding mirror, forms glide by,

Casting a shadow as if life were there,
So, o'er the mirror of my soul's rethought,
Rose up the home of childhood, wearing all
The magic bloom that memory giveth
Unto the things that have been, and are now
But present through her mightful influence.

"I pondered o'er the past, until my steps,
So hurried late, became all slow and sad,
Its spell was busy with my heart and brain,
Till in my thought I was once more a child.
Again I stood, a wild and joyous boy,
By the green shore of the rushing river,
Flinging therein full many a round stone;
And ofttimes numbering, with most earnest brow,
The little circles as they widened there.

"Again — a pale and dreaming youth — I lay
Beneath the shadow of the pine-trees dark
That grew around our dwelling; poring o'er
The lore of vanished ages, — weaving aye
High dreams and noble from the storied page
I loved so well. Our lonely home had been
The storehouse of all knowledge; garnered up,
Through the long lapse of by-gone centuries,
By those who cradled hope for future years
In those old records of departed time.
These precious tomes were to mine untried soul
A well-spring, quenching for a time its thirst.
So, from these musty chronicles I learned
The strength that bears all suffering and is still —
The spell that crowneth genius with its fire —
The lore that makes men great!

                    So passed my youth.
Then came the darker retrospect of death,
And I looked down upon the valley sods.
Three graves were lying silent at my feet,
And from my yearning gaze shut out, there rest
My parents and my sister. The first had laid
Themselves to sleep in the fulness of years
All ripened for the grave; but she, — mine own
And only sister, — she had withered — died —
Ere life's spring-time was over, — with its bloom
Yet fresh upon her cheek. She was so fair!
A gentle, loving thing that aye would creep
The closer to my side when storms were near,
As though my presence were a shield from harm,

She passed away so silently from life,
I knew not she had left me, till the moon
Flamed out, and showed the marble of the tomb
Too surely frozen on her Parian brow.
My hold on earth seemed shattered when she died;
And yet I've run a long and changeful course,
Since silence settled on my early home.

    " A gush of song — clear, joyous, swelling song —
From the sweet warblers of the wild green wood
Broke gladly on mine ear, and called my thoughts
From their sad wanderings to the present back;
And with a sudden shiver I awoke
From mournful memory's tenacious dream,
And turned me, as man ever turns at times,
To our kind mother, Nature, for relief.
Fair was the scene that lay before mine eyes;
Stretched out beneath, in wild magnificence,
Upland and lowland, forest, mead, and stream,
Diversified the plain.   All wore the garb
Of the sweet summer time — so brightly green,
So richly various.   Far to the west
The sleeping waters of a mighty sea
Lay bathed in golden splendor, glassing bright
The slanted rays of the uprisen sun.
There, gliding swiftly o'er the heaving tide,
Sped the white birds of ocean; while a sound
Of sweet and far-off music filled the air;
Soft flowing o'er the wave unto the shore,
The smiling summer shore.   Around me frowned
The cold and iron majesty of cliffs
That reared a stern and stately front to heaven;
While close beside me spread a sea of ice,
The slow, yet certain, work of centuries.
I, only, breathed the breath of human life
'Mid those white, shadowy cliffs, where evermore
Silence and desolation held their sway.

    " I turned me from those stillest realms of ice
Unto the plain beneath, where, in its pride
Of stately palaces and gardens rare,
Rose up a mighty city, girdled by
A ring of emerald.   I marked it well,
And thought within myself that I would be
A dweller in its walls.   So from the lone
And cheerless summit, with slow, weary pace,
I bent my steps and journeyed thitherward.

"It was a day of solemn festival,
And the great city, through its hundred gates
Poured forth its thronging myriads to the plain
Where, lone, majestic, rose a temple fair, —
The lofty Pantheon.   A dome of gold, —
A thousand columns the vast arch upheld, —
Loomed, high and central, o'er the lesser towers
That seemed as sentinels a watch to keep
O'er some great monarch's slumber.   All the wealth,
The gathered gems of twice ten thousand years,
Were lavished on the walls and archëd roof,
Till in the blaze of Day's bright burning orb
It seemed the various Iris had been won
From its high place, to gleam in changeful light
On the vast dome and its attendant towers.

"A burst of song — a sound as if all Earth
Woke the deep lay — swelled sudden on mine ear,
As with mute step, and scarcely throbbing heart,
I entered with the crowd, and stood beneath
The wide, o'erarching dome.   The light of day
Streamed never through those walls of clearest glass,
For o'er them laid were golden plates, and gems
That barred the rays of sun, or moon, or stars.
The vaulted roof was tinted like the sky
When stars shine brightest, and all diamond-strewed.
Till, in the pale, soft light of shaded lamps,
It seemed the arched and glittering firmament.
A thousand columns stood in circle round,
A thousand altars flamed on every side
And waving censers filled the perfumed air
With clouds of freshest fragrance; and the while
Soft tones of music, like to ocean waves,
Were ever floating through the sounding arch, —
A never-resting flow of melody.
A clear, sweet voice rang out above the swell
Of loudest music; and the gathered throng
Of worshippers bowed low the willing knee,
As if one soul had animated all.
And yet not all.   A fair and fragile girl
Stood lonely in the midst, — her eyes upraised,
And her slight fingers claspëd o'er her breast,
With such a holy calm upon her brow,
That in my heart of hearts I worshipped her.

"Alone she stood!   Receding from her side,
As from a thing that breatheth pestilence,
The crowd drew back, and, with cold looks askance,

And a strange dread quick settling on each brow,
They gazed upon her as on one accursed;
And, from the altars flaming round there came
A deep, stern voice, — 'Or kneel, or bear the curse!'
A shudder crept o'er all that living mass;
But she, that maiden lovely, trembled not;
And, with clear tones and lute-like, spake aloud, —
'I kneel not, save to God!'
        "Dark frowned each one
Of all that wore the priestly mantle there;
And with low, muttering tones, and eyes that glare
Beneath their cowlëd brows, they gathered near
The chiefest altar, and with hissing voice,
Bade that fair girl draw near; and then they spake
Such words as made me dream the old time back
Of torture and of fire!
        — " 'Thou that hast sought
Our holy temple but in mockery;
Say, whence the spell that giveth thee that look
Of high and holy calm?   And, wherefore thus
Insult the Deity in his own abode?
Nay, answer not! for, false one, on thy soul,
We, who know all things, see the signet dark
Of him who ruleth hell!   Ay, thou art one
Of those who bear them purely, holily,
In outer seeming; so to gather souls
From mid the shelter of our Mother Church.*
But well it is for all who unto her
Are servants true, that those who live like thee,
And prowl as wolves among the shepherd's fold,
Are doomed to meet discovery and death.
For still the church is armëd for such foes;
Her arm is mighty, and outstretched to save, —
Her eyes far-seeing, and her power great,
Omnipotent and ubiquitous evermore!
Yet thou, frail child of earth, hast dared to set
Thyself in opposition to her will;
And breathed forth heresy, e'en where her name
Is graven on yon mimic vault of heaven.

* The author begs leave to forestall any impugning of her orthodoxy by declaring that the self-styled "church" of which Regina's father speaks, is only another name for the Babylon of the Apocalypse; and is not, and could not be, "the Bride," the Church of Christ. In these days of many creeds, when much learning seems to make men mad; when all manner of opinions on the one great point are so prevalent, it behooves us who are members of the CHURCH, to beware, lest we trench, unwittingly, too nearly upon the strong lines of demarcation which sever the doubtful and the unbelieving from the true Christian, therefore if, in this her book, any opinions seem to savor of other than Church doctrine, let it be remembered that it is spoken only "in character." Further, the author has only to acknowledge her own most thorough belief "in Unum, Sanctum, Catholicum, et Apostolicum Ecclesiam," together with each and every article of the Nicene Creed; the "Filioque" not excepted.

Yet, yet, in pity to thy tender years
And seeming innocence, we give thee space
To win her pardon by thy penitence.
So speak, while yet thou may'st.' —

          — " ' But passing brief,
The space ye grant for penitence,' outspake
The maiden, as she stood, her meek hands crossed
Upon her heaving bosom, as to still
The ceaseless throbbing of her fevered heart.
' Yea, brief the space, but it sufficeth me.
What, know ye not, — ye who make your dwelling
In the high haunts of power, and bend men's souls
Unto your bidding with remorseless strength;
Making a sport and pastime of the tears,
And broken hearts, and lost souls of your race, —
What, know ye not, that oft-times in this earth
There comes an hour, when from the weary yoke
And crushing superstition of the few,
The fettered soul awakes, and spurns its bonds,
And, like a lion freed from hunter's toils,
Leaps forth, exulting in its liberty?
So came the day-spring rushing on my soul;
And, from the low, and dark, and crooked way
Ye have traced out for earthly things to tread,
I woke to tidings of a higher life,
To freedom and to God!   Nay, I must speak!
So call your hirelings back, and give me space.
What! did ye think that freedom was crushed out,
When ye made slaves of all the noblest gifts
That crown the human race?   True, ye have laid
Dull fetters on the mind, and taught the brain
To be your bondsman, and to work your will.
And well have they obeyed your lessoning!
Look forth upon our Earth, — the beautiful!
Its plains are clothed in freshest verdure fair;
Its vales are strewed with various-tinted flowers;
Its streams flow on rejoicing to the sea;
And all is bright, and pure, and glorious, —
Instinct with life and truest beauty.
But ye have made the pleasant homes of earth
A poison and a snare; have flung the blight
Of cold suspicion on each loving heart;
Till every household hearth, so sacred once,
Is now a dwelling scarcely fit for fiends!
Nay, frown not, for 'tis true! ye know it well.
Gaze o'er the earth.   Are not its valleys dyed
With the red stains of battle and of strife?

Flows not the blood of those whom ye have slain,
For that they dared to break your hateful yoke,
Unto the gates of yon all-seeing heaven?
A testimony true, and ceaseless evermore,
Crying unto the Holy One, " How long?"
Lo! Earth calls out for vengeance on the wrongs
That for ten thousand years have weighed her down,
And stained her patient brow!   And the hour comes!
Yea, — borne on the wings of all-subduing fire, —
Pale Pestilence stalking with its horrid tread,
As grim Avatar of the coming doom,
And Death, the pitiless, sweeping sternly on,
And leaving not a phantom life behind; —
The fated hour swift draweth near its birth,
And when it comes — as come it shall, and soon
In fearful darkness heralding your doom —
Then look ye to your power!   Its end is nigh.
Lo! a dark tempest sweepeth over earth;
And Ruin rusheth forth upon the wind;
And after cometh, with a flaming sword,
The Angel of Destruction.   Lo! your fanes,
All desecrate with blood, are tottering;
And from your shrines the idols are cast down:
And in their place sitteth a mocking fiend
With bitter jibe triumphing o'er the doom
That marks ye his forever!   From the sky
All light is blotted out, and o'er the world
Horror and Darkness, twin-born of the night,
Hold dread dominion.   On your guilty souls
The shadow of the doom to come sits darkly;
The voice of prayer is hushed; — and, 'mid the crash
Of wild collapsing elements, and the dim
And lurid light of flames that slowly fade,
Deep darkness settles on the universe,
And veils the vision of a dying world!' —

  " She ceased — and for a moment all was still.
Men's brows looked ghastly in the torches' glare,
And a dim dread of something undefined
Lay frosted on each heart; while every eye
On that inspired maid was riveted,
As though each thought on that prophetic brow,
As in the magic glass of olden days,
To read their final and determined doom.
And she? — Within her dark and flashing eyes
There shone the light of inspiration's fire;
While on her brow, peace, like an angel, shed
Its holy influence.

           "Not long endured
The silence and the fear. With ready tact
The mitred priests held out the sacred signs
Of their high office, and with deep, stern voice
They spake the maiden's doom; with words of death
Veiling their secret dread.

           — " ' Lo! ye have heard
From her own lips the fearful blasphemy
Wearing the guise of prophecy; and seen
How even now the fallen One doth strive
To lead men's souls astray. Our holy Church
Is watchful o'er her flock; and ever seeks
To save the faithful from the secret snare
That leadeth to destruction. Hear her doom;
And in your happy homes think of the soul
That goeth to its death. Apostate child,
And lost sheep of the flock! — thou that hast mocked
The gentle teachings of our Mother Church,
And flung aside the hand outstretched to save,
And uttered fearful words of blasphemy; —
Depart from us! The *curse* is laid on thee!
No heart may speak its blessing on thy path;
No hand come nigh in greeting unto thine;
No eye look kindly on thee, and no voice
Speak aught unto thee save an added curse.
Let earth refuse thee nourishment; the sky
Shed down no sunny influence on thy way,
And ocean bar thee e'en from sepulchre!
Go forth to loneliness and the desert —
The thorny pathway, and the silent sands —
Go from us — thou art doomed!'
             "The doom was said:
And instant from the crowd a woman came,
With hurried pace, yet soft and silent step.
She recked not of kind hands that would have stayed
Her onward motion. With a wailing cry
She clasped the doomèd maiden to her breast;
And 'mid the awe-struck stillness of the throng
These words were heard, ' My mother,' and ' My child!'

    " ' Forbear! she is accurst!' — with thundering voice
Began the cold and heartless priesthood,
The while their slaves with hands irreverent
Profanèd nature's holiest meeting;
With savage strength, unheeding their sad plain,
Severing parent and child. There rang a cry —
A wild, passionate cry — from 'mid the band

Of careless hirelings, as if some chord
That bindeth life to life were rudely struck,
And shivered 'neath the shock.   So full of death,
So sudden-sounding, and so sudden still,
Was that same bitter cry, that to mine ear
It seemed the death-shriek of a broken heart.

   " A breath of fire passed swift athwart my brow;
A strange, deep courage filled my burning heart;
And with extended arm, and gesture firm,
Indignant I broke forth : ' What! are ye *men*,
Yet trample thus upon a mother's love?
Think ye, your solemn ban and curse can chill
That ceaseless flow of love, or turn its stream,
So pure and sparkling, into bitterest gall?
As soon might ye essay with impious hope
And fond dream of success to win from night
The tiniest jewel in her starry crown!
Yea; stronger than the chains ye forge for souls,
Stronger than Death, a mother's quenchless love.
Ye have proved it well; and your cold hearts
Have seen how mightier far than fear it is.
It hath braved all things but to look again
On one dear face, and die !   Ay, die !   Look there !
Death is within your temple walls, and ye —
Ay, *ye* — have called him there !'
             " And, as I spoke,
I lifted from its gentle resting-place
The mother's lifeless form, and laid it down
Beside the altar-stone; whence the pale dead
With its so still and calm rebuking glance,
Looked upward to the arched and massive dome,
As if it sought from angel lips to ask
Beseechingly, ' How long?' —
             " Deep silence fell
O'er all that countless throng; and they were still,
For Death was in their midst, till o'er the hush
There rose a voice in wailing for the dead.
' My mother! O my mother!   Thou art gone;
And thy so loving heart may beat no more
Responsive unto mine.   From thy dear lips
I learned the earlier lessonings of truth
In sweetest teachings given; and now — and now —
O mother! silence is upon them set,
And they speak not, save in Heaven.   O Death !
Hadst thou but called me too, I had gone down
Smiling to the dust; for from thy dwelling
Short is the way that leadeth up to GOD;

And I should now be there with thee -- with thee --
My mother -- O my mother!' --
                   "While the voice
Of her low wailing fell upon mine ear
I watched the faces of the priesthood,
And only read in their so cruel mien
The maiden's sealéd doom. So, when she rose
From her dead mother's side, I took her hand,
And, in slow, solemn tones, I breathed a vow, --
Earth's holiest, -- and, turning to the throng
That stood around the altar, uttered it.
'Ye have sent forth from the known haunts of men
A helpless maiden; and, in mocking doom, --
For that ye shut her out, as one accurst,
From human love and human sympathy, --
Have made her life more bitter far than death.
Ye have spoken her doom; now, speak ye mine!
For know that, as her creed, so readeth mine;
And, before GOD, and in the sight of men,
I call her wife. Behold, our lots are one
Throughout this life, and for eternity.
Therefore, speak ye our doom; that from your path
Our own shall parted be for evermore!' --

" 'For evermore!' resounded through the dome,
As rude hands seized us, and, with hasty zeal,
Close chained us to the dead. Then darkness fell
Upon our eyes, and every sound of earth
Seemed hushed forever. And I thought that Death
Had broken those dread chains, and set us free.
And so I slept again. When next I woke
The night-winds swept athwart my fevered brow,
And on mine ear fell the cool plash of waves.
I strove to rise, but vainly; for the chains
Lay heavy on my limbs. I only saw
The far-off heaven and the shining stars.
And yet I knew I was not all alone
Amid that silence; for, close beside me,
And bound in the same fetters, lay the dead;
And, though I saw her not, I felt my bride
Had shared the self-same doom. I strove to speak,
But utterance was denied me; to move,
That I might look on her; the power was gone,
And I was weaker than the feeblest child.
Thought, memory, alone were left to me.
But they proved tyrants in that fearful hour,
And only brought me bitterest agony;
Conjuring up wild dreams of her despair

Till Reason tottered on its trembling throne.
But the night winds were cool, and so their breath
Soothed the wild fever burning in my veins,
And I grew calm, and very still, and smiled,
Thinking of Death.
        "I felt we were alone.
No sounds of earth came sighing through the night,
And all things human, save ourselves, were far.
Our boat, so fragile, tossed upon the waves
As 'twere a plaything yielded to their sport.
And if, from yon pale planets of the sky,
Angels looked down, what saw they on the deep?
A lone bark, bearing on its lighted prow
Two living forms yet chained unto the dead,
While Night and Silence, they lay over all!

"I watched the stars fade, — with a dim thought
That never more their gleam should meet mine eyes.
And, as the sun rose o'er wide ocean's breast,
There came a faint and feverish sense of thirst
Unto my parchèd lips; but vain would be
All effort for relief; and so I lay
Suffering in silence. The breeze had died
From off the ocean, and its waters slept
In waveless calm, beneath a burning sun;
And on its idle breast our little bark
As idle lay, and motionless. The sun,
That seemed to move amid a cloudless sky
A living ball of fire, shone on the sea
As though it sought to quench immortal thirst
In the unfathomed deep; and scorchingly
Its rays fell on mine unprotected head,
Till, in my fierce, impotent agony,
I prayed for death; but death was far away.

" And so the day wore on, — the same dead calm,
The same pitiless sun. But, ere it closed,
Far in the west there rose a small black cloud,
And fast it spread along the horizon,
Till, as the sun, a blood-red, flaming orb,
Departed hence to light another world,
The little cloud had darkened all the sky,
And wrapped the sea in night. A moment held
All things as chained in silence, and I heard
Only the gurgling gasping of my breath.
Then came the storm in all its fearful might,
Scooping the waters in its onward sweep,
And flinging the white spray from wave to wave,

As the wild ocean were a thing for sport, —
A feather in its path!   And the winds raved,
And moaned, and shrieked, in their demoniac glee;
While the racked waves, all torn and shattered, made
Treaty with the winds, and, with blended tones,
Sent fearful music on their maddened sweep.

"And our light bark!   How lived it through the gale?
I know not; but it seemed a charmëd thing,
And rode the raging billows as a bird
That findeth there its native element.
And I?   Methought my soul had found its sphere,
So fiercely it rushed forth and merged itself
In the wild strife of nature, only glad
To be so free once more!
                          "So glad!   So free!
That I forgot the iron on my limbs,
And felt my heart throb high in deepest pride,
And, for a time, — an hour of wildest mirth, —
Recked little of the hushed heart by my side,
Nor mourned o'er the fair victim lying there.
But soon there came, as fire-damp to the flame,
The hour of dull reaction; and my soul
Drooped from its soaring pinions, and so fell,
All crushed and strengthless, to the lowest depths
Of darkness and despair.   The storm raved on,
And the vexed ocean moaned in agony,
As mother o'er her dying child; while I —
The life of life, the trust in human love,
Was dying in my heart.   O'er my young bride, —
So lately known, — so loved, — death's wing had lain,
And I might look upon her gentle face,
And hear her soft and loving voice, no more.

"Was that the cry of some lone albatross,
Far on its daring way, or but a wail
Wrung from mine own convulsed and swollen lip?
Again it sounded, and, with one swift bound,
I burst my chain, and looked upon my bride.
Praise to the Life-Giver!   She was not dead;
Nor I left all companionless 'mid the waste
Of that wild ocean!   Through the fearful war
Of elements let loose; through all the long
And racking agony that I had borne,
She had slept calmly on, and felt it not,
Wrapped in that deep and blessed forgetfulness.
But now she wakened, and the dreamless trance,

That had so bound her senses, broke away
In the wild wail that had so startled me.

"Regina, I have looked on Death since then;
Have known of joy and grief most various thrill;
But never yet hath sound so full of joy, —
So rich in weight of blessing, — come to me,
As came unto my wild and fevered heart,
When her soft voice went sighing o'er the sea;
And every pulsing of her heart did say
That Life was throbbing where I looked for Death!

"Day after day our frail bark floated on,
Sole moving thing upon that dreary main.
But we recked little of Time's passing then,
Though Death glanced mocking from each crested wave.
But GOD was merciful. The gentle rain
Fell frequent from the clouds, with its cool drops
The torturing fever-thirst allaying still;
And Ocean brought us from no distant shore
A waftage of fair fruits, that still sufficed
To dull the hunger-pain. So the days went;
And still our slight, but angel-guarded boat
Moved onward o'er the ever-rolling sea.

"One morn — its beauty fills my vision now —
Sweet sounds, long silent, broke the spell of sleep.
The joyous song of birds, the wind's soft breath,
Made musical the densely foliaged trees;
And the clear rush of waters, as they dashed
Against the rocks and on the pebbly shore
Was heard through rustling leaves. All these were tones
That brought to eyes that had been burning hot
A flood of passionate weeping. On our ears,
Making them know the usage they had lost,
Those sounds fell sweetly as an angel's song.
For we — O joy too deep for utterance! —
Might tread the blessed mother-earth once more!

"Nor desolate, nor uninhabited
The land whereon the waves had drifted us;
For with the sun came voices to the shore,
Voices that spake the old familiar tongue
That lingered with my childhood; and the words
Thrilled to my heart as from the grave they came.
I could not speak, — I had no language then, —
And on my lips the words hung powerless.
I only pointed to the fettered form

That lay beside me; looking the wild prayer
I could not breathe in words, that they would break
Her chains, and bring her back to life again.

"They were of gentlest mien, that island race;
Of softest speech and eyes; yet were they framed
Of that stern stuff whereof men martyrs make.
Fragile of form, pale-browed, and golden-haired,
They had such look as meekest angels wear
When God smiles on them; yet beneath this veil
Slumbered the strength that triumphs over death
And darkness and despair.   They were of those
Who have outborne the worst of torture-pains;
And with true heart, and firm uplifted soul,
Have hushed in silence their lips never broke
The keenest pangs of human agony.

"Such were the hearts — so gentle, true, and brave —
Who spoke our welcome to their island shore,
And gave the exiles refuge and a home,
Till we forget, in that so blessëd rest,
The dread anathema that bade us live
As wanderers and homeless evermore.

"There was a quiet lake within that isle
Whose glassing waters knew not one deep sound
Of Ocean's mightier wave; and only sent
A rippling murmur from its grassy nest
To float along its shore, and blend alway
With the soft tonings of the earth and sky.
And by that lake, where through the dusky eve
The plash of coolest waters caught the ear,
Made we our home.   And the calm years moved on
With scarce a breath of change, till thou, my child,
Hadst counted seven summers; then there came
A day of darkness, blighting all this bloom.

"I was a wanderer ever, — restless,
And of unquiet mood; and oftentimes
Would spread a sail to catch the rising breeze,
Yet never went I forth companionless.
Thy angel-mother linked her fate with mine,
And braved the ocean-terrors fearlessly,
While thou, my child, with outstretched hands didst greet
The crested billows of the foaming deep;
And smile when o'er thy brow the spray-showers fell, —
For innocence like thine, a baptism meet.
So I read the sport of those wild waters,

And in my secret soul, I vowed for thee
Faith, Hope, Charity, and in fancy taught
All deepest lessons that to earth are given.
I knew thy lot was cast in troublous times;
And in thy young clear eyes, so cloudless yet,
There slept a shadow that might darken soon
And deepen into night.   And then I learned
Unto mine own tamed heart a higher trust,
And mightier strength to bear, so to give thee
Life's truest lessonings.   That task is o'er:
And I go down to silence and to dust
Where all these things are heard not; leaving thee
The seeds from whence life's great events do spring.

"But time wears on.   My tale is not yet told;
And this poor struggling frame must linger still
Upon its couch of pain.   A little space, —
A passing hour, — and this pulse of mine
Shall know ' the taste of rest,' never again
To throb in joy or pain!   Enough! the Past
Doth call me to itself.   My island home
Dawns on my vision, slowly — smilingly.

"It was a morn of spring.   That glorious time
When Earth seems born anew, and doth put on
The garmenture of youth, and looketh up
With a smiling brow to Heaven.   Our bark was moored
Just off the pebbly beach; and on its prow,
Ere yet the sun rose from his ocean-bed,
Thy mother sat, her arm around thy form;
Both watching me, as from its secret hold
I drew the anchor up.   Sail after sail
Was given to the winds, and long ere noon
Our fairy home, Exila's isle, had dipped
Below the horizon.   A night went by,
Another day was waning to its close,
Ere our wild ocean-bird, with willing speed,
Sought the loved shore again.   'Twas changëd all.
The spoiler, the remorseless, had been there
And death and silence were our welcome home!

"I mind me well how on my native hills
A stately forest grew, the peasants' pride,
Where never yet the sounding axe had been;
And in its solemn shadow all were wont
To roam at eventide.   Calm at its feet
A silent lakelet slept, whose waves scarce knew
The touch of sunshine, those far-reaching trees

Did so o'ermantle them; and so the dusk
Seemed ever o'er that stillest wave to glide.
One night, there came through all its holy hush
A hurtling sound, — a whisper gathering strength, —
A rush as of ten thousand battling storms
A moment passing — and then all was still
As death; cold as the silence of the grave!
Morn broke, and on the sickly eye of day
Flamed forth Destruction's aspect terrible.
The gentle hill whereon the forest grew,
The quiet lake beneath, had vanished,
And in their place a vast and fetid plain
Loomed low in all its dark deformity;
While o'er its lifeless waters, dull and green,
Already were the marish-mosses growing!

" So to that meek and gentle island race
The deadly hour of persecution came.
At morn, the holy song of praise went up
To Heaven through the soft and sweet spring air
From light and joyous hearts, — from young and old, —
And every pulse sang "Glory unto GOD!"
At eve, the worse than silence of the grave,
The desolation of desolation
Held its revel there!   Our holiest fanes
Were levelled with the dust.   Our quiet homes
Were scattered stone by stone, and o'er their place
Slowly the sea-bird winged its fearless flight.

"Lo! a voice upon that silence floating low
Soft, silver-sounding, but too sadly sweet: —

" ' Alas for thee, fair Island! thou wert doomed
To bear upon thy glad and sunny brow
Destruction's fatal seal.   Thou that didst rise
From the blue depths of Ocean, truest type
Of glory crowning labor, the sure seal
Wherewith success doth stamp slow, patient toil; —
Even thou, whose birth-hour breathed "Eureka,"
Must go down to very nothingness, and be
That which thou art and hast been, nevermore.
Thy doom was sung when first the sun beheld thee;
For the great deep but lent thee unto Day
That thy lone shores for a sad homeless race
A refuge and abiding sure should be.
They have departed, as the daylight fades
When the swift hurricane sweeps o'er the land,
And on thy shore, the strangers, only, breathe.

Their path is otherwhere.   They leave not here
Their dust for wandering waves to revel o'er.
They shall depart in other lands to keep
All saddest thoughts of their low-buried home;
But for the dead, who lie upon thy breast,
Pale martyrs unto Superstition's zeal, —
O'er their cold brows must ocean-waters flow.
Ay! over all; but only o'er their dust.
For twixt that morn and eve — when Murder stalked
Over man's erring soul predominant,
And deaf to Mercy's plea — a thousand souls
Went rushing up to GOD: before his throne
Outpraying thus, " How long, O Lord, how long? " —

      " 'Ye weep.   If for the isle, where first ye heard
The simpler breathings of that little one,.
I will not stay your tears.   But to the dead
Whose dust doth lie before ye, give no tears!
They have but fall'n as GOD appointed them;
And, for each parted friend, an angel more
Is added to GOD's host.   They have but gone
Before ye to their home.
                    " ' But haste ye now
And flee these doomèd shores; for, from the south,
All dark and sullen with the brooding storm,
Sweeps the low line of white and drifting clouds,
On-driven by the wind that moans along
The restless bosom of the unquiet deep.
Speed ye your steps!   The time is very brief.
Still your light bark doth rest upon the wave,
Calm as an infant on its mother's breast.
An hour hence, and the fierce winds, let loose,
Will scoop the waters into wildest forms,
And fling their foam-wreaths o'er that vessel's prow;
And ye, thus made of elements the sport,
Will know their very pastime terrible.
But fear ye not.   The Holiest is there.
The GOD who ruleth storm, and wind, and sea.
The GOD who loveth all!'—
                    " As dies the swell
Of some soft hymn upon the summer air,
Leaving a haunting echo of its tone
Unto the heart forever; so that voice
Fell faint, then soundless all.
                    " Slowly we went.
Our lingering feet seemed loth to leave the soil
They might not press again; our yearning eyes
Turned frequent to each fair and cherished scene,

Never to meet their longing vision more,
Save in some dream.   And I had lingered yet —
Perchance had perished with Exila's isle,
But that thy mother's hand fell soft on mine
With sweet, compelling sway; and so we went.
Forth to the breeze we flung our snowy sail,
And in the distance, fading fast away,
Sunk the lone islet, on whose pleasant shore
Looked never human eye again!
                              "Day passed,
And o'er the red and stormy sunset glow
The night came down, starry and beautiful, —
A night without a cloud!   The hornèd moon,
Just hovering o'er the dim and trackless verge
Of farthest ocean, slowly vanishèd.
And 'neath the soft and holy light of stars
I kept my lonely vigil, watching o'er
A sleeping wife and child.   For me the night
Had lost its slumbrous spell; my painèd lids
Were throbbing 'neath the weight of unshed tears, —
Tears that went flowing back upon my soul
Marking the pride that kept their flood-tide back,
Nor gave to grief its sweetest utterance.
Yet blessings on that night!   It gave me strength
To bear all after-growth of human ills.
Unto my soul it taught the lesson deep,
To suffer and be silent; asking not
Wherefore the doom to wander evermore
Was meted out as mine.   Gently the night
Shed o'er mine aching brows its cooling dews,
And o'er my heart, so fevered and so wild,
Its holy influence.
                    "There came a morn "
In rarest splendor garmented, — a day
All flush and glowing in the crimson rays
Of a more crimson sun.   In the far south
Vast piles of clouds loomed up magnificent,
Like mountain ranges, on whose snow-clad steeps
The roses of the sunset lingered yet,
Reluctant to depart.   Above, the sky,
Of deepest, darkest hue, was flecked with clouds,
Pale rose-leaves scattered o'er a field of blue;
And earth, spread out beneath that glorious arch,
Seemed not less fair, less bright, less beautiful.
She wore her robe of early summer beauty,
Her brow was crowned and radiant with delight,
And in her smile was joy that never words
Of mortal framing could link unto song!

"Such, and so fair, the morn when our frail bark,
From its long ocean wandering released,
Lay idly tossing on yon river's breast.
Thou know'st the rest, — how on that river's shore
We reared our quiet cot, and how the years
Went by so happily, till from our hearts,
God called an angel home.
                    "And now the night,
Whose morn for me hath other light than ours,
Doth verge upon its noon.   Ere thou canst count
The beatings of an hour's pulse, my life
Will be a part of what hath been; and thou,
Mine only one — motherless — fatherless. —
O God, who art forever, keep my child!" —

      Enough! there ceased the tale; and the dear voice
Whose music filled my life, grew hushed and still
Beneath the shadow of an angel's wing;
The passing wing of Death.   Alone, alone, —
From midnight unto midnight keeping watch,
I sat beside the dead.   I could not weep;
My tears seemed burnëd up.   I could not pray;
My heart had grown so cold.   And so — and so —
The hours drifted by.
                    Light came at last
On the darkness dawning.   I was athirst
For the cool waters of a sparkling spring
That flowed our home beside; and I went forth
From the still presence of the holy dead
Into the light of day, whose every throb
Was eloquent of life, making my heart
With all its fevered pulses doubly sad.
There went a sound of music past mine ear, —
A glad, triumphant strain, breaking the spell
That grief had woven round me, and I knew
How sorrow seemeth to the desolate.
So the hot, blinding tears came fast, ere night,
To fall upon a grave.
                    Sleep fanned my brow,
Soft stealing o'er my senses, and I slept;
Although the pillowing of my weary head
Was on my father's grave.   My dreams were strange,
And floated past my brain like phantom forms
That flit before the day.   Another world
Seemed opened unto me, — a world of light,
Wherein all things did wear some shape or form
Of deepest loveliness.   Methought, the sky

Was softer, bluer, than the sky which smiled
Upon my childhood, and flashing by me,
Its clear waves flecked with light, there rushëd on
A fair and glorious river, on whose breast
A thousand sails gleamed white beneath the sun.
Its shores were palace-crowned, and stateliest fanes
O'ertopped the proudest of the ancient trees
Whose foliage fluttered in the ambient breeze,
And made their very shadow musical.
Methought, while yet I gazed, and as mine eyes
Paid homage to this beauty, that there came
Between me and the glory of the scene
A form of darkness, moving swiftly on,
Filling, with its cold, impalpable gloom,
The very atmosphere. I inly shook,
And shivered with the frost that chilled my veins,
And pressed my cold hands on as cold a brow.
I looked again. The phantom of the night
Had passed away. Its destined work was done;
And that fair scene, so consummate in itself,
Was changed, as if the Angel of the Tomb
Had shed the poison from his folded wing
Upon its loveliness, blotting it out
From Earth's fair breast forever. Fearful gulfs,
Whence noisome vapors tainted all the air,
Yawned hideous in the midst. Rocks piled on rocks,
All black and smoke-begrimed, were frowning dark
Where late the river flowed so royally;
And not one stone of all those fairy domes
Was left to tell their fate. All, all, had gone.
Destruction, only, ruled where man had raised
The noblest fabrics of his daring pride.
The mighty earth, that bore them on her breast,
Was now their tomb, and all that breathing life
Went quick into the grave, — was swallowed up
In the passing of a thought!
                         I woke,
The river of my dream flowed at my feet,
And the great city, fancy made so fair,
Was present to my sight, no air-drawn shape
By dreaming pencil traced, but all instinct
With form and substance. It was no mirage,
No mocking vision that I saw, and yet,
How came I there? I know not, even now,
Save that sleep found me by my father's grave,
And when I woke, some hour after noon,
'Twas 'mid the splendor of that city fair.

I was alone — within a gorgeous room
Most royally apparelled, where the mind
Found fitting food for thought.   All forms of grace,
Breathing through marble as if life were there,
Were scattered round me.   I can see them now, —
Pale as the moonlight, soft, and white, and still,
And yet withal so wild and passionate.
My heart trembled with its rapture, and my soul
Was fillëd with their beauty, till my tears
Flowed fast and silently.
             There was a couch
Within a curtained recess, and I lay
Upon its crimson cushions, marvelling
If these strange changes were not shadows all,
And I a sleeper, and a dreamer still!
But, thinking so, there floated past mine ear
A strain of saddest music, wailingly,
Sighing itself to silence as it passed.
Again it sounded, sobbing, sorrowful,
As though it were a dirge o'er buried hopes
Poured forth by some lone heart, that only now, ·
When death was waiting for its parting throb,
Might give unto the feelings of a life
A brief, but all-sufficing utterance.

I knew it was the Death-Song of the Swan.

" And I must die!   From the sun-lighted river
    And from the glory of the summer-day,
I must depart; and where pale lilies shiver,
    There must the Swan pour forth his dying lay.

" I hear the fountains in the far woods rushing
    With silvery singing to the solemn sea;
I see the morn with rosy shadows flushing
    The free blue sky that smileth still on me.

" Life's pulse is throbbing round me, upward springing,
    As if no spell could tame its spirit-glee;
While I — the very dust to me seems clinging,
    Bearing me downward where no joy may be.

" Yet ere I go, beneath the death-wave sinking,
    To look on earth's soft beauty nevermore,
Let me but sing one song, that sadly linking
    My name to earth, may float along this shore.

"For I have loved it, with a full heart ever,
　　Though fate denied all utterance to that heart,
　And bade my joy be silent, speaking never
　　Till Death come unto me, and I depart.

"The voice of Summer on mine ear is stealing,
　　Sweet, clear, eloquent, as in years gone by;
　And the light falls on beauty, soft revealing
　　All fairest things that move beneath the sky.

"Bright in the sunshine rippling waves are sparkling;
　　Lightly they part them to my snowy breast;
　And 'neath the shadow of the trees lie darkling
　　A thousand haunts where I from sport might rest.

"Gladly and gayly, the laughter-loving hours
　　Hasten their bright and sunny way to tread;
　While, stealing perfume from the summer-flowers,
　　The wild, free winds go singing o'er my head.

"And I must leave all this! the full life glowing
　　Through all this beauty may be mine no more.
　Far from this pleasant shore my life is flowing,
　　And with my song its dream of joy is o'er.

"Oh! for one throb of the weak pulse now dying,
　　To breathe a song that might not pass away!
　In vain!　The shadow on the stream is lying,
　　And silence settles o'er the waning day."

　Alas! the Swan, its death-song sadly singing,
Mourning o'er fair things it might see no more,
Had roused my soul from its forgetful slumber,
To thoughts of buried love, and lonely graves.
I knew I was alone upon the earth;
No human heart claimed kindred unto mine;
And in my youth of years, and untried strength,
I must go forth to brave the armèd might
Of a cold, careless world, and struggle on
Apart, unaided, with no loving eyes
To brighten if I triumph; no fond hearts
To veil me with their love, and make their truth
Armor of proof, and buckler unto me!
The countless pulses of a city's heart
Were throbbing all around me, finding each
Their own responding thrill; but mine had none.
I was a stranger in a foreign land, —

A captive dreaming of my own far home,
And vainly pining for the pure fresh air
I might not breathe again!
          They gave to me
A home that kings might envy; rarely decked
With all that could give pleasure to the eye.
I liked it not. They gave me wealth untold
To lavish at my will, and power too;
For I was beautiful, and these stern priests
Were vassals to my smile, and willing slaves
To do my slightest bidding, and to give
All things save freedom; and for that I pined.
They called me free, and deemed me well content
To wear the fetters they had forged for me,
Because their hue was gleaming as with gold,
And they were flower-wreathed. But I had been
Free as the mountain air, and like a bird
Had wandered wheresoe'er it listed me.
They caged that bird. What marvel if it pined,
And beat its wings against the frowning bars
That stood between it and the free blue heaven!
What marvel if the gilded chains I wore
Soon pressëd deep their iron in my soul,
And I grew cold and hard like to their links,—
My woman-heart all silent, till its pulse
Seemed dead or dying. Little recked I then
If smile of mine gave pleasure or gave pain;
As little dreamed of hope, or love, so low
My soul had fallen in its apathy.

I knew that I was beautiful. Stern eyes
Melted into softness if their gaze met mine;
And changing cheek, and trembling hand and lip,
Were signs whose meaning I had learned full well,
But little cared to see. Time wrought its work:
And some who fancied they could love but me
Wooed other maids, and soon forgot me quite;
While two or three — the summer grass is green
Above their early graves, and they changed not,
But loved me to the last. And yet they all
Looked joyous in my presence, smiling still
With such sweet brows, I could not think their hearts
Were breaking all the while. I knew not then
How truest love may mask its secret pangs
With quiet smiles, that so the one beloved
May never know its bitter agony,
Or mark how fast the quick and fevered pulse
Doth beat unto the grave.

But one there was
Among the courtly throng that fluttered round,
Who loved me not as these, and only gave
Such love as brother unto sister gives.
But it sufficed me.   I gave him back
Like measure of affection, grateful still
For the pure stream thus offered to the thirst
That drained my heart-veins, slowly, painfully.
He was a fair, pale youth, with bluest eyes,
Most like unto my mother's, pure and sweet,
From whence an angel lookèd evermore.
He had a brow all white and undefiled,
Upon whose fair expanse the poet-soul
Had set its holiest seal; and archèd lips
That trembled to each feeling of his heart,
And only spake, in accents clear and low,
Such words as angels might not choose but speak,
Nor speaking, blush to hear.   He was of those
Whose hearts seem thrilling into music-tones, —
Who breathe away their very soul in song,
And die while singing!   He was as a plant
That hath one single stem and many buds,
But never beareth flower, and hath no seed.
I loved him; but it was with such a love
As hath its fruit in bitter tears, not joy,
Making us know earth's vanity.   With love,
O'er which the shadow of the doom to come
Is lying darkly, teaching to our hearts
The weary wasting of a dying hope.
I knew he could not live.   I saw too well
How the high soul was fretting 'gainst its chains;
And yet this fragile form, this fleeting life,
Was all to which my weary heart could cling, —
Was all that roused the woman in my heart,
Making it beat again !

One Autumn eve —
Whose glories robed the hills in burning gold,
And touched the clouds with crimson — found us both
Roving beside the swift and rushing stream.
Silent we moved, all conscious of the spell
Earth's dying beauty laid upon our souls,
So soft and dreamy in its glamourye.
Only our eyes spake, looking every thought,
In their mute language eloquent.   There came
Upon our trancèd ears, all sudden, swift,
A strain of muffled music; fearfullest
Of all that city's many harmonies,
For that it told of judgment dark and still,

And sure but secret doom.   We drew us back
Within the curtain of a leafèd tree
Whose branches fell around us shroudingly,
And watched the grim procession passing by,
In saddest silence still.
                                I might not tell
The fearful secrets of my prison-house, —
An oath had sealed my lips; but well both knew
That we were lost, did other eyes than night's
Peer through our leafy curtain; so we hushed
Our very breathing, and in silence gazed
On the dark line beyond.   Slowly they went;
The fearful music following their steps,
And in their midst, white-robed, and whiter-brow'd
A fragile maiden moved.   An ice-cold hand
Fell sudden upon mine, yet neither spake, —
A deeper dread had frosted o'er our lips, —
And we beheld that band, as midnight, dark,
Fade into shadow, and we said no word
Of all the anguish burning in our hearts.
The music died away; and that white shape
Passed into darkness, as into the grave!
Then from my brother's heart there came a prayer
On the hush trembling: " Have mercy, Heaven ! " —
Then wailing forth, through wan and ashen lips :
" O my beloved, would I might die for thee ! " —

    I asked no question of that breaking heart,
I knew too well that Earth had never balm
To soothe its agony.   No human aid
Could reach his soul's beloved; she was e'en now
Beyond redemption's pale.   The gentle dove
Was in the vulture's grasp; the secret doom
Had silent reached its victim; and I knew
It was too late to succor or to save;
To God belongeth vengeance!   So I turned
Me where my brother stood, and laid my hand
Upon his pale brow lovingly, so to say
He had a sister still.   He met my gaze
With such a holy calm upon his brow
That my wrung spirit bowed beneath its spell
Forgetful of its passing dream of vengeance.
For I so loved him.   Mournfully his voice
Went sighing past mine ear, for in its tone
There was a something caught from other worlds,
That made my wild heart tremble and grow still
In very dread of losing him.   He was more
Than all the world to me, and as he spake

I veiled my brow to listen, hoping still
He might not leave me.
      " Regina, sister,
Do thy tears fall sorrowing that I go
To join my loved ones in a purer world?
Rather rejoice, that from its earthly chains
The struggling soul shall be released at last.
The captive doth not love his prison-bars;
They come between him and the world without,
And mock him when he dreams of liberty.
Dost think he deems it an unwelcome hand
That breaks those bars, and makes those dreamings truth?
No! for the boon is very life to him!
And to the soul, whose fetters are of flesh,
It is the hand of Death that giveth freedom!
I fear him not. His aspect unto me
Is very sweet, most tender and most true;
And, with a loving hand, he leadeth me
Through a dark shadowy vale unto that land
Where living waters flow. And she — the maid —
Whom thou didst see but now, so meek and pale,
Found faithful unto death, doth tread with me
The same dark pathway to the one bright shore.
Thou knowest that I love her, though her name
Was never on my lips. I could not speak
Of love to one so fair, so beautiful,
When every pulse and throbbing of my heart
Was flitting to the grave. I could not bring
The shadow of my doom o'er her bright life
To darken evermore; and so I made
My poet-dreamings eloquent of her,
But gave unto my shrinëd love no name;
And yet she knew I loved her. Not a song
Wherein I sang to Fame, but had some tone
Wrung from the minstrel's heart, to tell its tale
Though only unto her. Death's touch hath drawn
The veil from off mine eyes, and well I know
That in the land to which we journey now
All things shall be revealed — nor more be seen
Darkly as through a glass. I know that there,
All sweetest dreams, all pure and holy thoughts,
That here found never echo, so were dumb,
Shall find a voice, nor longer mock the soul
With their unanswered longings. I have had
Such glorious visions of that Better Land
Whither my soul is tending! Dreams that made
All earthly splendor wan, and sickly pale;
Till the bright sunshine I shall see no more

Seemèd but another name for darkness, —
A shadow of the night. There were no clouds
To dim the soft effulgence of that light,
Radiant and far-shining, wherein the host
Of angels, cherubim and seraphim, found
The essence of their being and their life.
It formed the crown that rested on each brow,
Token of victory o'er spirit-foes,
And triumph over Death. For light — for crown —
God's all-approving smile! And this shall be
The meed of every patient human heart.
What if it suffer much? What if it know
The bitterness of life, and the light worth
Of earthly joy — draining unto the dregs
The seething cup of mortal agony?
What if it learn to bear through slowest years
The wasting torture of some hope deferred
That smiles, an ignis fatuus, but to lead
Unto a goal that hath no retrospect, —
No past, no present, and no future morn?
What if it die by inches, wounded, worn,
With no soft, loving hand to bind its hurt,
No faithful heart to shield it from the storm,
To rob misfortune of its poisoned dart,
Or blunt the arrow's head? And what, if thus?
So the poor bleeding heart rebelleth not
But own its trials just; so the true soul
But pass its earth-probation undefiled
By soiling of the dust that shrineth it;
What matter for the rest! Earth's years of pain
Thrown in the balance 'gainst eternity
Were very nothingness. Take from the shore
A grain of sand, and from the solemn sea
A sparkling drop. Dost miss the grain of sand
From the lone shore where it so long had lain?
Doth the great deep forget its time of flood
For that a drop was gathered from its wave?
And as the grain of sand from off the shore,
And as the drop of water from the deep,
So are the years of man, when weighed against
The endless cycles of eternity.
What matter, then, if this poor life of mine
Doth vanish from the earth? There will not be
A tear the more in any human eye
For that the minstrel of a fallen race
Is passing hence away. Sister, farewell.
The chill is on my brow, and I go hence
With all my dreams unanswered, and my hopes,

So proud and joyous once, must die with me:
They rise not o'er a grave.   No song of mine
May leave an echo unto after years
Telling of me.   No trumpet-voice of fame
Will float above my grave, and tell the world
'A minstrel sleepeth here.'   And yet I go,
Resigning me to earth's forgetfulness,
Content to know that in the Spirit Land
My soul shall quench its thirst in purer streams,
And from the burthen of this mortal coil
Shall rest for evermore.   Sweet sister mine,
Lay thou thy gentle hand upon my brow
As I in very truth had been thy brother.
So — so.   Twin stars have fallen from the sky,
And one is mine.   The other — Agatha!
Mine own — Agatha!"
      Hush! was it a voice,
Or but the flutter of an angel's wing,
That floated on the wind, as in reply
To my young brother's cry of " Agatha "?
It faded, blending sadly with the moan
Of waves that glide by night, and with the fall
Funereal sounding of the autumn leaves.
Slowly I lookëd up, and dimly saw
A pale, cold shadow creeping o'er the sky;
And heard the wailing of the soughing breeze,
The sobbing, wuthering wind; and well it told
What angel stood beside me.   Shuddering,
I drew my hand from off the icy brow
Where it had laid itself so lovingly,
And bowed my head upon my claspëd hands,
Weeping such quiet tears as soothe the heart,
And leave no death behind.   Yet was my grief
Most certain and most deep; for I had lost
The only thing I loved, and knew too well
The meaning of that saddest word " Alone."

A peal of bells rang out the midnight hour.
And, as their silver chiming died away,
Over the hill-tops rose the clear, cold moon.
Its pallid rays lit up my brother's brow,
And on that face, so beautiful in death,
I saw the smile all holy and serene, —
The smile that never living features wear!
It hushed my grief and unavailing tears;
And, as I watched beside, I heard the night,
With all its solemn voices, gathering round,
Wooing my soul from all its saddening thoughts

With whisperings of reunion in a land
That hath no graves, of hope the fatal bourn,
O'er which young, loving hearts may break and die;
And I grew calm and still.
      There fell a step
On the brown, crispèd grass, so slow — so slow —
As though it kept true time unto a heart
Whose pulse was weary with its load of woe;
And yet so firm as if the soul had strength
To bear its burthen bravely, hopefully!
I lookèd up, and met the steady gaze
Of earnest eyes, — such eyes as read men's thoughts,
Yet tell no secrets, and are faithful still.
I met their gaze, so solemn, questioning,
With the brief words, " My brother, he is dead."

Gently he spake to me, with soothing words
Stealing into my heart like a sweet strain
Of softest music.

Leon.   GOD comfort thee, poor child!
Thou art so young for such a grief as this.
Yet thine is no lone fate. It comes to all, —
This doom to see fair flowers perishing
And passing from our sight; yet to live on,
As though these things were not, and did not leave
Their impress on our lives. Gentle maiden,
How called ye him who lieth there so still?

Regina. Eugonäis.

Leon.   The minstrel of my race!
The tendril frail, that still, when sterner men
Disowned, betrayed, did cling so faithfully
Unto our fallen fortunes, — hath he gone,
Brave heart — true soul — unto the silent land,
Leaving the young oak on the desert plain
Alone to battle with the storm and blast?
He was my foster-brother, and his heart
So strong and pure in its unselfish zeal
No time could teach it falsehood, and no art
Debase its native gold with foul alloy
Of meaner metals. And this noble soul,
This gentle heart, " sans peur et sans reproche,"
Hath gone before me o'er the breezeless sea.
May I but meet him on the further shore,
Where he is resting now! But thou, poor child,
With thy so quivering lip and pallid brow,

Where dwellest thou? For the night wanes to morn,
And thou art all too frail to linger here.·
Whither shall I lead thee?

Regina.   Dost see yon palace,
With its terraced walks and shady arbors,
And the one fountain sparkling in the midst?
There, where the moonbeams fall so softly now?

Leon.   Is it there thou hast thy dwelling? Then I know
What name thou bearest, lady; and thy home
Doth shelter one who for long years hath been
My dark and secret foe. Yet can it be
His blood flows in thy veins? Thou dost not move
With the cold, haughty tread of those who claim
Near kindred to that house; and in thy voice
There is no sounding of their mother-tongue.
Thou dost not bear their name?

Regina.   Kind stranger, no!
They hold me captive in their golden cage;
And I am but an alien to their race,
An exile in their halls. Far, far away,
Towards the region of the setting sun
Doth lie my native valley; and the name
I bore in happier hours is mine still,
And I am called Regina here.

Leon.   Lady,
Forgive the stranger that he knew thee not,
And spake perchance too roughly. I have been
So long a rover on the tossing deep,
That it hath taught my voice a ruder note
Than greets thee from the smooth-lipped courtier throng.
I saw thee once. The rosy-cheekĕd morn
Smiled gladly on the sea, and thou didst sit
Beside the sun-touched shore, while my bark slept
Full softly on the wave; and I, alone,
Was standing on its prow. I saw thee then,
And felt — no matter what! Is this thy home?
Lady, thy brother's dust shall have from me
Such rites and homage as all true hearts claim
From our humanity.

Regina.   A moment yet.
Fain would I follow that belovĕd dust
Unto its silent home; but watchful eyes
Will be upon my steps. I cannot break,

As once this night, through sentinel and ward,
To wander where I will; and yet — and yet —
When that fair form is borne unto its rest,
I must and will be there.

 Leon.   And so thou shalt!
They shall not bar thy will by open force,
Nor yet by secret guile, if thou rely
On my sure promise, and wilt meet me here
When the night stealeth o'er the morrow's eve.
And yet, not here, but where he lieth now:
For none will follow there! The place is cursed
By the dark memory of a fearful crime.
But fear thou not. The moon will light the dark;
And, trust me, lady, I will guard thee well.

 Night came, and with it came the weary rain,
The drear and sobbing storm. Yet went I forth,
With stillest footsteps gliding through the dark,
But fearless, as had ever been my wont.
I was no trembler. Never had my heart
Known the quick throbbing that doth stifle breath
And soundeth loud like the dull beat of drums
Heard through the quiet night. Yet, as I passed
Beneath the shadow of the fir-trees dark,
And heard their long leaves whispering as of yore,
I almost paused to listen, as in dread
Of what might be before. The moment's thought
But added wings unto my lingering feet,
And I sped on, till sorrowing I stood
Within the shelter of the same sad tree,
Where I had left my brother slumbering.

 He was not there! Only a silent void —
Only the stillest shadow greeted me!
Irresolute I stood, while through the leaves
The rain-drops filtered wearily — wearily.
A moment, and a voice spake in mine ear,
" Lady, we wait for thee." I turnëd quick,
For well I knew the voice of yestere'en,
And gave my hand, and followed where he led.
But ever as we went, the wind's dull moan
Came sobbing round us, and our hearts grew still
And very sorrowful. Some slowest steps
Did bring us to the green and sedgy marge
Where the wild river flowed most dreamily;
And there, on whitest bier, all wreathed with flowers,

Two veilëd forms were lying, robed and crowned
As for a bridal; but no earthly one,
For the pale likeness of a parted soul
Looked coldly from each brow.
                        All words were said —
All fitting rites were o'er — and calmly, we,
Unto the keeping of our mother Earth
Did yield our parted treasures, as in trust
Until that day when all shall meet again,
And earth and sea have never more a grave!

We count not moments, in this life of ours
As parts of time, but only as they leave
Some deeper impress on the heart or brain.
And so the days that went between that grave
And the first after dreaming of my life
Are less than nothing in this retrospect,
And died from out my thought, for that they had
No place in memory.
                        One winter morn —
The snow lay deep on every threshold stone,
And the trees glittered in the sun's clear rays
As every branch were strewed with diamond dust —
I sat alone, slow poring o'er a tome
That I had rescued from the dust of years.
It was the saddest book, wrought in a brain
That never saw the fruit of its vain toil,
But perished immaturely. Even now
Through all the turmoil of uncounted years
An echo from its leaves comes to my soul,
And I hear its voice full slowly chanting
A measure like to this: —

" What matter if the dust we blindly tread
Was once instinct with life, and moved the earth
In likeness of ourselves, and linked itself
To beauty and to bloom; and left a name
For some few years to garner, then to die
Without a record of its well-earned fame
To tell the world how from its circles wide
A noble soul had passed!   What if this be?
Little it touches us; since years will come
When o'er our silent hearts, all carelessly,
Will fall the footsteps of a future race.
As all unconscious they that their swift tread
Is on our crumbling ashes, as are we
In this our busy life, that evermore
Around us and beneath us lie the wrecks

Of a forgotten and a buried Past.
But from these wrecks, unto the prescient soul,
In stillest whispers cometh '*resurgam*.'
And as from burials of ages gone
The long entombëd cities of the East
Rose up, dim phantoms of their golden prime
To greet some bold son of the present day,
Rewarding thus his long and patient search; ·
So shall the dead from their still cities rise,
And glide, pale shadows of their former selves
In our mind-pictures of their passëd days.
But only rise, silent to sink again
To their forgotten graves!"—
                         "Well do we know
That the dry dustings of a thousand years
Are lying thick upon their old renown.
Yet shall a breath, from lips all touched with fire,
Far to the free winds scatter every atom,
Till the pale shapes of a diluvian race
Rise up majestic from their slumber long,
Called thence by genius' magic spell, and walk
Through the old temples we have raised for them
In our imaginings, as if they were
But things of yesterday."—
                         "I mind me well,
How in my frequent poring over books,
I read of one whose conquering eagles flew
From the hot desert to the bitter frost,
Yet never rested till the midnight looked
Down on a sea of fire; and then they drooped
Never to soar again! And how fared he
Who led them on to victory and fame?
He died, an exile on a distant shore;
And the wild moan of waters was the dirge
That sang him to his rest. Earth never saw
A man like unto him, and yet his name
Has died from out the memory of the world;
And but some legends old keep record brief
Of that far-reaching life and lowly grave!"—

    I turned the page, but still more sad the strain;
As if, the while the poet traced the words
His own heart-pulsings echoed every line;
But ere I read, a shadow crossed the brook,
A shadow that I knew—it might be, loved.
'Twas his—the gentle stranger—by whose side
I stood all weeping, when to earth we gave
The form of my young brother.   Silently

I placed within his hands the mournful page
And bade him read to me.

    —" To wait and hope!   It is a weary task
When the young, fiery spirit fain would rush
Exultant to the goal!   To wait — to wait, —
That is a lesson youth but rarely learns,
And never willingly.   There is a grave
Beneath the shadow of a mountain cliff, —
A quiet grave, — and he who lieth there
Did wear that bitter lesson on his heart;
And watched, in meekest patience, through long years,
Waiting the dawning of a most sweet hope
To which his youth was consecrate.   But days
Went slowly, slowly by; and the fair bud
So fondly cherished by that jealous heart,
Grew never into leaf while one warm pulse
Was throbbing in his veins.   As through the night
Some tender plant will rear its drooping head,
And greet the morning with a perfect flower,
So from the ashes of that silent heart
An after age did form the consummate flower, —
The reverent love that clingeth round his name,
For which he lived, but did not die, in vain."—

    —" Pour out upon the dry and thirsty sand
Fresh life-drops from thy heart, and dream the while
They color all the earth!   The next hour's rain
Will blot the red stains out, and leave no sign
To tell where late such dark oblation fell.
Is it not so with our fond hope of Fame?
Do we not fling upon its thousand steps
The gems of mind, — the aloe-blooms of thought, —
And the wild breathings of the poet-lore
With its frail passion-flowers?   Do we not pour
Upon the ashes of Fame's altar-fires
Pale beads of dew from pale brows gathered slow;
And crimson drops, wrung from the tortured heart
To bear o'er earth its seed, and through all time
Its heritage of fame?   Vainly they flow,
Those crimson drops; vainly it falls, that dew;
For the dry dust on life's arena flung
Drinks the poor wasted offering, so to leave
No witness there.   Or the hot rain of tears
Down-falling on some lone, untimely grave
Doth wash the record out as silently,
And what remains to us?   A quiet spot,
Wherein we rest, forgetting all our dreams.

For the *dead* dream not; neither do they hear
The busy turmoil closing round the scene
Whence they have been removed.   And for this death
Through perished hopes — and for this noteless grave,
We make our youth a desert, and our prime
A ceaseless struggle 'gainst that darkest tide,
The ebbing tide of life; to find ourselves
Stranded at last, and all our fair hopes wrecked
Upon an opening grave.   Yet it may chance
That for a passing time our name may rest
Upon the world's cold lips, and sweetest praise
Thrill to our yearning hearts.   Earth's gifted ones
May yield to us the hand of fellowship,
And call us brothers; while the vassal world
Doth greet us with a triumph.   But the boon
Long sought, long waited for, is as the fruit
That grew in Hades, — tempting fair without,
Within but ashes found, and bitterness.
The wreath we strove to bind upon our brows
Is resting there; but it hath sharpest thorns,
And they pierce deep; mocking our throes of pain
With words like unto these: 'Ye won the crown;
Now wear it! though its weight press on your brain,
And though it woundeth sore.   To win that prize
Ye made your hearts give up their precious things,
And laid their secrets bare, and reft your souls
Of all their hidden jewels.   Now the world
Hath won them from your keeping, and they are
Your very own no more!' —
                    'What if the fame
Come never in our lives, and only light
With the far-spreading splendor of its beams
The silent halls of Death!   'Tis worthless, then,
For the closed eyes see not that shining light;
And the dull ear of dust doth nothing hear.
And yet not worthless all, this after-fame;
Since Death would find us calm and all resigned,
Did we but know that on our graves would rest
That after-smile of fame!"

   Leon.   This pleases you?
It is by far too sad a strain for me,
And chimes not well with such rude tones as mine.
So, by your fair leave, I'll read no further.

   Regina.   Then sing to me.   The cloud is on my soul,
And I am dull to-night.

Leon.   Then you shall hear
Some most rare music.   I have such a voice!
My comrades say its melody was caught
From ocean in its ire, or from the winds,
That sing like trumpets through the shrouds at night.
Nay, you shall hear it!   Seldom gentle ears
Are greeted with such music!

SONG.

" The early dawn was breaking
    On the sunny hills of Spain,
And the morning wind was shaking
    The dew-drops down again;
But the sun's first rays were glancing
    Where an army on its way
— The light on gay plumes dancing —
    Sang aye ' *viva el rey!* '

" There was mourning heard at even,
    There was deep, triumphal glee,
For the dead who went to heaven;
    For the glorious victory!
But the foe, while dastard flying,
    Learnt our watchword well that day:
For our living and our dying
    Sang aye ' *viva el rey!* '

" And the future, too, shall hear it,
    Though they've hushed its music long;
And our foes shall learn to fear it
    When it bursteth into song.
From our old ancestral towers
    Shall the silence pass away,
And we'll hail far brighter hours
    With the song ' *viva el rey!* '

" From the dust where hope hath slumbered,
    Lo! she riseth once again,
For the days of doom are numbered,
    And forgotten is our chain.
Through the din of coming battle,
    When the smoke shall darken day, —
Through war's sharp, continuous rattle,
    Comes the song ' *viva el rey!* ' "   .

            So he sang;
And evermore, around me, and beneath,
Choral voices echoed " *viva el rey!* "

There came a rush of quick and hurried feet,
And through the arched portals of the hall
Swept the poor hirelings of their master's will;
Intent on bearing to a secret doom
The daring singer; but they found him not.
He passed, — I know not how, — but he was gone,
And those poor slaves dreamed not of questioning me.
And so they turned to go; but, as they went,
Once more the mocking chorus echoed back
The chaut, " *viva el rey !* "
                    Words have I none
To tell how from each pale, awe-stricken face
The secret dread looked out. They dared not speak,
And shuddering glided from the haunted hall.
I knew they thought it was no living voice
That in the fatal covert of those walls
Dared breathe that rebel strain; and so they went;
Fear, like a touch of frost, through all their veins
Diffusing ice; and on their ashen lips
Setting the seal of silence.
                       Evening came,
And Leon sought me once again. He stood
Beside the open casement, where the light
From moonbeams shining on a field of snow
Fell softly on his brow; and, as I gazed
On the stern beauty of that lighted face,
There came a wistful meaning to mine eyes
His read full easily.

Leon.   Lady, the moon
That shines so coldly on the winter-earth
Hath looked on other scenes with gentler smile
Than she doth wear to-night. I've seen her rays
Stream down through orange-bowers far away,
And light up brows whereon a tropic sun
Had left a dusky shadow. I have seen
This same cold moon, full-orbed, and red as blood,
Rise up o'er ocean's dark and tossing tide,
In its deep crimson heralding the storm
Yet cradled in the west. And one calm night
She walked the sky like some pale vestal pure,
All marble cold; while 'neath her chastest beams
Such bitter tears were falling. But her smile
Grew never less serene, and only seemed
To mock the grief poured out upon the dust
That once had been a mother! I have been
For some brief years a rover on the deep;
And still through all my dreamings goes the moan

Of never-resting waters, and I hear
The same wild music sounding on mine ears
As made my youth's first joyance.   Even now
My heart is thirsting for the trumpet tones
Of ocean in its strife.   But Fate hath cast
My lot for other calling; and I wait
The coming hour when all the world shall know
How Leon the Rover fought for vengeance,
And won the freedom of his native land!
Ay, lady, even so! Your paling cheek
Doth show my name no stranger to your ears,
And beareth witness how they spoke of me.
But false the tale, and never friend that told it.
I know they called me " traitor," " infidel "—
And worse than these, if darker names there be.
But hear me; and if then you still should shrink
As doubting if I be not all they say,
I will be patient, and in silence go,
Shutting the sunlight from my lonely path
For evermore!
                    Days were when I was young
And very proud; for I, so noteless now,
Came of a noble race, upon whose brows
From sire to son in long unbroken line
A kingly crown had rested; and their rule
Was strong, yet gentle, too, and they were loved;
For the leal hearts upon a thousand hills
Were sword, and shield, and buckler unto them.
But Craft, with outward garb of softest smiles,
Came hither, and, like a thief in the night,
Did rob the people of their brightest gems,
Deluding them with somewhat semblant things,
That shone with a false lustre.   From our faith,
So pure and hallowed in its simple creed,
They sought to win us; and with deepest guile
Raised phantoms from the dust of ancient graves
Whereof to make them idols for the shrines
They reared by thousands in our once free homes.
Woe to the day when o'er our happy land
These harpies winged their way, scattering such seed
As left a harvest of the foulest weeds
For after reaping!   Ere that dark day came
My father died, and rested from his toil.
He sleepeth well, but I am desolate.
The golden circlet crowning once his brow
Did never rest on mine; for I was born
Of a high race that never stooped to guile;
And when the serpent-brood who so well wrought

The viewless fetters binding all the land,
Would have me wear as gift from their false hands
The crown that should have been mine own of right,
I spurned their mocking proffer, and did go
From out their loathèd presence, as doth one
Who feels he is an exile evermore.
Alas for thee, my country! Thou dost wear
Upon thy bleeding breast and marrèd brow
The impress of all scorn; and thou dost bend
All pale and shrinking, when thy iron heel
Should crush the dark oppressor in the dust!
A day shall come, when for this bitter shame
There *shall* be retribution; when the land
Shall break, like morning, from its trance of death,
And like a giant from his long sleep waking
Assert its right and title to be free!
But for our Present — woe that it should be!
We have no Present, we, save that which lies
In the pale likeness of a fettered slave
All trembling at our feet; with no more life
Than the vile modicum which doth suffice
To make it feel the lash, but not to turn
And rend the hand that so dishonors it!
And for our Past — we dare not speak of it
In this our low estate.   It had brave deeds
For after years to emulate, — high themes
Befitting well a minstrel's song of fire, —
Yet have they died from out the thoughts of men,
As in the evening of the tropic clime
The sunlight dies from off the glowing earth,
And the night follows quick upon the day,
No hour of dusk between!
                  My native land!
That ever sons of thine should stoop so low
As wear a foreign yoke! And yet — and yet —
They *were* a noble race; not smooth of speech,
As are these courtier-priests, but free and bold,
And somewhat rude withal, but true as steel!
What are they *now?* Slaves that have borne the yoke
And bowed beneath it servilely; as death
Were not more welcome than a life of chains!
Yet are there some true hearts this race among,
That have not bent to the usurping sway
Of a smooth priesthood, nor bowed the knee
At altars where pale shadows sit enthroned
As fittest shapes for lowliest worshipping.
Ay, yet there are — I glory in the truth! —
Some high and noble souls who keep the faith

In which our fathers died; who would not yield
Its glorious promise for the highest meed
Of earthly fame or honor; who would die
The slow and fearful death of sacrifice
Ere to the idols of a darker creed,
They bent submissive knee!
                                        I see a stream,
Its sluggish current all encrust with mould,
Whereon no bark may sail — no breezes blow —
'Mid whose green slime and floating wreck of weeds
A nameless race slow vegetate and die.
It hath its source within a fenny wild
O'er whose dank sods the mournful cypress sheds
Its wealth of shifting shadows; while the oak,
All gnarled and stunted in the ungenial soil,
Lets fall its scanty leaves with little moan,
Though pining in its hard, distorted heart
For the fresh mountain air!   Lone in the midst
There is a clump of dark and tangled pines;
And at their roots where never sunshine came
A dull, cold fount flowed out all noiselessly,
And crept through shadow and through darkness on
Beneath its pervious shroud of yellow moss;
Emerging from its still and secret way
Where first the sullen waters of the stream
Met the bright eye of day, but smilëd not.
And as that stream, all dark and deadly cold,
Flows on, in a far cavern's sunless gloom
To pass from mortal sight, so doth our fate
Move on remorseless to as dark a close.
Our present is stagnation — and our pulse
But throbbeth unto death, as if the grave
Were only bourn to which our sad hopes tend.
So they die early — wherefore should they live?

Regina. Nay, hope thou still! For from the burning sand
The secret spring may rise o'er desert-wastes
To spread some oasis of living green;
And, from the ruins of a buried age
Where long the fox hath dwelt — the bittern cried —
Another race may bid fresh cities rise,
Till grace and beauty, like a Phœnix, spring
From the funereal ashes of the past.
What wouldst thou more?

Leon.   The death of this despair
Fierce gnawing at my heart! I cannot still
Its restless fever. Keen are its pangs, and dure;

And evermore it crusheth out sweet hope
As if no flower, fair, and bright, and pure
Might bloom where it held sway.   Oh, I could fling
My very life upon one only die,
If but the shadow of that venomed shape
Would vanish from my heart!   It sitteth there
Defiant, flinging over cherished dreams
Its veiling darkness and funereal pall
Till all my life seems blending with the dust
Of cold and silent graves; and all my hope,
So buoyant once, dies out with those poor dreams.
Vain hopes, and vainer dreams!   I loved ye once;
For in my passionate youth I dreamed such dreams
As never feeling of more sober years
Doth shape into a likeness of our thought.
Such dreams as rounded nothing into beauty;
Pleasing our fancy with unreal types
Of that we fondly deemed some future day,
Pregnant with fate, would fashion into form
Making our visions more substantial seem.
So did I dream; so revelled in the bliss
That seemed to come, but never came to me.
As the lone traveller o'er burning sands
With painful pace and slow, and all athirst
Doth see the waters of a quiet lake
In the far distance shining, and doth haste
In the cool, sparkling wave to quench his thirst,
But, coming nearer, findeth the bright stream
Nought but a mocking mirage; so youth's dreams
Show fair and glowing in the early dawn
Of the heart's spring-time, but they mock us too;
And, when we seek to grasp them, they do fade
As shadows, and our path lies stretched before
All parched and arid 'neath a burning sky.

Regina.   Yet have thou hope; for life is often long,
And in the years to come fruition's hour
May crown the hope so all uncertain now.

Leon.   Lady, thou art so young.   Thou hast not known
As yet the torture of a dying hope;
Or the wild agony, slow, but very sure,
Of trust whose stay proved but a slender reed,
That broke with leaning on.

Regina.   Hush! hush! be still!
What if some hopes have fled, some visions died?
Life has a thousand, into being springing

With but a thought conceived; and these are thine,
Veiling the dead dreams that have passed away
As flowers blooming on a quiet grave
Do shut the dweller in that narrow spot
From the cold winds of earth.

   Leon.　　　　　How wouldst thou weave
The tissue of a dream?

   Regina.　　　　　With such bright hues
As youth's gay fancy tints the sky withal;
And each most joyous shape of earth and air·
Should show itself upon my tapestry.

   Leon.　I, too, have woven dreams; but aye the night
Did color warp and woof.　While sorrow, care,
And many another shadow of the world
Shed frost on every flower I could wreathe
That mournfullest web among.　I have walked
Through the wild mazes of a tangled wood
Where aye the shadows deepened as I passed,
And heard no voice on the lone silence breaking,
Save where the pines, a dark and stately race,
Moaned out through all their branches as the wind
Did rock them to and fro.　I was young, then,
Light of heart, and thoughtless; and as I walked
I plucked, in very sportiveness of mood,
The pale wood-flowers that grew beside the path.
My quick and fevered grasp was death to them;
And they fell, wan and fainting, from my hand,
The restless moaning of the tossing pines
Their only requiem.　So with the dreams,
Whose golden tissue glowed with all delights
While in the distance shining.　They were bright,
Preëminently beautiful, as they smiled
From out the future's portal; but the hour
That hailed them *present*, robbed them of their light,
And as the touch of a too curious hand
Doth rub the down from off the gauzy wings
Of some gay butterfly, so my wild heart,
In its too eager haste, did crush its dreams,
Even in the time when they did seem
The nearest to fruition; and they died
From out my world forever!
               There was a time
In my lost youth when Fame sang unto me,
Till on my brow its glory seemed to rest,
And its wild thirst was burning in my veins.

I saw the mighty dead, with solemn brows
And eyes all fillëd with a changeless light,
Move by me; and with haught and daring pride
I looked unto the time when I should be, —
As each had been through silent centuries, —
A star, clear-shining through the firmament.
Such was the thought, that in my fevered youth
Was very life of life; ever tinting
All dreams of future glory with its hue.
But in my wiser manhood I have learned
How futile was the dream.   Yet was it long
Ere the fond hope died out; and even now,
Through all the silence of forgotten thoughts
Its siren voice sounds in the distance, singing
The same sweet song that charmëd me of yore.
But the spell is broken; and golden Fame,
That did but mock me with its promise fair,
Hath lost its beauty of eternity.

Regina.   Nay, Leon, must thou share my sad mood too?
Come, cheer thee! for the night hath reached its noon,
And thou must wear a smile ere thou canst go
From out these halls.   Nay, smile; thy brow should have
No place for shadows, but be bright as mine
On that fair morning in the golden spring
When first I saw thee, standing on the prow
Of thine own bark.   Methinks a change hath swept
Over thy spirit since I saw thee last.

Leon.   Thou speakest truth. The change is written here;
And wouldst thou know the spell, — 'tis told full soon.
Lady, I love thee!

             To my cheek the blush
Rose sudden, deep, and my wild heart stood still,
So fierce the moment's rapture.   On my brow
A kiss pressed lightly; a few murmured words,
Not yet forgotten, — linked my fate to his
Through life and death.

Leon.   I see thee, O beloved!
Not as I saw thee once, when thou didst wear
An aspect mournful unto loving eyes;
For, as a lily drooping on its stem,
Thy form bent earthwards and as clouds
Float darkly o'er the clear midsummer sky,
So shadows of thy sorrow seemed to glide
O'er thy life's heaven, veiling all its stars.

Then tears were in thine eyes; and for the dead, —
The young, true heart that in its light of dawn,
And dream of fame, grew silent at thy side, —
As April shower on the soft green grass
Did fall thy heart's sad, quiet rain of tears.
I saw thee then, with brow so wan and still,
And eyelids drooping so, that to mine eyes
Thou seem'dst to be some vision of the grave.
I see thee now, no more a lily pale,
But robed in beauty as the queenly rose,
Joy's radiance on thy brow.   As the fair morn
Doth grow in glory with the rising sun,
So o'er thy brow where sorrow's shade did lie,
The sun of love shines crescent; and as earth
Doth welcome aye the sunburst of the dawn,
So to thy heart, that living fount of light
Comes fresh and glorious, steeping all thy life,
As with the golden splendors, tropic dyes,
That mark the tinting of some northern skies,
When the day dieth on the western sea.

    Even as Leon spoke, the rising wind
Flung wide the lattice, and a sound came in, —
The stir of a great city, and the rush
Of gathering multitudes.   Through the air
Streamed myriad signals of far-passing strife,
And from the starry dome, on high uplift,
Flamed out the crimson banner, sign of war,
And nearing battle-hour.   Swift through the streets
The armèd cohorts swept, all crimson-robed,
And bright in war's yet stainless panoply.
How shall the morrow find them?   Low in death,
Or flushed with pride of hard-won victory,
Forgetful of the dead who have no pride!

    Clouds had swept o'er the sky, and soon the rain
Came down from heaven fast and silently,
Wasting the pure white snow with magic speed;
And darkness veiled the night, but could not still
The restless feet without.   Through all the sounds
That rose beneath me, Leon's voice was heard
Breaking a moment on the ceaseless plash
Of falling rain-drops, murmuring full low,
"God's blessing on my own," — and then it ceased.
The silence gathered round me, cold and still,
While over all there floated, as through dusk
Of evening glides the reflex of a cloud,
A likeness of the darkness yet more dark.

"Where art thou, Leon?"—But no voice replied.
Only the ceaseless tramp from out the streets, —
Only the plashing of the weary rain, —
Fell on my thirsting ears.
      From out the dark,
And on that moment's loneliness, there broke
The olden chorus-song, "*Viva el rey !*"
With startled sense, I woke from my sad dream,
And, as I looked, across the darkening hall
A darker shadow passed; a shapeless thing,
With mantle loose and flowing, black as night
When storms are brewing, and as fearful still.
I strove to speak, to question its intent,
But utterance was denied me, and the words
Fell still-born from my lips.   It came, and went,
Most like the phantom of a fevered brain,
And left me lone again, dreaming once more
Of new-born hope and joy.
      I was beloved!
Not deepest night could dim the quiet light
In which henceforth I lived; nor fear, nor death,
Steal from my lips the sweetness of the draught
So lately drained.   It seemëd to my heart
As if the thought so long in secret nursed,
Had sprung to life and glory, as of old
Aladdin's palace rose, reared in one night
By the all-potent genii.
      Enough !   Enough !
The morrow came, all ushered in with gloom;
Never a ray of sunshine for the earth,
And only tears for me!   Far to the north
The tide of war had swept, and darkly red;
Its frozen plains were covered with the dead
Who there had striven on a stricken field.
But they who fought against the church's power
Proved victors in the strife; so from the dome
Where it had floated long triumphantly,
The priestly conclave took the banner down,
And flung its crimson foldings to the breeze
That sent it northward.   Thither they, too, moved
To win by cunning what they lost in war;
Fit heralds of the mighty armament
That followed slow upon their devious way
As engine of their will.
      I saw them go, —
And dared to smile, as in recovered freedom.
Too soon the mandate came, that I must join
Their armëd host, with this poor bloom of mine

To grace their triumph, or to share their fall.
I went, — wrenching apart all closest ties
That late had bound me to my prison-walls;
And wearing on my brow the marble veil
That shroudeth ever secret agony.
While coldest eyes, and lips as cut from stone,
Told nothing of the warm heart crushed beneath,
And breathed no word of all the secret tears,
The very wreck of dead hopes garnered there!

Tempest and storm were heralds of our way;
And the cold North did send its terrors forth
Daunting the boldest hearts of all our train.
The sky was racked with clouds; the wind's dull moan —
Demoniac scream — went sounding through the pines
Whose mournful shapes loomed sadly from the snow,
Dark sentinels of death!   Huge, stern-browed cliffs
That reared their giant heads, encrust with snow,
Did bar our onward way.   Wild torrents rushed
Athwart our path, all cold, engirt with ice
That gave no resting for the weary foot,
And plunged adown deep gulfs where darkness held
Its undisputed sway.   The avalanche
Fell rude and sudden from the topmost crags
Hurling swift doom to thousands; yet our lords
Still urged us onward.   Little did they care
How fared the common herd, so that their rule
Lost never one poor state.   "Onward! onward!
Though the dead fall fast as the autumn leaves,
And Azrael stand before!" — was still their cry,
And onward did we go!   But all the land
Was up in arms.   The very earth did seem
To join the league against the priestly host,
And the stern Winter laughed in coldest scorn
At all our futile efforts!   Inch by inch,
The invaders pressed towards the utmost pole,
But found a desert, bleak and desolate,
With never a living thing!
                              Yet once — once —
A breath of human life did cross our path.
Our way was o'er that very battle-field
Where late the children of this frozen zone
Stood victors, and the dead lay resting there
As softly, silently, as if night had sealed
Their eyelids unto slumber.   Them amid
A woman sat, pale-eyed, with saddest brow,
And lips all white and wan.   Alone she sat;
The pale night gathering as a cloud o'erhead,

And the stars shining down so pitiless.
Poor child! poor child!   The very sky did frown
Upon her wild and passionate agony,
And the cold winds went moaning past her ear;
They could not say " Be still!"   *Alone* she sat,
There was no fond heart now to soothe her pain;
No tender hand to wipe away her tears;
And she had nothing, for the grave had all! —
The gráve that rose between her heart and hope,
And shut the sunshine from her quiet life! —
The grave, that like a miser, clutches *all*
And giveth nothing back!   Yet she had been
A joyous creature; all her bounding life
Sent out in motion, light as any bird's;
And evermore, far-ringing on the air,
Was heard her laughter, musical and clear;
A sunny joyance in its cadences
That made your heart throb quick, as if its pulse
Had caught that merry chiming, and did send
As gay an echo back.   The battle-day
Dawned darkly on the land, and her young hope
Drooped dying in her heart.   Fate gave to her
A bitter cup, all drenched with saddest tears.
She drained it to the dregs; and then hope smiled —
The hope that looketh to another world —
But only that she died.   She sleepeth well.
Not deepest wailing, and not wildest tears
Can wake her from that slumber; and her heart
With all its weary pulsings is as still
As death can make it.   Peace unto the dead!
The white snow drifteth o'er their crimson couch,
And the pure stars do watch them, as with eyes
Of pitying angels.
                        We left them there
And hasting went on our unholy quest.
Unholy, — for the land had burst its chains,
So that with purer rites, more simple creed,
Their sons might worship GOD.   To bind those chains,
So lately broken, closer on the land
The fiery children of the fervid South
Had left their sunny clime.   For this the priests
Had donned their martial robes, and sounded forth
The clarion of war.   For this they braved
The unknown terrors of the frozen zone;
And left pale thousands sleeping by the way
Who never woke again.   Death had put on
His kingliest aspect, and where'er they went
They met their Master; till the clear cold stars

Looked only down on graves!   Yet pressed they on
Until the silence of the Polar Sea
Stretched vast and lone before.   A dreary void,
With only the smooth and the glassy ice, —
Only the drifted snow.   High over all
A glittering sky arched down with all its stars,
Brilliant exceedingly, but oh! how cold!

Torrent and tempest they had braved full long,
Nor turned aside for the swift avalanche;
But that still sea, so dread because unknown,
To traverse that, how might their skill avail?
But "Onward!" was the cry.   They might not pause;
And so the march went on.   O'er smoothest ice
The crimson cohorts swept.   Enough for them
Their priests did lead the way.   They followed slow;
The chill frost stealing o'er their weary limbs;
And day by day, some poor hearts fell asleep
Cradled to endless slumber on that sea.
Quietly they rest; but in far hamlets
Fond, loving hearts do watch for their return.
Vainly they watch, — for the dead return not,
Neither do they hear in their so silent home
Earth-voices any more.   Alas! the hearts
That must be wrung with anguish, when years go
Bringing not the absent back!
                              One swift day
The flush of morning lit up mountain cliffs
Born of the Frost-king's breath, and struck with light
As with a shower of roses.   All the night —
The long, still night Polynia calls its own —
Had we o'erpast in journeying hitherward.
Now the day dawned, as on our glad eyes flashed
Polynia's fair, but giant-guarded soil.
The day had dawned; but to the unhappy land
Our coming was as night; for torture, death,
Did follow in our footsteps.   Stanch the hearts
And strong the souls that made their home beside
The Sea of Shadows, and their simple faith
Proved mightier than the terrors of the Church.
Vain were its tortures, crushing out all shape
Of sweet humanity.   Vain were its words
Of mocking promise too!   They could not quench
The soul's deep thirst for truth.   They could not still
Its earnest longings for a purer life;
Nor stain its holier prompting with the taint
Of worship offered unto sainted names,
Or lower still, to dust!   And day by day,

Life torn from quivering limbs did send its cry
Accusing unto Heaven!   O God! to see
What fiends may wear Religion's sacred garb,
And veil beneath its holiness such deeds
As were most fitting unto darkest hell!

I saw not aught of this.   I only heard
Of silent fields made populous by graves!
They barred me from the day, that so mine eyes
Might see no shadow of the passing crime.
They could not chain the flight of freest winds;
And on their pinions, borne unto my cell,
Came saddest wailings from bereavëd hearts,
And oft the sighs of death.   I needed not
A human voice to tell me how the Church
Doth woo rebellious spirits to its breast;
And well I knew, how, through that summer-time,
Innocent blood was, like to water, shed.
Wherefore?   So that within the Church's pale
The souls that burst its fetters should return
Obedient slaves once more.   The task was nought.
Souls yielded on the rack — wrung from the clay
By slowest agony — were not less free!
The passing hour but severed every chain,
And human malice was the sport of Death, —
Of Death, against whose silence — as the waves
Beat on the stubborn rock — they dared to breathe
Their vain anathema.   On the quick frame
They wreaked their utmost vengeance; but their wrath
Soon stilled the senseful life, and gave the soul
Eternal freedom.   Joy to the redeemed!
The holy ones who trod the martyr-path
Of suffering unto God!   Hail to that band!
Not one had turned aside for offered life;
Not one had proved apostate in the hour
Of sharpest agony.   Calmly they saw
The flaming torch applied; and their freed souls
Went up through fire to God!
                              I knew all this.
My pulse was hourly throbbing unto pain
I could not still nor soothe.   Once I had prayed
For ceasing of this strife.   Once I avowed
A faith like unto theirs for whom I prayed.
They spurned me as a thing for mocking made,
And bade me pray unto my prison-walls.
I never stooped unto their scorn again.
I did but wait the coming of the end;
For death seemed very near; my life had **grown**

So aimless and so still!
                    One quiet eve
My prison-doors were opened, and they bade
Me wander where I would. Slowly I went,
The warm air touching into quicker play
My languid veins. The sun that never set,
But only circled round the horizon
Through the long day that stretched to triad months,
With rays aslant, did tint with emerald
The wide glaciers, while far away and near,
The slumberous sea lay silent and serene,
All blue and smiling as the heaven above.
Green, sunny slopes rolled downward to the sea.
And, in the valleys, herds of tiny deer
Did crop the tender herbage. Fairy trees
Were on the hill-sides growing, and the bloom
Of sweetest summer crownèd all the scene.
It was so fair that in a moment's space
My thoughts flowed back to that soft southern clime
I scarcely hoped in life to see again;
It was so far away.
                    Stern voices broke
The enchantment of my senses, and I saw
The dark tribunal looming at my side;
The darker yet by contrast with the sky
That smiled so bright above. There sat the judge,
With lips compressed and locked by force of will.
And brow dark as a storm-cloud, yet all flushed
As by some secret pang. Against the bar,
Pale as a shadow from the spirit-land,
A shape was leaning, on whose beaded brow
The veins like cords were lying, swollen thus
In very silentness of agony.
This palest shape was in its morn of life,
Beautiful as a dream, but drenched with pain
As flowers by the rain.
                    Outspake the judge,
With accents cold and sharp as edgèd swords.
—"The Church doth proffer pardon; gives thee life,
So thou but kneel repentant at her feet,
And own her judgment just. 'Twere vainest hope
To look for safety elsewhere than with her.
And soon the land, so late rebellious grown.
Shall new allegiance pay, and ye be free
As in the olden time."—

                    —"Free! when the yoke
Must lie the heavier on our weary necks!

Free! when our fathers' faith must be betrayed,
Our country fettered, and our GOD denied!
Call you *this* freedom?   And the early doom
Your word hath laid on warmest, truest hearts, —
Can we forget the loved whom ye have sent
Through torture to the grave?   Will no voice rise
From their still realms to haunt our paths for aye,
If we blot out their memory from our lives?
For ye, — who shut stern Justice from her seat, —
Not wealth of tears, nor years of vain remorse
Shall hush remembrance in your haunted souls!
Go, fling the dust upon a thousand hearts;
It will not still the voice that from their graves
Doth rise, accusing ye!   What though the dead
Come never back to tell us of their fate, —
Yet, from their very ashes, rise such words
As waken nations from their slumbrous calm;
Till, borne on lightning wings from soul to soul,
The spell like magic works, and all the land
Exultant springeth from its lethargy!" —

— "Dreamer!" —

    — "Am I a dreamer?   Nay, if so,
Then are these fetters nought but fantasy,
These weak and tortured limbs a fearful dream,
And all my visions of the death to come
As baseless as your daring hope of heaven!
But, fit negation of your scornful word,
Hear you the shout out-ringing through your streets?
A people up in arms do send it forth,
Sounding defiance to your mailèd bands,
Your dull, obedient slaves.   And, though I die,
My heart's blood drained in agony, yet I go
Rejoicing on my way; my soul upheld
By a high hope you know not, and a *Love*
That walketh with me through this darkest hour
And stilleth all my fears.   O GOD! my GOD! —
So take me to thy rest!"

            His brow drooped down,
An awful shadow creeping o'er its snow,
As the slow pulse was dying in his heart.
Then silence fell upon him, as a frost
On quiet river, and his life went out
With never-flickering motion.
                    "He is gone,"
Murmured a peasant voice in deepest tones.

"His heart will never throb to pain again,
And his poor body I must beg of you,
To give it fitting rites of burial.
You will not wreak your vengeance on the dust
Of your once brother?"—

     —"Call him not brother;
I know not such a name! and for this thing
Do with it what you will; only the Church
Doth bar the faithless from sepulchral rites
And rest in holy ground. It goes not there!
Fling it to the waves, if so you will it.
They'll not refuse a grave, though they may make
Rare sport with the poor waif!"—

     He ceased, frowning,
And so he turned away; but, as he went,
A form stood in his path,—a childish face
Looked questioning in his own, quick reading there
The things that had been; and with keen regard,
Stealing the secrets from that haughty heart.
—"Where is thy brother?" spake the little child,
Laying her small hand on his nerveless arm.
"Where is thy brother?—he who once did brave
The unchained fury of a swollen stream
To rescue thee from death, and almost gave
His life as price for thine. His loving heart
Was thy sure shield in battle, and his life,
With all its hopes, was so bound up in thine!
Yet where is he? For all his earnest love
What hast thou given him? Not equal love;
Rather most bitter hate! For the pure faith
Ye both had gathered from a mother's lips
He gave himself to torture and to death.
And thou stoodst by, and coldly looked on this!
Dost hear? He *loved* thee! And now, never more
His voice may come to thee save in thy dreams.
A word from thee had saved him! Now the dust
Is on his fair hair lying, and the grave
Hears never wail of sorrow. To thy soul
Remembrance cling as some sharp scorpion sting
That beareth agony, but doth not kill!
And through the night a voice come unto thee,
Asking, in clearest accents evermore,
'Where is the brother who so loved thee?'"—

Pale grew the brow that had so sternly frowned,—
The strong frame shook and trembled as a reed,—
And the lips they spake not,—the cold eyes glazed

Into cold silence. 'Twas but a moment,
And the fierce anger clove its way through fear
And a strange sense of awe.
                    — " Dost question me
Of the poor phantom that thou call'st my brother?
Go ask the sea, within whose secret caves
His corse will soon be lying! Ask the grave
Of all that lies beyond its quiet bounds,
And question Death where the warm Life did go
When the keen torture wrenched it from the frame
Of him thou call'st my brother! question *these;*
They have some claim upon the senseless dust.
I have none!"—
                    — "And yet he was thy *brother!*
O stern and hard of heart! Thou didst not love
The warm true heart that battled by thy side;
Thou dost not fear the dead! Yet from the deep
Beneath whose mighty wave he soon shall rest
A sound shall come around thy couch at night
To wail most mournfully, filling thy brain
With bitter thoughts. And from the mightful Past
A shape like his shall glide; with tender smiles
And murmurings of gentle words and deeds
To rive thy very soul with vain remorse,
And vainest yearnings for the silent heart
Thy word hath stilled so soon. GOD pity thee!
Thou hast a fearful doom!"—
                    And the child ceased.
The soft tears trembling in her full dark eyes;
But he passed on, in all his spring of years,
But winter of the heart; from that dark day
To have the shadow of a tortured form
Haunting his waking and his sleeping hours,
And resting nevermore! He passéd on;
And all the pageant of the judgment-seat
Did seem to vanish with him. But the child
Did linger yet. I called her unto me
And questioned of her friends.
                    — "I have no friends.
They left me long ago, and yon bright heaven
Is all their dwelling now. I may not see
Their faces more till GOD doth call me home."—

Regina. Poor child! poor child! I read within thine eyes
— So full of meaning in their speechless gaze —
The thought that I am stern. Thou canst not pierce
The mask that time hath moulded, not yet know
How throbs the poor and aching heart beneath.

Come hither, child. Thou hast the brow and eye
All clear and dark of mine own distant land,
So tell me of thy home.
                        — "It is not here,"
The child replied, — "not here where evermore
The pale frost glitters on the dwarfèd trees;
But far away; in that all lovely land
Where the sun shineth softly, and the sky
Is yet more blue, more tender than thine eyes.
I know a song, — my mother taught it me, —
Wouldst have me sing it?"

Regina.   Ay, sing it, my child!
And I will listen, — calling buried thoughts
The while from their still graves.

THE CHILD SINGS.

"Where the skies shine ever bluest, and the glorious sun
        looks down
In his deep effulgent radiance from a heaven without a
        frown;
Where the day it passeth dream-like, and the hours their
        pinions fold
As the sunset poureth over earth its crimson and its gold;
Where the night's serenest forehead, as an angel's brow
        is starred,
While angels o'er its holy sleep, seem ever keeping guard:
There my home, in all its beauty, rises slowly unto me,
As an island riseth upward to the mariner at sea.

"Oh! the forest, the old forest! beneath whose shade I
        strayed,
Flinging laughter back in answer to the echo laughter
        made;
In its silence of past centuries, how evermore it grew
More silent and more beautiful till I grew silent too.
And the torrent leaping downward, — leaping downward
        past our door, —
How wild and thrilling was the hymn I heard amid its
        roar!
But I loved not much its music, though it ever floated near,
For the rush of swollen waters sounded harsh unto mine
        ear.

"Oh! the sweet, the blooming flowers that around my
        home there grew,
From off whose fairy petals the morning kissed the dew!
And, oh, the quiet garden where the orange-trees were seen

With their golden fruitage gleaming through their foliage
    dark and green,
And o'er the little arbor with its tracery of stone
— The work of fairy fingers — bloomed roses, many a one;
And through the carvëd trellis, in the sunlight's glowing
    sheen,
The purple clusters of the grape hung rich and full be-
    tween!

"Where the wind goes ever singing, as it had no note of
    grief,
And the forest knows no shading of the sere and yellow
    leaf;
There my home is softly smiling with the gentle smile of
    yore;
And I — my heart is dying — I shall see it nevermore!
Only in my earnest dreaming, — only in some hour of
    sleep, —
Do I tread the olden pathways, and the olden footsteps
    keep.
Only then, — alas! I waken from the vision all too soon
But to see the ice-fields glitter 'neath a cold and glittering
    moon!"

So sweet had been the song, that it did bring
The restless music of a torrent's bound
Close to mine eager ear, till my thoughts flowed
Back to the river of mine early days.
I woke as with a start. 'Twas but the rush
Of hurried footsteps through the pavëd street,
And the wild swell of voices, eloquent
With all that teaches unto Power fear.
Hast ever heard the dash of angry waves
Upon some storm-swept coast? So came the sound
Of those fierce voices on the free wind's wing.
In their guarded walls the tyrants trembled,
For well they knew resistance were but vain
When the roused anger of an outraged race
Had torn asunder all the bonds of fear,
And risen up insurgent.
                We were safe.
No arm of all that host would touch the life
Of woman or of child; and yet I wept.
For the swift thought of all the many homes
That strife must darken rushed upon my soul,
Clouding it with tears. Death had been lying
A quiet shadow on each household hearth;
But those who slept had trod the martyr's path,

And on each mourner's brow a strange joy smiled.
Now strife had gathered o'er the fated land
And closest bonds a moment's breath must break,
Severed by death upon the battle-field
That might not bring them victory. Vain tears,
For they were wasted! GOD stretched out his hand,
Hushing to silence all the wrath of man,
And every heart grew still!
     What of the child
Who paused a moment on my line of life?
Our paths crossed nevermore. In that same night·
A wind went forth, wandering through the land,
Mild as a zephyr, but it breathèd death.
GOD sent it, gathering thus into the fold
The Shepherd's chosen flock; and then they said,
The little child went home!
     From out that land,
Dispeopled all, and eloquent of death,
The invaders fled. Not as they entered in,
A mighty host whose banners met the breeze
All fearless of dishonor; but as those,
Who, few in number, and in courage weak,
Do call the night and darkness to their aid,
And choose the coward's part of flight and shame.
And I went with them. Death came not to me,
Though it had been most welcome; and my way
Turned southward once again, and through my soul
There thrilled the hope of meeting Leon yet.
Death had been very busy, but his wing
Might have passed Leon by. So I lived on, —
Upheld by that one hope.
     Our little band
Moved slowly on, beneath a sky all black,
From out whose deepest shadow flashed the stars,
Blood-red and burning; while the Frost-king held
Such revels all around us as might tame
The proudest spirit into abject fear.
Still we went on; for that before us smiled
The hearts that best did love us.
     One calm night
I lay beside the watch-fire, with closed lids
That veiled no slumber, for my thoughts were sad
And would not yield to weariness their sway,
Nor vanish into dreams. Above my head
A pine-tree waved its branches moaningly;
And at my feet, but far below my couch,
A torrent rushèd by, with such a song
As only distance bringeth to our ear.

Voices broke on the night, scarce startling me.
I listened dreamily, as oft doth one
Who thinks he is asleep, yet sleepeth not.

FIRST VOICE.

" She was robed most royally, as an eve
Purpled with sunset; and her scornful eyes
Looked down upon me in superbest pride,
Scathing my soul with light.   Yet I loved her;
Bowing my neck beneath her haughty smile,
And well repaid if for my lowliness
I won the shadow of a glance."

SECOND VOICE.

" Poor slave !
And thou didst think to win her!   Why, her pride
Doth grasp the world within its boundless sweep,
And would not stoop so low, e'en in its dreams,
As mate with thee!   Content thee with thy lot.
The falcon's wing flies far, but doth not soar
As the eagle's to the sun."

FIRST VOICE.

" Then I will be
E'en as the eagle, and with equal force
Soar proudly to my goal!   Oh! I will make
The very time my slave, and through the wreck
Of war-tossed nations make a name to lay
Its laurels at her feet.   She shall be mine,
If I do peril worlds to win her!"

SECOND VOICE.

" Worlds !
Nay; worlds on worlds would fail to bear thee there!
Her heart doth keep still vigils o'er a grave;
And aye within the ramparts of her pride
There sits the shape of one pale memory;
And her whole being, soul, and life,
Are only true to that.   To seek some star
That only mocks thee with its far-off light,
Were surer proof of wisdom than to pour
Love on a shrine so cold and dead as this!"

FIRST VOICE.

" Then farewell hope, and welcome be despair!
My heart is but a grave where all sweet dreams
Lie early buried, as are frailest flowers

Beneath some late spring snow.   True to the dust
Thou sayest is her heart; and mine shall be
Yet truer to its love.   I will not die
Till the wide world doth crown me with its fame;
So that her lips may one day breathe my name
As one, not all unworthy of such love
As might have blessed my life, had her heart been
Free as I dared to hope it !   O sweet hope !
Thou liest on the bleak shore of my life
As some dead mariner on the cold sands
Of ocean's wildest verge ! "

       I heard no more,
For the wild storm-blast swept athwart the night
Armëd with wrath; and the old stately pines,
Beneath whose shade our band lay slumbering,
Bowed their dark heads unto its force, and fell
Supinely to the ground; never again
To point unto the sky.   Clouds, dim as night,
Rolled up the zenith, shutting out the stars;
And with the blast, the King of Terrors swept
All grimly on his way.
       I bowed my head.
Methought the terror was upon my soul,
Claiming its ready prey.   It passed me by,
To silence every pulse that yestere'en
Was throbbing unto memories of home,
And thoughts of swift return.   Vain dreamings all!
The word " return " was blotted from their lives;
And they lie sleeping on a foreign soil,
Dreaming of home no more !   Sadly I gazed
Upon the stillest hearts that slept around,
And as I gazed there came unto my soul
A feeling of unrest, — a longing wish
To tread again the sunny land of flowers.
Perchance their beauty might assuage the pain
Fierce gnawing at my heart; and so I went
From out the voiceless presence of the dead,
Turning my footsteps to the golden South,
Whose sparkling waters knew no touch of ice.
Too long my home had been amid the white
And stony giants on Polynia's shore;
And I was weary of the terror-shapes
That heralded but death, and filled my dreams
With darkness and despair.
       Slowly — slowly —
With weariest steps I trod the fated way,
As one who journeys on a dreaded path

That hath no turning back.   Day unto day
Did tell the same dull tale of weariness
That knew no resting, for my soul asked none.
Rather it murmured at my progress slow,
And with a fevered pulsing questioned aye,
"How near unto the goal?"   Alas! my heart,
If but thy questioning had won from earth
A shadow of reply, how still, how cold,
Had been thy after-beatings!   Now the thirst
Of wildest yearning, and of hope deferred
Burns quenchless in thy veins; and all life's strength
Seemed slowly ebbing from my weary frame;
For I have borne so much!   Yet doth my soul
Preserve its strong, unconquered energy,
Bearing me up with true and steady force,
To tread the homeward path.   O home, sweet home,
That smilest where the sparkling waters play!
Thou risest to my vision, soft and bright,
With such a glamour, as if angel eyes
Were looking into mine, with their clear light
Scattering afar the shadows on my soul!
O home, that in the distance waiteth me,
If but my feet were wingéd as my thought
I might be with thee now!   "O pining heart,
Rest quiet still!   All shall be thine at last,
If only thou have patience to the end,
And yield not to despair."   So spake the deep
And potent oracle of my secret hope;
And thereunto I listened with a smile,
And went upon my way, so weary late,
With lightest step, as one who garners joy
Unto the coming day, and in his heart
Hath smiles wherewith to crown the future.
Morn,
In all the glory of its first-born smile,
Moved radiant o'er the earth, whose garmenture
Told of the ripest spring.   I paused awhile
To trace upon the tablets of my heart
So fair a picture; and my weary eyes
Were fain to linger on the quiet dell,
Whither night had led my steps.   Wanderer
Had I been long, and 'twas foretaste of joy
To look on scene so calm and sweet as this!

   A fairy cot, with ivy curtained in,
A murmuring stream that rippled past the door,
A stately tree, o'ershadowing the cot,
And some few flowers, did form the magic spell

That bound me with the might of loveliness.
Too soon the glamour faded; and I knew
No spot so fair, but sorrow creepeth there.

I heard the echo of a weary step,
And, turning, saw a feeble, shattered man,
Dragging towards the fairy cot his feet.
His face was wan, and in his darkened eyes
There sat the shadow that aye marketh one
Who beareth evil tidings. Swift my glance
Was on the cottage bent; and a girl came
Into the presence of the glowing morn.
She stood within the porch, with keen regard
Watching the far-off pathway. On her cheek
The pale rose trembled; in her radiant eyes
Sat joyous expectation, and her heart
Was beating high in earnestness of hope.

Who cometh yonder o'er the short, crisp grass,
Slowly — slowly? No messenger of joy
Is he who moveth with such lagging pace;
And her prophetic heart doth feel its doom
Ere yet the words are spoken. Hast thou seen
A lily floating on some swiftest stream
Down to the soundless sea? Didst watch it pass
Into the distance from thy earnest eyes;
Feeling the while it went but to its grave,
And would be seen no more? So fled her hope
Of joy in life. There needed no vain words
To tell her heart that on his fair young form
The silent dust was lying. One long look
Upon the face of him who brought the tidings, —
One upward glance to heaven, — and she died.
Now, o'er her virgin beauty grows the grass,
All fresh and greenly, as if never heart
Most true and loving rested silent there.

Life! life! Thou hast a fragile tenure here.
'Tis but a thread of gossamer that doth hold
Thy spirit unto earth; and one poor breath
May snap that frailest band, and all thy pulse
Be still for evermore. And yet we count
Upon thy length of days; and weave such dreams
As only years can ripen into fruit;
Forgetting, all the while, that every throb
Sent from the busy heart is so much time
Lost from our span of life. We think not so,
Or if the thought should come, we do but say,

"Some may die young, but we shall have long years
Wherein to make our dreams reality." —
Blind mortals that we are! One onward step ·
Towards the goal where all our wishes tend,
Doth bring us to the grave; and all our dreams
Shall end, as we, in dust!
              These saddest words
Came floating through my brain, as I stood there,
And saw dark tidings on that girlish brow
Set the cold seal of death. O happy one!
I gave thee never tears, for thou wert blest
So early called from Earth. In thy soul's home
Thou dost not feel the woes that day by day
Drain blood from living hearts; and thou art free
From the dread yoke of Sin that cannot dim
The glory of the crown that marks thee now
Redeemëd from the world!
             O Land so fair!
O Shore that lies beyond the waves of Death
Whither that soul hath gone! how may we look
Upon thy glorious beauty and yet live?
How in our idle dreams we picture thee
Fairer than thousand earths, yet come not nigh
The veriest shadow of thy loveliness!
O Land! eye hath not seen thee! never dream
Of poet-heart yet pictured aught so bright!
Only when our poor hearts are turned to dust,
May our enfranchised spirits find in thee
The mansions GOD doth give to his beloved.
Yet to our fettered fancy, in the still
And solemn watches of the holy night,
There floateth, oftentimes, a seraph song, —
A psalm of strength, — and we go forth at morn
Comforted and sustained by a deep sense
Of GOD's abiding presence. Oh, the love
That links eternity with this frail clay, ·
And turneth not away for all the sin
Wherewith we stain our souls! How poor, how mean,
How little worth in his all-sinless eyes
Must our vain longings be! and yet our GOD,
The High and Holy One of Israel,
Watcheth and loveth us!
             Back to the earth,
O thoughts of mine! — back to the earth again;
Ye are not free from its cold bondage yet;
Life's tale is not yet told.
             Silent I stood.
I had seen the flower perish, heard the cry

Wrung from the ashen lips of that pale man,
As o'er the beauty of her sunny face
Fell the gray shade of death; and then I moved
Unto the cottage porch, and laid my hand
On the dead maiden's brow; and with wan lips
Did murmur o'er such soft and soothing words
As stole the sting from his poor, sorrowing heart,
And hushed its wail of grief.   Yet still the words
Came frequent from his lips, and thus he spake, —
Many a pause between:
                              — "She was my all, —
The only thing that loved me, — yet the grave
Must be her resting now.   And she so fair,
So loving, all the pulses of her heart
Beat but in answer unto his and mine;
Her lover's and her brother's.   He hath gone
Before us to his rest.   The storm-wind swept
Athwart our quiet slumber, and its breath
Laid low the stately pines; and where they fell,
Beneath their darkest pall, some gallant hearts
In death lie sleeping, crushëd out of life
In the passing of a moment.   I am here
Of all that martial band, and bannered host
The only living one; and my poor life
Will vanish with the day, and with the sun
Its waning lamp die out." —

Regina.   Hast thou no friends?
No loving ones to watch and care for thee?
No hearts of home and hearth, whereon to rest
Thy weary brow?
                              — "I had a mother once.
But little love had she to give the boy;
And now, the man, returning weary, worn,
And stricken unto death, may yearn in vain
To feel the impress of a mother's kiss
Upon his dying lips.   Mother! — mother! —
Couldst thou but see thy child!" —
                              As ceased his voice,
From out the silence of the shaded cot
A woman moved full slow.   Her eyes were dim
With length of years; and in her trembling hands
She held a staff wherewith to guide her steps.
Those steps are stayed — wherefore?   Before her lies
The child of her old age, — a lovely form,
That hath nor life nor motion.   She sees not
That other child, so long unloved, unknown,
And doth but weep above the breathless clay,

As one who knows what shape Death's Angel wears
When with the silence of his unseen hand
He striketh down the beautiful.
              — " Mother ! " —
In saddest accents came the man's deep tones,
And struck upon her heart, unsealing there
The long-closed portals, and the buried love
Rose living from its grave.
                From out the West
The setting sun a flood of glory sent;
And through the foliage of a stately tree
Its golden rays streamed in upon a brow
Whereon the signet of life's passing hour
Had left its shadow gray. They passed beyond
And rested on a form that never life
Could robe in beauty more, then faded all;
And in the darkening room we sat, and watched
The spirit in its flight, and heard the words
That fell so slowly from those pallid lips.

  — " I stand within thy solemn presence, Death,
And all earth-visions fade from out my life.
I hear the rush of wings that bear me on
Through thy dark valley to the further shore;
And all my soul is filled with dreamings wild
Of that which is to be; of glories vast
O'erpassing all our human thoughts of Light;
And of a Love that weigheth all things down
In its unapproachable purity.
Yet through all these there floats a mournful song
Wherein the dust doth breathe its life away.
With swiftest face, and brow all pale and wan,
A saddest shape flits from me, and I feel
It is the Present I may claim no more.
The Future that doth wait beyond the grave
Is all of Time for me. The Past is dead,
And all its deeds are written in the Book
Wherein my doom was tracĕd long ago.
O Death! my dreams are of thee, nevermore,
For I am thine. Thy hand is on my brow;
Thy coldness stealing to my fainting heart;
And my poor mother's form hath grown so dim,
I cannot see her now! One kiss, — the last
From those fond lips. Nay, weep not; only smiles
Are in the angel's eyes. 'Tis very dark, —
Surely the night hath come, and I shall see
No more the dawn of day. Mother — thy hand —
So — so — "

                    Awhile he lay with that thin hand
Clasped in his own, and we, who watched within
The quiet chamber, thought that sleep had hushed
That voice of music, and in stillest mood
We waited for the morn.   "The morn is here!"
Went sounding through the hush; but as the sun
Looked in upon the watchers, a low cry
From the pale mother's lips told every heart
That Death had given to a parted soul
Another morn than ours!
                              I went forth,
From out the presence of that silent heart,
Into the flush and sunshine of the morn
So gloriously beautiful!   Earth! — Earth! —
Thou hast so many graves yet smilest still!
Smilest, as if no shadow of man's grief
Could dim thy splendor or attaint thy bloom.
I love thee, Earth!   Unto mine earnest eyes
Thou hast the virgin beauty of thy youth;
The cloudless aspect of thine earliest morn.
I've seen thee when thy brow was all alight,
And day's resplendent beams did crown thy head
As with a diadem of living fire.
I've looked upon thee when the burning noon
Flamed hot and lurid on a desert's sands,
And deemed thee not unlovely.   When the snow
Lies pure and spotless on the year's cold grave
Thou hast a sadder seeming, yet most sweet;
And liest in thy shroud, as some fair child
Unto whose dreams death whispered silence;
Silence that stilled the pulse, but could not tear
God's signet from the pure and holy brow!
Yet most I love thee, Earth! when heaven's arch,
Glorious with stars, doth watchful bend
Above thy quiet slumber.   Then my soul
Doth spurn the bonds of Time, and through all space
Doth seek to hold communion with its GOD.
Nor fruitless quite the search; since oft the Night,
From out its sibyl caves, yields to our quest
Oracles more potent than the dazzling hopes
Wreathing life's early days.   Spirit-voices
Floating through shadows aye, — prophetic tones
That sound upon our souls, and bid them wake
Unto a higher life wherein the strife
Is for a deathless crown; — and far-off songs —
Fragments of angel-anthems borne through night
And silence to our hearts — are oracles
That only touch the soul, and rarely die

Unanswered from the world.   Beautiful Earth!
Hadst thou no graves wherein to gather life, —
If but thy love had immortality, —
We would not leave thee for the promise rich,
Heralding the Better Land!   Enough!   Enough!
For thou *hast* countless graves; and Time, and Change
Do scatter ashes on our weary hearts
Ere Death doth still their pain.
                              Day waned to night,
And night to morn; but ere the hornëd moon
Had stooped again adown the western sky,
Two little mounds were looking up to heaven.
I stood beside them, as the sunlight died
From off the distant hills, and in the blue
The pale stars trembled; and I inly thought
How quietly they sleep! the peaceful dead,
Around whose dwelling never care may come.
They see no clouding of the summer day,
They hear no turmoil of the restless world,
Though loud and fierce above their quiet home
Its jarring voices clash, as swords that cross
On the wild battle-field.   They feel no more
The ceaseless rush of life's unresting stream;
For the cold waters of a darker wave
Have borne them onward to that shoreless sea,
Eternity!   They pass from out our sight,
And on their slow and mournful exodus
Mists gather silently.   Not yet may we
Look on the Promised Land!
                              A falling star
Flashed sudden through the night, and in the South
Vanished in darkness.   With a fearful heart
I marked the omen, and with hasty steps
I followed where it fell.   I thought not then
Of the poor mother, and her lonely hearth;
Or how she'd sit, through many a summer eve,
And in her faithful heart, as in an urn,
Gather sweet memories from her household graves.
Not then gave I one thought to that lone heart
So patient in its sorrow; for my own
Was thrilling to a dread I could not master.
Leon — or dead, or dying — was the theme
Of every thought and dream.
                              But all my haste
Was labor thrown away.   I did but tread
The same wide circle ever.   Weary, worn,
With every nerve a torture in itself.
I laid me down to sleep, but in a mood,

When every sense that should have dormant been,
Was quickened into action.
                          Round me strewn
Were moss-grown fragments of that olden day
When men reared temples from the rudest rock,
And thought to vanquish Time. Time mocked them all,
And saw the domes they deemed imperishable
Totter, and fall, and crumble into dust.
Around me, too, were stones of later date ;
Pale marble cenotaphs, on whose furrowed plane
Some names were deeply cut ; forgotten names
That died upon men's lips long years ago.
O'er all had Nature's kindly spirit flung
A veil of greenest leaves and brightest flowers ;
While, towering high above man's feeble work,
The grand old trees did rear their giant heads, —
The tireless growth of o'erpast centuries.
The grand old trees ! How in their thousand years
They laugh to scorn our puny boast of life,
That only stretcheth to threescore and ten !
They flourished, green in youth, in those old days
Whose record is tradition ; and the hour
When Time's death-struggle is of Earth the doom
Shall find them in their prime. Their fragile germs
Awoke to life amid the mouldering dust
And stately monuments of crownëd kings,
Who, in their time, were what the world calls great,
And rulers of mankind. As dies the sun,
When all the west is crimson as with blood,
And the low-hanging clouds do mantle him,
So they died, royally ; dying, as those
Who know and feel an after-day must come,
When Fame shall twine its laurel for their brows,
And loving memories of a grateful land
More fit ovation be ! They slept in death,
And o'er their graves men reared fair sculptured stones
That should outlast all time, and be for aye
Memorials of the dead. Alas for fame !
Its symbols perished long ago, as dust
To mingle with the dust ; while the frail germ,
That slowly crept into the outer air,
Hath felt the heat of ages and their dews,
And flings its shadow far and wide above
The sepulchre of kings !
                          My wandering thoughts
Full soon flowed back unto my place of rest ;
And then I saw a lonely monument,
Upon whose marble white no stains of Time

As yet were dying. Two were sleeping there, —
A brother and a sister, — and my heart
Did trace their epitaphs, and thought it read
The writing on the dull and silent stone.

I.

" Her life was as a stream, whose placid breast
No breeze went rippling o'er. Her thoughts were dreams,
So sweet she never gave them utterance,
Lest darker blendings should their light destroy.
Her dreams were shaped by love that lonely dwelt
Its secret shrine within, and looked not forth
Lest the cold world should mock its humbleness.
And she had known the fulness of all joy
In resting on a heart that gave back love,
In measure such as generous hearts should give.
But Fate had mingled in her cup of life
One deep, abiding sorrow. Soon the grave
Did bear unto its silence the true heart
Whereon she rested all her earthly dreams;
And she was left alone, save for the love
Her brother's heart within. How flowed her life
When thus the joy departed? As a stream
Upon whose waves the tender moonlight plays,
Shedding soft radiance there. From out her heart,
So silent in its sorrow, came sweet songs
Of earnest life, and solemn psalms to GOD;
And at her hearth dwelt meek-eyed Charity,
Working in secret aye, and all her life
Was ' holiness unto GOD.' When she slept
An angel went to Heaven." —

II.

                    — " He who resteth here
Did live amid the dreams, wild, fanciful,
Of the old days that were dark ages called.
For him the stars had voices, and the night
Did ope to him its solemn mysteries,
And told him all its secrets. On his head
Snow-flakes had fallen, blanching all his hair,
Yet was his brow as smooth as any child's;
As sweet and gentle too. His soft, low voice
Was full of music in its clear accords,
And had an angel's lovingness of tone.
The years that work such changes came to him
As to the promise of a golden summer
Doth autumn's wealth of fruits. Only the dull

And frozen winter followed not thereon,
For, in the fulness of an honored life
The old man fell asleep; the quiet stars
Filling his last of earthly visionric."—

Such were the lines methought I tracëd there;
And o'er and o'er I read them, till each word
Seemed as a living thing, and took strange shape,
And gathered round me with a rush of sounds
I could not choose but hear.   But through all these
There stole the far-off murmur of a brook
That sang unto the stars, and on mine eyes
The sweet sleep laid its spell, yet not of force
To shut out visions from my restless brain.

I heard the sighing of the soft south wind;
I saw the blossoms of the orange-trees;
And in their glorious beauty rose the domes
Of the fair southern land that was my home,
In those bright days when Leon told his love.
Not yet had dawned the day; but morn's first beams
Shone pale upon the horizon, and the streets
Were filled with human life.   It seemed to me
Some day of festival.   And yet not so.
There were no signs of light and festive mirth
On those care-wrinkled brows.   No joyous mood
Is that which stamps resolve upon the lip,
And arms men with the sword.
                         My gaze passed on,
— Mid all this crowd, it found not what it sought,
In search of one too well-remembered face.
Nor long my quest.   Methought my steps were stayed
Beside the Hall of Council.   On its porch
A shape was standing armëd for the field,
Above whose stately form a white plume waved
Shadowing the brow.   'Twas Leon's self I saw;
And yet I could not reach him.   Something stood
A barrier between us, and my heart
Constrained itself to silence, and was still.
Another shape came gliding by me soon,
With pale and quivering lips, and took its place
My Leon's form beside.   He spake to it.

Leon.   Wherefore so sad, my friend?   Thine's not the
      brow
To bear the brunt of battle, or the fate
That gives us death, but never victory.
How now, Velasquez, why so sad, my friend?

Velasquez.   Leon, the dust is lying on her brow;
And from her grave, O friend, I come to thee
For comfort.   Canst give it?   Leon! — Leon! —
The world has vanished from my broken life;
And in its stead a shadow sits enthroned,
A thing of dust, that calls me to itself
With potent spells, teaching unto my heart
Throbs intermittent, — pulses speaking aye
Of the near and quiet grave.   Still I hear
The far-off murmur of the busy world,
And catch the heavy swell of dull applause
That hath no music now.   Hushed is the voice
That ever woke soft echoes in my soul,
And when it died in silence, all my life
Grew hushed and silent too.   The sun departs,
But the day lingers long, though that which made
Its glory is no more.   So lingers life,
When all that made it beautiful hath gone hence
Bearing its joy away.   So clings the heart
Unto some phantom shape of memory,
When that which gave unto the shadow form
Doth rest beneath the mould.   O vainest love,
That could not shield nor save!   What matter, now,
That this poor heart doth tremble unto pain?
Will it not so the sooner silent be?
The sooner journey to that summer shore
Above whose flowers Death's shadow never floats?
Shall I not be at rest?

Leon.   Rouse thee, old friend!
Life was not made to waste in vain regrets
O'er the returnless dust.   Keep, if thou wilt,
Her shrinëd image in its olden place,
But give thy life to action.   Dream no more
Of the still shadows on thy hearth-stone lying;
Dreams bring not back the lost; and man's true realm
Is never memory!   Life summons thee
Unto its noblest battle, where the crown
Is ever to the victor.   Lift thy brow
From out thy claspëd hands, and with stout heart
Look Sorrow in the face, and she will seem
Less dark to thee.

Velasquez.   In vain!   Thou hast not known
The grief of gazing on a face beloved
That looked not love again!   Thou hast not felt
The wordless agony of breaking hearts
When all that made life sweet doth flee away ·

Into the darkness of the closèd eyes, —
The silent heart!

   Leon.   Be still! for who may count
The lost graves of a lifetime? Who may know
What shapes lie buried 'neath the quiet smiles
That only speak content? Sweet hopes that shared
The rainbow's promise — golden dreams that made
Our youth most glorious — silent joys of heart —
Pale, passionate thoughts of love without return,
And lone despair, have lived their little life
And died from out our lives as flowers die
From off the summer earth. We bury all
In coldest silence, and so forget them,
Till our later years glide smoothly onward
Reckless of the storm and turmoil of their youth.
I tracèd, once, a river from its source.
Swift from a mountain's brow, the water rushed,
Fretting and foaming on its downward way,
Now lashed to anger 'gainst the upheaving rocks,
Now soothed to music 'neath the sun's soft rays,
Through olden forest, and primeval gorge,
Through silent dells where never sunlight came,
The stream went on its way, and grew at last
A broad and mighty river; all its days
Of restless striving, shadow, and of storm,
Forgotten in the glory of its prime, —
The fulness of its rest!

   Velasquez.   Thou reasonest well;
'Tis thy brain speaks. Thy heart hath never stirred
Unto the breathing of a woman's name.
Thou hast not loved!

   Leon.   Little thou knowest me.
'Tis that my heart *hath* trembled, and grown still,
That I can counsel thee, in this thy need.
O friend, I envy thee! *Thou* hadst the bliss
To watch o'er thy beloved, — to whisper hope.
Thou couldst smooth the way of darkness, — show the light
That breaketh from on high; and in thy grief
Thou hast her grave whereon to shower tears.
I have nothing. This poor heart may not know
Where its beloved lies sleeping. May but learn
From stranger lips, that o'er the mighty host
With whom she journeyed, death hath flung the pall.
Her fate lies dark as night; and in my heart
The sweetest fountains of its secret love

Lie buried evermore. Enough! *that* life
Hath lost its glory. Not the less doth *this*
Call on our souls to work its high behests.
Our country needs her sons, and base were he
Who, in *her* hour of peril, sighs o'er graves.
I know thee, gallant friend! No coward, thou!
But look! O'er yonder hills the morning sun
Doth dawn apace. Each to his destined post!
And, in the coming strife that waiteth us,
God grant us victory!
                              So they parted,
And the vision ended. I saw no more;
But heard the quick and measured tramp of men
As they went marching by to cover earth
With dying and with dead. My thoughts did pass
Beyond the coming time. I saw a field
Crimson with blood, and heavy with the dead
Who had not yet found sepulchre. I saw
Fair, pleasant homes, wherein War's breath of fire
Had scattered desolation; and I heard
The wail of stricken hearts o'er some beloved
Who had in battle fallen. Not a hearth
Within the City of the Seven Hills
But had "some vacant chair." The restless tramp
Of that vast army marching to its doom,
Dying on mine ear, a moment lingered;
And I awoke, to look on graves again.
And see the moonbeams glimmering through the leaves,
Shadowy, like ghosts.
                              Again I slept;
Again the vision came. I saw a plain
Whereon the grass was springing fresh and green;
And in the first rays of the morning sun
The dew-drops glittered bright. A bugle note,
A trumpet's call to arms, and in the stead
Of glittering dew-drops moved a serried band,
All eager for the strife. A moment's pause, —
Then came a rush — a whirl — a clang of arms,
In the fierce melée meeting! Through it all
I caught the glancing of a steel-clad form,
The waving of a plume as white as snow,
And with a fevered pulse I watched that plume,
And found it ever, floating white above
The thickest of the strife. All else, save that
Had vanished from my sight. I recked not how
The tide of battle flowed. I did but see
The snowy plume above that calm, pale brow,
And shivered as I gazed. A muffled sound —

The beating of ten thousand arméd hoofs
Upon the yielding turf—a rush—a whirr
That drowned all other sounds; and then the plain
Rose up to view again, all still and dark.
The strife had ceased. That charge had mowed all down,
As mowers mow the grass. I saw him fall,—
The steel-clad leader with the snow-white plume,—
I caught the gleaming of a broken sword,
And darkness sealéd up my dream.
        I woke,
To fill the night with laughter, and to be
Myself no more.
      Years sped; I know not how.
The chambers of my brain were tenantless,
And gave free scope for airy shapes therein
To hold fantastic revel. All these years
Were to my soul as one long, dreamful sleep.
I woke at last, "clothed, and in my right mind;"
Awoke—to find my youth had gone from me,
Bearing my beauty in its silent flight.
A mirror hung before me. On its face
I saw a shape, the shadow of myself.
Eyes wild and gleaming with the fever-fire;
And scattered tresses on whose raven hue
Pale silver threads were lying soft like snow.
My cheek was flushed, but not with health's warm tint;
And all my strength was less than any child's,
I was so changed, so helpless, and so weak!
Where was the bounding step, that in the days
Of my bright youth could bear me o'er the earth
Tireless and resting not? And where the strength
Succumbing not to pain? Departed all.
I could not raise my hand from off the couch
To brush aside a tress that on my brow
Lay heavily. 'Twas wearisome to think.
And so I slept away full many weeks,
With little sense or motion. Dreamily
The days went by, while health through all my veins
Diffused its quickening pulse.
       'Twas autumn time;
A day of Indian Summer, when I woke
From that long death in life. Idly I lay
And watched with childish eagerness of eye
The falling of the leaves that fluttered past
The open casement; and I counted o'er
Their number as they fell. Their hue was red,
Or burnished as with gold; and they seemed bright
To my regardful eyes. Far off—far off—

A sweet, young voice was singing. Soon it came
Nearer, and yet more near, until I heard
The wording of the song.

Song.

"The leaves are falling — falling; and the day it is so still,
That you hear them rustling far away upon the crimson
    hill, —
Upon the crimson hill-side, where the fading light of day
Reflecteth back the glory to the crimson wave alway.

"The leaves are falling — falling; and I hear their sighing
    breath
As they go floating downward to the open lap of Death.
As the Dolphin, when it dieth, bids the rainbow mark its
    doom,
So they bear their strange, wild beauty to the cold and
    wasting tomb.

"The leaves are falling — falling; and the night doth fall
    above.
Doth it send its starry heralds on a message full of love?
I know not; for I cannot hear what song the stars do
    sing:
It needs must be a sad one, for the flowers are withering.

"The leaves are falling — falling; and the stateliest trees
    are bare.
How they seem to shake and shiver in the clear and frosty
    air!
And the flowers by the brook-side, and the daisies in the
    grass,
In their sweet and modest beauty, as a vision from us pass.

"The leaves are falling — falling; dost thou hear them, as
    they fall,
Saying unto human creatures, 'As we perish, so must
    all'?
For our fate is as the falling leaf's: we mingle with the
    clay,
With a far more glorious body to rise and live alway."

The fair young singer in my chamber stood;
Her youth enfolding her as rose-leaves lie
Around the rose's heart. Within her eyes
There burned that steady light clouds cannot darken;
And her full lip was archèd with the smile
That makes home beautiful. Her quiet heart

Was formed for sunshine, but had strength as well
To meet the storm unshrinking. Oft she came
Unto my stillest room, cheering its gloom
With the old songs she sang.
                              One dusky eve
A shape of other mould did stand within
The circle of my gaze; and it had been
The fairest thing on earth, if but amid
That glorious mould of form had dwelt alway
A loving human soul. I read her heart,
As with a curling lip and scornful eye
She looked down coldly on the feeble frame
That could not cope with fever, and yet bear
No tokens of its dark and cruel strife.
She had a proud beauty. There was a glance
Half-scornful, half-defying, in her eyes;
And on her brow, so calm in self-control,
There sat a veilëd splendor, as of skies
Where light clouds flecked the sun. She was most fair
To look on; but her full and curvëd lip
Had long forgotten smiles; and for her heart, —
The bitter fruit beside the Dead Sea growing
Were likest unto it. It had no love.
Above that fountain sweet, pride's desert sands
Had long been drifting; and the pleasant stream
Was buried at its source, and gave no more
Its silvery singing as a tribute meet
From loving heart to Love. As she stood there,
Frowning defiance to my searching gaze,
There stole into my heart a memory, —
The voices I had loved on that dark night,
When, 'neath the pressure of the fallen pines,
The relics of an army breathless lay,
Crushed into sudden death. Was this proud thing —
This shape without a soul — the queenly dame
Of whom that fond and fiery lover spoke,
Ere love and all its visions died in death?
She read my thoughts as if on open book
They had been traced.
                       — "And so the poor fool died?"
The words came slow and hissing from her lips.
— "He loved me once, and dared to tell me so!
The crouching slave! I could have struck him down
As you would strike a snake! I did but smile,
And on that mockery he builded hope.
He was a poet — I laughed his rhymes to scorn —
And dreamed of fame; I bade him win the wreath
Ere boast of wearing it. He had a friend

Who loved him; and to that friend's simple heart
I seemed an angel, all too high above
Mere worlds of feeling, for a child of dust
To hope for love from me.   I mocked him, too,
By seeming that I was not; and both went
From out my presence as my palest brow
Were crownëd with a star.   They could not raise
The veil from off my heart, or pierce its gloom
To learn how my soul did mock them! "

Regina.   Lady,
Dost know thou shouldst speak gently of the dead;
For what the earth doth cover is henceforth
No theme for jibe or jest.   Lady, the twain
Of whom thou makest sport, died far away.
A night of storm came, full of death to them;
And on the morrow fell the soft white snow,
Alike their shroud and grave.   And on his lips, —
Thy poet-lover's, — when the summons came,
A woman's name was trembling.   Hast no tears
For the swift doom that struck that name beloved
Into dull silence?   Hast no pity left?

— " Pity? dost think the falcon mourns the dove
Whose heart it hath torn out?   Dost think that I
Would grieve above the dead?   I tell thee, no!
Not if my life's blood should pay the forfeit!
Shadow which liest there, — with such pale cheeks
And so rebuking eyes, — little thou knowest
How in the heart of woman broken faith
Doth bury deep all sweetest, purest thoughts;
As the hot ashes, showered o'er pleasant fields
In the volcano's wrath, enshroudeth all
In everlasting darkness.   Once the queen
Beloved and cherished of a mighty realm,
Behold me in my desolation — lone —
Discrownëd — yet still regal in my hate."

Regina.   Thy hate!   Oh! not on woman's lips that word
Should find accustomed greeting; and as thou
Dost hope for pardon in thy dying hour,
Tear from thy soul that demon dark and foul,
And love and trust again.

— " Thou mockest me!
I love!   *I* trust again!   If thou didst know
How once I trusted, till the thing I loved
Was steeped in shame, as the night in darkness!

I was so happy once; but baleful tongues
Shed poison on the fame of him I loved.
Then my pride woke, and I flung off the heart
On which my faith was stranded; flung it off
As 'twere the basest thing in all the world;
And in my pride I stood aloof, and smiled
The while men's voices lashed him with their scorn.
Wouldst thou have loved him still?" —

    Regina.   If I *had* loved him,
Never breath of shame should blight the feeling!
If once my hand had rested within his,
Not bitter jibing, nor yet scornfullest eyes,
Should tear it from his grasp. 'Twould only cling
The closer there, and with its gentle clasp
Bear witness of the heart so fond and true
That could no touch of worldly changing feel.

    — "What if the world turned coldly from his name,
Tainting his honor with its meaning laugh
And half-breathed whisper? What if these things were?"

    Regina. If I did love him, little would I heed
What others said of him; and my full love
Should robe him royally, so to mask the shame.

    — "What if he stood alone, — the mark of scorn, —
Bereft of friends, — the brand upon his brow
So steeped in crime that the cold world doth say,
'The very dust he treads would be defiled
But that God made it'? Couldst love him still?"

    Regina. If friends forsake, then the more need that love
Should draw its tendrils closer, so to veil
The guilt it cannot see!

                   "If this be love,
Then what am I? My heart had never veil
Above my lover's darkened fame to fling.
Nay; I did mock him with my taunting smile,
Marvelling how aught so base dared speak of love,
Or hope to keep it! I crushed him with such words
As only anger clothes the lips withal;
And then he left me; all his hopes in life
Flung, dead and dying, on my scornful self.
And for a type of such despair as his,
A vessel floating on a shoreless sea,
Were fittest emblem."

Regina.   Thou couldst do this thing!
A woman, thou, yet crush the broken reed!
Thou didst not *love* him! Love would but have clung
The closer for the guilt; and flung aside
The scorning of the world, as one who runs
A race unto some goal doth fling away
All that doth stay his progress. Hadst thou loved,
And o'er his fallen spirit shed the bloom
Of thine own truth, the world had scorned him less.
For love doth sanctify what it doth touch;
Redeeming in its own eternal light
What else had been but darkness. But thy heart,
In falling from him, left no staff in life
Whereunto hope might cling, and it may be
He died without a smile.

                        — " Nay : never so.
He was too proud of soul. There are who wear
Upon the sweetest feelings of the heart
A masking veil, that so the idle world
May have no knowledge of the secrets hid
Within that heart's lone cells; upon whose lips
Bright smiles delusive play, while in the soul
The gnawing worm of bitter musing holds
Its dark, and grim, and solitary sway,
Warring with life! And he was one of these;
And when he died, there was no word of moan.
Brief space had he to learn how much man's heart
May suffer and yet live. My words were death.
The morrow's sun was shining on his grave;
As brightly, smilingly, as if no heart
Were slumbering beneath."

Regina.   Alas! that thou
Didst let the sun go down upon thy wrath;
Since ere the morrow with its glory came
The heart that had offended thee was dust
And could not hear " forgive!" O child of clay!
How couldst thou cherish anger, when the grave
Doth lie so near the hearth? If but thy voice,
So bitter once, could pierce beyond the tomb,
And through its silence plead for pardon sweet
How eloquent thou'dst be! Too late! — too late!
The soul that hath departed hears no more
The voice of earthly friendship; nor responds
Unto its wail of grief. Thou hadst *this* life
Wherein to prove thy love. If thou didst fail
Through all the passéd years, not wildest prayer

Can call the soul back from its wanderings
To hear thee tell the love that never deeds
Could shape into reality! Too late!
The grave hath set its seal upon the past.
Too late to win him back; but not too late
To learn the lesson death hath left to thee.

— "Be still! I will not hear thee! What art thou,
That thus thou schoolest me? I would not stoop, —
If from his grave he rose to hear the words, —
I would not stoop so low as say 'Forgive.'
What dost thou here? I did not bid thee come.
Hence to thy grave!" —

                        As thus the proud one spoke,
I saw a pale, wan shape, ethereal
Float through the moonlight, with a lambent brow,
And eyes that burned like stars. A soft, low voice,
Clear as the echo of an evening bell,
Thrilled on my heart; it was so strangely sweet;
And thus the spirit spake : —
                        — "Poor, erring child,
That will not bear rebuke. I come to thee, —
GOD hath permitted it, — and in my love
I have o'erswept the dark, dividing grave,
Dimming my glory, so to rescue thee.
Thy youth — thy beauty — are as upas-trees,
Blighting thy soul's true life. I blot them out.
The worm is gnawing at the flower's heart;
'Twill soon be withered. Years are granted thee,
Wherein to sow such seed as yet may bear
Fruits that may ripen in eternity.
Remember, O proud heart, 'they who love much
Are forgiven much.' O Father! in whose sight
Earth's children are as dust, yet who didst yield
Thine only Son to death that we might live;
Hear us, we pray thee, and in thy good time
Redeem this soul; for not alone by tears
Can sin be washed out. 'Tis only Love
That — shining from above — can take away
The Shadow from the Cross!" —

                        Serena's step
Light echoed from the porch. Her voice in song
Broke musical upon the solemn pause
That filled my haunted room. The spirit's brow
Did grow more human as those soft tones rose
Clear, full, and rounded, yet so sadly sweet;

And in his starry eyes a shadow dawned;
A passing touch of mortal sympathy.

SERENA'S SONG.

"The night is on the river,
    And the stars they shine so pale;
And the floating lilies shiver
    As they feel the autumn gale.
The willow boughs are sweeping
    Down upon a quiet grave;
For Eulema lies sleeping
    Where the wave sings to the wave.

"As a wail o'er autumn flowers
    Doth our heart's sad moaning ring
Through all the winter hours
    Till the coming of the spring;
But we think amid our weeping
    Of the life beyond the grave,
Though Eulema lies sleeping
    Where the wave sings to the wave."

Ere the last words had died upon mine ear,
The spirit-shape that in my chamber stood,
Had passed from out the moonlight into shade.
I saw a hand — within its grasp a cross —
From out the shadow come, and on the brow
Of the cold-hearted maiden plant a sign, —
A white and burning cross; and in its light
I saw her beauty as a ruin foul;
For GOD had smitten her with leprosy.
She felt her doom, and fled from out my sight
With a wild, bitter cry, — "Unclean! unclean!" —

"GOD pity her!" I said.

                        — "He pitieth all,"
The spirit-voice replied, "and his great Love,
Exhaustless in itself, doth watch and keep
The children of the dust. With tenderest care,
As loving Shepherd of a wandering flock,
GOD seeketh out the lost, and leads them back
Unto the fold. His ways are not as man's,
Nor yet his thoughts. Therefore, rest patient, thou;
Nor in thy hasty mind dare question why
Evil or good be wrought. Enough for thee;
GOD ' doeth all things well!'" —

                                        I veiled my eyes
Beneath the burthen of that grave rebuke;
And in the drooping of the heavy lids
The spirit passed away. Again I heard
Gentle Serena (so they called the maid)
Soft singing to the night a song of sleep.
O'er all my senses stole the soothing strain,
And straight I slept.
                         The morning broke in clouds;
And through the spaces of the leafless trees
The wind moaned restlessly. Gray, rifted clouds
Full slowly floated up the grayer sky, —
A sky all dull and cold. A little brook,
That had been singing all the summer long,
Was very sober now, and put on gray,
Glassing the skies it mirrored. Some few birds,
Clad in the same sedatest coloring,
Were searching wistfully on the cold, gray ground;
And all the landscape, with its quiet tints
Was as a prophecy of snow. It came;
And as it fell in soft and feathery flakes,
Filling its mission with so little stir,
It minded me of good deeds done in secret;
Of deeds that had no fame, and were but known
To some poor hearts and Heaven.
                                Serena's voice,
Full of a new-born feeling, tuned my heart
Unto another key; striking such chords
As called the master-passion into life,
And broke the slumbrous pause of memory.

Serena. Lady, the world is stirred as with one pulse.
A name is throbbing on its mighty lips;
And a great deed hath late been chronicled, —
A deed that flings its shadow on past time,
And looms up grandly 'gainst the future's disc.
A fate hath been fulfilled most gloriously,
An ancient realm redeemëd from its grave,
And on the noblest brow in all the land
A crown is resting lightly. A bold soul
Hath left its signet upon all these things,
And lighted the whole world with its renown.
Wouldst thou hear his name? Leon the Rover! —
Rover no more, but lord of all the lands
His fathers held before him! —

                                As the sun,
Breaking through clouds, defineth everything,

Making each outline stand out bold and sharp,
So came that name unto my twilight brain,
Unsealing the closed leaves of memory.
And I bethought me of that vision dark, —
The field of battle, and the rushing steeds, —
The silence and the pall.   He died not, then,
My noble Leon! yet, what matters it?
He knows not I still live; and in his heart
My old-time place hath silent been so long!
He had no room for grief.   Far nobler themes
Were stirring in his brain; and evermore,
In this strange life of ours wherein we move,
The world of action calls us, and we leave
The dead to sleep.   Why call pale shadows up
From their lone rest to haunt us?   Why install
Within our hearts an image that doth keep
Alive old agony?   And yet, — and yet, —
To be forgotten by the one we love, —
Forgotten, when our every pulse doth beat
Only for that one!   Is not this torture
Stilling all other pain?   O loving heart,
This must be, and hath been; so be thou still
And very patient.   Never faithful trust
But found itself rewarded in the end,
For all its weary waiting.
                         Softest eyes
Looked down on mine the while I thought all this;
And in their gaze there was a meaning sweet
I read full easily.   Serena's heart
Had learned my secret, and its quiet pulse
Was throbbing fast as mine.   I spoke no word;
I could not then reveal my inward joy;
It was too deep for speech.   She spake again
Veiling emotion as I veilèd mine,
With many words on other themes of life.

Serena.   I had a friend once, who was a poet,
And his very talk had music in it.
He was a pale-faced youth, with no more bloom
Than showeth in a moonbeam, and the world
Could find no beauty in him.   He had eyes
That were all heart and soul; and, seen but once,
Their lambent light would follow you alway.

Regina.   And this young poet, — loved he Serena?

Serena.   Nay, he loved another, who had no love
To give him in return, but only scorn.

For she was proud and very beautiful,
And prized not the heart the poet proffered;
And yet she smiled on him.   And for that smile, —
That empty trapping of a scornful lip, —
He wove him dreams of fame that was to come
And crown his brow; and these he told to me,
And sang in songs he thought would never die.
Alas, poor Ion!   Save for one sad heart,
His sweetest strains had perished long ago.
It seems to me that in its thirst for gold,
The world cares little for its gifted sons;
And but that genius lives beyond the sky,
There finding native soil, 'twere far more wise
To silence all its breathings, and to keep
Them holy unto Heaven!

  Regina.   Nay, Serena.
No truest life was yet lived out in vain.
What if it silent glide, as some still stream
That never saw the sun, and pass away
With never glory of the golden light
To dance upon its wave?   What if it be
A glorious river, flowing swift and far
Unto the soundless sea, through all its course
Rejoicing in the clear and cloudless day?
Or diverse still, with all the Protean forms
Wherewith the earth doth gift its progeny?
Little it profiteth — when the dust doth fall
Alike on all — that the light world did smile
Upon the foolish, frowning down the wise.
Little it profiteth.   Time's passing tries
As in the fire the worth of all these things.
And Folly's children reap a field of tares
From the wild sowings of a foolish sire,
Who scattered bitter seed.   A wise man's words
Are germs that blossom in some after time,
And ripen into rich and golden fruit.
"By their fruits ye know them."

  Serena.   What, then, avails
The idle breath of human sympathy?
Why strive for fame, if all its incense be
A foam-wreath on the wave?   Passing away,
It may be, long before our mortal dust
Hath mingled with the clay that lies around
Its silent resting-place.   Why weave bright dreams
And clothe their beauty in immortal verse,
If they must die with us, and be no more
A glory on the earth?

Regina.   Why dost thou keep
So closely shrinëd in thy heart of hearts,
The faded memory of one poet's words?
Are they not dear to thee?   Woven amid
The pulsings of thy life?   Yet askest thou
Why men do work for fame?   Ofttimes their hearts
Are twinëd in with every word they write,
And thoughts of self are blotted from the scroll,
Or Fame doth woo them with its siren song;
And but to hear that veriest mockery
They'll pour their heart's blood on life's desert sands,
Nor think the red libation poured in vain!

Serena.   Yet why not rest in full and calm content;
Nor link the future with the present hour,
Filling the soul with visions that must break
The stillness of repose?

Regina.   Thou askest this?
O simple heart!   Art thou content to dwell
In dust forever, climbing not the skies
That shine so blue above; nor risking aught
To gain a fuller knowledge than thou hast?
I tell thee, thou art nothing, if this be.
Thy heart hath never throb, thy soul no wings,
If in the dulness of content thou dwell,
Nor aim at higher things!   Man cannot rest.
The spell of progress on his spirit lies;
And till the grave doth set that spirit free,
Its course is downward, onward, or upward,
As unto good or evil it doth tend.
God never meant life's fountain-spring to be
A dull and stagnant pool!   And, oftentimes,
The fame thou slightest is a holy thing,
So we but use it rightly.   If it be
The motive power unto some highest end,
And lead the soul into those sacred paths
Where God and angels walk, wouldst think it then
So very slight a thing?

Serena.   If this were so,
I'd shrine it in my heart, as some pure shape
Whereon the light of Heaven did shine alway.
But in my soul a latent shadow lies,—
An oracle of grief, —and well I know
By the sad wisdom of one poet's life,
That Fame as written on the walls of Time
Is but a bitter mockery at the best;

And, like the ivy round the ruined tower,
It decks the genius that it feedeth on!

Regina.   Serena, in thy heart there is a thought, —
A deathless memory.   Thou dost garner it
As a most precious gem, and with its hue
It colors all thy life.

Serena.   Well, be it so!
I know it, and I feel it.   Evermore
A voice is sounding in my thirsting ear,
And I cannot forget!   Hush! — let it pass!
I know a story of a faithful heart,
And I will tell it thee.   'Tis very brief,
Like all the things of earth.

The moon's cold rays
Were gleaming down upon the moaning sea,
Whose restless waters surged upon a shore
Against whose senseless rocks, for countless years,
That sea had beat, yet left no impress there.
My childhood's home was by that surging sea;
And aye its solemn song went sounding past
The threshold of our dwelling, filling all
My dreams with its deep swell.   There was a grave
— A lone and lowly grave — within a dell
Whose waters flowed down silent to the sea;
And my fleet footsteps by that little mound
Were often stayed.   I loved to linger there,
And weave bright garlands o'er that grave to hang;
For I had heard that youth and beauty there
Had found an early resting.

One fair eve
— A summer moon was floating through the sky —
I stole back thoughtful to my quiet home.
My mother met me by the trellised porch.
"Be very still, my child.   An old-time friend
Long absent from us hath come home to die.
Go to him, if thou wilt; he ever loved
To see child-faces near him; and thy brow
Hath that will win his love." — With stillest feet
I passed into the chamber, hushed and dark,
And crept unto his couch, and laid my hand
Within his thin white fingers; and they closed
So tenderly on mine. — "Love me, my child.
My life is passing as a dream away,
And I have need of love, whereon to rest
My pained and weary heart." — For sole reply

I laid my head upon his breast, and wept;
For, as I bowed my head, I heard the loud,
Dull beating of his heart, and knew too well
Unto what bourn that muffled sound was tending;
For so had beat my father's patient heart
Ere it grew still forever. — " Nay; little one,
Thou shouldst not weep.   Thou art too young for tears.
Come, talk to me; for I can listen still.
Dost thou love the sea? " — So I nestled close,
And told him how I wandered, day by day,
Unto a lonely grave, there weaving wreaths
Wherewith to garland it. — " Thou goest there!
Where *she* lies sleeping, crowning with sweet flowers
Her early grave?   God love thee, child, for this ! " —
And on my brow his quivering lips he pressed.

He was not young, — this poor death-stricken man,
Round whom my heart's fresh tendrils twinëd soon, —
He was not young; and in his saddest eyes
There burned a light which was not of this earth,
And told of other lands whereto the soul
Was winging its swift way.   One quiet eve
I heard him singing to himself these words : —

    " Alina, in our golden days
        The summer hours were far more sweet;
    And pleasure with its sunny rays
        Came speeding aye, our smiles to meet.
    But with the passing of that time
        The light grew fast with darkness rife,
    And rain of sorrow's bitter rime
        Did flood the fair fields of my life.

    " Alina, all these weary years
        The cloud hath been upon my way;
    The ceaseless fall of endless tears
        Hath shut the sunshine from the day.
    I tread not now the olden ways;
        I hear no more the low, sweet song
    That ever, in those happy days,
        The waves were singing all day long.

    " Alina, in thy quiet grave
        My hopes were buried, one by one,
    And now beside the restless wave
        I listen for the sea-bird's moan.
    I listen, — but I do not hear;
        My thoughts are only of the dead.
    The shadows of another year
        Will never darken o'er my head."

As ceased the music of that softest voice,
My pale-browed mother stood within the room,
And, with a gentle motion, she flung wide
The darkened casement, till the moon shone in. —
"Art better, Walter?"—softly questioned she.
—"Better? yea; for I am dying,—dying
With the same fever burning in my veins
That burned there long ago, — ay, long ago;
When all my dreams in their bright flush of hope
Did turn to ashes on a young girl's grave!
How beautiful she was!   I see her now,
Her golden tresses veiling o'er a brow
As pale as any lily, and her eyes
So soft and brown, sweet smiling down on me.
She was so beautiful!   How could I dream
That fading — death — was written in each line
Of that fair, blushing face?   How the round moon
Doth smile to-night!   So did it seem to smile
When last we met beside the summer sea.
Alina mia, how thy tears did fall
When by the margin of that silver wave
We breathed adieu!   The moon was on the wane.
Ere it had filled its horn, I stood again
Beside the sea.   Alina was not there,
And the cold moon was shining on her grave!
'Twill shine on mine to-morrow!   Thou smilest.
Dost think I dream?   O friend, I hear the swell,
The far-off murmur, of the rising tide
Forever beating on the shores of Death;
And in my heart there is an answering sound,
A welcome unto death; and I go hence,
More blest in dying than I was in life.
An angel beckons me.   *She* told me once,
How 'God, he giveth his belovëd sleep,'
And I shall sleep ere morn.   Hath the moon set?
I cannot see her grave." —
                              And so he slept.
They laid him where Alina long had lain,
And the soft singing of the solemn sea
Floats sadly o'er their rest.

                              Serena ceased.
Her voice died into silence, as the sun
Below the purpled hill-tops sank to rest.
Soon in the cold and stormless winter sky,
A lonely star shone out.   A ghastly shape
Rose up between us and that palest orb;

And, shuddering, I turned me from the loathèd sight
Of the proud maiden in her leprosy.

  "Why do ye shudder at my mourning robe?
For it becomes me well, since in the grave
My lover lieth low.   And thou, fond fool,
That kneelest there, and dar'st not look on me,
Why hast thou not a mourning garment too,
Since he thou lovest perished long ago?
I sent him to his doom; and he doth sleep
Where never wailing from thy loving lips
Can break his rest."—
                    How our poor hearts do cling
Unto the veriest fantasy of hope,
Though the wan ghost doth mock us evermore!
So had Serena clung unto the thought
That in some day, though far away and dim,
Her poet-lover would return to her.
Alas, poor child! the dead return no more!
I saw her drooping, as the words came fast
And bitter from those white and leprous lips;
And then—and then—I looked on death again!

  A wan, pale face that had no hue of life;
Dark tresses heavy with the dew of death;
Cold eyes slow glazing 'neath the moveless lids;
And lips all still, as frozen into stone.
What needeth more?   The arrow had struck home,—
The death was in her heart!
                    Seraph, they say
Ye have no part, no sympathy with our race;
And that ye only pity the wild love
That breaketh human hearts.   If this be so—
Nay?—then I'll mourn not o'er Serena's grave;
For in her youth she passed away from earth;
And in that world where all blest spirits are
She hath forgotten tears!

                    I stood again,
When some long days of travel had gone by,
Within the City of the Seven Hills.
The pestilence was abroad: and all the streets
Were filled with living corpses.   Like a ghost
I glided through the dread and silent streets,
Seeking one form I dared not hope to find;
Yet found at last within the palace hall
Where first he said he loved me.   Lone he stood,

And shadow-like, the white plume waving still
Above his palest brow. "Twas Leon's self,
Changed, but the same; and ere my lips could breathe
The name so long beloved, he turned to clasp
Regina in his arms. O joy past hope,
To rest again upon that faithful heart!

Regina. Canst love me yet? I am not what I was;
For lonely thoughts have robbed me of my youth.
Once thou didst call me beautiful, — in days
When joy sat crescent on my radiant brow;
And sorrow lurked unseen and silent all
In the dim future's horoscopic glass.
Now all my beauty fades, like as the summer,
Into the wan and sickly autumn leaf.
Dost love me yet?

Leon.   Ay, by my father's faith!
Thou hast not changed to me. Thy brow wears still
Its angel aspect; and thy quiet eyes
Smile on me, as of old. What matter, then,
If some frail bloom hath faded from thy cheek?
So that thy heart doth keep its wealth of love
Sacred to me I cannot ask for more,
Yet claim no less. Let but propitious fate
Set on my brow the crown my fathers wore,
And thou, Regina, shalt be queen indeed.
The day that calls thee mine e'en now lights up
The far-off horizon of my dawning hopes;
And soon the world, through all its circles wide,
Shall ring with tidings of a battle won;
An ancient crown redeemed.

Regina.   Not yet redeemed?
Nay, then the world hath falsehood on its lips.
Leon, dost know that I was waiting death
In calmest patience, when I heard thy name
Heralded as conqueror crownëd in the strife?
It woke me from my dream of Leon dead;
And, in my heart, where long pale shadows sat, —
Strange, mocking visions of a fevered brain, —
Love throned himself again, and Reason came
Unto its ancient seat.

Leon.   Regina mine,
That thou shouldst so have suffered! But, enough!
We will not dull this meeting with a thought
Of what hath been. Wouldst see mine olden home?

My bark is tossing idly on yon sea;
And some few hours would bear us o'er its foam,
Unto the summer-land. Nay; fear thee not,
There is no danger lurking on the deep;
The breeze is steady, and the sky is clear;
And in my home there are true, faithful hearts
To greet my gentle bride. Ay, bride! This night
Shall see thee mine by all the holiest vows
Wherewith our faith doth temper human souls.
What ho! Velasquez! We must forth to-night.
And to thy gentle care I leave my bride.
Be thou her brother till the church shall give
A husband's right to me. Thine eyes are swords;
I fear them not, old friend. 'Tis no new love
That throbbeth in my heart, and long ere morn
We will the tale rehearse. But now the breeze
Doth murmur at delay, and we must be
At home ere the high noon doth blaze adown
The burning summer sky. To thy true care
I leave the life that's nearest unto mine.
And thou, Regina, love Velasquez well.

Regina. Nay, Leon; that were surely needless word.
For where thy heart is mine must always be,
And whom thou callest friend is mine also.

Velasquez.   Thanks, gentle lady.

———

                    Some brief hour hence
Our bark was speeding o'er the sunlit sea;
And at high noon a castle's hall was decked
Meet for a bridal. When the even came
Leon and I were wandering on the shore,
Talking as lovers talk; while on my hand
The circlet glittered bright, — the little pledge
That marked us one forever.

Leon.   Thou smilest.

Regina. And wherefore not? I am so happy! I rest
Upon the very fulness of content,
And want not anything. And if I smile,
'Tis that my heart concealeth not its joy.

Leon. Dost love me, then, so well? What if the world
Had marked me with its scorn, and sealed my brow,
As in the former ages GOD sealed Cain's?

Regina.   I care not what the world doth think of thee;
For in my loving heart thou sit'st enthroned
In likeness of an angel. Thou art more
Than all the world to me, and my fond eyes
Do crown thee with perfection. So thou lov'st,
I could content me with the whole world's scorn,
And bear myself as should Golconda's lord,
So rich my life would be! O noble heart!
So gentle, loving, true, yet firm withal;
Upon thy throbbing pulse I rest my soul,
Nor fear its trust will prove a broken reed.
I could not doubt thy truth; for that were doom
More dark and deadly than if death should come
Between our hearts forever. In the grave
If thou wert sleeping, I might watch above
And guard thy rest; till in the Silent Land
Our souls should meet again. But, wert thou false, —
If mingled darkly in my cup of life
That bitterest drop should be, — I could but pray
In its first agony to droop and die.

   Leon.   Nay; fear thee not, mine own. No chill can
         come
Between our loves, till that last one of earth,
When death but parts us for a little space,
To join our souls for all eternity.

   Awhile we sat in silence; on each brow
The quiet sunshine of our full content.
The evening faded, and o'er smoothest sea
The night came down, with pale, moonlighted eyes.
A shadow crossed us. 'Twas Velasquez' self;
And with his mournful voice he broke the spell
Of happy silence and of loving eyes.

   Velasquez. The moon rides high to-night. Look how
         her smile
Doth light the waters where the green isles rest;
And see, where, in the shadow, calm and slow,
Yon swan floats graceful o'er the yielding tide!
Would I were like that swan! to dwell alway
Where the bright summer lingers long and late,
Nor yields to winter's sway. So might I 'scape
The waning splendor of the dying year;
Nor, with wan autumn's wail o'er perished things,
Blend my sad sighs for dead and buried hopes
That in their graves lie wretched and forlorn!
There is no resurrection-morn for them;

And they will be forgotten, long ere dust
Is lying on this throbbing heart of mine.
O restless waters! Some brief moments since,
And ye were slumbering as infants sleep.
Now the swift breeze goes rippling o'er your breast,
And into thousand tiny waves ye break,
Mocking the moonbeams in your sportive play!
Far-reaching Ocean! I have loved thee well;
But thou art fickle, treacherous, and false;
A very Proteus, full of changes swift.
I had a brother, once, a fair young boy,
Within whose eyes sat daring; on whose brow
Pale fear had left no impress. He was aye
Our mother's darling, and I loved him more
For that his mood was little kin to mine.
He was a lover of the wild, wild sea,
A scorner of all book-worms; yet I think
He loved *me* well enough; but then he was
A sometime dreamer in his quiet moods.

Leon. I care not if youth dream, so it but be
Such dreams as herald greatness. But to waste
Life's morning in inaction, weaving webs
Of folly, soft as silk from Indian looms,
And with no stamina; ay, this, indeed,
Were forging fetters for all after years,—
Such chains as those wherewith dull, senseless sloth,—
A worm—doth eat away the soul's true strength,
And leaves it barren and unfruitful all,—
A dry and withered tree.

Velasquez.   Not such was he.
The life was there, a fierce and restless stream,
And all his dreams were rounded into action.
I was of other mould. I lovëd books,
And gleaned from them the language of all souls
That there have written worlds; and in my heart
I treasured all their glamourye. Days came,
When nations called me to the Council Hall;
And to my lips, in fierce and fiery flow,
Rushed the keen, pointed words. Never till then,—
Never till then, had eloquence so swayed
Contending passions. On each angry brow
Soft smiles descended, and hands claspëd hands
That some few moments since had only met
In wild and bitter struggle. Leave we this.
There was a golden morning of sweet June;
A day that touched e'en my slow veins with fire,

And lured me from my books to breathe the air,
That swept o'er waving fields as o'er the sea.
My brother rushĕd past me to the beach,
His golden curls flung backward, and his eyes
Laughing a welcome to the rising breeze.
With eager haste he caught the waiting oars,
And urged his tiny bark far o'er the wave.
I stood, and watched him.   How the water flew
Before that sharpest prow, and his slight arms
Seemed dowered with strength to ride upon the deep.
I lingered long; scarce conscious that the wind,
So tempered late, was gathering its powers;
Till, scattered at my feet, torn branches lay,
And the white foam went rushing on the shore,
Hissing concordance with the raving wind.
With beating heart, I glanced far out to sea,
And saw my brother battling with the storm,
And heard the ocean roaring for its prey,
While I was powerless, and could not save!
The gallant boy!   A moment's space he stood,
His fair face turned unto his childhood's home:
A moment, and the angry waves o'erleapt
The little boat, and never human eye
Looked on my brother's slender form again!
Our mother—see! yon willow waves its boughs
Above her quiet grave, and evermore
The song of ocean floateth o'er her rest
As if it held no dead.   Thou treacherous deep!
Look how it smileth, basking in the rays
Of the full harvest moon!   Out on these tears!

My brow was resting on my Leon's breast,
And when I lookĕd up, Valasquez' form
Into the shadow faded, while the night
Was verging on its noon.   A pale blue flower,
Snapped by his hasty step, lay at my feet,
The dull dust staining all its velvet leaves.

It seems a little thing, with iron heel
To grind the flowers beneath us in the dust,
And yet GOD made them!   Gentle, lovely things!
How with your delicate beauty ye bring back
To the old, furrowed earth its dew of youth,
Till her worn brow looks fresh and smooth again
And to our weary hearts, what are ye not?
A sweetness and a glory evermore!
The child doth grasp ye with its tiny hands,
That scarce can hold the tiniest of you all,

Loving your changeful hues.   Youth breathes the love
That dares not speak, with offerings of flowers;
And maiden-brows that know not summer yet,
Ye deck alike for bridal and for bier!
Methinks that when the High and Holy One
First smiled upon the world that he had made,
Your various tribes sprang up beneath that smile,
To fill the conscious bosom of the earth
With an eternal memory of bliss, —
A shadow of GOD's smile forevermore!

Enough of all this dreaming! I must turn
From pleasant fancies unto earnest life.
Fain would I linger, 'mid the charmèd scenes
That made one brief, bright time a joy for aye;
But time forbids; and, seraph, in thine eyes,
I see the hour draws nigh, when this fair Earth,
Still so fair, shall be no more forever.

Two seasons white with snow, and two that blushed
With summer's wealth of roses, passèd on.
The outer world knew little of them all;
But in two hearts their light is chronicled
With all sweet things that may not pass away.
Then came a time of darkness, — days that saw
The pall's cold shadow glooming on the earth.
Awhile the echo of a child's sweet laugh
Was heard amid the silence of my heart;
Awhile its light, free steps went sounding by,
As if no sorrow could arrest its speed;
Awhile soft kisses, on my pale lips pressed,
Awoke my soul with thrillings wild and deep;
Awhile all these things were; and then Death came,
Stilling the throbbing of that little heart!
We murmured not.   We knew that we had given
An angel unto God; and so we left
With bleeding hearts, yet meek, resignèd souls,
The shadow of our beautiful to dust;
And our sad hearth was childless evermore!

Ere yet the grass was green upon that grave,
Dissension sowed its seeds through all the land;
Engendering strifes that ripened all too fast
Into most bitter fruits.   And Might put forth
Its daring hand to wrest from us our faith;
And in the dust to trample out our souls
For that they lovèd freedom.   But the land
Rose, as one soul did animate them all,

To meet the proud aggressor.   As the gift
Of their untrammelled will, they placed the crown
Upon my Leon's brow.   'Twas his of right,
Since it had rested on his father's head;
And when again a living brow it ringed,
Uprose the battle-cry of former days, —
"*Viva el rey!*"
                    Men armed themselves in haste,
And in groups gathering, questioned, each of each,
Above what plain the vulture army winged
Its dark, predestined flight.   "We know not yet," —
Some gravest voices murmured in the crowd,
— "But yesternight the dark and serried clouds
Met other clouds in strife, and all the winds
Were tuned to battle-music.   O'er the hills,
An echo floated downward, swiftly borne,
That told of burning cities, tombless dead;
And in the council hall e'en now are met
The rulers of the land.   Some talk there is
Of shapes that love the darkness, and go forth
Through silence of the night to make themselves
Haunts in our quiet homes.   Dark traitors, they,
That dread the daylight, lest the sun reveal
The blackness of their souls."

                    While thus they spake,
The carvèd pillows of the Council gate
Rolled backwards, and the eager crowd rushed in
Panting to learn what manner of defence
Had been resolvèd on.
                    Leon, the King,
Sat crownèd in his place, and him around
The best and bravest of our fair Castile
Sat sternly mute, while in the midst, and lone,
His clenched hand quivering on the marble stand,
His blue eyes flashing out a lurid light,
Pale Juan Gomez stood; the while the king
Struck home some sharp and ringing words of scorn
That had a sting.

Leon.   I call thee *friend* no more!
Go! fling the dust upon thy old renown,
And to the silence of all ages leave
Thy heritage of shame!   Why com'st thou here?
Hence! for thy country owns thee not as son;
In her large heart there is no room for thee.
Away with thee!   Why dost thou linger still
When every sword is thirsting for thy blood?

And but for some poor touch of ancient love
"Twixt mine and thine, I'd let them loose on thee!

   Juan Gomez.   Nay; spare thy taunts. I go, but I return;
And when the foe is thundering at thy gates
The bravest hearts in all Castile shall rue
Most bitterly this day. And then, fair sirs,
If on this threshold Gomez stand again,
Methinks your greeting will be unlike this,
And on your brows will rest another look,
More courteous far. If there be any here,
Who fain would know how ringeth Gomez' sword,
Let them come on, and try! What! not a word?
Nay? then I fling back coward in your teeth;
And if when next our armies meet the foe,
My banner floats not on Castilia's side,
Then call me " traitor," " coward," — what you will, —
I'll never question why!
                  With arm outstretched,
And eyes that flashed more darkly, as the crowd
Of people swept into the Council Hall,
Outspake false Gomez; veiling o'er his guile
With smooth, deceitful words.

   Juan Gomez.   Hear me, people!
And if, when having heard, ye blame me still,
I will bow meekly to your hearts' decree
Nor murmur at my fate. If I have wronged
A son of fair Castile, — if on my soul
There lies one stain of darkest treachery,
And ye can plant it there, — then let me go
From out your presence as the vilest slave
That e'er defiled the earth! If I have sought
By word, or deed, to spoil my native land,
Then send me forth a branded traitor knave,
Or slay me where I stand! Ye answer nought;
But questioning turn to where your king doth sit,
As if to ask his will. Ye are not *slaves.*
Your breath did place him there, — your breath can take
The sceptre — crown — away. What! are ye mute?
They call me traitor — spy. They say my tongue
Hath learned the cunning of another land.
I fling the falsehood back! If any here
Deserve the name of traitor, 'tis your king;
And on his head, for broken faith and oath, —
And on his head, for realm and hearth betrayed,
Be all your vengeance poured!

　　　　　　　　　　　　　　.　As at the cry
Of some fierce beast of prey the jackals speed,
So did the artful wording of that man
Arouse the populace; and they shouted "Death!
Death to the traitor king!"—　　　'
　　　　　　　　　　　　The few, who stood
Beside their king, had drawn their ready swords.
He waved them back, and reared his stately form,
And with uplifted brow, and smiling eyes,
Strode forward some brief space, flinging aside
The slender corslet that he wore.

　　Leon.　　　　　　　　　Lo! I cast
The last frail barrier down; and on the prey
That waits your hatred, rush, O people mine!

　　Serene he stood; smiling to meet the death,
As if the doom were only joy to him.
At that mild aspect, all their fury died.
"Live, live!" they cried, "and battling by thy side
We'll prove us better patriots, than if hands,
Yet white, were dyed to crimson in thy blood.
Thou art no traitor, else thy cheek had paled
When all the people shouted for thy death.
Live! live! and we will make this hour's shame
A lesson for our future. Nevermore
Will voice of ours be lifted 'gainst thy cause.
Henceforth 'tis ours also, and we will pour
The last pale drop of blood from our stout hearts
Ere it be championless!"—

　　Leon.　　　　　　　　Enough! I knew
My people would not slay me, nor forsake
The simple creed in which their fathers died.
For thee, O Gomez, thou hast heard thy doom.
Go, and return no more! We love not much
A traitor in our councils, so depart;
And, gentle friends, lay no hands upon him.
Let him go free. We will not touch his life.

　　From out the hall, the baffled traitor passed,—
From out the hall, where never more his shape
Left darkest shadow; and his ancient home
Knew him no more.
　　　　　　　　　There were no woman-tears
Poured forth like rain-drops, when my hero went
Unto the battle-field. I gave him smiles
And high and hopeful words, and bade him go;

But bring me back, sole thing of all I prized,
The heart that lovëd me.   I watched him pass
Beyond the circle of my yearning eyes,
Then turned to weep alone; yet smile the while,
To think he nothing knew of all the pain
Fierce gnawing at my poor and fevered heart.
Mine was no feeble love, to falter, fail,
When days that called for strength, and marred all bloom,
Rose slowly, darkly, o'er life's horizon.
Love borrowed strength from Love, and smiled serene
O'er darkness and despair; as smiles the moon
Through rent clouds looking on a stormy sea,
As never thence the cry of drowning men
Had risen unto heaven.   I could not rest
Within my lonely home, and so I went,
Clothed as a page, to join the armëd host,
A shadow ever at my Leon's side;
And in this garb I followed him alway.
I guarded him as only Love can guard.
I stood between him and the assassin's knife
In that dark hour when Gomez stained his soul
With thoughts of murder; and above my heart
There is a silent witness of my love,—
A crimson scar that never told its tale.

    An eve of shadows.   All the forest gloomed
Beneath the darkness of o'erhanging clouds, —
Thick clouds that shut the dying sun from earth;
And in the close aisles of the tangled wood
I wandered wearily.   My thoughts were sad,
For I had learned that Murder was abroad, —
That in my Leon's heart, the dagger's point
Would soon be driven home.   A fevered pulse,
A throbbing of unrest, had sent me forth
From the wild tumult of the bivouac
Into the hush and slumber of the wood.
My roving feet, unconscious, led me on,
Till every sound of stirring human life
Had faded into distance on mine ear.
Then rose a single voice, though low, distinct, —
A voice that filled the empty space with sound,
And thrilled upon my heart.   'Twas that of one
Upon whose fatal hand my Leon's life
Hung as a thread.   And thus he spake; and still
I listened eagerly.
                    — "I sit alone.
Through silence and through darkness of the night
I hear a soft voice singing evermore
The same sweet song that in my sinless days

My mother sang to me.   Be still, sad song!
Why dost thou haunt me with thy mournful tones,
Filling the pauses of my memory
With a reproachful wail o'er wasted life
And hours unredeemed?   Why comest thou now
To wake my soul with a vain dream of home?
I hear thy music ever, all night long,
And through the busy day it floats alway.
I hear thee, and a vision passes by:
A shore whose air is faint with orange-blooms;
A sun, set round with purple-tinted clouds,
Slow sinking down upon the western sea;
And, looking on all this, still, patient eyes,—
Soft eyes of one who had come home to die.
When midnight came, I stood beneath the stars,
An atom in the infinite!   What! tears?
Methought their fount was drainëd long ago;
Drained by the fire that doth sear men's souls.
Tears! tears! could ye but pour a flood to drown
All record of my manhood, I would bless
The olden song that brought the healing stream
Up from its sacred source!   Enough of this!
Tears make not ready for a deed of blood,
And are as palsy to the shaking arm
When the strong hand should send the dagger home!"—

A voice from out the darkness echoed back
The last word, "home."   A low, sweet woman's voice,
That had a solemn cadence like a chime
Sent from the spirit-land.   Unto his knees
It bowed the conscience-stricken; and he flung
The glittering dagger in the still, dark pool
That gloomed beside.   That instant, on the night,
The evening chimes rang out, "Glory to God!"
And on the trembling soul the holy words
Smote hard, as Moses' rod upon the rock,
And the pure waters flowed out full and free,—
The healing stream of tears!
                                    The work was done.
Silent I came; as silently I went;
My full heart pouring out a psalm of praise
For a poor soul redeemed!

                                    In every heart
Lie hid the germs of darkness and of light,
Of darkness leading downward to the dust—
Of burning light that looketh aye to Heaven;
And as we follow either, so our lives

Grow dark as night — a night without a star,
Or rich in splendor as the cloudless day!   .

   A day of battle dawned, — of fiercest strife, —
And I was far away!   Leon had won
From my pale lips a pledge to rest within
The silence of our home, while he went forth
Unto that darkest field.
                Some days went by, —
Long days that aged me more than weary years.
There came no tidings from the armëd host;
And Rumor, with her thousand tongues, awoke
To scatter falsehood as youth scatters flowers.
Sternly I schooled my fevered heart to bear
The wasting torture of that dread suspense,
And smilëd still!   I knew that my calm brow
Was as a beacon unto every eye;
And so it told no tales of all the fears
Thick gathering round my soul; and I moved on,
Through the dull routine of this daily life
As death could never reach my Leon's heart,
Nor Victory, flush from fields of battle won,
Desert his crownëd brow.
                Alas for smiles! —
Too soon came tidings that were cold as death, —
A tale of darkness heralding defeat;
And the poor remnant of our gallant host
Came back to die around their household hearths.
But for the hearts that throbbed so high yestere'en,
Their names were on the roll-call nevermore.
They fought as heroes, and as heroes died,
For from that fatal field was no return,
Save for a few who round their king kept guard;
And they returned to meet another doom, —
To die as martyrs die, and yield their souls
Through agony to God!
                One struggle more!
One final throe ere freedom could expire;
And then! — and then! —
                The royal city slept,
While on its walls true hearts kept watch and ward.
Great need was there of both; for armëd hosts
Hemmed in the doomëd city, and we knew
That death was nearer unto us than life.   .
And yet we faltered not in our poor task
But bore us bravely; while on each pale brow
Sat expectation, as a buried hope
That riseth not again.   Night o'er the world

With all its soothing influences reigned;
But o'er my pulse its holy spells were nought.
A fever of unrest was on my soul,
And the still night was rife with visionrie.
It brought me shadows of the future hour,—
Dark thoughts that robbed my painëd eyes of sleep,
And dowered me with gift of prophecy;
Till to my prescient soul the coming doom
Was as a written scroll. I read it all;
And then the terror seized upon my brain,
Aud swift I fled unto my Leon's side.

He stood alone upon a bastion's verge
That loomed majestic o'er the vale below;
And on his kingly brow there slept no shade,
And in his eyes there sat a firm resolve,
Whereof my prescient soul, too prophet-like,
Knew well the meaning. All the future rushed
With bitter clearness on miue aching eyes.
Vainly I flung it from me,— vainly strove
To shut the vision and the terror out.
Darkly it loomed before me, and my lips,
Wan iu their agony, slowly moanëd forth
" Have mercy, Heaven!"—and my Leon heard.

Leon.   Regina, thou! This is no place for thee!
Those clasping fingers, I can read them well;
So rest thee there, sweet wife. My heart can yet
Thy shield and buckler be. How still the night!
The moon is up; but through the veil of mist
Her light shines dimly, and the holy stars
Seem blotted from the sky. There breaks no sound
Upon the dread repose of that dull sea,
The sea of mist; yet, far beneath our feet,
The quiet vale is all astir with life.
The foe lies there,— the wary, restless foe;
And in their thought to-morrow seals our doom.
To-morrow? It is here! For through the mist
Float rosy shadows; and the golden morn
Of our last day is breaking on the world.
Is it not gloriously beautiful?
This world that man scarce darkens with his crimes;
This world that God hath made!
                              A solemn pause.
The kingly brow was bared unto that Name;
The warrior-knee was lowly bent in prayer;
And as he knelt, I, silent, looked on him.
I saw the angel glory in his eyes,

The will so firm, the meek submission too, —
I saw the shadow of the dread To Be, —
I saw the doom!

   Regina.   Would I were nearer thee!
O Leon, best beloved! I came to warn,
To counsel flight, to share thy changing fate.
Nay, frown not, thou! I know thy soul is brave;
But couldst thou bear the prison and the chain,
The torture and the doom? Oh, I have seen
Such fearful things since in the olden time
We met and parted. Death was everywhere
Haunting my steps as it my shadow were;
I could not fly its path. And now, and now, —
When every pulse should throb for thee alone, —
The same dark shape is on my footsteps still.
Thou dost not see it. To thine earnest eyes
It brings no trouble. On thy soaring hopes
It flings no darkness. I, only, see it;
Feel its presence, know the ending near,
And yet am powerless! Last night, the spell
Of prescience was upon me; and I saw,
As in a dream, the shadows of To Be.
Thick darkness was upon my painëd eyes,
And through its curtain lurid flames soon broke,
Revealing phantom-shapes that to and fro
Went shudderingly; moaning out sad words
That had no meaning to me, — yet I knew
They were but wailings for a dying world.
The end of all things was at hand; and Earth
Would have no witness to its agony,
So veiled itself in night. And yet I saw, —
It was not night to me. Shadowy shapes
Loomed up through shadows; things that had no form
Came flitting by me; but I marked them not,
For my thoughts were full of thee. Where wert thou?
As by a magic word, the veil of night
Was drawn aside; and, on my awe-struck gaze,
A city rose from out a cloud of mist;
All clear, defined, as mountain-peaks stand out
Against a wintry sky. Thou knowst it well.
It sitteth as a queen on seven hills,
And all the world are vassals at its feet.
I saw it in my dream arrayed in blood,
And from its prison-cells a cry went up, —
"How long, O God! how long!" Without the gates
A host did make them ready for a feast, —
A sacrifice of blood. Leon! Leon!

Thou, too, wert there; and on thy marrĕd brow
Red drops stood out like beads; and thy white lips
Were set in firm endurance of all pain;
And I, who saw thee thus, felt in my heart
Each pang that thou hadst borne.   And must this be?
Is there no refuge left?   No hope in flight?

Leon.   I cannot fly!

Regina.   Not, Leon, when the doom
Prepared for thee is torture and the stake?
Dost know they will that I should present be?
Oh, spare me that!   How could I look and live?

Leon. Is this poor Earth so lovely in thine eyes,
That but to win some brief years' longer stay,
Thou'dst have me fly, or else betray my GOD?

Regina.   Not that!   Not that!   I'd sooner see thee die!
O Leon, husband, pardon these poor tears!
I shall be braver when the terror comes.
But now to lose thee, — now, — when all my dreams
Had rounded into so much happiness,
And all the world was smiling at my joy!
Is not this bitter? — turning day to night ?
Nay, look not thou so stern.   I'll still this pain,
And shut it in my heart; so nevermore
It burn upon my lips; and for my tears
I'll give thee only smiles.

Leon.   O truest wife!
Dost see how our old dreams of earthly crowns
Were mocking shadows all?   And yet, I err;
For still, on yon dread field, a time of strife
Is waiting for our souls; and Heaven hath crowns
For every conqueror there.   And what is Earth,
That we should fear to leave it?   What our life,
When in the future God doth give to us
A Life that hath no death, and never grave?
What is Death that we should fear it?   Darkness
Clothing the body, — touching not the soul, —
A silent shadow by the life-tree sitting, —
A shape that follows from cradle unto grave, —
An angel on whose brow a star is shining,
Veiling the sadness in his holy eyes, —
A breath from GOD's own spirit, — summoner,
From this brief life to Life that knows it not!
Look up! my life.   Is not the morning here?

The clouds are lifting, and their shadows fade
While the bright sun doth shine out gloriously.
And see! o'er mountain-peaks, serene and high,
The bow of promise bends; a token sweet
That smiles shall follow quick upon our tears.

While yet he spoke, the golden morning broke,
And gave to view a stately bannered host
Set in array of battle 'gainst our walls;
And what had we of gallant souls and true
To stem that fearful tide?   I said, but now,
The royal city slept; the words had weight.
It slept the sleep of death!   The few who 'scaped
The battle doom of yesterday had borne
Their death-wounds from the field; and in the night
Their souls were summoned hence.   Each at his post
We found them still, guarding in death the land!
Yes! they were gone, — sleeping their final sleep;
And they were dwellers in the Silent Land
While yet we watched for morn.   Not wildest prayer,
Not life for life, could win one sleeper's soul
Back unto Earth again!

Leon.   It is enough!
Man's wrath is nought.   It cannot harm them now.
And we can bear our fate, whate'er it be,
With calmer brows, than if these franchised hearts
Still lived to share our agony and death.
Fling wide the gates, and let the spoilers in;
They cannot touch the dead!

Regina.   And Leon, thou?

Leon.   I can but die!   It matters not how GOD
Doth call the spirit home.   'Tis but one pang,
And earth can claim us not; and we are free,
Dwellers no more in darkness, but in light.
Save for the rending of some closest ties,
Save for the breaking of some hearts, — it is
A little thing to die.   And thou — mine own —

I saw the quivering of those firm-set lips —
I felt the heaving of his mighty breast.
"Fear not for me," I cried; "is not God good?
Will he not guard?" —

Leon.   God love thee, my true wife!

With swiftest feet we trod the silent streets, —
Flung back the massive portals so to give
The foe free entrance; and we then went up
Unto the Council Chamber, there to wait
The coming of our fate.   Far-off — far-off —
We heard the stirring battle-music break
In rolling waves of sound; and through it all
The tramp and martial clang of armëd men, —
A proud, victorious host.   I turned mine eyes
Where, far below, the close and serried ranks
Pressed onward to the walls.   They neared the gates.
The swelling music died into a wail,
Then ceased; and with bent brows and paling lips
They entered on the void and voiceless streets
Where absence of all sound seemed to proclaim
A city of the dead!   Yet on they came;
An ocean-tide when at its time of flood,
Filling the empty streets with waves of life.
I watched them as they swept upon their way,
Nearer and yet more near! then turned to rest
My throbbing heart upon my Leon's breast,
As if all peace and safety nestled there.

What needeth more?   Through all the weary day,
The rampant army feasted in the halls
That death had left so cold and masterless.
All day they feasted.   When the evening came,
There rose a stir among the armëd band
That kept a watch upon the Council Hall,
Our prison-tower now.   Some briefest words
Taught me the bitter meaning of that stir;
Yet I spoke not.   I stood apart, silent;
For I had nerved my shrinking soul to bear
This last, most sharp of earthly agonies,
That so I could smile on him to the last.
They bore him from mine eyes; and the cold night
Crept shudderingly down on me.   I knew no more
Until the morning glared so mocking bright,
And then I shivered back to life again.

The year was in its summer when the foe
Did hang victorious banners on our walls,
And gave them to the breezes.   Roses blushed
In every palace-garden; and the vales
Were rich in sweetest flowers.   Earth and sky
Were full of beauty, but we saw it not.
How might it enter in our lonely cells?
Flowers love the sunshine; never one bright ray

Might smile upon our darkness!   All the light
That we could hope to have was but a shade
Of lesser night, that crept through some cold bars
We knew not whence; and did but serve
To make the darkness terrible.   The only thing
That stirred the pulses of those secret cells
Was the unending drip of water-drops
Upon the cold, damp floor.   Day after day
The ceaseless drip went on.   But little sound
It made when first we heard its monotone;
Daily it grew more loud; till at the last
The brain was fillèd with its dreariness,
And painèd unto bursting.   Nay, had burst,
But that one night a peal of thunder broke
Above our dungeon, and the lightning smote
The mortised rock, and gave unto our eyes
The clouded heaven once more.   The rain-drops fell
With magic coolness on mine aching brows;
And reason, that was tottering on its throne,
Resumed its wonted sway.   Not long to me
Was left that wealth of clouds and cooling rain.
That boon was all too precious, for a heart
That dared to brave its gaolers' ire, and keep
Its faith untainted still.   That far-off gleam
Of the blue heaven, and the few bright stars
That smiled on me at night, through the rent roof
And shattered wall of stone, was all too much
For such a thing as me; and so they bore
My drooping form unto a closer cell,
Against whose outer wall the freest winds
Might play at will.   They might not enter in,
Though there a living creature pined and prayed
For one pure breath of air.   And pined in vain;
For if the boon were granted, 'twas with such
Accompaniment of fearfullest things
As made my very soul in torture writhe.

I tell thee, seraph, in thy blessèd home
Thou knowst no terror of that awful shape
Which mouldeth human hearts to mock all ties
Of sweet humanity.   From out my cell —
Where life did sleep — dost know they brought me forth,
And made me look on scenes that only fiends
Could prompt wherewith to wring a woman's heart;
And I had been a mother — was a wife! —
A wife! there spoke the spell that conquered me.
If e'er mine eyes were closed unto the sights
That made my heart to bleed; if e'er mine ears

Were shut to moans that could not be repressed, —
They whispered "Leon," and my soul was crushed,
Submiss and patient to their cruel will.
The GOD who giveth strength unto the oak
Doth dower therewith the frailest flower also;
Or childhood had not borne with unmoved front
The same fierce agony that paled man's lip
With its too real, but unspoken torture.
Yea, they gave children — young and tender things
That smiled upon you with their loving eyes —
To the sharp mercy of the living flames,
Nor shuddered at their work! I blessëd GOD
For that my child went home so long ago;
And prayed that strength to Leon and myself
Might still be given, so to bear the fate
I knew must close the measure of our lives.

The year was dying.   Last of all the years
That Earth had counted since the primal morn
When all the morning stars together sang
Sweet praises of the world that GOD had made.
The year was dying; and its pallid brow
Was frosted over by the coming death;
The death that never more might reckon Time
Among its victims.   The year was dying;
Death was in the world; and yet the nations
Sinned on, unconscious of the day of doom.
Though — told by thousands upon every shore —
Pale corses strewed the Earth, and floated thick
On the sick waters of the loathing Sea.
Dispeopled cities, lying waste and lone; —
Wrecks of lost nations, holding once a place
Amid the mightiest of the earthly realms,
But scattered now and nameless; — ruined shrines —
(Worshipped and worshippers alike were dust),
That yet polluted Earth with memories; —
All these, and more than these, were fearful types
To herald forth the doom; and yet, none saw,
None heard, nor heeded; and the world went on
Its olden way of sinning, and to sin.
Yet had it known some fearful judgments.   Lands —
Whose habitants had drained sin's bitter cup
Unto the very dregs, and so shut out
All thoughts of good — had from the face of Earth
Been blotted as a scroll.   Cities that rose
To power and glory, through long lapse of years,
Waxed proud with growth, and in their leprous sin
Forgot the hope of heaven, and knew not GOD;

So perished in their darkness; and the world
Found them no more! These things had surely been;
But the blind nations took not home such truths.
They saw no warning in the cities struck
From off the roll of Earth. They gave no heed
Unto the prophet-voices of the past.
Famine — plague — that decimated nations,
Were, in their darkened vision, little less
Than vanity; a little more than dreams!
All ancient shrines were desecrate with blood;
And altars were not holy any more.
The living had no faith save that which yields
Homage unto idols. The dead went down
To silence and to dust, and had no hope!
And very few the souls that in the world
Yet knew and lovéd GOD! The Earth was ripe
And ready for destruction; — full of sin.
The pleasant Earth, that GOD had made so fair
And called "good," was as a fearful blot
Upon the stormy scutcheon of the skies.
Soon GOD will wipe it out; and it shall be
No more a dwelling unto Sin and Death!

The year was dying; and a word went forth
From out the City of the Seven Hills
Summoning all men unto a sacrifice, —
A holocaust of blood, what time the year
Was breathing out its life. The hour came;
And to the dread arena gathered fast
The children of the world; a race as cold
And full of guile, as if from Satan's realm
They rose to darken Earth. I, too, was there :
To suffer, and be patient as of yore.

Slowly the red day dawned, — the day of days, —
The last of all the years. Slowly it dawned;
And Earth, whose brow but now was dusk and wan,
Flushed red as blood in the hot, lurid glare
Of the late risen sun. The hours wore on.
Slowly the multitudes gathered; and the day
Was verging on its noon, ere yet they called
The victims forth unto the funeral pyre.
They came at last, — a glorious martyr-band;
Some, paler than the marble that they trod,
And swaying like the reeds. Oh! who shall say
How much the human frame may bear, yet live?
Or who shall say unto the weary brain,
"Thus far, and no farther," when these had borne

All tortures that man's cruel art could bring
To bear alike on body and on soul?
Their souls had conquered pain, and smiled serene
From heights man's malice sought in vain to reach.
And now they came, with painful steps, and slow,
Once more into the sunshine, but to die!
Death had no sting,—no terrors left for them.
Smiles lit each patient brow, and in their eyes
A strange, deep joy was burning, as a star
To light them to their home.
        He, too, was there;
Mine own true Leon; yet I trembled not.
I knew that we were treading the same way.
I knew that some poor moments were the all
Between our souls and heaven. Heart answered heart,
And on our lips there was a voiceless prayer.
God heard it.
      In the North, a cloud uprose.
Slowly it gathered strength. Far off—far off—
I saw its shadow darkening over Earth,
And knew it was the Avatar of doom.
But the blind multitudes, they saw it not.
Their gaze was on the dark arena bent,
Eager to look on Death; unconscious all
That Death was waiting for his triumph hour,
Sure that it would not fail! A rush of winds,
As hot, and dry, and burning as they came
Fresh from Sahara's desert; then, o'er all
The darkness fell, as thick, impervious night,
Shutting the red sun out. Earth opened wide
Her heaving bosom, and the city fell
A ruin in that grave; fierce tongues of flame
Lapping her fallen towers. A bleeding form
Had caught me up, and borne me from the death;
And I was resting on a green hill-side;
While, far below, a black and hideous gulf
Yawned where the City of the Seven Hills
Had late in glory stood. Through all the world
One word went sounding as the breath of doom,
And mercy there was none. The beautiful
Had perished, and her place was desolate,—
Her crown had passed away.
       I turned aside.
My Leon's form was bleeding at my feet,
And from that truest heart the tide of life
Was ebbing slowly—slowly. Me he saved;
For me his life was given. On my breast
I laid that palest brow, and patient saw

The death-dew lying there.   I was alone,
Watching the shadows vanish.   My last hope
Was fading from me, as a lonely leaf
Borne out to ocean by receding tides,
And never brought to shore!   I could but fold
My patient hands in prayer, and silent watch
The ebbing of his life.   A breath of wind
Touched my hot brow to coolness; and a dream
Of soft, warm skies, of summer, and of song,
Came floating by me as on angel's wings.
I heard the rippling on the pebbly shore;
I saw the sun gleam on the river's breast;
I felt a kiss pressed soft upon my brow,
And murmured "Mother!"   In a little space
The vision faded, and the silence fell
Again upon my soul.   In all the world
There was no sound upon that hush to fall,
Save the dull throbbing of my beating heart.
In all the world there was no life save mine!
He had gone from me in that passing dream,
And left me lonely; waiting with still soul
The solemn presence of the Summoner.
The Earth is rolled together like a scroll,
And through the shadows I look down on dust,
That once was life and beauty.
                              Holy One, —
Beneath the shadow of whose folded wings
My soul is gathering its strength to try
The unknown pathway to yon blessèd land, —
Father in Heaven!   I yield me to thy will;
And meekly as a child, upon thy love
I rest my weary soul.   Be with me now.
Uphold me, lest I falter, as my way
Leads through the Valley of the Shadow of Death.
Thou art All Good, All Merciful, O God!
I rest on thee!   "O Death, where is thy sting?
O Grave, where is thy victory?"

CHORUS OF ANGELS.

" Slow the world is dying — dying;
    And the shadow and the gloom
Over earthly things is lying;
    All doth mingle in the tomb
        That is aye dust's destiny.
From the silence and the dread,
    From the fierce-destroying wave,
From the company of dead,

From the darkness of the grave,
God hath redeemëd thee!

" Earth is fading; Earth is mourning
O'er its beauty and its bloom;
Unto Chaos all returning,
Buried in one common tomb,
Silent for eternity!
Give thou glory to the Father!
Child of earth, the gulf is passed;
And around thee angels gather;
Thou art free, O soul, at last;
God hath redeemëd thee!

" God hath redeemëd thee!
All glory be to Him,
The Holy One, beneath whose eye
Dwell cherubim and seraphim
Through all eternity.
From a world whose loss is gain,
From the dust where dust doth rot,
From the endless torture-pain,
From the worm that dieth not,
God hath redeemëd thee!"

The "Pacific" Lost at Sea.

O Sea! whose restless waters now are sleeping
In the soft sunshine of the early spring,
Dost hear, upon a thousand shores, the weeping
Of some poor hearts who, faithful still, are keeping
Alive some hope that should be withering?

O Sea, thou smilest, and thy great heart, beating,
Hath not one tremble for the mourners pale
Who cling so wildly to the hope of meeting
Again on earth their lost ones, — all unwecting
How brief their record, and how sad their tale!

" Dust unto dust " is but a saddest saying,
When from our eyes the loving pass away;
But *we* have watched, 'mid tender care and praying,
The wasting form, and kept from darkest straying
The soul that hath gone upward unto day.

Our eyes have met the last look of the dying;
  Our lips have rested on their palest brow;
Our ears have heard their last of earthly sighing;
And on the quiet grave where they are lying
  Our hands may scatter sweetest flowers now.

But when, O Sea! unto thy sternest keeping
  The loved and loving of the earth go down,
We see them never more, and all our weeping
Doth only bring them from that ocean-sleeping
  Our midnight dreams with mocking shapes to crown.

O Sea! remorseless, — flowing on forever,
  What is our wailing and our moan to thee?
Thou renderest back no gift; returnest never
The life that storms crushed out; and wide dost sever
  The dust of hearts that in one grave should be.

Roll on, O Sea! in thousand billows breaking;
  Not long shall thy vast deeps a mystery be.
The dead, who in thy caves repose are taking,
Shall from their stillest slumber rise awaking
  Unto the words, "Give up thy dead, O Sea!"

"Christe Eleison."

CHRISTE eleison! for we are sleeping
  The sluggard's slumber, when we should arise
From our dull sloth; and, faithful vigils keeping,
  Prepare our souls to seek the upper skies.
                    Christe eleison!

Alas! the world — its toils around us clinging —
  Doth give no stamina unto our soul;
We hear its siren voices ever singing
  A song that lures us to a darker goal.
                    Christe eleison!

Yet home, and home affections they should gather
  Our wandering hearts unto the better way;
Should teach us ever of the eternal Father,
  And bow our spirits to his gentle sway.
                    Christe eleison!

The dust is erring, and forgetful ever;
  It knoweth life; life's end it cannot see.
O Father! hear us, and forsake us never;
  There is no hope, no refuge save in thee.
                    Christe eleison!

When earth is fading from our darkened vision,
  And slowly shadows gather on our way,
Then through the echo of a world's derision,
  May we but pray, and in our praying say,
                    Christe eleison!

When foes do scorn our mournful plain and weeping,
  And earthly joys are parting like a dream;
When our beloved in stillest rest are sleeping,
  And on our stricken hearts no light doth beam;
                    Christe eleison!

When life is passing, and our soul doth gather
  Its all of strength to tread the unknown way;
Be thou our guide, — a tender, loving Father, —
  And teach our poor hearts evermore to pray
                    Christe eleison!

"Coming Home to Die."

THERE is a fever burning at my heart,
    A silent summons to depart,
      And yet I cannot go!
For me earth wears its robes of beauty yet,
    Its brow with tears hath not been wet, —
      Brightly its waters flow!

My heart hath known no shadow of despair,
    My life lies stretched before me, fair
      As morning's cloudless sky.
Fond hopes, bright dreams, that might a lifetime crown,
    Are by one breath flung sudden down;
      For I come home to die!

To die! Low falls the utterance of that word;
    A death-sigh in its echo heard,
      A cadence of farewell.
And yet, what are we when they fling the clay
    Upon us? Things of yesterday,
      That went far off to dwell.

Shadows are calling to my restless soul, —
    Shadows that beckon to the goal
      Where the dust meets the dust,
I have no fear. I do not dread to go, —
    But parting pains the spirit so;
      Yet part we do, and must.

For I come home to die!   My own fair home,
        Again unto thy hearth I come;
          Never to leave it more,
Save for the dwelling that is dark and lone;
        A rest, when life's last work is done,
          Life's "fitful fever" o'er.

The day is fading, and the sun hath set;
        My life is passing, too; and yet
          I am so young to die!
Be still, poor heart!   What need is there to weep?
        "God giveth his belovëd sleep."
          So wait thou patiently.

A Prayer Answered.

FATHER! be with us now!   The shadow lies
   Upon our quiet hearth; the shadow dread
That yet may darken over closëd eyes, —
   That yet may shroud the dead.

Our hearts keep silence in unspoken fear;
   We dare not ask each other of the thought
That broodeth there, lest haply some swift tear
   Be with our meaning fraught.

Father! be with us now!   The very air
   Though fresh and cool it sweep athwart our brow,
Seems laden with the gaspings of despair.
   Father! be with us now!

We know that thou art gracious, and we rest
   Our weary souls upon thy promise fair.
Earth hath but silence in her mighty breast;
   Thou dost silence despair!

Father! be with us now!   And not for sin —
   Though on our garments fair its hue of red
Is darkly lying — let the death come in.
   As yet, we have no dead!

Our household hearth hath never given up
   Unto the dust one warm and throbbing heart;
We have not drained that sad and bitter cup
   Whence smiling doth depart.

Father! be with us now! for thou canst save,
  Let not the earth be filled with our moan;
Let not our loved go down unto the grave
  Leaving our dwelling lone.

   .   .   .   .

And thou hast been with us, O Holy One!
  The shadow hath departed from our hearth;
The cloud hath lifted, and the fear hath gone
  That darkened o'er the earth.

For thou didst hear our prayers, and gavest back
  The soul we thought was hastening far away
Upon the lone and unreturning track
  That knoweth not our day.

Father! be with us ever; so to keep
  Our feet from straying, and our souls from wrong.
We know thou dost not slumber, nor yet sleep;
  Be with us, all day long!

And when the night shall come, — as come it must, —
  And we lie down unto our last, long sleep, —
When o'er our graves sounds "dust unto the dust,"
  Do thou our spirits keep!

And in the other world, where soul meets soul,
  And Love is Love's eternal shield and guard,
Whence all thy children see the darkness roll, —
  Be thou our "sure reward"!

Winona.

They err, who say our land hath no romance:
"Blue though your sky, free though your waters glance,
  They have no spell of olden days to shed
A mystery around them. All your tale
Is but the sighing of a passing gale.
  Ye have no history, — ye have no dead!"

Such words are spoken, but they err who speak.
Where'er a thought hath crimsoned woman's cheek,
  Or stilled the life-throb bounding in her veins;
Where'er a noble deed claimed human hand,
Or men have perished for their native land,
  A poet finds fit theme for all his strains.

'Tis true; that in our century of years —
A life-time shadowed out by hopes and fears —
  We claim no heritage of old renown.
Our boast is but of deeds our sires have done,
Of fetters broken, and of freedom won.
  We have no tales of temple or of crown, —

Whereto the willing fancy lendeth ears.
Not ours the long array of countless years
  Crimsoned with war, and darkened by old feud.
We have nor fallen towers, nor ruined shrine.
The halo sleeping upon Palestine
  Rests never on our mountains, vales, nor flood.

Yet have we battle-fields whereon the brave
Laid down to slumber, finding but a grave
  Which yet was dearer than a life of chains;
And scenes of strife, where our star-banner rose
Victorious, o'er the dark array of foes
  Who vainly gave the life-blood from their veins

To check our giant strides for freedom's goal.
And such the themes that light a poet's soul
  With purer flame than if old Europe gave
Her wealth of storied crime and high renown, —
Her thousand tales of temple and of crown, —
  To fill the measure of each studied stave.

There are who say that no romance have we, —
That some brief tales of hard-won liberty
  Are all that we may glean from passèd years.
They err, who speak. There's not a flowing stream,
Nor yet a haunt whereon the sun doth gleam,
  But hath its own old tale of loves or fears.

Around Montaup the glamour lingers still;
King Philip haunts his own belovèd hill;
  And far away, in the fair land of flowers,
Where nature in her bounty doth rejoice,
Memories of Osceola's soft, low voice
  Yet sadly blend with sighing evening hours.

Ohio's waters have full many a tale,
And every rushing of the western gale
  Doth chant some half-forgotten deed of yore;
While Mississippi, in its mighty wave,
Doth shroud the beauty of a maid, who gave
  Unto its depths, a heart that hoped no more.

Towards the regions of the setting sun
A world our eyes have never looked upon
  Is filling slowly with the waves of life,
Whose onward flow hath swept old landmarks down;
Crushing memorials of old renown
  Won 'mid the ravage of some border strife.

A land, far-spreading to the setting sun;
A mighty river, that doth swiftly run
  Unto the confines of a soundless sea;
Tall trees, beneath whose shadow things of old
Are slowly wasting, blending with the mould;
  A sky, o'erarching all eternally.

Up from that river's cool and darkened breast,
A cliff doth rear its stern and rugged crest,
  With beetling brow, o'erglooming the still wave.
Thick o'er its sides the tangled forest grows
With rustling foliage, troubling the repose
  That should lie sleeping on a maiden's grave.

A maiden's grave — a woman's breaking heart,
That could not live and see its dreams depart,
  Hath here found silence and forgetfulness.
It could not bear the burthen of its woe;
So o'er that restless heart the waters flow.
  No more it throbs for weeping or to bless.

Vows early plighted, and a fond heart given
Unto the love that seemèd true as heaven;
  A brief, glad season following thereon;
A fairer face, that crossed her path in life;
A change, with bitterest agony rife;
  A lover false who fled, but not alone.

Alas, Winona!   All thy young heart sent
Of love, of gladness, and of full content,
  A precious venture upon life's wide sea,
Was wrecked before the sharp and sudden blast;
And all thy fond hopes, crushed and dying, cast
  Upon a shore, drear as thy destiny.

Alas, for breaking of a maiden's dream!
Sweet flowers flung upon a rapid stream
  Fleet not so swiftly as the hope that flies
From out the future of a loving heart
When falsehood blights its glory.   All time's art
Brings rarely sunshine when the love-hope dies.

What needeth more?   'Tis but an old time tale.
The moan of waves, the sighing of the gale
  Are not more changes of our daily life
Than is the ringing of that bitter chime
Which bears a loving heart before its time,
  Unto the resting from all earthly strife.

What needeth more?   The Indian maiden gave
Her waning beauty to the quiet wave,
  There finding rest that knew not human love.
Self-sought her doom.   What matter unto her
How slept her heart, when never it might stir
  Unto a loving eye that watched above!

Quietly she sleepeth.   The false one now
Sees never shadow resting on her brow;
  Hears never wailing from that broken heart.
And in the world where the freed spirit dwells,
There sounds no echo of the earth-farewells,
  And earthly love is as a thing apart.

Old days have been forgotten, like a dream;
Old things are passing, as the rays that stream
  Soft on the waters, ere the sun departs;
Old names yet linger, as memorial-stones
That for a time may cover o'er the bones
  Of the great dead, or rest upon their hearts.

Old names yet linger, and old legends still
Make haunted places of each vale and hill
  That knoweth yet the Red Man's gliding feet;
And Mississippi on its restless shore
Hears yet the murmur of the olden lore
  That hath no voice where mart and city meet.

———◆◆◆———

“Priez pour les malheureux.”

I was in France.   The morning sun was low;
And all my steps were weary, faint, and slow;
  I had been journeying the long night through,
When, by the road-side, from the velvet grass
A cross did rear itself.   Pause, ere you pass,
  And let its rude inscription meet your view:
      “ Priez pour les malheureux.”

Alone it stood, defined against the sky,
As if it only lookëd up on high,
    And nothing had in common with the dew
That glittered at its feet. Yet from the stone
A simple sentence, and a mournful one,
    Brought to your heart a feeling sweet and true:
            "Priez pour les malheureux."

I knelt and prayed.   My heart's first impulse o'er,
I sat me down beside the river-shore
    And gazed in silence on its waters blue;
Marvelling, the while, how many had knelt there
In eager hope, in fear, in wild despair,
    To murmur o'er with that lone cross in view,
            "Priez pour les malheureux."

"Consumption."

My life is fleeting like a stream away,
And all earth's sounds go rippling past the shore
As waves that die in silence, and return
No echo to the ear that marketh them.
All day I lie beneath the shade of trees,
And hear the summer-winds play through the leaves
Whose rustling falls like music on mine ear.
All the cool air is redolent of life;
And many birds are singing everywhere,
Rejoicing in this summer of the year.
Flowers by thousands in the fields are springing,
And every breeze that floateth o'er my couch
Hath touched their fragrant lips, and wafted thence
A world of sweetness.   And I lie idle,
While the world's astir with throbbing pulses!
I have no strength to strive; no goal to reach.
The vulture gnawing at Prometheus' heart
Is but a type of the chained soul's unrest,
Or of the fever of the fretted heart
Preying upon itself.   I look abroad
O'er all this fair and glorious world of ours;
Its beauty feeds my senses, yet I lie,
As doth a slave, bound down by heavy chains
To a couch of sickness.   My soul drains deep
The cup of sensate pleasures, loving well
The outward glory of this earth, yet pining
For all the stir and hum of busy life,

The sounds that only reach it, as the roar
Of far-off ocean moans through forest trees
That never saw the gleaming of its waves,
Nor knew the baptism of its cooling spray.

My life is fleeting as a dream of night
That never knew completion.   All my hopes
Were shadows, still-born; and my love is dust;
It never woke to life.   My youth is age;
For I, though young in years, have never known
The full and bounding pulse of early days.
My life was measured by a broken rule;
And all mine hours were numbered, and are few;
Few, yet they linger, lengthened out by pain.

My life is fleeting, and I feel it go.
The sands are falling in the fatal glass;
And, as I watch them, earthly things grow dim.
A veil hath fallen on the light of day,
But, through the shadow, angels come to me;
And from their lips fall holy words, and prayers
That seem to pave the silent road that leads
Unto the City of the Heavenly King.
My weary feet already touch that road;
And to my soul a new-born strength is given.
I may not falter now, though dark the path;
Though lone and still the way.   I may not shrink,
For angel-voices whisper unto me, —
"Fear not, O Soul!   God, who redeemëd thee
Once trod the path thou treadest, and became
First-fruits of them that sleep.   Have thou no fear, —
He, that so lovëd thee that for thy sake
He gave his only Son unto the cross,
Is with thee now.   Lean thou upon his arm,
And his great love shall shield and buckler be!" —
As through the darkness of a night of storms,
The clear outringing of some convent-bell
Doth guide and cheer the wanderer on his way;
So to my soul, float echoes from that world
Whither its course is tending; and the grave
Hath lost its victory.   Do I not know
"That my REDEEMER liveth"?

The Old Year and the New.

The year is dead! Cold in its grave it lieth;
  But not to silence hath the year gone down;
For of the Past the world's voice ever crieth,
  And oft its deeds find afterward their crown.
The year is dead; but evermore life bringeth
  Back from that passèd time, or thought, or deed,
Whose issues seemed forgotten, till it flingeth
  Upon some quickening soil a little seed.
A little seed, — a fragile thing, and lowly,
  Yet bearing in its germ a world of fate;
A little seed, that gendereth surely, slowly,
  That which the sower would have crushed too late.

The year is dead; and on its throne is sitting
  A radiant stranger, strong in heart and limb.
He seeth not the mournful shadow flitting
  Into the darkness; what is it to him?
Little he recks who wore the crown he weareth;
  Nothing he feeleth of its thorns, as yet;
And nobly, as a kingly soul, he beareth
  The royal state that soon his heart will fret.
What matter? Let the Future darken o'er him;
  He sees not now the far-off cloud of fate;
The world is fair, and lieth all before him;
  His brow is smiling, and his heart elate!

And we, — the dust that at Time's feet is lying, —
  Have we no greeting for its crownèd king?
Some song that hath no shadow of vain sighing,
  Some strain that like a trumpet-note doth ring?
Ay! that have we! Onward and upward ever,
  Floateth the glorious music of one song;
The only strain that knoweth silence never, —
  The only song that riseth graves among.
It breaketh from the heart all crushed and bleeding;
  It falleth from the lips death soon must seal;
It fills our souls when this poor life, receding,
  Withdraws the veil, Heaven's glories to reveal.

Know ye the song? The angels sing it ever,
  And o'er our cradle float its harmonies;
But we are moved by many a passion-fever,
  And in our human hearts its echo dies.

Wherefore so? It needeth tender keeping,
  And gentlest nurture in our early years;
Give it but this; and in its spring-tide leaping
  Forth into song, it shutteth out our tears.
Onward and upward! Look not back for sighing,
  Nor bury any hope beneath the pall.
What matter if the years of life are flying,
  When Heaven is so near, — GOD over all?

"A Little While."

A LITTLE while! O Earth, give happiness
  Ere I am summoned hence away.
O Love, thou hast the means, the power to bless,
  Pour thou thy sunshine on my waning day.

A little while — and my once home shall boast
  A silent presence then and evermore;
A voiceless shadow, of the loved and lost
  Whose feet are treading the eternal shore.

A little while — and echoings of my name
  Shall sound no more where the bright waters flow;
A little while — and all my dreams of fame
  With "dust unto the dust" shall silent go.

A little while — and this poor heart of mine
  No more shall tremble unto throbs of pain;
A little while — and other suns will shine
  Upon the grave where long my dust hath lain.

A little while — and all these things shall be;
  And to my quiet place there will not come
One lingering step in memory of me,
  And I shall be forgotten in my home.

A little while — and all this breathing mass
  Shall be as shadows fading in the night;
A little while — and every hearth, alas!
  Will know how sorrow darkens over light.

A little while — and this fair earth of ours
  Shall shrivel as a scroll, and all the dead
Shall rise, and in this last of changeful hours
  We all shall know by what way we were led.

A little while this weary earth to tread;
  A little while to kneel upon the sod;
A little while to rest amid the dead;
  And then to be for evermore with God!

A *little* while; then let us patient be,
  And softly fold our hands, and ever pray;
And bear life's crosses meekly, cheerfully,
  Waiting the dawning of eternal day.

A *little* while!   O restless heart, be still;
  Nor murmur thou beneath so light a cross;
But bow submissive to our Father's will,
  And know thy grief is rather gain than loss.

A little while to fold our hands in prayer;
  A little while to fit us for the sky.
Rest we content; for our beloved are there,
  And God doth watch o'er all eternally.

"There went out a Sower to sow."—Mark iv. 3.

A SOWER went out to sow,
  And with unsparing hand
The good seed and the precious seed
  He scattered o'er the land.
And some fell on the beaten path,
  Some on a rocky bed;
And the fowls of the air they gathered the first
  When the last was withered, dead.
And some of the seed 'mid thorns
  And choking brambles fell,
And it never knew the time of fruit.
  But only God can tell
Why the good seed the Sower sowed
  Should perish at its birth,
Or grow awhile but to die without fruit
  From off the summer earth.

A Sower went out to sow,
  And he scattered goodly seed,
And some fell on a richer soil,
  Was not choked by thorn nor weed;
And the grain increased, and grew strong,
  And the sun shone on it still;

In the harvest the reapers gathered in
  A hundred fold at will.
Know ye who the Sower is?
  The God who loveth all;
And he soweth seed in human hearts
  There to grow, or there to fall.
May his sun shine aye upon it,
  And his rain fall soft and slow;
And the seed that our Father hath planted
  To a goodly harvest grow!

My Picture-Gallery.

I.

A QUIET vale, wherein a lowly cot
Reared its moss-covered roof. Spring's magic touch
Had loosed the fetters from a little rill
That flowed adown the vale; and tiny blades
Of grass were growing greenly, and some flowers —
Some pale blue flowers — looked up from out the stream
As it had caught bright fleckings from the sky
And gave them back unto the light again
Fresh-clothed in beauty, and new-shaped as flowers.
A child was lying 'mid that soft green grass,
His naked feet white plashing in the wave
With whose cool spray they sported. Clearest eyes
Were looking up into the bluest heaven
With half-pleased wonder; while one restless hand
Was filled with the blue flower "forget-me-not."
Stern cliffs, white-browed with snow, were looming cold
From out the distance; frowning, silent, pale,
On all the youth and beauty at their feet.

II.

A palace-chamber, crimson garmented,
Wherein an infant slumbered; quietly,
As if upon her brow there rested not
The shadow of a crown. Her tiny hand
Doth hold a mimic sceptre in its grasp;
And scattered round, meet for a royal child,
Lie jewelled toys, and fairy crowns, not flowers.
The world doth gift her richly; but the earth
With all its wealth of beauty hath no part

In aught that pleases her. She lieth there,
Unto her mother's heart a thing of joy,
A child within its cradle sleeping, yet
In some far-seeing statesman's eye, a queen!

III.

A forest-opening where through archéd trees
The morning sun looked in upon a scene
That stirred some finer pulses than if life
Had been a stranger there. A princely child,
That scarce had seen ten summers sweep the earth,
Leaned white and cold, against a sturdy oak,
Her darkening eyes yet fixed upon the foe,
The dreaded wolf fierce ravening for her blood.
Betwixt them both, a boy, a stripling, stood,
With lips compressed, and brows resolved, though pale,
His ready dagger gleaming in his hand.
Far-off, were dark blue mountains, purple-tinged
In the cool light of morn; and at their feet
A gleam of silver waters. Through the trees,
There stole faint glimpses of the arching skies
That smiled so blue above. Fair all the scene
That nature called her own; but fairer still
The drooping, girlish brow, so white with dread,
So veiled with waves of bright and golden hair.
The gallant boy, also, his dark eyes filled
With all a man's true daring, standing there
'Twixt the gaunt wolf and his expected prey;
Content to die — if such fate waited him —
So that grim wolf shall bear him company.

IV.

An ancient hall, hung round with banners old,
Wherein the pride and flower of the land
Were keeping stately revel. Rainbow groups
Were scattered here and there, with brows unbent
From all the cares of day, and fullest lips
That only curled to laughter, or light scorn;
Such scorn as sitteth mocking on the arch
Of some sweet girlish lips. The merry throng
Had drawn aside, and down the central space
The queen and star of all the festival
Moves slowly; yet with such unconscious grace
That every eye doth rest upon her form,
As loth to turn away, and, turning, lose
The sight of such rare beauty. Soft brown eyes
Wherein the soul yet slumbered; brow as white
As lily-flower just opening to the sun;

And archèd lips, now wreathèd with a smile —
Yet firm withal, as if in danger's hour
High noble truths, and words that vanquish wrong
Might issue through their arched and ruby gates;
Thick, heavy braids of soft brown golden hair
Rolled round the Grecian head, and shadowy fell
Upon the snowy temples.   Robed in white,
She stood amid the rainbow-colored throng
As some fair lily in its dew of youth
Doth stand amid the roses in their bloom.
All eyes were bent upon her.   Some that looked
The love that never found an utterance,
But silent lived; prompting to noblest deeds
That so themselves might win a quiet place
In her true memory.   But one who came
Within that lovely presence gathered hope,
Though he was young and nameless, peasant-born;
And went upon his way, with nothing more
Than one sweet smile to cheer him; yet it made
Sunshine within his heart forever!

v.

A field of strife, wherein the peasant-born
Did link his name to glory, and became
A heritor of fame, and all to win
A thought from one who never could be his!
Deep on his heart that bitter truth was stencilled,
Yet none the less its every throb was hers.
What though her brow was ringèd with a crown,
And might not lie upon a peasant's breast?
What though the gulf between them was too wide
E'en for ambition's leaping? Yet his love
Might come betwixt her and some threatened hurt,
As in the passèd time his young, strong arm —
Her only refuge in that fearful hour —
Had smitten down the fierce and eager wolf.
And so he led her armies to the field,
Turning the tide of battle when it ebbed;
And hasting on the day, whose time of flood
Crowned the long strife with Peace!

VI.

                    — "Alone!
Do I not know the meaning of that word,
Written in fire on my heart of hearts?
Doth it not burn, yea, quiver there alway,
Torturing my soul with restless agony?
Alone! — alone. There flows no kindred blood

In any veins of earth.   There beats no pulse
That might keep measure with mine own, and give
Some little warmth to me.   Alone — alone.
Crowned and anointed queen, but nothing more;
Nor wife — nor mother — mated but to pride,
That wears my heart away!   Would I could crush
Beneath my feet the crown that doth enring
My forehead as a curse, and be as free
As is the meanest peasant in my realm!
Then might I hope for something of the joy
That smiles on humble homes, yet passes by
The palaces of kings!   .
          There is a dull pain gnawing at my heart —
What if it be thy slow precursor, Death?
The foe is thundering at the city gates;
My country needs its queen; I cannot die!
Yet to my worn and weary spirit now
Pale death would seem an angel sent from God;
And I would greet him as the captive greets
The light of day once more.   Be patient, heart!
I say not yet to thy wild throbs " be still."
There are some duties that do bind me here,
And I must work, although it be alone.
Alone — to bear the brunt of this fierce war;
Alone — with none to comfort if I fail;
Alone — yet I must live ! "

VII.

          Back to the city of that fairest queen;
Back to the city he had saved for her,
Came the proud victor; but no flowers strewed
The path he trod.   The very streets were still,
As the inanimate stones were stricken dumb
By some great sorrow.   Banners that were flung
Victorious to the breeze were trailing low
As every fold were all instinct with grief.
How still had grown the victor's bounding pulse!
Yet stayed he not. — " Lead on!   I pause not here."

VIII.

          Within a royal abbey's sacred walls
A queen was sleeping; guarded right and left
By all the best and noblest of the land.
Robed all in white, no mocking emblems there;
The crown and sceptre lying at her feet,
She slept.   No sounds of earth might waken her.
A wail was on the air that none might still,
For every heart was chanting requiem.

A stir without. His forehead bared, unarmed,
The peasant victor knelt before his queen.
— "Lady, this day I bring thee back thine own.
Thy cities are untouched; thy land is free;
Thy foe hath made such peace as leaveth him
No shadow of old boasting; and thy realm
Is all thine own again." — The soldier ceased :
And from the crushed heart of the lover swept
Its wail of agony. — "And I return
To look upon thy dust! I thought to hear
Some kind and gracious words; to meet thy smile, —
I never hoped for more, — and *this* is all !" —

   .   .   .   .

The next of line sat on the vacant throne,
But in his Council Hall the peasant-born
Had never place. The armies of the land
Were led to battle by more noble chiefs;
And the proud victor of a passëd strife
Was never heard of more. He left no name
To gift the world withal; and passed away
In the same hour that gave that fairest queen
Unto the silent keeping of the earth;
And none knew how he died, nor where the dust
Was lying on his brow.

"Youth ever loves to Dream." — Bulwer.

WHO loves not dreams? What matter if they flee,
  Or pass from out our hearts as leaves that glide
On some swift-rushing river to the sea
  That but engulfs them in its mighty tide?
What matter if they fade? They have been bright;
  More sweet than any other fancies were.
O'er some brief hours they poured a flood of light,
  And something of past glory lingers there.
What matter if they die? As in an urn
  Regretful sorrow shrines them; and they bring —
Though never in their glory they return —
  Back to our hearts a memory of spring.

Who loves not dreams? Yet often they may have
  Such bitter fruit of loneliness and tears
As shuts life's joyance in an early grave,
  And leaves a shadow on its after years.
We weave them oft; we bind them on our hearts;

We give them rarely to the light of day;
For in the sunshine all their charm departs.
  Break but their silence, and they fade away.
Do ye love dreams? Then guard them as a name
  That ye have given to the grave to keep;
Be they as secret as a deed of shame
  Whose very uttering were tears to weep.

Who loves not dreams? Yet what, in truth, are they?
  Mere idle phantoms of the heart and brain;
Woven of the sunshine, — formèd from a ray
  That *hath* shone brightly; shineth not again.
We like them well. We see them as we see
  The motes that cross the sunbeam; but they fade
And give no token of reality;
  The dusk receives them, and they die in shade.
We know all this, and yet we cherish dreams,
  Though scarce we know in what we place our trust;
We follow still their ignis fatuus gleams,
  And half our lives are wasted on their dust.

Sorrow.

As one, who, standing in some place,
Doth see before him, face to face,
  A shape that shape hath none;
Whose brow grows moist, whose heart grows still,
All power lost to turn at will
  From the thing he looks upon;
So do we stand, with hushed heart-beat,
When first upon our path we meet
  The sorrow of our life.
Vainly we strive to turn away,
Or shut without our walls of clay
  The pain with which 'tis rife.
I counsel not to drive it hence.
How do we know from Whom, or Whence
  The dreaded shadow came?
It hath a visage cold and stern;
It treadeth some funereal urn
  Or telleth of some shame.
All this may be; but I would clasp
The sorrow with as warm a grasp
  As if some friend it were.
Weary and sad may be the task,
  Bitter and dark to me;

But a day shall come, when falleth the mask;
  When the cold, stern face
  Shall not have a trace
Of its olden shape and mien;
When a glory shall rest, as a golden sheen,
On the sorrow past, and I shall see
  God's angel smiling there!

A Reverie.

I AM sitting by the fireside
  In the dusk of the day,
And I watch the fire-sparkles
  As they flash and fade away;
Till into my heart there glideth
  Some dreams of golden glow;
And they gleam as if their glory
  Had not perished long ago.

I am sitting by the fireside,
  As in those pleasant days
When all our dreams seemed full of life
  Caught from the cheerful blaze.
I hear the old, sweet voices
  That knew not sorrow's tone;
And I see the glad, young faces,
  So joyous, every one.

I am sitting by the fireside;
  But my heart is otherwhere;
I look upon another scene,
  I breathe another air.
I hear the breezes, flying
  O'er the waters in their play;
See the autumn-flowers dying
  On a hill-side, far away.

I am sitting by the fireside;
  And my thoughts are flowing back
Like a murmur of sweet music
  To my childhood's early track.
And I dream of sunny hours
  That may come no more to me;
Though the present gathers flowers
  From the past of memory.

I am sitting by the fireside,
  But none sit there with me;
And merry voices, loving hearts,
  Are only memory.
Through the day I may be lonely,
  But the evening hour doth bring
Unto my heart all gentle things
  It lovëd in the spring.

I am sitting by the fireside,
  Watching the shadows pass
Across the mystic jets of flame
  As in a magic glass,
Till echoes of soft foot-falls
  Sound on the oaken floor;
Yet I know those feet are treading
  A far and silent shore.

I am sitting by the fireside,
  And on my heart there lies
A memory of clasping hands,
  A thought of loving eyes.
A mist falls o'er the firelight,
  A sob is in my breath;
Those hands lie folded evermore,
  Those eyes are sealed in death.

I am sitting by the fireside,
  And I hear what none may hear
Save those whose souls are passing
  Away with the passing year.
A mournful chant and sighing,
  Half silenced with a song
Of praise and glory unto God
  That riseth graves among.

I am sitting by the fireside,
  And the shadows gather there,
And their wan, wan lips are moving
  In a murmur as of prayer;
And I hear, far-off, the flowing
  Of a river that doth run
Through morning, and through evening,
  Unto the setting sun.

I am sitting by the fireside,
  And patiently I wait
The breaking of my prison-bars,
  The opening of the gate.

The bird is weary of its cage;
　　Pines for the free blue skies;
Break but its bonds, — with tireless wing
　　Upward the freed one flies!

"Give Thou no Tears to Me."

GIVE thou no tears to me.　I'll have no weeping
　　When for my soul the welcome angels come.
Rests not the dust within the Father's keeping?
　　Goes not the spirit home?

Give thou no tears to me, when from this dreary
　　And restless world I go but to be blest.
Wherefore should I linger?　I am so weary;
　　Shall I not be at rest?

Give thou no tears to me.　My dreams of morning
　　Lived not the full and glorious day to see.
I know their light on other hearts is dawning;
　　They gave but night to me.

Give thou no tears to me; but keep thou ever
　　Within thy heart one thought that is all mine;
And I will bless thee, ere the grave shall sever
　　The bond 'twixt mine and thine.

Think of me kindly, as of one who, sleeping,
　　Hath buried all her faults from memory;
But keep thine eyes from shadow of vain weeping;
　　Give thou no tears to me.

An Incident.

MORNING dawned
O'er the far-reaching prairies, lighting up
Their waves of green; and resting, as a swan,
On the broad bosom of the flowing river.
Soft sighed the breeze along the silent shore,
Singing through stately trees that knew not yet
The white man's fatal axe.　Not long endured
That happy ignorance.　Even now a sail

Flashed white against the forest's wealth of green;
And swiftly, as a thought, it rode the wave
That ne'er had known such rider till that morn.
It paused upon its way; its sails were furled;
The bark was moored beside the western shore;
And on its deck a sad band gathered slow.
We ask not wherefore, since a shrouded form
Was lying in their midst.   They had but paused
To give unto the keeping of the earth
A woman's silent heart.   It beat yest're'en;
Though faintly, as a strain of dying music
That fadeth into silence with a smile.
And she died smiling, as a child in sleep
That resteth quiet on its mother's breast.
Some tender hands were with her when she passed
Unto the Better Land; yet strangers all,
That scarcely knew her name, nor yet her life,
Save what she murmured to herself, ere death
Brought silentness.
     —"I joy that I am dying.
I hear the river rippling as it glides,
Bearing me far away.   It brings to me
A dream of yore; a memory of days,
When all my youth fled from me, as a stream
Doth lose itself within the mighty deep.
Coolly the waters glide, and musical;
And in my heart an echo answers them.
I tread once more my far-off father-land;
I see its skies blue smiling down on me;
I hear sweet voices that have long been still;
A merry laugh is ringing on mine ears,
And restless feet fall lightly on the turf
I may not tread again!   All this, and more,
Is present to me; and my weary heart
Doth beat as if it nothing knew of dying;
And yet the rising of yon setting sun
I shall not live to see!—
     —"I fear thee not,
O quiet Death!   O still and dreamless sleep,
That soon shall cover me from pain and tears!
I see a vision of a churchyard green,
With mossy head-stones, and sown thick with graves;
Where, in the shadow by the old tower thrown,
My mother long hath slept.   Another grave—
It seems to me as if but yesterday
The earth fell heavy on the coffin-lid—
Lies there beneath the stars that never veiled
Their glory when he died.

         — " I wandered, once,
Out in the ruthless storm, unto the shore
Whereon the living waters foamed and dashed.
Madly the billows curled, and on their crest,
A moment seen, a dead man's face gleamed white.
The next they dashed it to my very feet!
And from those sands the eyes looked cold on me
That ever were so loving. Cold and still,
Beside my mother's grave, I left him sleeping;
And, where they rest, my dust shall never be.
How fast the river runs! It flows from me, —
I cannot hear its ripple, — but I see
A church-yard green with graves, and mine not there!
I am so weary; let me sleep — sleep — sleep." —

And so she slept; to wake no more on earth.
She parted ere the morn. At set of sun
Strange hands had made her grave, where still the flow
Of Mississippi's waters murmured soft
A song of sorrow.

—◦◦—

Song.

SILENTLY, silently fleeteth the day,
  Softly and slowly the night cometh on;
So the light of my youth it is passing away;
  It came as a dream; as a dream it is gone.
      And I sit and I sing,
      By the old mossy spring,
Of the days that forever are gone;
      And I hear, once more,
      The voices of yore,
Till I feel no longer alone.

Merrily, merrily, passed the hours,
  When my heart was as blithe as a bird;
And my feet they were pressing the brightest of flowers,
  And sorrow's wild moan was not heard.
      When I sang but one song
      All the merry day long,
And the song was as glad as could be;
      But it floated away
      With the passing of day,
Till it died into silence for me.

Wearily, wearily, goeth the day; ·
For my heart is more weary still;
And vainly I strive to make time pass away, —
   'Tis a riddled cup I fill.
     But this wasting strife
     Is as death to life,
And I shall not be weary long.
     Soon a place there will be,
     And a rest for me,
Earth's thousand graves among.

Under the Sea.

I saw, as in a dream.   My spirit walked
The waste of ocean; and the deeps gave up
Their solemn mysteries.   Strange things were there.
Rare palace-chambers, lighted up with gems
That once, perchance, had decked Golconda's lord;
Or shone with mocking radiance, 'mid the plumes
Of some dark-browed cacique; torn thence to grace
The noblest dames of Leon or Castile.
Yet destined ne'er to sparkle on a brow
Of earthly loveliness.   The sea gives not
Its priceless treasures up; and so it kept
Within its secret caverns and its cells
The ravished jewels as the fruits of crime
The spoiler might not reap.   Yet hath the sea
More lovely things than these.   Anemones,
Half plant, half animal; coral groves, that mock
The marble domes and palaces of man,
For that their fairy structure was the work
Of some poor feeble insects, yet endures
When marble domes have crumbled into dust;
And shells that lie upon the ocean floor
As stars do fleck the sky.   Pale shells whose hue
Doth show beside the blush-rose lovelier;
And some that mock all tintings of that arch
Which spanneth heaven as a type of hope,
A promise of To Be.   And yet the deep
Hath costlier things than these; for human hearts
Have striven, and grown still, amid the foam
That floats so lightly o'er their secret graves;
And in its palace chambers, soft and still,
A thousand, thousand hearts are lying low.

I saw, as in a dream, pale shadows flit
Across these palace-chambers, — shapes that once
Made light and sunshine in some home of earth,
Yet perished far away amid the storm
And never came to shore; dark brows of men
Whose hearts were darker with some crime or shame
That gave them never rest, though death had stilled
Their fevered pulse to silence. Many forms,
That once were of the earth, came gliding past,
Seen but to disappear as silently.
Yet some moved slowly by, speaking the while
What seemed to be a record of their life.

A shape rose up beside me, stately-browed,
Yet fair withal; her voice not soft and sweet,
But full and deep, as any man's might be.

— "I was a woman; but my father taught
Unto my soul such deep and bitter lore
As made me more akin unto himself.
I was his only child, and wildly loved;
Yet trained by him as I had been a' man,
And fit to heir the greatness of the schemes
He thought would crown him king. They did but stain
His memory as a traitor's, false alike
To country and to home. In his counsels
I shared not then, nor ever. When he crept
Unto the happy hearth-stone of his friend,
A serpent in its Eden, leaving there
A loathsome slime upon its fairest flower,
I had been sleeping long. When on his brow
The name of 'traitor' burnëd as a flame,
Mine ears were deaf unto the world's sharp scorn,
Mine eyes saw nothing of that brand of shame,
My heart knew never one wild pang of pain,
So still and deep its slumber.
                              "One fair morn,
Our path was o'er the ocean, and our bark
Swept on full proudly o'er the restless sea,
Whose surges sang so sweet and sad a song.
I sat upon the vessel's prow; mine eyes
Bent downward as to pierce beneath the foam
And learn what language wave did speak to wave
So mournfully; till, wearied out, I slept.
I saw not, in my sleep, how in the South
A sail loomed white against the horizon;
Nor watched it grow into a stately barque;
Nor felt the terror, nor the anguish knew

That throbbed so keenly in some stoutest hearts.
But there came a swift and dark awakening.
A battle-cry rang out upon mine ears;
A sound of hurrying feet that swept the deck,
And sabres clashing for the briefest space.
Then all was silent, save some moans of pain
That might not yet be stilled. From out my lair—
They had not seen me yet—I looked, and saw
The hapless dead tossed to the hungry waves
That closed above them soon. I saw the plank
Run out to leeward; saw the few yet left
Of those who fought so bravely tread its length,
And so go down to silence and to death.
Ere yet the wave had settled o'er the last,
A white shape flashed athwart the buccaneers,
And stood, unfaltering, on the narrow plank
Yet poised above the deep. I had my choice,
To live, and be a thing for my own soul
To mock at evermore; or to go down
Quick into the grave, and—I am here!"

I saw, as in a dream, an ancient ship,
With sails all set, yet cold and motionless;
All ribbed with ice, and still as any stone.
A man sat at the helm; and by his side
A fair-haired child was leaning, with blue eyes
That had no child-look in them. Still she sang:—

"Father, the sun was high in heaven,
    And praise unto Mary Mother was given
        For the fair and cloudless day
        The morn we sailed away;
        And merrily we went forth
        O'er the waters to the north
            Whither our course did lie;
    And my song it floated over the sea
        Merrily—merrily.

"Father, the moon looked so pale last night,
    That I scarce could see in the misty light
        What shadow was passing me.
            But it turned its face,
            And I then could see
        Of my mother's form some trace;
    And she touched my brow with her shadowy hand,
    And it felt as cold as the white ice-land
        That I saw but yestere'en;

And my heart beat fast, as when long ago
They left my mother to sleep 'neath the snow
      Near the kirk of Eiladeen.

"Father, the sun did not shine to-day,
      And the sea moans wearily;
The cold, wet sleet driveth fast on me,
      And I cannot move away.
The sails do not flap, and the crew lie so still,
      I hear not any breath;
And your face is as white as my mother's, and chill
      As hers when her sleep was death.
Let me hold the helm. You are weary; sleep,
      Till the morning comes to me.
Dear Mary Mother, watch over us keep,
      As we sail upon the sea."

The morning came, lighting with coldest ray
The pathless ocean; but that ancient ship
Had silent vanished; and the blue-eyed child
Saw never earthly morning dawn again
To light her to her mother's far-off grave, —
The lonely grave near kirk of Eiladeen!

I saw, as in a dream. A woman sat,
Self-crownëd and alone, upon a throne
Herself had reared beneath a lofty dome;
But seaweed tangles were amid her hair,
And sand and shells strewed thick upon her robe.
Not fair, nor yet ungentle, was her brow,
Though she had veilëd womanhood with a mind
Most like a man's; and all to win a place
Was never meant for woman. Let her speak.

"I left the home I loved not overmuch,
And did unsex myself, that I might be
A dabbler in diplomacy, and learn
What secret wires did make the puppets move.
I went abroad; and made my home for years
Beneath the shadow of a papal dome;
And noted petty trifles, — little things
That yet do make the sum of royalty, —
And weighed them leisurely. Full well I knew
Which scale must touch the beam. I wrote a book;
And thought to fill the wide world with my name;
But, ere I gave its pages to the day,
The doom was meted out to me and mine;
And all my life, half wasted, incomplete,

Was dashed out at one blow; and I left nought
Behind me save a name with never work
To crown it, as I do crown myself
Knowing what would have been, had I but lived
And worked out all the purpose of my soul."—

I saw, as in a dream.   A dark-browed man
Did stand before me, wearing the plumed hat
And peakëd beard of Isabella's reign.
A man, whose foot, disdainful, trod the sands;
Yet sorrow had been busy with his brow,
Leaving rude traces there; though the proud lip
Had never tremble in its curvëd lines
To show how throbbed the poor and tortured heart.
Silent he stood before me; cold and stern;
Until the o'ermastering soul compelled him speak,
And as he spoke his eagle eyes grew soft.*

.   .   .   .

A Pebble.

Go, fling in the river that glideth by
   A pebble caught up from the shore,
And look on the stars and the quiet sky
   That never shall see it more;
And give, if you will, a passing moan
   To some belovëd at rest,
Or unto some hope forever gone;
   Then look on the river's breast!
No trace of what has been is left;
   Onward the troubled wave hath swept;
   Right softly the waters flow;
And they tell no tale to the grassy lea,
And they bear no murmur unto the sea,
   But the pebble lies below.
     And it keepeth its place,
     Though never a trace
Of its grave shall the pale stars see!

Maud.

O Maud, my little Maud!
   Art looking to the skies,

* Unfinished.

As if from those far fields of blue thou'dst won
　　The color of thine eyes?
Or from those rays of morning light
Hadst caught the tinting warm and bright
　　That on thy tresses lies?

　　O Maud, my little Maud!
　　Thy hand rests in my hand,
With more tender trust, truer lovingness,
　　Than any in the land.
There is no fear within thine eyes,
Nor shadow of a shy surprise,
　　To break my fairy wand.

　　O Maud, my little Maud!
　　Thy life hath but begun,
While mine hath travelled for many a day
　　Toward its setting sun.
Ere the full morning of thy day,
My passëd one shall flee away
　　As with a race that's run.

　　O Maud, my little Maud!
　　Leave me not yet alone;
Thy spring will be flush with its fairest flowers
　　When I am dead and gone!
I fold my weary hands to pray
That through thy bright or cloudy day
　　God keep thee, little one!

　　O Maud, my little Maud!
　　Yet closer to my breast,
That on thy brow, that on thy cheek, thine eyes,
　　My pale lips may be pressed.
Smooth with thy hand my gray hairs o'er,
For only this once, — nevermore,
　　For I shall be at rest.

　　O Maud, my little Maud!
　　My feet press on the shore,
Where the faithful of earth may not fear to tread,
　　Since Christ hath trod before.
O little Maud, when I shall sleep,
May God our Father watch and keep
　　And love thee evermore!

1857.

The last morn of the year
In its earliest dawn is here,
But clouds upon its cradle hours are lying;
For through the starless night, but now o'erpast,
The rain fell thick and fast;
And through the leafless trees
The phantom of a summer breeze
So wearily went sighing.
But the wind hath gone to rest
As a weary child in slumber blest;
And o'er the hill-tops, dim and cold, appears
The pale ghost of a day,
All wrapped in clouds, and cradled unto tears;
As if all hope of sunshine were a dream
Too brightly glorious to gleam
On that dull shadow's way!

The last day of the year;
And from its cradled sleep the morn is waking,
And through the storm-clouds breaking,
Far-off the blue and smiling skies appear.
A type of hope,
That to the heart grief-riven,
Doth softly ope
The golden gates, the everlasting doors of Heaven!
O tender Hope! that with thy angel hand
Dost wipe away our tears.
O glorious Hope! that lightest up the years
Till on the silent shore
(Where the heart and time beat nevermore)
Our failing feet shall stand;
Till o'er the bitter wave,
That floweth to the grave,
A light shall dawn as from eternity;
Till, guided by thy hand,
Within the portals of the Better Land
Thou leavest us, — as those
Who, having found repose
Beneath the Love of God, have no more need of thee!

The last day of the year!
What memories doth it bring
Of crownèd summer, and of autumn, bright
With the promise of the spring!

Earth hath not failed to yield
Her ripened harvests to the reaper's hands:
And every waving field
Hath paid the tribute that hard toil demands
And freely given up
Its wealth of golden grain.
But for the poor man's cup,
Who shall replenish it?   In vain
Shall his children cry for bread.
The heat and burthen of the day he bore;
The earth was heavy with his tread,
And with pale drops his weary brows were wet.
He brought the ripened harvests to your door,
Laying up treasures for you; and yet
The fire is cold upon his hearth;
Famine at his threshold stands,
And he lieth upon the earth.
Or he watcheth, with folded hands,
For the dawning of that day
(He thinks not far away)
When the Hunger-pain shall cease,
And the Fever-thirst be quelled!
When the pining soul that had rebelled,
Owning its judgment just,
Shall fling aside the dust,
And the worn heart be at peace!
Yet, "blessèd are the poor!"
For the *Holiest* came to them.
The sceptre of all the worlds he bore;
The stars were under his feet;
And his Father's love was the diadem
Enringing his brows, as the crown most meet
For the Child of Bethlehem!
Yea; "blessèd are the poor;"
For the gospel was preached to them;
And the Lord of all as a poor man came
To the world that he had made.
And he suffered alone — alone —
The Highest, Holiest One;
" Enduring the cross, despising the shame,
For the glory before him set."
O Man! thou art very poor;
Grim Want is standing at thy door;
But, forget not, 'mid Poverty's sharpest stings,
Or, as onward is sounding thy weary tread,
That the *Lord of Lords* and *King of Kings*
"Had not where to lay his head!"
Remember! the brow of thy God hath been wet

With the blood of agony;
And the Lamb that was slain for the sins of the world
Laid down his life for thee!

Depart, Old Year! thy work is done;
Thy task complete; thy destined mission o'er;
And thou mayst calmly sleep;
Thy race is run!
But some poor hearts of earth shall throb and beat
With a bitterness, evermore,
Unto an agony and horror, meet
For a deed that thou hast known.
The sound thereof hath flown
To the remotest strand;
And the nations tears of blood shall weep
O'er a sin-defilëd land,
Till its name shall be blotted from the scroll,
As of that which hath long been dead;
And it go down to dust, as a corse whence the soul
With the life forever hath fled.

The last night of the year!
· Slowly the moments go.
I hear, far off, the unending flow
Of a river that runneth near;
And, through the hush that the wind doth mock,
I hear a clear bell's chime;
The striking of the clock.
It numbereth o'er,
With an echo " nevermore,"
The throbbing pulses of the passing time,
The dying of the year!

O year that diest,
Going we know not whither, but never to return,
Pale on thy wintry couch thou liest,
And for thy funeral urn,—
Thy only landmark in the long To Be,—
The morrow's dawn shall bring thee memory.
We have no more:
Save bitter thoughts o'er that which *might have been,*—
The unattainable of the passëd year,
Which holdeth yet uncertain tenure in the days
That stretch so far and wide before,
And are not seen,
But with a veilëd mien,
And through the reflex of unsteady rays
Caught half from Hope, and half from Fear,

And mocking our poor bosoms evermore!
    O hopes of earth, that faded long ago;
    O dreams of joy, that never saw the day,
About your graves a mournful chant doth flow;
The dirge of time o'er fair things passed away.
            And *we*, too, wail and weep
        O'er all the beauty that doth sleep
Where hearts are silent; and o'er all the love
That hath gone from us to a Better Land.
        And with veiled brows we stand
            Around our lonely hearth
        (So lonely now, so very desolate),
            Yet feeling that, above
In calm repose, our lost belovĕd wait
Till God our fetters shall unbind,
    And we in yon bright Heaven find
The love and beauty that hath gone from earth.

        The bell hath ceased its chime;
            The year is dead.
        We move o'er the grave of Time,
            And softly let us tread.
Softly, — as if our best belovĕd lay beneath,
Hushed in the long and silent sleep of death;
    Softly; for the bell hath ceased its chime.
            The year is dead!

H. B. H.

FATHER in Heaven!   We bow before thy throne,
    And for an erring soul we lift the prayer;
Thou canst release from sin, and thou alone!
    Let not our plea be wholly lost in air,
        And turn not from us in our need;
        For humbly do we plead.

Father in Heaven!   Be thou about his path,
    And win him gently from the downward way;
And lovingly, in mercy, not in wrath,
    Make him to see thy everlasting day;
        Nor dread its coming, as a soul
        That wanders from its goal.

Father in Heaven! Not doubting do we pray.
    We have the promise of thy Holy One, —
"From him that pleads I will not turn away;

And he that trusts I will not leave alone.
  Who asketh shall receive of me
  Life for eternity."

Father in Heaven!   We know in whom we trust;
  There is no shade of turning found in thee.
On thee, as on a rock, we worms of dust
  May build our hopes, and know they will not flee.
    Therefore we come, and at thy throne
    Plead for this erring one.

His feet are straying in forbidden ways;
  Bright seems the world that he hath entered in;
His soul is caught in its deceptive maze,
  And feels not yet its fetters are of sin.
    Thoughtless he wanders from the track;
    Is there no turning back?

The world lies all before him; veiled in light
  That masks the darkness brooding underneath.
Life's web seems woven of all hues, most bright
  With hope and pleasure; but the woof is Death!
    He sees not dark, because of light;
    Yet surely cometh night!

Father in Heaven!   For this poor child of earth
  We fold our hands in prayer; beseeching thee
That thou wouldst lead him from the way of death
  And give him life that is eternally.
    Keep o'er him here true watch and guard
      Through morning and through night;
      And, in "the world that makes this right,"
    Be thou his sure reward!

Thoughts.

          O HEART of mine,
Speak thou!   Is it so sad a thing to die?
Dost weep because the mandate hath gone forth,
That calls thee hence away?   What though thy path
Is flush with summer roses, and no blight
Is on their beauty?   Said they not of old
"Whom the gods love die young"?   And yet they knew
No hope beyond the grave, save for the great,
The crownèd ones of earth.   But for the meek,

The lowly, and the poor, this world was all.
Warrior and prince, and bard and priest alone,
Had place in their hereafter.   Peasants died,
As of the "earth, earthy," without a hope.
Children, that with their merry voices made
Sunshine within a gentle mother's heart,
Were laid like broken flowers in the dust,
And were not any more.   And woman's love —
The love that crowned as mother and as wife —
Was but a thing of earth, and perished all
With the warm heart that gave it utterance.
This earth, unto the loving hearts of old,
Was all in all.   But unto us it is
As the passing of a night whose stars shall fade
Before the dawning of eternal day.
We have a Hope, not builded on the sand,
We have a Joy enduring through all time,
We have a Faith, God-given and most sure,
A Trust that fadeth not away forever;
We have the promise of the Holy One,
The GOD who cannot lie!   And when we give
The dust of our belovëd to the dust,
We know it is but for a little time, —
The passing of a night, — that with the morn
Shall come reunion.
                    Life is a shadow, —
A cloud may blot it out; a breath of wind
Suffice to change it into nothingness,
Or still its throb forever.   Yet we cling
Unto this shadow as a drowning man
To any straw that floats upon the wave.
We dread the hour when the sun shall set
And the shadow fade into the darkness, —
Darkness that is another name for Death!
O Life of Earth! — the shadow that doth flit
So swiftly past our souls, yet as it flies
Doth break our chain, and set our spirit free;
O Life of Earth! a Proteus-shape is thine;
Changeful and various; a feather, swayed
By every breath of wind; a flake of foam,
Tossed to and fro upon the ocean wave;
A mote that danceth in some sunny ray,
Yet dieth in the shadow.   Unto all
Most frail and lovely things is this our life
Resemblant; and yet hope, and love, and faith
May give it strength to suffer and endure
Such sharpest agony as pales man's lip
E'en in remembering.   Ofttimes life dureth,

Ephemeral, the bursting of a spark
That flashes but to fade; or it may have
A longer term of being, and yet fall
Like earliest blooms of spring, touched by the chill
Of winter's lingering frost. Some pulses keep
Such even measure through the gliding years,
They scarcely jar the secret springs of life;
So the oil wastes silently, and at last
They bow their heads as some o'erweary child,
And so they sleep. But other hearts there be
That beat themselves away in fever-pulses;
Finding no rest, no peace, save in the grave;
That quiet bourn where hearts beat nevermore!

O Life! O Death! fierce is the war ye wage;
The earth is rank with blood, and green with graves,
And yet ye meet at last within the heart,
Contending there as for a citadel.
The walls have long been sapped; and, as they fall,
Death rushes in, and, victor, as he thinks,
Doth stretch his hand to grasp the laurel-wreath
That falls in dust and ashes at his feet;
While Life, true conqueror, relumes her torch,
And, crowned with amaranth, breaks every bond
Of time and sense; and with untiring wing
Doth take her flight sublime unto the realms
Where *Death* is powerless, and *Life* supreme!

It should not be so sad a thing to die.
Life is not worth so much that we should hope
To have our sole abiding city here.
What though the morning dawn without a cloud?
Ere noon the tempest may sweep over Earth,
And all the promise of the early day
But end in desolation and in death;
The darker doom because of suddenness.
O Life! while yet unconsciously we stand
Upon thy threshold, knowing not the hues
Wherewith thy woof may yet be deeply dyed;
How like a vision fair and glorious
Doth show the vista that before us lies!
Earth hath no after-bloom like that she wears
When the *young* heart drinks in her loveliness.
The sun shines never with such radiant light
As in life's morning freshness; and the skies —
Though still serene they smile above our heads —
Are never half so blue, as when they flashed
In fulness of their glory on the heart,

The passionate heart of youth.   And oh, we dream
Such wondrous dreams of that which is to be !
Shaping these fantasies at our sweet will,
As sculptors see within the marble block
The perfect image of their unborn thought.
But not as they carve from the living stone
The likeness of their thought, may we give shape
And substance to our dreams.   They mock us still;
Far-off, and gleaming as the stars of heaven
That shine far down within the river's heart,
Yet stoop not from their thrones, albeit to bless.
And as those stars grow dim before the dawn,
So hopes of youth are slowly lost to view
When life's more earnest themes do fill the soul.
And as the stars are lost in light of day,
So youth itself dies into stately prime;
Forgetting its time of dreams.   Silently,
The hand that labors, and the brain that works,
Fling dust upon our fancies, till we see
Their old familiar faces nevermore ;
So deeply they lie buried 'neath the sands
Blown o'er their graves by such destroying winds
As custom and as change.   And years glide on,
And darker changes come; and in the cares,
The petty troubles of our daily life,
All memory of our early dreams dies out;
And we forget them, as they had not been
The sunlight of our youth.   Yet were they fair, —
Those golden shadows of an inborn light
That never more may shine upon our path;
The light of youth and love.   It faded all;
But our tried hearts are stronger and more pure
For the fire that made ashes of our dreams.
The mirage fades that with delusive scenes
Had veiled life's desert-sands; the quiet wave,
Wherein we thought to quench our burning thirst,
Is but a mocking semblance; and is gone
Ere we can tread its shore.   Some weary hearts,
Faint with the agony of hope deferred,
Lie down and die.   They have no strength to tread
The widening wastes that seem to stretch before,
And so they fall asleep, with never thought
Of that fair land where living fountains flow.

   Youth passes from us with its careless smiles,
Its bounding pulses, and its laughter sweet;
And passes from us never to return !
For with our years come sadness and regret;

Our smiles less frequent are, and often forced;
Our hearts beat slowly; painfully, perchance.
And all our laughter is as crackling thorns;
And for our tears that were so swift to flow,
Their stream is bitterness, or stagnant all.

Life seems so fair, — veiled in such golden light,
When first we tread its mazes.   Hope doth stand,
With such a glory on her radiant hair,
Her white hands beckoning the young heart on
To scenes that seem the fairer for the charm
That distance lends them.   Joy scatters flowers
Upon our path; and flowers, so rich in bloom,
Of such rare fragrance, that our eyes see not
The dust from whence they sprang, nor yet the death
That lurketh under all their loveliness.
Love, riseth, too, upon our trancèd sight
In likeness of an angel; and our hearts
Go forth to meet him with such eager trust,
And crown him with a garland; give him place
Within the secret temple of our life,
And make him priest of all its mysteries.
Yea; crown him king of that wild realm, the heart,
Unknowing what we do.   For weal — for woe —
The tyrant angel comes; and we take home
Life's deepest joy; or cherish in our hearts
The serpent that shall sting us unto death.
Worth more than these, another shape shall rise,
White-robed and glorious, changeless as the star
That guides the mariner o'er ocean's waste.
More steadfast far than human love can be;
Stronger than death, — *eternal, as is* God!
Faith, meekest angel of the host of heaven,
Thou movest o'er the desert, fainting not;
Thou treadst the waters with unshrinking feet;
And walkest through the furnace, as the flames
Were harmless breath of cool and summer-winds!
No broken reed art thou, but as a rock
Whereon we lean, and fear not any more.
Patient we tread Death's Valley by thy side,
Upheld by thee; and though our feet recoil
— We are but mortal — from the river cold,
It is but *dust* that struggleth with its doom.
The *soul* doth look beyond the waters dark;
And eyes, not sealèd yet, rest on the shore
Where stand the " shining ones;" and ears that hear
No more of earth are open to the song

The waiting angels sing; while on the lip —
That never more speaks lovingly to us —
A smile is lingering, as a shadow caught
From the dawning light of heaven!

"Alone."

THE moon hath set; and in the darkened skies
  Only the pale, pale stars are shining now:
A passing ripple o'er the river flies,
  But no wind comes to cool my fevered brow.

Vainly mine eyes do pierce the shades of night,
  As if they thought some loving eyes to meet.
Vainly I listen for a footfall light;
  Unto my heart was never sound so sweet.

The darkness mantles me as some thick cloud;
  The night falls round me as a heavy pall;
Before me lies a shadow, and a shroud
  That veileth o'er that shadow, — this is all.

O eyes, close-sëaled from the light of day!
  No more to linger lovingly on me;
O lips, whose music hath been stilled for aye!
  Ye leave me nothing but a memory.

O hands, crossed meekly on that quiet breast!
  Your tender clasp shall comfort me no more;
O gentle heart, the truest and the best!
  Your life is living on another shore.

Belovëd, on thy lips I press mine own.
  They have no kiss for me — there is no breath.
My heart is beating, but it beats alone;
  I am alone with silence and with Death!

"Broken Hearts."

WHO spoke of broken hearts? It well may be
  There are such things in this sad world of ours,
Wrecks scattered lie upon the glorious sea,
  And no poor land but hath some broken flowers.

Who spoke of broken hearts, as if in doubt
  That hearts could break? Are they not formed of dust?
They throb, and beat their little tenure out
  In grief or joy, till death stills all their lust.

Some hearts break easily. O happy hearts!
  O'er their warm tide doth pass an icy breath;
They linger not till every hope departs;
  For the quick pulse is sudden stilled by death.

And some hearts break, yet live! Their crimson tide
  Doth ebb and flow, and on the surface lies
No telltale wreck.   'Tis buried deep by pride;
  The waves of daily life above it rise;

Their mocking spray doth blind all other eyes;
  Their wreaths of foam are as a veil o'er all
The deadly ruin that below them lies;
  And jest and smile are of that corse the pall.

Yet lips writhe sometimes, and hot tears will start;
  The torture of the rack must wring some moan;
But unseen these witnesses of the heart
  That breaks perforce, and yet must break alone.

Who spoke of broken hearts? Oh, count them not!
  Let them go down to silence and to sleep;
Their anguish stilled, their weary pain forgot,
  No more to throb, and no more tears to weep.

Spring.

Wʜᴀᴛ dost thou bring unto us, O Spring?
  A Summer whose roses are dead;
A lightning gleam of an old-time dream
  Whose glory forever hath fled.
A bitter wail in thy softest gale
  Sounds sadly upon our ear;
And mournful tones, and requiem moans
  Are in every song we hear.

What dost thou bring unto us, O Spring!
  But a mocking memory
Of joys gone by, as old landmarks fly,
  When we sail upon the sea.

Vainly our hands, over barren sands,
　　We stretch to the pleasant shore
That from us flies, that behind us lies;
　　We never shall see it more.

What dost thou bring unto us, O Spring!
　　But a bitterness of regret?
A knell that rings over sweetest things;
　　A dirge we cannot forget.
What dost thou bring?　A shadow to fling
　　O'er roses that soon may bloom;
Some drops caught up from life's bitter cup;
　　Some memories of the tomb.

What does thou bring unto us, O Spring!
　　But a shadow of the past;
A thought of light o'er whose day the night
　　A gathering gloom hath cast.
A thought of eyes on whose glory lies
　　A seal that we cannot break;
A yearning deep for the hearts that sleep
　　Nevermore on earth to wake!

What dost thou bring unto us, O Spring!
　　With thy sunshine and thy flowers?
A loveliness and a holiness,
　　Of another world than ours.
A star whose light shineth through death's night;
　　A hope that shall never die;
And one pure dream with its holy beam
　　Of life's immortality.

What shalt thou bring unto us, O Spring!
　　When our hearts are still at last;
When o'er our rest in the earth's cold breast
　　The Winter storms have passed?
A veil of green, as a memory seen,
　　To be woven o'er our sleep;
Roses to bloom o'er the silent tomb;
　　And the night soft tears to weep.

What shalt thou bring unto us, O Spring!
　　When the years have passëd by;
When every one who loved us is gone,
　　And we have no memory?
Sunshine and flowers o'er this dust of ours
　　The returning years shall shed.
　　11

Until the day when our GOD shall say
  To the graves, " Give up your dead ! "

What shalt thou bring unto us, O Spring !
  When we lie in our last long sleep ;
When the poor clay that mouldereth away,
  We give unto GOD to keep ?
Softly the years that do stanch all tears
  Shall vanish within time's urn ;
Till that bright morn when souls shall be born
  Into eternity !

White Violets.

O VIOLETS, pale violets,
  That scattered at my feet do lie ;
Not less the sweet for all the tears,
The gathered drops of many years,
  That fall above them silently.

O violets, pale violets !
  How sadly does your sweetness cling
To all that was most dear in life !
Past moments, that with joy were rife,
  Are rich with memories of the spring.

O violets, pale violets !
  The dust upon your beauty lies ;
And broken petals, bloom destroyed,
Have left within your world a void
  No after-growth of buds supplies.

O violets, pale violets !
  A bitter lesson ye recall ;
How all the hopes, so bright, so fair,
Have left me nothing but — they were !
  They budded, blossomed ; this was all.

O violets, pale violets !
  I fold ye gently to my breast,
As if your fading brought some spell ;
A whisper of one low farewell,
  To sound when I shall be at rest.

O violets, pale violets !
  I do beseech ye that your breath

May float around my lowly grave.
'Tis but a simple boon I crave;
   Yet granting it will sweeten death.

O violets, pale violets!
   Would I might breathe a spell o'er ye;
A spell of might that still should keep
Some leaflets green above my sleep, —
   Some ivy leaves of memory.

A Broken Dream.

O DREAM, that was so golden sweet,
   That never hadst a shape of ill;
Thou liest at my weary feet
   A pallid corse, most cold and still.

Back to my heart, O Dream, and there
   Find fittest urn of burial;
The shadow of its lone despair
   Shall fall above thy dust, a pall.

Rest thou in peace! Spring bringeth back
   A beauty to the earth and sky;
But o'er thy unreturning track
   No after sunshine soft shall lie!

O Dream that faded like a dream!
   I scarcely moaned, I scarcely wept,
O'er the swift dying of the beam
   That in mine heart of hearts had slept.

And it is dead! Its light hath gone
   Forever from my weary way;
With never wailing, never moan,
   I saw the night flow o'er my day.

O Dream! O heart! O corse! O grave!
   Keep silence in your agony;
Nor let the empty worldling crave
   Such bitter theme for mockery.

A Picture for my Gallery.

BREEZES were blowing through some ancient trees,
Whereon the faintest tracery of green
The spring had pencilled. A voice of waters
Did blend itself with sighing of the wind;
And, from the midst of myriad blades of grass,
Was breathed the breath of sweetest violets.
A road wound through the forest, rarely used.
Pleasant it was, as any hope of youth
That makes itself a path through fairest scenes,
And dreams not of the storm. There came a sound
Of beating hoofs, that on the stillness broke
Like earliest patterings of a summer shower
Upon low cottage eaves. A little spring,
That seemed to nestle 'mid the spreading roots
Of an old giant oak, flashed on the eyes
That else had lingered not; and they drew rein,
Won by the quiet beauty of the spot.
Young were the riders; merry-hearted too;
Gentle and loving, — so they lighted down.
And on the margin of the silver spring
Reclining sat, the while their lazy steeds
Did crop the tender herbage. Life did wear
Unto those hearts a glory not its own,
But borrowed from the future. Both were young;
And one was lovely as a poet's dream
When first he dreameth. Silently they sat,
And idly, but content; since each to each
Was all in all. They spoke not of the past,
And had no thought for that which was to be.
Enough for them the present with its joy.
They saw fair flowers blooming at their feet;
A cloudless sky blue arching o'er their heads, —
They did not look beyond; and, hand in hand,
Heart throbbing unto heart, they whiled away
Some hours of sunshine, — hours that did seem
Stolen from Paradise, they were so sweet. Night,
Starry-crownèd, found them lingering still,
Unconscious of time's passing. Then they woke
From out their happy dreaming, and went home
O'er dewy turf, by lone, moon-lighted ways,
Saying "the day had never been more fair,
Nor night more beautiful!"

Lines for Music.

Recitative.   I that live; I that tread the earth to-day, —
I sing of the belovëd who lie sleeping
Where our voices may not reach them any
more.

Air.   They sleep the sleep that knows no waking, —
Above their rest the summer morn is breaking,
But they see not any day:
And at their feet a mountain stream is leaping
Unto the sea, with music flow, on sweeping,
And fast it glides away.
But they who rest beside that silver river
Hear never flow; see not the lilies shiver
Where the waters touch the shore.
They dwell in silence; and, while time is fleeting,
They count it not by weary pulses beating;
They feel not any more!

"Day of Small Things."

DESPISE not thou the day of little things.
Take heed;
They are the seed
Whose germ shall ripen in some stateliest tree,
That a great shadow flings
Across some quiet lea;
As a mystery and a memory
Above a thousand springs.
They are the echo of a word
Which sharper far than any sword
Doth cleave through boundless space;
And leaving, in passing, scarce a trace,
Doth wound some gentle heart
Unto the death;
So no physician's art
Can stay the feeble, fluttering breath,
Or heal the bitter pain,
And raise the broken flower up again.
One forward step, one footprint on the sands,
May leave such impress on the land
That all the rain of all the years
Can never wash it out.
A half-breathed thought, one idle doubt,
Though in itself ephemeral

And dead beneath the pall,
May prove the source of bitterest tears,
That shall forever flow
For irremediable woe.

Despise not little things.   The hand's caress,
The word of tenderness,
Are quick to bless,
And have long life in some true memory.
The cup of water, given by thee,
From out thy heart's deep charity,
Hath a savor of sweet sacrifice,
That shall to Heaven arise
And bless thee in the giving
Even in thy earth-abode,
As a proof of holy living
And of walking with thy GOD.
The warning word that in some heart takes root
And beareth noble fruit;
The lesson sweet that left its seal upon the soul,
And winged the spirit to its goal,
Ye count but little things;
And yet they never die!
But as the rays that from one focus dark
Do light on every part
Of the vast circle, so each little thing
Hath many diverse rays to fling
Abroad upon the earth.
We may not know what gave them birth;
We only feel they do not die,
But mingle with eternity.
So humble, fervent prayer;
Its breathings are not lost in air,
But float around the strings
Of those sweet harps the angels strike in praise
Of YAHVEH, "ANCIENT OF THE DAYS."

———◦◦———

"Let the King's Justice pass!"

A STIR upon the river's brink, —
A rush of wildly hurrying feet, —
A thing from which all seem to shrink;
While pale looks every face you meet,
And a horror sits thereon.
Up, into the morning fresh and fair
Out of the river-slime

They have drawn a body. It lieth there,
Dead in that summer time!
It lieth there; and the pitiless sun
Stareth down on the pitiful sight
Of a thing whose race is run.
It lieth there, with a cheek as white
As the hawthorn blooms above;
With a gleam of gold on the tangled hair
Amid whose tresses, rich and fair,
Lingers no touch of love!
They bore
The still white corse within their cottage door.
To them it had no name.
No bitter thought of shame
Made their hearts hard, and tenderly
They laid their burden down;
And then they saw
The words of him who wore their country's crown,
Whose word was law.
"*Let the king's justice pass!*"
Alas!
Swift to the waiting river borne,
And in the face of morn,
They flung that fair corse in; and let it go
Where'er those waters flow;
And made that wave
A dark and unrevealing grave.

Captive and Monk.

A Picture for my Gallery.

Monk. Nay; fret not o'er the Past, nor cling o'ermuch
Unto the Future. Patience becometh
A captive in his cell. Have patience, then.

Captive. "Patience!" ever "patience!" Is there no word
In all your tongue but "patience," which to choose,
As a text for daily preaching? "Patience!"
Have I not had it? All these weary years,
That unto *you* brought sunshine and sweet flowers,
Have found and left me in a prison-cell.
Alone, dost hear, *alone?* And not *one* smile,
One look from loving eyes, to cheer my soul!
Not e'en *one* hope to linger in mine heart;
And yet to *me* you talk of "patience!" Time,
That ancient mocker of poor human dreams,

Hath brought to me one bitter lesson home.
Forgetfulness — yet I cannot learn it.
Soft to my heart glide thoughts of former joys;
And on my dungeon-walls, all moist and cold,
My fancy pencils pictures of delight, —
Green lawns, cool waters, and thick-foliaged trees,
Amid whose beauty I recline at will;
And o'er them all I throw the soft, warm rays
Of an unsetting sun; and in that glow
— What though imaginary? — my spirit basks
As never in the sun that shines for all.
Yea, shines for all; and yet ye shut me out.
What have I done, that on my limbs the chain
Should drag so heavily? I — who was free
As any breeze in Alpine valley blowing.
O happy breeze! would I were but as free,
So I might rest once more beneath the roof
That sheltered me in childhood, and there die!

Something about Love.

THE love that trusteth is a holy thing;
Oh, guard it well! Let no doubt o'er it fling
The shadow which is death; but to thy breast
Fold thou it closely; it will give thee rest.
Fear not, nor falter. Terror may assail;
The fearful racking of some worldly gale
May wring thy spirit with the sharpest pain;
But one *true* heart will bring thee peace again.
Stay thou on it, as on a rock, thy soul;
And fiercely though the waves of trouble roll,
They shall not tear thee from that faithful breast;
They shall not bar thee from that perfect rest.
Certain and sure thy refuge. " Carking care,"
Unquiet hope, and unrest come not there.
"Tis as a shrine wherein life's holy things
Are treasured; as a harp whose sacred strings
Sound not to any fingers save thine own,
For thou art master-spirit, — thou, alone!

The love that sleepeth. 'Tis a jewel rare
That, guarded in some casket, wasteth there
Its brightness; and its beauty hath no place
Amid the glory of the day's glad face;
And is no more than the poor clay inurned,
Which, lovely once, is dust to dust returned.

The love that sleepeth is a mocking thing;
A shadow, and no substance; with no ring
As of true metal when we strike its chords;
And all its music is as empty words
That mock us with their hollow nothingness;
And have no meaning, own no power to bless.
The love that sleepeth is a lifeless germ,
That finds no fruitage at its being's term;
A bark, left stagnant on some Dead Sea wave;
A star, which hath the human heart for grave;
A changeless monotone; an aimless strife;
A pulse beating idly; and death in life!

The love that clingeth.   Take it to thy heart,
And make it of thy very self a part.
It will not leave thee, though the darkness come;
And where thou art, it only feels at home.
The love that clingeth seems a feeble love,
And breezes light its gossamer fabric prove.
But let the storm come fierce, and loud, and long,
And this so fragile thing grows deep and strong,
And dares, in majesty of unbroken might,
Alike the burning day and darkest night.

The love that hopeth hath an angel form.
As a white dove it flitteth through the storm
Unto the light that shineth far away.
Through gloom of night it sees the dawning day;
And in prophetic vision treads the shore
Where the poor heart shall hope and fear no more.
What though the darkness shroud it as a pall,
And the wild tempest rock it?   Still, through all,
It sees the blue sky smiling; and its trust
O'ermasters all the quailings of the dust.
What though the spirit, sick and shivering, turn
From the near prospect of the funeral urn,
And cling to life with such despairing zeal
As only those who hope no heaven feel?
Yet love that hopeth, pointing to the sky,
Can bid these dark and fatal terrors fly;
And lead the parting soul, with gentle hand,
Into the haven of the Better Land.

The love that weepeth.   Who shall count its tears?
Have they not fallen since the Eden years
With all their smiling vanished?   In the prime,
The golden fulness of that Eden time,
Tears were not known; nor could they be, when GOD

The fair and Paradisal garden trod.
Sin entered there; and tears were unto Death
As the dew on graves scattered by the breath
Of some cold wind; and no more might the heart
Of man beat out its life, and have no part
In aught that summoned tears!   Their lava tide
Hath burst the strongest barriers of pride;
And loosed life's crimson torrent, till its flow
Did meet with Death, and could no further go.
Their stream, congealed, falls on the heart a stone,
Until all kindly feeling thence hath gone.
Or else the burning drops suffuse the brain,
Till Madness cometh with its mournful train
Of mocking laughter, and of wailing moan,
And plants itself on Reason's vacant throne.
Force back no tears.   Let their sad fountain flow;
They bring relief and respite to our woe,
Easing the surcharged heart.   Why should we check
Their grateful stream, nor have them at our beck?
For tears are sweet, yea, holy, when 'tis love
Doth shed them; and oft times they fall above
Some one beloved who strayeth from the light
Into the shadows of eternal night.
And love that weepeth may have power to win
The erring spirit from the way of sin;
Wrapping it round, as with an angel's wing,
So safely home the wandering soul to bring.
Are not tears sacred when they fall above
The dust of that we dowered with our love?
And shall we, like the stoic, sternly keep
Our grief in thraldom, and forbid to weep?
Behold, some Rachel for her children weeping;
Some Rispah, desolate, her lone watch keeping,
And with the stoic bid that fount be sealed!
Hath not GOD blessed it?   Hath not GOD revealed
That tears are holiest, since he hath kept
One sweet and gracious record, — "Jesus wept!"

And silent love, that seemeth aye to say,
Am I so cold?   'Tis but an outward veil;
'Tis but the ashes covering the fire
That smouldereth beneath.   Let but a breath
Scatter their ashes, and the flame leaps up
A quick and living thing!   Am I so cold?
The wave that's stillest is the deepest ever;
And love that waiteth ready on the tongue
Is not the truest when the darkness comes;
Clingeth not closest! —

The love that prayeth.   Cast it not from thee;
It armeth thee as with a mighty sword;
It hath a spell to shield thee from all harm;
And bears thee up, and dowers thee with power
As 'twere to tread on ploughshares burning red,
And from the fiery ordeal walk unharmed!
It doth not trust in mortal hand alone;
It knoweth well how weak such stay would prove.
But, resting on an Arm, strong, though unseen,
And mindful of a Promise broken not,
It lifts pure hands unto the Mercy-seat,
And pleads for its belovëd; feeling aye
The love that prayeth is the nearest GOD!

The love that keepeth.   Only GOD can keep;
And he who keepeth Israel doth not sleep.
On the wide world his eye, all-seeing, rests,
Marking the pulsings of our human breasts.
Dust as we are, 'tis granted us to meet
JEHOVAH's smile; and yet beneath his feet
A million worlds are trembling to their doom.
Dust as we are, so dust unto the tomb
We daily give; believing that our GOD
Will burst the fetters of the valley clod;
And, in the hope that he that dust will keep,
We leave our best belovëd to their sleep.
And, folding meek hands on a patient breast,
We wait the hour shall summon us to rest;
And, when it comes, GOD makes us down to lie,
In the sure hope of Immortality!

A Torn Leaf.

FADING! you dream!   The rose is on her cheek;
The gladness in her eyes; and in her step
There is no languor.   I mark no decay
Of any one of life's sweet attributes;
And in her voice the same soft music dwells
That stole of old into my heart of hearts;
And yet you say " fading " is written there!
I see it not.   Nay, more; I will not see it!
" Fading! " you said it — " fading " and my love
Not yet hath compassed hers!   Look on her now.
The sunshine falling on her shining hair,
The warm blood mantling on that smoothest cheek,
The full lips quivering, as if her heart

Were touched to sadness by the rhyme she reads.
Is she not beautiful?   And yet you say,
"Fading!"   I'll not believe it!   She sees us,
And the smile upon those sweet lips breaking,
Is light unto my heart.   Nay; cease, old friend;
I will not hear that bitter word again.
Know thou I love her, and one look of hers
Is all the world to me.   ·   ·   ·   ·
         ·   ·   ·   Rejected!
And yet so gently, — with such faltering voice,
As if she felt herself the pain she gave me.
O Imogen!   I ne'er loved thee half so well
As when you dashed all my poor hopes to earth
With but one little word!   Dear Imogen!
I marked her when she spoke it, and her cheek
Was whiter than the lilies at her feet.
"Fading!" — how the word haunts me, and my love
May never come between her and the grave!
      ·   ·   ·   ·   ·   ·   ·

Dead! and the dust is lying on her heart!
Dead! and mine eyes shall never see her more!
Mine Imogen, whom I loved!   Life seems dark,
And very lone without her; yet I live.
May live, perchance, to number o'er long years
And count them wasted, since bereft of her.
Wasted? not so; for life hath other needs
Than love; and I may hope to give some joy,
Some happy moments unto other hearts.
My heart hath closed itself, as with sealed doors,
'Gainst all sweet household joys; but in their place,
The whole wide world hath leave to enter in!

Books.

I HAVE read much; and some old strains, and sweet,
That made soft music in the Long-Ago,
Lie nestling in my heart, as if they knew
They were beloved of me.   When I am sad,
They bring me gladness, such as smiling Spring
Bestows upon the pulses of the earth
Long chilled by Winter's sharp and icy breath.
And when I would be glad, they ring, as bells
Whose chiming floating o'er the summer sea
Doth bring to some poor lonely mariner
A thought of home, and all sweet homely things.
Therefore I gather books; yea, garner them,

As Love doth keep the things that were the dead's.
I knew not those who wrote them; but their souls —
A part, at least, of that which is their soul —
Do speak to me from every living page;
And my soul answers back the voiceless words,
· And thrills as unto music from the grave!

The Years.

How the years glide from us when our first youth's past!
    They fleet away as some wild dream of night
That holds our spirits bound in fetters fast,
    But is as nothing; and forgotten quite
When earth lies fair and smiling in the morning light.

Time treadeth softly, moveth very slow,
    In life's sweet spring-time; for our childish feet
Bound lightly where the valley-waters flow;
    Lightly as any antelope, and fleet;
Yet pause, the while, to gather every flower that we meet.

These years pass, — lingeringly, yet they pass;
    And youth's keen, fiery soul contemns the vale
That childhood found so beautiful.   Alas!
    When driven to and fro by passion's gale,
For that green valley lost, the weary heart may wail.

Steep is the path youth's eager feet must tread;
    And clouds lie thick upon the mountain brow.
They see no steepness; and the clouds o'erhead
    Are veilèd by the brightness of the glow
That from the unclouded sun of early hope doth flow.

High is the hill whose weary steep we climb;
    Yet often half the rising way is passed
Ere we do feel the toil, or count the time
    That we have spent or wasted; and, at last,
The summit gained, perchance a backward look we cast.

Is that the path that our poor feet did tread
    But yesterday? Or hath some fairy wand
Left its kind glamour there, that in the stead
    Of sterile rocks that frowned on every hand,
We see a glory lying dimly on the land?

Ere yet we left the vale, Hope's magic glass,
  Held up before our eyes, gave to the way
Its own soft tints of rose; but they did pass;
  Or slowly change into a motley gray, —
The sober hue experience wears, — so poets say.

But looking downward from the summit gained,
  A softening veil o'er the rough path is thrown;
And fairer far than all we have attained
  Doth seem the parted joy, the bright hopes flown,
The olden faith, now dim, the time forever gone!

The years that have been passed full slowly by,
  Reluctant, lingering, — as if they, too,
Toiled up the hill, and saw *above*, the sky
  That smiled upon them from its depths of blue;
And knew that at their feet were flowers and sweet dew.

The steep is won. For some brief space we pause.
  A retrospective glance our sad hearts may
Give unto that which has been, and its cause;
  Then, faltering, take the path that winds away
Towards the far-off regions of eternal day.

The path leads downward; and the swift years go
  As doth a ball rolled slowly down the steep.
We give ourselves the impetus, and so
  Roll as the ball, — all obstacles o'erleap, —
Till in the silence of the Silent Vale we sleep.

The path leads downward. This of dust is said;
  The dust that mingleth with the valley clod.
Our way it lieth where do sleep the dead;
  So we must share their rest beneath the sod.
Onward and upward is the path that leads to GOD!

In that path the spirit walketh, keeping
  Itself unspotted by the world's cold lust;
Meekly it walketh, watchful, lest sleeping,
  It wake to wail an overweening trust;
To find its hopes of heaven were but builded on the dust.

Father in heaven! Our times are in thy hand;
  We are but dust and ashes in thy sight;
Yet in thy love thou hast prepared a land,
  A " better country " for us; where no night
May enter, for thou art its everlasting light!

And to that land, grant that our footsteps tend,
  And that our feet in the straight way may be.
Keep us, O Father! through life unto life's end,
  So every year but bring us nearer thee,
Till our poor life hath blended with eternity.

----♦----

A Prayer at the Institution of a Minister.

FATHER in heaven!
Thou that hearest, and in thine own good time
  Dost answer all our prayers;
Hear us, and answer now, as, with clasped hands
  Hushing our own poor cares,
We kneel before thy glorious throne,
  And plead for one,
  Who, with bowed knee,
And lowlier heart, himself hath given
Unto the temple-service and to thee!

Hear us, O Father!
And bless our prayers indeed
With all fulfilment. Bless him, also,
For whom we pray. Grant that the seed
His hand may scatter shall find goodly soil,
  To a rich, ripe harvest grow,
Repaying hundred-fold the sower's toil.
  Grant him a glorious crown,
In that bright day, when, putting in his hand,
  The Reaper gathers the full harvest in,
From the seed the sower hath sown.
Hearts ransomed from the yoke of sin,
And souls led onward to the Better Land.

Hear us, O Father!
And, if it be thy will,
Grant him long life, — the fulness of all years;
  Pour thy true sunshine on his pathway still
And with thy loving hand stanch all his tears.
  Or, — if this may not be, —
If our poor prayers may have no power to bless;
  If pain and weariness,
And broken hopes, his sad allotment be;
  Then grant that he may see
  Only thy love in all;
And, burying each grief beneath its own dark pall,
  May look beyond to thee;

Content with knowing this, —
Enough for him of bliss, —
That thy smile is not growing dim;
That thou, his GOD, hast not forsaken him!

O GOD!   Our Father!
Look down upon him now, and, in thy love,
Make smooth his onward way;
And with thy strong and tender hand remove
All shadows from his day;
That in the broad, clear light,
As righteous in thy sight,
His walk on earth may be.
So thus,
That we who follow where he leadeth us,
May, treading the same path,
Be found accepted in the day of wrath.
So, when thou countest up, as in that day,
Thy jewels, both himself, and we,
And all who neath his ministry
Shall hear the Word of Life, and learn its way,
May be of that bright band
Who stand at thy right hand:
Redeemëd from the world, to share with thee
The unfading glories of Eternity!

Dec. 8, 1858.

1858.

COLD on his bier a crownëd king is lying;
" About his couch doth go "
The soft white flakes of snow,
And, o'er his quiet heart, and pale, cold brow, —
So painless now, —
Wildly the winter wind is flying.

He sleeps, not royally; but as the dead
Who have no dreams, and know no waking;
And, as he sleeps, the crown falls from his head;
And, from the nerveless hand,
The idle sceptre, that chill grasp forsaking;
Falls broken to the ground.
And far and wide, through all the land,
Doth go a mournful sound;
A wildly wailing, momentary knell, —
A passing bell!

Lone on his bier the poor old king is lying;
The courtiers all have fled.
Little they cared for the dying,
But less they care for the dead.
So alone the old king lieth,
Alone upon his bier;
And the midnight hour flieth,
But there are no watchers near.
No watchers?   Yet soft in the starlight,
Pale, dusky phantoms glide,
And with soundless footsteps, as of night,
They gather on every side.
No watchers?   Yet thoughts most tender and true
Linger lovingly round that bier;
And memories, sweeter than morning dew,
Rest on it, like dew most clear.
No watchers beside that forsaken bier?
When the thoughts that around it cling
Are as many as sands on the widest mere,
Are various as flowers in spring!

What shape have the shadows that gather there?
They come from each home of earth, —
The belovëd who seemed to us most fair,
The light of our quiet hearth,
The father, or mother,
The sister, or brother,
Who have passed away from earth!
And that crownless king, as he lieth there, —
The snow-flakes falling on his hair, —
Worketh strange glamourye
In human heart and soul;
Till, standing by that solemn bier,
As by an altar to the Past, we see
The shapes that have been and are not arise
And pass before our eyes;
Fading in the dusk beyond the goal;
That goal, the grave, so near.
We see *them* once again, — the fair, the loved,
Who in the old time proved
As sunshine to our hearts, and made them glad.
We know they may not come
To cheer us now; yet we are rarely sad,
For GOD hath called them home!

What thoughts are lingering where that pale king
Lieth cold upon his bier?
The fruits of an autumn, or summer, or spring,
12

Are gathered and garnered here.
But many a seed that our hands have sown
   Was blighted, or dead, or lost;
And some, that unto the harvest had grown,
   Were killed by an early frost.
And the few we bring to that old king's bier.
   As a tithe that we offer him,
Are all we could save from the autumn sere,
   And their glory is passing dim.
Yet we make us wreaths of these perishing things,
   These fading fruits and flowers;
And Memory o'er them its glamour flings,
   And we fancy their beauty ours.
But a little time, and these thoughts shall flee
   Into silence, when the heart grows cold;
And it matters not what their tale may be
   When the graves of each life are told!

Cold on his bier the dead king lieth.
   'Tis the mid-hour of the night;
And the by-gone time, with its shadows, dieth
   Out in the morning light.
So we bury our dead from out our sight,
   All under the white, white snow;
And we turn to greet, in the morning light,
   A shape that we do not know.
As we leave the grave by the frozen rills,
   Forgetful of moan or tear;
With a stately step, o'er the wintry hills,
   Paceth the coming year.

———•◦•———

It is not Long till Morning.

UNDER the shadow of a time-worn bridge
   A woman sat, cowering. At her feet,
Through the dark arches of that fretted ridge,
   A mighty stream was flowing far and fleet.
Little that silent watcher heeded aught
   That passed around her. On her patient breast
A child was lying in its dreamless rest;
And through her lips broke words her life had taught, —
      ·   "It is not long till morning."

In that meek trust she waited. Yet earth's morn
   Brought nothing unto her save warmth and light.
Yet was this much for one to whom the scorn
   Of the hard world was clinging like a blight.

For she had fallen; yet not hers the shame.
　Lower in the slime she would not sink;
　And, evermore, while sitting on the brink
Of that cold wave, she murmured o'er the same, —
　　　" It is not long till morning."

It may be she had thought how still and deep
　The unseen depths of that dark stream must be;
And dreamed they might her bitter secret keep,
　In their cold silence, everlastingly.
But if these things had been they were not now.
　Some chance words uttered by a loving heart
　Had given her strength to play her weary part
On life's dull stage.　A hope lights up her brow, —
　　　" It is not long till morning."

" It is not long till morning."　Few the words.
　Her heart was burning with the bitter wrong;
Her soul on fire, when, striking on their chords,
　Came that sweet refrain of a maiden's song.
It quenched the fever; prayers learned long ago
　Broke from her lips; the story read of yore, —
　Of *Christ's* sweet charity, " Go, sin no more " —
Was heard again in that soft music's flow.
　　　" It is not long till morning."

Patient and meek, this woman; yet her lot
　Could scarcely be more dark and desolate.
By all the world forsaken and forgot;
　And yet submissive to her cruel fate.
Repining not, because of deadly sin
　For which she suffered; and content to bear
　Her heavy burden and yet not despair;
Her sad voice breathing through the city's din,
　　　" It is not long till morning."

Patient and meek this woman.　What are we
　That from the burthen of our light despair
Our hearts should turn; and moan so bitterly
　O'er clouds that gloom the skies but now so fair?
Beside that woman let our footsteps pause,
　And hear her wan and sickly lips repeat
　The words that for our own had been more meet,
For *her* despair had had most bitter cause, —
　　　" It is not long till morning."

How wide the gulf between her lot and ours!
　Yet we, poor erring children of the dust,

Because our footsteps are not all on flowers,
  Murmur, and dare to say "God is not just;"
And with rebellious spirit tread the way
  That broad and long but leadeth down to hell;
  Nor turn aside; but let our future tell
Its own dark tale, nor with that woman say,
              "It is not long till morning."

Or else we boast, as did the Pharisee,
  That we are not like this frail child of clay,
That no stain lieth on our purity;
  And with a haughty head, pass on our way.
But in the trial of the Judgment-Day,
  This woman meek, though erring, whom our pride
  Would crush to earth, shall be found justified
Rather than we. She, sinful, weak, did say,
              "It is not long till morning."

The Flower and Dream.

I watched, once, a flower from its birth.
  My hand had giv'n the little shining seed
Unto the silent keeping of the earth;
  And, day by day, I waited for the meed
They told me would be mine. One quiet eve
  I saw, just peeping through the dark brown earth,
Two tiny leaves. I scarcely could believe
  Such little things would to my flower give birth.

Daily I watched it; and through gentle rain,
  Sweet sunshine, and soft dews, the small plant grew.
Some brief days I was absent; when again
  I looked upon the plant I scarcely knew
If it could be the same; so sweet, so fair;
  Flush with the glory of its crimson flowers.
Thoughtless, I gathered all; their bloom to bear,
  A gift, unto a loving friend of ours.

They died! — what more? Nay, nothing but a thought
  Of one bright dream they shadowed. In my heart
I raised a golden palace; and I wrought
  Rare work of carving, sweet device of art,
To deck its fairy chambers. One clear breath
  Of truth revealed its emptiness, and it fell;
But with me lingers still its moan of death;
  And through my life sounds evermore its knell.

"Make no long Tarrying, O my God!" — Ps. xl. 21.

BEHOLD! the shadows lengthen, and the evening comes!
  Yet to my soul it will not bring the night.
Twilight is stealing over many happy homes;
  And some sweet eyes are smiling — smiling bright
Greeting to loving meeting, but to part at morn.
  Unto such meeting oft my feet have trod;
But now they linger sadly, yet not far the bourn.
    "Make no long tarrying, O my GOD!"

Behold! the shadows lengthen! I have lived my life;
  A life not all unhappy; and I go,
Beyond the restless murmur of yon city's strife,
  Where I shall hear no more its river flow.
Long since, Peace folded gently o'er my weary heart,
  A scroll caught up where many feet had trod.
I hear its echo round me now when I depart, —
    "Make no long tarrying, O my GOD!"

Forebodings.

A DAY of spring-time! Soft and warm, the air
  Doth kiss my lifted brow; and in its breath
There is a spell that could withstand despair,
  And quench the fever that betrayeth death.
Life, fresh and full of vigor, seems to start
  Anew into existence, when I feel
Such balmy breezes; and my beating heart
  Throbs gladly as the sun-rays o'er it steal.

A day of spring, — of sunshine rare and sweet, —
  Bathing my temples in its hazy glow;
And life springs up exultant, as to greet
  The glorious day; and yet — all sure and slow —
Its pulses beat a death-march, soon to cease.
  Yet none the less doth the poor heart rejoice
In present bliss, for that it heareth "peace!"
  In the low cadence of an inward voice.

Be still, sad voice! I will not hear thee now,
  But bask in this sweet sunshine, as if doom
Were not a word of earth, nor on my brow
  Long written. All the year is in its bloom;

And I, too, will be glad and blithe, and give
  My soul up to bright dreaming; and be free
To think how glorious a thing to live;
  Not counted with the " have been," but " to be."

Be still, sad voice! What! must thy murmur rise
  To darken o'er my gladness evermore?
Behold the glory of the soft blue skies;
  The warm light resting on the wave and shore;
See quickening life in every swelling bud,
  And hear the ripple as the stream glides by.
Clear through my veins doth bound the living blood,
  And yet, thou echoest through all, " to die."

And must it be? O'er this quick pulse of mine
  Must silence, as a mighty river flow?
And laughter, and sweet song, and gay sunshine,
  Bring never to my heart the old-time glow?
Yet I have lived a fuller life than most;
  If I have suffered, I have joyed as well;
And from my past there riseth no pale ghost
  Of bitter wrong, or secret sin, to tell.

I am so happy! Full the cup and sweet
  That stands before me; yea, full to the brim!
But ever, as the passing hours fleet,
  I see more clearly, resting on the rim,
One bitter drop, that, falling in, would break
  The cup as it were Venice glass. A breath
Might make it fall. No after care we take
  Would aught avail. The bitter drop is death!

Yet only bitter for that life is sweet.
  It ever seemeth hard, when life doth wear
The golden crown, and royal sceptre, meet
  For its full glory, that pale Death should bear
Us down to silence from the light of day.
  Yet let us think *Whose* Hand doth lay us low,
Whose Love will yet redeem us from the clay,
  And calmly meet the seeming cruel blow.

Brightly the sun shines on our pleasant way,
  Softly life's river floweth to the sea;
Our future dawneth as a summer day,
  And robed in glory seems the long To Be.
But what are we, that we should question aught
  The Holiest may do? Our race is run.
Enough to know our work hath all been wrought;
  And for the rest, GOD'S holy will be done!

A Picture for my Gallery.

I saw a picture, once;
A woman's face,—no more. A white, white face,
That from the shadow of the thick dark hair,
Gleamed out—a tomb-stone in the dusk of night.
A brow nor high, nor low. A mouth most sweet,
But, as you longer gazed, a gathering sense
Of hidden pain came stealing to your heart;
Until you thought you saw those full red lips
Quivering to agony, whose bitter sting
Not yet had been crushed out. And in the eyes,
That seemëd evermore to meet your own,
A still, grand patience dwelt; a godlike strength,
If not to conquer, calmly to endure.
'Twas but a pictured face. It had no name.
No story, half-remembered, linked itself
Unto that shadow. None knew whence it came,
Or cared to know. The years had come and gone;
Found it, and left it there! The house was old;
And they who dwelt therein were simple folk,
Honest and true, but with more heart than soul.
They did not like the picture. In their eyes
There was no meaning in it. O'er their lives,
So calm, serene, no feeling like a flood,
Had swept destroyingly. No conquered pain
Had set upon their smoothest brows and lips
The signet of endurance; and no chord,
In their rough hearts vibrating, thrilled response
Unto the meaning of those patient eyes,
So womanly,—so sad!

Trust!

Trust, O heart! for doubt is deadly;
   All its growth is bitterness;
And its poison, slow distilling,
   Takes from joy the power to bless.
Dark and deadly, sure and slowly,
   With life's purest streams it blends,
Till the crystal waters darken,
   Till each stream in ocean ends.

Trust, O heart! for doubt is torture,
   Overpassing other pain;

As a poisoned arrow hanging
  To the heart it clove in twain.
Every thrill is added anguish,
  Every motion racketh thee;
Till thy very breath is laden
  With intensest agony.

Trust, O heart! for doubt doth madden
  More than any other pain;
Till the fevered pulses triumph
  O'er a wild and fevered brain;
Burning out, like to a fire,
  All the chambers of the soul;
Leaving but the blackened ruin
  Over which the smoke-clouds roll.

Trust, O heart! and thou shalt gather
  Flowers, where doubt findeth weeds;
Thou shalt bring home a rich harvest
  While doubt soweth worthless seeds.
Trust, and though the desert widen
  With its trackless wastes of sand,
Pastures green, and quiet waters,
  Wait thee in a Better Land.

Trust, O heart! The life before thee
  May have sorrow dark and deep;
But we know strength will be given, —
  He that keepeth doth not sleep.
In his arms he takes his children,
  Bears them on his mighty breast
Into Heaven. So our Father
  Giveth his belovèd rest.

"Show me thy Way, O Lord!"

Show me thy way, O Lord! Make clear the night
  Wherein mine erring footsteps blindly stray;
Mine eyes are dim; I cannot see aright,
  And far I wander from thy holy way.

I am so weak. I have no strength to keep
  The straight and narrow path; but turn aside,
And daily, hourly; for that I may sleep,
  For pleasant toys, for weariness, for pride.

Vainly the boon of liberty I seek;
  I cannot break the bonds that fetter me.
Strive as I may, my spirit is too weak,
  And all mine efforts are as vanity.

I know that I am nothing without thee;
  That blindly evermore my feet would stray
But that with gentlest Hand thou guidest me
  Within the circle of thy Love alway.

Keep me, O Father! from the snares of sin;
  Bow thou my spirit to thy gentle sway,
That so my footsteps may not enter in
  The path of death, but choose thy perfect way.

Show me that way, O Lord! Make clear the right
  Wherein I wander blindly. Grant me grace;
That I may walk, not darkly, but in light,
  Through all the changes of mine earthly race.

----•••----

"An April Day."

An *April* day! Nay, you do laugh at me,
In saying so. Methinks this breeze, so rude,
Hath caught the music of that roaring glee
From some rough air of March's brotherhood.
No low, sweet strain, befitting April's mood,
Is that, which sweeping past us mockingly
Doth seem to shout, "Where are your quiet days
Of sunshine soft and warm? Where the bright rays
In which your spirit basked rejoicingly?
One breath of mine hath scattered all your dreaming,
And rolled thick clouds between you and the sun."
With such sharp words the wind's rude blast is teeming,
Nor uttered half ere its swift race is run.
An inner voice replieth unto him:
" Truly the sunshine waneth, and is dim,
And clouds do shadow all the pleasant sky,
But only for a season. Light is shining
Beyond the cloud-land as a silver lining,
And the veiled sun will smile out by and by."

An *April* day! yet by the fire I sit
Indulging in a moralizing fit;
The subject clouds and sunshine; yet no day

Is this of April.   No sweet changes play
Across the aspect of the sombre skies;
And from the troubled waters moanings rise;
No gentle ripple o'er their surface flies;
For the rude wind strikes hard the river's breast,
And wakes its current from its seeming rest,
Till white caps dance upon each curling wave
A measure, suited to the frolic stave
Of the wind's piping; neither sad nor slow;
And true time keeping, swift the waters flow.

An *April* day!   I think March had some days
It borrowed from sweet April.   Now it pays
Them back with usury.   Would that the debt
Had been forgotten utterly! and yet
'Tis better as it is.   We know not all
The worth of what we have, until the pall
Hath shut it from our vainly longing sight
As with the blackness of a starless night.
Our eyes are darkened, and we do not see
How full of blessings our life-cup may be;
Till our poor hands, too hasty, not too slow,
Do make the sparkling treasure overflow.
The dry dust drinks it up, and we have lost
That we soon learn to prize and value most.

"What! moralizing yet?"—
                                        Ay; even so.
My fancy trips on no "fantastic toe."
No April garb is hers, but sober gray;
And slow she paces on her quiet way.
Nor April mood hath she, save for swift tears
That leave their impress upon all the years,
Making the gray more gray.   But I, apart
From this same Fancy, am of other heart;
Not over sad, nor changeful much of mood;
But like the rest of my still sisterhood;
Or like a child that pleased is with slight things,
While slighter yet may have some sharpest stings.
A word, a look, hath aye the power to bless
And fill my quiet heart with cheerfulness.
The shadow of a tone may darken day,
And shut the sunshine from my lonely way.
The first I treasure as a holy thing,
And keep it in my heart, and crown it king
Of its peculiar time; and so to be
Held ever sacred in my memory.
The last may torture for a little while,—

May rob my heart of light, my lip of smile,
But I am patient.   In my little hand
I shut the shadow, that would else expand
And darken all my life; and so it dies;
A painless shadow in my hand it lies.
Above its grave, a quiet rain of tears
May fall as Lethe.   In the coming years,
No pallid ghost from that still grave shall rise, —
No after-shadow on my pathway lie!
Once in its grave, it hath no more To Be.
'Tis but a wind-breath that o'er water flies, —
A cloud-wreath sweeping through a summer sky.
I give it not a place in memory.

To S—.

CLING to thy home!   It hath sheltered thee
    In the old days, long and sweet;
When 'neath the old rafters echoed free
    The patter of little feet.
Rough and rude are the chambers old,
    But they seemèd not so to thee;
And the wainscot low, with its stains of mould,
    Hath its place in memory.

Cling to thy home!   For the world, though wide,
    Hath not in its weary round
A joy more sweet, or holier pride
    Than may in thy home be found.
For the gentle clasp of a loving hand
    In the light of loving eyes,
Is more to the heart than the fairest land
    That lieth 'neath sunny skies.

Cling to thy home; while it yet is thine,
    And love the dear ones there.
Who knoweth how long the sun may shine,
    Or the sky be bright and fair?
Honor thy father!   His hairs are white,
    And his step is faint and slow.
Make thou the burthen he beareth, light,
    And smooth the way he must go.

Love thou thy mother!   Let no one take
    Her place in thy heart's best love;
And cling to thy home for her dear sake,
    Nor far from its shelter rove.

Wander away — and a day shall come,
    — Oh! far may it be from thee ! —
When her loving lips shall be cold and dumb
    To thy wail of agony!

Cling to thy home! and for evermore
    Pray GOD to make it thine;
And keep thee pure, lest its gate before
    A flaming sword should shine;
And thou be shut out, as Adam and Eve,
    From thy childhood's Paradise;
Through all thine after-life doomed to grieve
    The lost love in thy mother's eyes.

Cling to thy home!   It hath all in all
    That this poor earth giveth thee;
Though the years may come when its flowers shall fall,
    Yet they leave thee memory;
Sweet thoughts of departed love to keep
    The valley of silence green;
And a tender faith, that, most strong and deep,
    Is a rock whereon to lean.

Day-Dreams.

I DREAM, and bright the land, and very fair
Wherein my spirit enters.   No despair.
    A cloud athwart the sunny sky is glooming;
    No desolate hope, its weary self entombing,
Breaks up the sod that green is evermore.
    No heart that moaneth o'er its bitter pain,
    No soul that wanders lost upon life's main,
May see the glory of that pleasant shore,
Or linger in the light that falls its valleys o'er.

I dream.   O'er far and shadowy hills
    The morning steps with light and rosy feet,
Soundless; and yet they wake the forest rills
    To utter their soft music, so to greet
The golden-tressèd herald of the sun!
    Unto my brow, the breezes, cool and sweet,
    Come softly.   From the distance, far yet fleet,
All murmurous sounds of day not yet begun
    Are stealing to mine ears; and, in my heart,
    Some throbbing pulses take their fitting part
In Nature's song of praise; and, with it, rise
Into communion with yon glorious skies.

I dream.   And noon is lying, like a dream,
Upon the bosom of the quiet stream, —
  A stream whereon no warring nations glide.
And in the blaze of sunshine clear and bright
The world is bathed as in wide waves of light, —
  Wide waves that seem to have no ebb of tide.
Deep calm is breathing from the soft, warm breath
  Of the sweet South; faint with the rich perfume
  Caught up from every valley's wealth of bloom;
But laden never with the curse of Death.
  No dew-drops sparkle on the open flower;
But flowers and leaves distill a fragrant balm.
  The day is at the zenith of its power,
And over all things broods a slumberous calm.

I dream.   The eve is fading in the west;
  Its purple light falls soft on every vale;
Its golden glow yet lingers on the crest
  Of eastern hills; the dusk is in each dale;
And through the woodland, sighing, steals the wind
  That beareth coolness on its passing wings.
The light slow fadeth; following behind
  The shadows creep.   Murmurs of bubbling springs
Do fill the air as with a voice of June;
And in the eastern sky doth float the full-orbed moon.

I dream.   The stars are shining, and their light,
So pure and holy in our human sight,
  Falls shadowy on the earth, as if a veil
Were drawn between their glory and our eyes,
Like that of flesh, which bars us from the skies.
  The stars are shining; but their glories pale
Before the dawning of the coming day;
  And as I look upon them, in my soul
There dawns a vision, clear, yet far away.
  A vision of the time, when, as a scroll,
The earth shall shrivel; when our God shall take
  Unto himself his own, and gather in
The souls his love redeemèd from their sin,
Counting them his jewels; when he shall make
  New Heavens and Earth. —

           I dream; but I awake
My hands lie folded on my weary breast;
  My heart is throbbing as it fain would break
Its bonds, and be for evermore at rest;
  And the poor soul is struggling to be free.
Be still!   Live out the life that waiteth thee;

And do thy work, O Soul! as if each day
Brought never morrow to thine earthly way.
The passing hour reveals the hidden sword;
Work, and be patient, waiting on the Lord!

------••------

"In Cœlo Quies."

ART weary, heart?　'Tis all too soon
　To lay thy heavy burden down;
Thy day hath not yet reached its noon;
　Thy summer weareth still her crown.
What if the path be steep and lone,
　And stainéd by thy bleeding feet?
As herald of thy journey done,
　There soundeth forth a promise sweet, —
　　　　"*In cœlo quies.*"

Lift up thy burden; lift it high,
　As if it were life's helmet-crest;
Nor murmur that no help seems nigh,
　That time stays not to give thee rest.
Behold! within thy heart there lies
　A little seed that GOD hath sown;
A germ to ripen for the skies.
　Heart, o'er thy burden do not moan;
　　　　"*In cœlo quies.*"

What! still repining?　Think, O heart!
　Of all this life of ours may bring,
Until thy burden seem, apart
　From darker griefs, a little thing;
Until, compared with other woe,
　Thy grief shall wear a friendly guise;
And from the load thou bearest, lo!
　A murmur soft and sweet replies,
　　　　"*In cœlo quies.*"

Lift up thy brow; and to the skies,
　That seem to frown above thee yet,
Turn thou the gaze of fearless eyes,
　That with no coward tears are wet,
And bear thy burden patiently.
　Fall not thy feet upon the moss?
Grows not thy burden light to thee?
　Shines not the crown above the cross?
　　　　"*In cœlo quies.*"

The Olden Time.

THE olden time!   As in a dream,
I see the broad, deep river gleam
    Beside my childhood's home;
And, broad as is that ancient stream,
    The waves of memory come.

A child, with the cool waves I played;
A maiden, by its shores I strayed,
    And wove me golden dreams.
So, through life's sunshine, through life's shade,
    The broad, deep river gleams.

The olden time!   O time most sweet,
That heard the bound of little feet,
    The laughter of the heart!
How could your sunshine fade and fleet?
    How could your mirth depart?

The olden time!   It seemeth rare,
For that it had nor grief nor care;
    And often our poor eyes
Look yearning to the land so fair,
    That far behind us lies.

Could we regain that far-off shore,
And tread its golden sands once more,
    The olden time would die;
An airy fabric, fashioned by
    Transmuting memory.

N. F. M.

"Young, Loving, and Beloved."

"YOUNG, loving, and beloved!"   What more?
The wave that falls on yonder shore
    Hath swept above his grave.
Down where the billows lie like lead,
Pale Death has pillowed his fair head,
    Down in some ocean-cave;

And, far away upon the earth,
There sitteth by a quiet hearth

Some one who waiteth him;
Upon whose heart, through all the years,
The burden of unanswered fears
  Hath left its shadow dim.

A mother, watching, sad and bent,
As the slow years they came and went,
  And brought him never yet.
The thought of him long since hath gone
From every memory save her own;
  But she cannot forget.

She hears a hand upon the door,
A footstep on the oaken floor,
  And turns her child to see.
Alas, poor mother! on this earth
The child to whom thou gavest birth
  Can never come to thee.

The foot is slow that was so light;
The soft brown hair is thin and white;
  The eyes are sad and dim.
Earth's ties have broken one by one;
She sitteth by a hearthstone lone:
  Yet still she waiteth him!

Poor, loving heart! that will not let
Its worn and weary self forget
  The one it loveth so!
Watch — wait — since best it seemeth thee.
GOD, in his own good time, will be
  The healing of thy woe.

* * *

Wait!

It is so hard to wait;
To move, a very tortoise, or a crab,
When the keen soul would speed unto its goal,
As thoughts to the beloved! yet wait we must;
Most oft in silence, since we dare not breathe
Our secret dreams, but must suppress them still.
Buried — as low and deep as if our hearts
Were but so many graves wherein we hide
The dead from sight.   But not from memory,
Nor yet from hope; since, in the coming time,
We look to greet their resurrection-morn.

Rarely it cometh!   Life's unresting stream
Doth bear our dreams, like as ourselves, away.
Ourselves, as trees, do float upon the tide.
Our hopes and dreams, as leaves and blossoms torn
From those poor trees, are scattered far and wide,
Or sink beneath the wave.   Better such grave;
Since no unfriendly, no malignant eyes
May pierce the veil of waters to our dead, —
The dead who have for urn the human heart.

It is so hard to wait!   We know it well.
Life hath no lesson half so deeply graved
Upon the heart; for we repeat it oft;
Yea; make unto ourselves strange luxury
Of repetition.   It *is* hard to wait.
Yet could we better bide the hope deferred,
But that our soul, with bitter prescience feels
How all unlike the thing we long for now
The granted boon will be!   As if, in youth,
We gathered store of fair and golden fruit
Against a day of festival; and found
Our golden fruits were Sodom-Apples all!

It is so hard to wait.   Yet must we bear
This trial of our patience patiently.
What though the spirit fretteth at its chains,
And beat its wings against its walls of flesh?
Vain must the struggle and the battle be,
Since finite warreth with no finite fate.
Yet from this strife, unequal though it prove,
Oftimes a patience, kingly, grand, doth rise,
To whom our spirit yieldeth willingly
True homage and allegiance evermore;
Till in our *patience* we possess our souls.

Say and Seal.

SAY whatever is most loving;
 Be thou patient, tender, true;
All the future shall be proving
 What one loving heart can do.
Say, unto poor hearts that sorrow,
 Christ himself hath wept as ye;
Seal it, telling of that morrow
 When nor grief nor sin shall be.

Say kind words, — they oft are needed;
  Scatter far their precious seed;
Though they seem to fall unheeded,
  Never fail they of their meed.
Seal them, by thy earnest praying
  O'er the seed thy hand doth sow;
Soon or late, thy toil repaying,
  For God's harvest they shall grow.

Say the words most sweet and holy,
  Such as pure lips, only, speak;
Seal them, by a life most lowly,
  By a spirit true and meek.
Say — it may be, words of preaching,
  Though thou be no priest of God;
Seal them, by the silent teaching
  Of the ways thy feet have trod.

Changes.

TIME works sad changes. Life, that seemed so fair,
Doth lie before us, as a desert, bare
Of all the sunshine of its early day;
Its freshness and its beauty passed away.
And we, in very bitterness, look back
To the lost glory of its trodden track;
Look back, to find its flowers faded, dead,
And all but Memory's clinging fragrance fled.

What solemn stillness o'er the past is shed
As o'er some lonely city of the dead!
All broken friendships, buried loves are there;
Bright hopes, sweet dreams, poor tombstones of despair,
That in the church-yard of the past gleam white;
Pale, shadowy phantoms of some old delight.

Back into the sunshine! Let the dead Past
  Bury its dead! For the heart loves the light, —
  All lovely things are precious in its sight, —
And singeth evermore, — "Night cannot last,
  And the sweet morning dawneth!"
                              Ye who weep,
  Ye who mourn o'er the Past as o'er some grave
'Neath whose cold sod the heart's belovëd sleep,
  Look up unto the skies that o'er ye smile,

And read therein your future. No cloud there
  But yields to sunshine. Fiercest storms awhile
May shut the brightness out; and winds may rave
  As in discordance of a dark despair;
But lo! between us and the blackest night
  The bow of promise shines; God's signet fair
Bridging the gloom with rays of living light.

Nothing.

When the years shall have brought you loneliness,
  And your home hath never sound
Of the old-time voices clear and sweet,
  And the laughter ringing round;
When there shall come to your aching heart,
  'Mid the silence and the chill,
A thirst for the touch of one little hand,
  "And the sound of a voice that is still!"

Through the long, long hours of the evening,
  In the same old room and place,
You will pine for the smile and the greeting,
  And the quiet, loving face;
And "nothing" shall meet your vision,
  Not a shadow, not a trace,
Of the little form that was wont to be
  In the old familiar place.

Through the long, long hours of the evening,
  You will sit alone for aye,
For you know that *she* cannot come again
  With the coming of the day.
You feel that no sense of your yearning,
  No tender and loving thrill,
Can bring her back to your side again
  From her chamber low and still.

The night with its wealth of dreaming
  Shall ever the past renew;
In its silent watches bringing
  Sweet memories unto you.
You will see her beside the old casement,
  Mark the blushes come and go
'Neath your gaze, while her busy fingers
  Ply the needle to and fro.

All night you shall be dreaming
　　Of fond fancies like to this;
But the dawn of day shall crumble away
　　The poor fabric of your bliss.
For the sun on her grave is shining,
　　And the grass long since has grown
Where the dust in its silent keeping
　　Holds the heart that was all your own.

And never, for all your moaning,
　　And never, for all your pain,
Will the tender light of those sealèd eyes
　　Look love to your own again.
Her heart has forgotten its throbbing, —
　　Her pulse thrills not to your hand;
And the dust keepeth all in its silence, —
　　Silence of the Silent Land.

A Picture for my Gallery.

An evening of sweet June, serene and still.
The moon yet lingered o'er the western hill;
And sweet and low the perfume-laden breeze
Went whispering by the scarcely trembling trees.
Most fair the night; but in proud, lighted halls
The revel had begun; and light foot-falls
Kept time to merry music in the dance.
　Apart, alone, a man, all weary stood,
　With brow all bent, and look as if his blood
Had frozen long ago, so never glance
From sunniest eyes could make it warm again.
A shape moved past him with most queenly grace;
He saw the profile of a sweet, pale face,
　Whose bloom had stirred his heart in other days,
And was not yet forgotten. His calm blood
Gave one wild bound — no more; and then he stood
　Transformed before her, meeting the still gaze
Of eyes that had no smiling in their light,
Nor aught of gladness in them. Coldly bright,
They stabbed him through and through with their deep
　　scorn,
And left him only night for that brief morn.
Not wild regrets, not passionate wealth of tears,
Not all the love of all those perished years,
　Could win her lost love back!

Coldly she met him, — coldly touched his hand,
With one brief word, he well could understand,
    To cross no more her track;
Then turned aside, and went upon her way,
As if no thought of him had e'er held sway
O'er her calm pulses, stirring them to know
Life's sweetest gladness, and life's deepest woe.

Thanksgiving, 1861.

A THANKSGIVING! Be it rendered
    For the fair fruits of the earth;
For the blessings GOD hath given
    Unto every human hearth;
But far away the fields lie wasted,
    And the only harvest there
Is of blood, and spoil, and carnage,
    Death, and anguish, and despair.

A thanksgiving! May GOD grant it!
    So the wild and fevered prayer
Borne from many a quiet homestead
    Sound no more upon the air.
Prayer, from hearts' suspense is breaking
    For the loved to battle gone;
Prayer, whose only hope is Heaven, —
    He hath left his dwelling lone.

A thanksgiving! . Who shall reckon
    All the agony and tears
That have been already lavished,
    And must be, through coming years.
Closest household ties are broken, —
    Scattered far and wide that band;
Brothers now are meeting brothers,
    But a sword is in each hand!

A thanksgiving! Who shall utter it?
    Shall it sound from battle-plain,
'Mid the moans of wounded, dying,
    O'er the last sleep of the slain?
Shall it sound where streaming banners
    Wave o'er Victory's crimson path;
A grand Te Deum o'er the thousands
    Falling on that day of wrath?

A thanksgiving!   As if given
  For the dark and deadly strife;
An Io Pæan 'mid the battle
  For the waste of human life.
For the waste?   What other naming
  Since our brother is the foe?
Most unholy waste and slaughter, —
  God and angels call it so.

And it matters not what meaning
  Men may put upon their deeds;
In the high and holy Heaven
  Is a record no one heeds;
One that fadeth not, nor changeth,
  Aye unalterably the same;
Only cancelled, if in season
  The angel of repentance came.

A thanksgiving!   May God grant it!
  For sweet Peace, — soon may it come,
Hushing all discordant voices,
  Bringing joy to every home.
No wild moaning, no heart-breaking,
  Crushing out the gladness then;
But a spirit all things ruling,
  Breathing good will unto men.

Killed in Battle.

"Dead!" and my heart gathered up in one minute
  All the sounds of the battle;
  I heard the death-rattle,
And I saw the red blood, and he lying in it,
  My brave one, my only!
I thought not of this when I smiled on his going,
  So proud of his beauty.
I knew that he went at the summons of duty;
  And in my gladness
  No vision of madness
Came, telling how soon his heart's blood would be flowing
  Away with the battle-hours,
  Staining the flowers,
  And I, left all lonely!

"Dead!" and I know not where he may be lying!
The hands of the foe gave our dead to the earth;

And *I* could not be with him when he was dying;
    Yet *I* gave him birth!
    And to see him no more, —
    Oh! but this falleth sore
On the heart that had only one treasure;
  And I let him go from me, my pride, my pleasure,
    And I waited the flying
Of the days of his absence, till that day should come
Which should bring him to me.   I waited at home,
    And he — lay a-dying!

I would I were mad, and I think I must be
When the thought of that battle-field cometh to me;
    And I see his life-blood flowing
With no hand to stanch it, and over him going
    The dark tide of the battle!
While I, by the light of the home-fire, warm gleaming,
    Had been dreaming
    Of my brave one, my only!
Of his soon coming home, to leave me so lonely
    Nevermore.
And he? the swift sands of his life had been flying,
    . And ran out 'mid the rattle
    Of the death-shots above him;
    And none that did love him
    Cheered his way to that shore
Where the sounds of the battle shall be heard nevermore!

"Dead!"   O GOD! and the mother that bore him
    May not look on his face again;
May not know where the grass groweth o'er him
    On that far-off battle-plain!

——◆——

Luisa.

WHAT more can I give than that I have given?
    All my life was your own;
Save some love for my mother, and one hope of heaven
    That I would not disown.
Oh! well I remember an evening of summer, —
    The roses were blooming, I know, —
When a heart and a hand were given away,
    Full twenty years ago.

That hand, though you never have claimed it,
    Hath been kept from other men;

And the heart then placed in your keeping,
    Is as true to you *now* as then.
Is as true; but you care not for it,
    As you would were it not your own;
For the charm of the winning is over,
    And what is won you disown.

Was it well to have burdened a lifetime
    With a love so exacting as yours,
That asked all, yet gave nought in requital
    Save the strength that in silence endures?
Was it well? It was not; and I know it;
    Have known it for weary years;
The years that have proved you self-lover, —
    The years I have counted with tears.

It may be that you have forgotten, —
    It was *twenty* years ago, —
How full of life and life's sunshine
    Was the heart you have tortured so.
It may be that you have forgotten;
    Did you dream that *I* could forget
That far-off summer, whose glory
    Is lingering round me yet?

You came to our quiet homestead,
    Not once, but ever and oft,
Till you wiled my heart from its haven,
    With your voice so low and soft.
And I gave it. Had I known to what keeping,
    I had laid it, still and low,
Where the sentinel stones of yon church-yard
    Are standing amid the snow.

Perchance you may weep when I'm dying,
    May miss me when I am gone;
But tears will not blot out self's record,
    Will not for the past atone.
Yet I love you — have loved you — must love you —
    Though I know you are not worth
One little throb of the patient heart
    You will give, so soon, to earth.

You will give? — even so; for your footsteps
    Will be traced on the broken sod
They will fling aside from my last long home,
    When my soul shall have gone to GOD.
You will follow my dust to its resting, —

The dust you once called so fair;
And go back to life, never more to think
Of her who is lying there!

The Leaves are beginning to Fall.

OH! soft and sweet through the green old forest
Floats the chime of the mountain rill;
As merry, as glad, as never upon it
Fell the shadows solemn and still.
The flowers are blooming, the birds they are singing,
Sunshine and summer are over all;
But the worm, Decay, feels his latent triumph, —
The leaves are beginning to fall!

More softly sweet than the stream of the forest
A voice is singing to me
A low, glad song of the days so golden;
But a shadow is on its glee.
Though the words ring out like a child's sweet laughter,
Yet the voice it trembles through all;
And the lips of the singer are white and quivering, —
The leaves are beginning to fall!

Oh! brightly the rose on that cheek is blushing,
And the brow is saintly fair;
But the spell of change on the heart now lying
Will soon be written there.
Life's cup so sweet hath grown strangely bitter,
She hath tasted of its gall;
And over life's sunshine the shadows gather, —
The leaves are beginning to fall!

GOD help thee, poor heart! thy summer is over;
Its blossoms are withered and dead;
And the sharp, keen blast of the coming winter
Is sweeping above thy head.
Yet bend thee low to the blast so deadly;
It hath come — must come — to all;
For no heart of earth but hath known that anguish, —
The leaves are beginning to fall!

Oh! soft and sweet through the green old forest
Floats the chime of the mountain-rill;
As merry, as glad, as never upon it
Fell the shadows solemn and still.

The flowers are blooming, the birds they are singing,
　　Summer and sunshine are over all;
But the worm, Decay, feels his latent triumph, —
　　The leaves are beginning to fall!

Annie.

UNDER the snow she lieth, pale and cold,
　　This quiet winter morning,
For Death has gathered to his silent fold
　　The heart you broke with scorning.
The white, white brow, the lips apart,
　　Are all in marble moulded;
And lightly over the pulseless heart
　　The little hands lie folded.

Under the snow she lieth.　Had you not come
　　With your soft voice and smiling,
From out the haven of her quiet home
　　That gentle heart beguiling,
Under the snow, so silent, and so pale,
　　She had not now been lying;
While over her moans the winter gale,
　　And the winter wind goes sighing.

Under the snow she lieth.　We, alone,
　　Are by our hearth-stone weeping.
We miss the presence of our only one
　　Out in the church-yard sleeping.
But you are jesting with the courtly throng
　　In yonder halls, fair lighted,
While she is lying quiet graves among, —
　　The loving heart you blighted.

Under the snow she lieth, pure and sweet,
　　With stillest heart forever;
And all earth's hours, cold and fleet,
　　Can bring her to us never.
And you may come to-morrow, false as fair,
　　The olden vows repeating,
To find the silence of our life's despair ·
　　Sole answer to your greeting.

Sweet Dreams.

SWEET dreams! ay, and many;
  Fair and glorious, pure and bright,
Filling all night's darkened chambers
  With their own unshadowed light;
Till the darkness seems to vanish
  In the broad blaze of the day,
And, from the sorrow at your heart,
  Your soul is borne away.

Sweet dreams! ay, and pleasant!
  Let their witchery come to you
As the light of olden friendship,
  As a throb of love most true;
Till your heart hath gathered gladness
  From those visions fair and sweet,
And its pulses bound most lightly,
  So radiant shapes to greet.

Sweet dreams! ay, forever,
  Might my wish but prove a spell,
All fairest hopes should crown your life,
  All bright things with you dwell!
Let mine be all the darkness,
  Let mine be all the pain;
It will matter little unto you,
  And I will but call it gain.

Sweet dreams! ay, the sweetest
  Man ever wove on earth,
Fill all your life with pleasantness,
  Crown most lovingly your hearth.
And I? — but it doth not matter,
  On Death's cold and silent shore,
If my love be all forgotten;
  Yet GOD keep you evermore!

Wishes.

I WOULD that my heart had armor of proof,
  Such as no woman can wear
Till her brow hath lost its glory of youth,
  And the snow lieth on her hair.
I would weave its chains, so close, so close,
  That no arrow could enter in;
And he must be the most cunning of foes,
  From its covert my heart to win.

I would that I had the strength of a man,
   When the days grow weary and long,
So my hands might work out what my head did plan,
   And be, for all labor, strong.
It were better for heart, and better for brain,
   To have work, and enough, to do;
So to shut out the dull and the throbbing pain
   That stealeth all senses through.

But my hands had no strength for the work to be done,
   So their labor is little worth;
And I leave behind a low burial-stone,
   And nothing more on earth.
And there was no armor of proof for me;
   My heart was stolen away;
And, far and lone, by the sounding sea,
   They are making its grave to-day!

Oh! vain are all wishes that cannot bring
   Their own fulfilment with them;
That have no promise, as of early spring,
   For the summer's diadem.
We breathe our wishes; but the hour flies,
   And their graves are at our feet.
They have died, as the glory of autumn dies
   In the winter's snow and sleet.

Oh, well for our souls that the shadows come,
   To darken the sunny day;
Else we might not think of that other home
   Where the light fades not away.
And GOD be blessed for the lack of love,—
   Love, making earth so bright;
Else we might not strive for the world above,
   "The world that makes this right!"

"The Night is far Spent; the Day is at Hand."

LOOK up, belovëd. Dark and drear the way,
  Wherein our weary feet are blindly straying,
But cheer thee still! Not far off is the day;
  And it shall come, if but for earnest praying.

Look up, belovëd. All our life o'erpassed
  Is but a shadow to the life before thee.

Earth's hours are fleeting silently and fast,
  And Heaven's light will soon be shining o'er thee.

Look up, belovĕd! Think not thou of me;
  But give thy thoughts unto yon Heaven only.
The days must go, and I shall be with thee
  Ere summer comes. I shall not long be lonely.

Look up, belovĕd! For the night doth flee;
  The stars are dim; the day is swiftly dawning!
Cold! cold! and there is only night for me,
  But never tears; for thou hast found the morning.

—————

"Nella."

O EARTH! the snow is lying on thy breast,
  And thy brow is pale and cold;
  Canst thou not give to me one little fold
Of thy white shroud? Canst thou not give me rest?
  I am so weary!
The life before me seems so dreary,
Under a cloud it spreadeth far away;
Silence and darkness are upon its day;
And from the storm there is no place of hiding.
No "Shadow of a great Rock in a weary land"
  Is there for me abiding.
  Without the gate I stand!

O Earth! thou seem'st so fair and sweet,
  In thy large mother heart
  Is there not room for me?
For I have borne a lone and bitter part
  In life's poor realm so long.
  Fain would I come to thee;
  And rest my weary, bleeding feet
  Thy graves among!

O Earth! I bring thee nought,
Unless it be a pale and sad despair.
I have no offering rich and rare,
  To win a boon from thee.
The little work that I have wrought
  Must die with me,
  Or is not mine to give;
  I could not even make
Life sweeter seem for the dear sake
Of one I loved. Why should I linger here?
  He hath no need of me!

O Earth! to thee I come;
Take thou thy poor child home,
And give me, give me rest,
I am so weary!
Rock me to slumber on thy loving breast;
And, from this world so dreary,
"Where men must work, and women must weep,"
Let me pass away in sleep.
There are no tears
In the green valleys where thy children lie;
Silence is with them continually.
And all the coming years,
Whose warring voices may not cease,
Shall bring them only peace!

Cobwebs.

I HAVE read in a childish rhyme,
Of a woman weird and dry,
Who evermore, in that ancient rhyme,
"Sweeps the cobwebs from the sky;"
And she had a broom of fashion rare.
Could I find its like again,
I would sweep away, with a breath of air,
The cobwebs from my brain.

They are delicate, fragile things,—
These cobwebs slight and thin;
But each, like a chain of iron, clings
To the chamber it enters in.
And my brain hath many a room
Where they gather so thick and fast,
That it seemeth to me a cloud of gloom
Is over my spirit cast.

I have seen the cobwebs, by thousands, caught
On the slender blades of grass;
And each gossamer thread with dew o'erfraught
For a string of gems might pass.
But the burning day riseth from the sea,
And each tiny jewelled string
Yieldeth all its glory and beauty to be
Its earliest offering.

But alas! the cobwebs that cross the brain
Are not so fair to see;

And I wish that old woman would come again,
    And bring her broom to me!
And I'd sweep away with a steady hand,
    Till there were no cobwebs left,
And the neatest dame in all the land
    Should praise the hand that swept.

But it needeth a touch as light as air,
    And an eye most sharp and keen,
And a broom of fashion strange and rare,
    To sweep those chambers clean.
For the human brain is a fragile thing,
    And in brushing the webs away,
We may break some tender and viewless string
    That is Reason's only stay.

I know all this; yet these cobwebs small
    Do weary me, night and day;
And I wish for that broom, so to sweep them all
    From my restless brain away.
Oh, that ancient rhyme, how it haunteth me,
    With the woman weird and dry,
Who, with her broom, ever merrily
    "Sweeps the cobwebs from the sky!"

A Thanksgiving.

For strength that could outlive all pain,
    And conquer silently;
Yea, still the tumult of the brain,
    O'ermastering agony;
        I thank thee, O my GOD!
For joy that came to lighten gloom,
    And dissipate the night;
That bade the early spring-flowers bloom,
    And made the summer bright;
        I thank thee, O my GOD!
For Hope, whose token-rainbow fair
    The cloudy heaven doth span,
So shutting out all dark despair, —
    A promise sweet to man;
        I thank thee, O my GOD!
For trust unquestioning and deep,
    Long cherished, and long proved;
That looks beyond the quiet sleep
    Thou givest thy beloved;
        I thank thee, O my GOD!

For Faith o'erpassing death; for all
That thou hast given me;
For rest in hope when earth-clods fall;
For Immortality, —
I thank thee, O my GOD!

To F. M. S.

WHAT shall I wish thee?   Earthly dreams are wasted;
False as fair, they perish, dying on life's strand;
And ere the draught earth proffers hath been tasted
The very chalice turns to ashes in our hand.
So I hold it not to thee.
What shall I wish thee?   Joys of earth endure not;
Fading and dying, they vanish from our way.
Only joys of heaven, brightly pure, that lure not
With a false lustre, may never know decay;
And GOD grant them unto thee!
What shall I wish thee?   Life, it beareth slowly
Pleasant things of earth, and mortal hopes away.
Hopes of the Hereafter, meekly kept, and holy,
Shall bear both fruit and blossom, in GOD's day.
May he give them unto thee!
What shall I wish thee?   Life is full of changes;
Sore and bitter trials of our constancy;
But in the Better Land, GOD so arranges
That there are no changings in eternity.
May it dawn in joy for thee!
What shall I wish thee?   Hopes that have no fading;
Holy joys that linger through the long To Be;
Faith, upon whose brightness cometh never shading;
And the rest GOD giveth.   May all these things be
Treasures that he giveth thee!

"Heimweh."

PINING,
For the bright sun shining
O'er mine own hills far away;
Till the glory
Of life's one angel story,
Seems to darken from my day;

Longing,
As memories come thronging,
For home voices evermore.
None so sweet
May here my name repeat.
Their echo floats not on this foreign shore.

Lonely,
With unfamiliar faces only
To meet my wearying eye;
Yearning
For the long way unreturning,
For the old home ere I die!

Dying
By weary inches; worn out with vain sighing;
Mine own land to see no more;
Never,
Through all the long forever,
To leave my dust on that beloved shore!

At the Chapel School.

THE little rain-runlets are flowing,
  And swift down the hill they go;
While the autumn wind is blowing
  The dead leaves to and fro.

Out on the breezy uplands
  The sheaves they are standing still;
And far away by the brookside
  I hear the click of the mill.

But the huskers are not in the corn-field,
  For the furrows are full of rain;
And the miller thanks GOD for the shower
  That helps him to grind his grain.

The crow flies over the tree-tops,
  To his nest in the old pine-tree;
And he caweth,—caweth hoarsely,—
  Who hath such a cold as he?

But little he cares for the weather,
  And less he cares for the wind.
So only the man in the corn-field
  Will leave a few ears behind.

The merry song-birds of summer
  To a warmer clime have flown;
And the robins, and later, the snow-birds,
  Have the fields to themselves alone.

But the fields they are white in winter
  When the snow is on the ground;
And the poor little robins and snow-birds
  Oft wonder where food may be found.

And ever nearer and nearer,
  To some friendly house they come,
Searching for crumbs that are scattered,
  Till they feel themselves at home.

So all through the cold, cold winter,
  GOD giveth the birds their food;
Till the first warm flush of the spring-time
  Melteth the snow in the wood.

Till the tender blades of the grasses
  Are green on each sunny slope,
And the swelling buds of the forest
  Are as harbingers of hope.

Softly the waters go flowing
  Through plashing meadow and plain,
Till the sun, in its thirst, hath drained them,
  And the sods are all dry again.

Then back to their nests come the song-birds,
  And the furrows are green again;
And the crows caw loud in the tree-tops,
  As the farmer sows his grain.

My rhyme it is well nigh ended,
  But is there no moral here,
That the earnest spirit may gather
  From the changings of the year?

As near to the footsteps of winter
  The promise of spring must be,
So after Death's final changing
  Comes the dawn of eternity;

And it needeth that we be ready
  When the summons comes, to go, —
When the winds of Death shall be blowing
  Our dead leaves to and fro.

How dieth the Day?

As a child that is grieving o'er some broken toy,
  Half teased into laughter, half tempted to tears,
Doth show us a smiling, part sorrow, part joy,
             As best suiteth his years;
   So dieth the day!

As a maiden who foldeth her hands unto sleep,
  With the first dream of love nestling warm at her heart,
Doth smile in her slumber, while soft blushes creep
             To her cheek, and depart,
   So dieth the day!

As a man o'er whose passing the tempest hath rolled,
  Shutting out the sweet light of the sun;
Till the death-hour comes, as the night on the wold,
             And the life-race be run;
   So dieth the day!

As a king who lies shrouded in purple and gold,
  The glory of empire veiling the pall;
The perfume of incense sweet over the mould
             That of earth is the all;
   So dieth the day!

As a priest who has stood by the altar of GOD,
  With pure hands uplifted in prayer and in praise;
Whose feet in the pathways of sin have not trod,
             Nor forsaken his ways;
   So dieth the day!

The Forest Grave.

In the green flush of summer's glorious noon,
The ancient forest reared its waving crest;
A world of various foliage. Rocky glens —
Their steep sides clothed with mosses and pale flowers;
Unresting streams that won their devious way
Now here, now there; their ripple, musical,
Just touched to silver by some transient ray
Of curious sunshine peeping through the shade
That was not all impervious; — hidden dells,
Alive with shadows from the tall trees thrown,
Full of all slumbrous sounds; low murmurings

Of leaves that whispered to the passing wind;
And sleepy echoes of the brook that wooed
The little forest-flowers;—all this, and more,
The grand old wood did hold within its heart.
All sounds of insect life, all songs of birds,
Did make themselves a home amid the leaves;
The leaves that stirred like pulses, full of life,
And green with summer beauty. Silently,
With steady, ceaseless flow, a river ran
The forest aisles between. A mighty stream,
That for a thousand miles had wound its course,
Nor yet had seen the sea. A thousand more
Must be o'erpassed ere with the tidëd main
Its inland waters meet, and, meeting, blend.
A virgin river yet, it had not known
The keel-compelling bark; nor heard the song
Of the rough sailor singing o'er his work
Some old familiar strain. No woodman's axe
Had left its impress on the forest groves;
Nor foot of white man trodden the free wilds,
Unchartered yet, and consecrate to peace.

A sail upon the waters, and a sound
Breaking the stillness other than the song
Of bird or insect; even the low hum
Of distant voices, singing some sweet hymn
To soothe the dying. Nearer and more near,
The solitary bark came on; a wail
Hushing the solemn hymn. And so Death came,
The one inevitable, certain guest,
Upon that river, to that unknown shore!

Slowly the vessel came up in the wind,
Drooping its white wings. Swiftly the anchor fell.
When evening came, serene and beautiful,
The weary bark did seem to lie and rest
Upon the quiet waters, as a child
Rocked into softest sleep. Above, around,
The night was holy with its burning stars, —
The stars that seemed, like angel eyes, to keep
Watch o'er a slumbering world. Within the bark,
They kept sad vigil o'er a sleep more deep
Than night can scatter from her poppy crown,
Or woo with aconite.
                              How still she lies,
The pale, pale maiden, with close-sealëd eyes!
Her little hands are folded on her breast,
Released forever from all earthly toil.

The little feet are crossed; so, never more,
To tread the paths of earth; and, at her heart
There is no beating of the throbbing pulse
To measure out the moments as they fly;
Silence is thronèd there!
                 Was it for this,
The mother, from her home amid the hills,
Had brought her only child? Was there no room
Beside the old church in the Vandois vale
For one so young and fair? Alas! the sword
Had gone through all the land. The little church
Had not one poor stone left to mark the spot
Where prayer and praise had once gone up to heaven;
And o'er the graves the heavy plough had passed,
Effacing all. The land had been bereaved
Of all its children. They had no place there
In life or death; nor church, nor home, nor grave!
So o'er the sea, unto these forest wilds,
The mother brought her child. And this the end.
The little feet touched never foreign strand;
Though by the margin of that mighty stream
The little maid is sleeping.
                 To the shore,
When morning dawned, a sad procession came.
Slowly they moved unto a grassy slope
Whereon the rising sun was shining warm,
Silently sipping dew from flowerets;
And there they laid the little sleeper down;
Smoothing above her rest the soft green sods
That ne'er before had known such saddest use.
Low at her feet a wild sweet-briar bush
Was set in silence. At her head, a cross,
Carved rudely from a simple block of stone,
Was raised 'mid prayerful voices; token sweet
That on that shore, in the far wilderness,
A child of GOD had found a quiet rest,
Waiting the resurrection!

———◦◦◦———

A Dirge.

SLEEP! for the day is dead;
  The night is coming on;
The stars are out in the skies o'erhead,
  But the harvest-moon is gone, —
The harvest-moon that was shining bright
  On the river far below,

When last we met in the hush of night
  One little week ago.

Sleep! for thy toil is o'er;
  Thine idlesse hath been won;
And thy hands may lie folded evermore, —
  Lie folded under the sun.
Never thy feet shall be weary now,
  Never thy step be slow;
The earth it is lying above thy brow,
  The waters beside thee flow.

Sleep! for thy rest is come;
  Thy work hath all been done;
Thy soul hath entered another home,
  Thy spirit's goal is won.
But some hearts of earth are throbbing yet,
  With a pain they cannot lull;
And oh! the world of sad regret,
  And the life that seems so dull!

Sleep! so to dream no more
  Of the tempest on the sea;
Of the waves that dashed on a stormy shore;
  Of a strong man's agony.
So to hear no more, through the long, long night,
  The cry of drowning men;
Or to shudder at sight of the sea so bright,
  That was so pitiless then.

Sleep! for the day is dead;
  The throbbing heart is still;
And the winds go moaning o'er thy bed, —
  That little grave on the hill.
Sleep! life's bitterness is all past,
  And far from thee removed;
Thine aching heart hath found rest at last;
  Sleep long and well, beloved!

A Nation's Prayer.

SEND help to us, O GOD!
  Behold a mourning land;
In all her pleasant places death
  And desolation stand.

Our homes in ashes lie,
  Or own another lord;
Thy temples are a mockery,
  Unhonored by thy Word.

Send help to us, O GOD!
  Our sons lie low in death;
Our daughters dwell in ruined homes;
  And wait, with stinted breath,
News from the battle-plain.
  While on that battle-plain,
Blood floweth in a crimson rain, —
  Earth wears a crimson stain.

Send help to us, O GOD!
  Bid the wild carnage cease;
And grant unto our bleeding land
  The blessèd boon of peace.
End thou this agony;
  This bitterness assuage;
And blot from out our history
  This dark and fatal page.

Send help to us, O GOD!
  In this our sore distress;
Let thy right hand be strong to save,
  To succor and to bless.
Behold our native land,
  Do thou her peace restore;
Her brow is red with Cain's dark brand,
  Thy judgment woundeth sore.

Send help to us, O GOD!
  And heal the bitter strife
That strikes such deep and deadly blows
  At all the nation's life.
Hear thou our earnest cry;
  We stretch our hands to thee;
Thou, only, canst all aid supply,
  Now, and eternally.

Send help to us, O GOD!
  From out thy plenteous store,
Until sweet Peace her olive-branch
  Shall stretch from shore to shore;
Until the stain of blood
  Be blotted from the land;
Until the dear old brotherhood
  Once more clasp hand in hand!

My Home.

WOULDST see my home? Come, ere the spring departing
  Leaves its rich promise to the summer's bloom;
Ere yet the roses from their green nests starting,
  Load lightest breezes with their sweet perfume;
Come — where the restless breezes, idly blowing,
  Bend low the grasses on the summer lea;
Where the old river with its wealth is flowing
  On to the margin of the soundless sea;
Come to my home; and thou shalt find me sleeping,
  Lying with still hands folded on my breast;
With eyes close sealèd from all earthly weeping,
  And pulses silent, and a heart at rest.

A Thought.

I SOMETIMES think
This life of ours a strangely tangled maze,
Wherein we wander blindly; seeking still
In our bewilderment, some clue to find
That, followed closely, shall bring us at length
Unto some beaten track wherein our feet
May walk assuredly. But we find it not:
Unless GOD leadeth us with loving hand
By ways we have not known unto himself.
Behold! the paths we shape at our poor will
Wend in and out, — hither and thither turn, —
But only shut us deeper in the maze
We fain would quit forever. Of ourselves
We have no power to break the secret spell
That still doth hedge us in. Impalpable
Are the strong chains that bind us, and unseen;
We know not where to seek them; how to break
The yoke our flesh must bear. We murmur oft;
Yea, in our impotence, do vainly rage,
As ocean fretteth 'gainst the senseless rock.
Of what avail? Not ours the hand to break
Those viewless fetters. Only in *his* time
Will God take off the yoke. And then he sends
The Silent Angel of the Silent Land
To set the captives free.

"Out in the Bitter Cold."

Out in the bitter cold!   Ay! past your door,
   A little child is straying —
A little child — like to your own Lenore,
   When first she went a-Maying.
The snow is falling on her shoulders white,
   She is footsore and weary;
She hath no shelter from the cold and night;
   And the streets they are so dreary!

Out in the bitter cold (the wintry street
   Her home, she hath no other)
Are lingering yet the little naked feet;
   Poor child! she hath no mother!
What if your own Lenore were in her place?
   Ay! pause, and on it ponder;
The same keen hunger in *her* little face
   As in that poor child's yonder.

Out in the bitter cold! and night is near;
   And on the chill earth lying,
(While at your hearth are warmth and pleasant cheer,)
   The little child is dying.
Above her form the snow-wreaths, falling fast,
   Thicker and thicker gather.
God takes the little one home at last, —
   She had no other father!

Out in the bitter cold!   And you let slip
   The chance that had been given;
You turned the chalice from your careless lip
   That was foretaste of heaven.
Bethink you of the solemn judgment-day,
   And — " Inasmuch as ye
Poured never sunshine on that poor child's way,
   Ye did it not to Me!"

Bold in Youth.

Ay! youth is bold!
It flings the gauntlet at a world of foes;
Says " I am ready! " ere the battle-hour,
And panteth for the strife.   It hath no fear
Of what the bitter morrow may bring forth;

It pauses not to count the costly price
The future payeth for the present joy;
It hath no looking back!   It nothing knows
Of doubts and fears that still perplex the man,
Bidding him pause, and think.   It rushes on,
And will not tarry for precaution's sake,
Nor yet for fear of that which cometh after;
And in its faith how beautiful is youth!

How beautiful! yet full of fancy, too;
For in our youth we do create a world
Full of all pleasant images.   The shapes
That glide across our dreams are robed in light,
And are not shadows in our eager eyes;
For we look only through a tinted glass,
Rose-coloring all we see.   A veil of flowers
Doth float between us and the naked steep
Our feet must learn to climb.   Ay! though they leave
A crimson stain upon the pitiless stone,
It may not be untrod!   As time flies on,
We learn how falsely fair our dreams have been;
And Life, with its realities, doth wear
A visage strangely stern.   The rosy tints
Have faded into gray.   The veiling flowers
Have felt the early frosts, and fled before
Those heralds of the winter coming on.
The first bright vision of our sunny youth,
O'er which we trace, with fingers trembling, cold,
The bitterness of " changed," is but a type
Of all that follows after.
            Peace and Hope
In time, may be companions of our way;
And sweet Content, a blessèd spirit, dwell
Within our quiet hearts.   But weary days,
Alternate grief and pain, all pangs that still
The human heart can bear, must first have wrought
The work they had to do.   Then, calm, resigned,
Our souls sure anchored on a changeless Faith,
We may front life with an unshrinking eye,
And say " the bitterness of death is past! "

Under the Snow.

LIGHTLY my boat on the river tosses,
   But I am lying low,
Never again the light oars to feather,

While the bright waters flow.
    Little it troubleth me,
      Under the snow.

In my own garden weeds may be rampant,
  And the green grasses grow;
Never a flower left, my hands had planted,
  Never a rose to blow.
    Little it troubleth me,
      Under the snow.

In the old orchard the sweet apple-blossoms
  May make as goodly a show;
But bloom they freely, or bloom they rarely,
  I shall not see them blow.
    Little it troubleth me,
      Under the snow.

Down in the valley the little brook runneth,
  Down where the violets grow;
But never this hand of mine shall gather
  Flowers where the brook doth flow.
    Little it troubleth me,
      Under the snow.

Oft on the shore of the glorious river,
  Idly listening to its flow,
Passed I the hours; still, softly singing,
  Onward the tiny wavelets go.
    Little it troubleth me,
      Under the snow.

On the old homestead the doom may be written,
  And the old walls lie low, lie low;
Over my birthplace, so fair, so pleasant,
  Over it all, the plough may go.
    Little it troubleth me,
      Under the snow.

From the old hill-side the pines may vanish;
  Where they were darkening, grass may grow;
Out in the sunshine the storms may gather,
  Wearily, drearily, winds may blow.
    Little it troubleth me,
      Under the snow.

Ione.

WHAT! must I barter my hand for gold?
  Forge myself the chain that must fetter me?
Myself for myself weave the Nestus-fold?
  Low in my grave I had better be!

What hath my youth with his age to do?
  Quick are my pulses; his slowly beat.
Dearly and lifelong this moment I'd rue
  If ever my soul with its twin soul should meet.

I do not love him; and what have I done
  That my life should be poured as on sand is the rain?
To mate my young years with his wintering sun,
  Were like chaining the quick and the dying again!

But I? — See, the blood floweth free in my veins!
  I have health, youth, and beauty; but what has he?
A house like a palace, and some ill-gotten gains;
  But what is his wealth or his palace to me?

You say that my hands are too small for toil;
  Too soft and white for the winning of bread;
I would work day and night through the darkness and moil,
  Ere stoop to the fate I despise and dread.

Would you chain a lark to the dungeon floor,
  Where never the light of the sun may be?
On its life and its song would you shut the door?
  Let it die in darkness and agony?

You would say that the bird had no part in the gloom;
  That ever it singeth at heaven's gate;
Yet my youth you would give to a living tomb,
  And my heart to a darker and deadlier fate.

What! must I barter my hand for gold?
  Forge myself the chain that shall fetter me?
Myself for myself weave the Nestus-fold?
  Low in my grave I had rather be!

Little by Little.

LITTLE by little the blades of grass
Through the brown crust of the earth shall pass;
Till a thousand plains are all green and fair
With the blades that are waving in summer air.

Little by little, and one by one,
Flow the tiny drops from the rifted stone;
Till a mighty river doth downward sweep
So to meet the waves of a mightier deep.

Little by little, and grain by grain,
The sands swept over the fertile plain;
Till they buried the cities of old so low
That the feet of the traveller over them go.

Little by little, yea, inch by inch,
The mighty rocks that would scorn to flinch
At the tempest's wrath, by attrition worn
Shall become the dust they may seem to scorn.

Little by little, — the breadth of a hair, —
Shall the moaning sea make itself a lair
In the cavernous gloom; or wear away
The haughty cliffs that once faced the day.

Little by little the acorn swells
The folding valves of its tiny cells;
Little by little, its growth shall be,
Till it spreadeth abroad a grand old tree.

Little by little — so man doth change
Till his old self to himself would be strange;
All that is left of it is but a shade;
Quietly, silently, that, too, shall fade.

Little by little life from us doth go;
But heedless are we of its ebb and its flow;
Till suddenly, strangely, we find ourselves cast
On the shore of the grave, and stranded at last.

Little by little we heap to ourselves
Riches and pelf; that, like trickiest elves,
Now here, and now there, shall elude us at last
When fondly we hope that our grasp holds them fast.

Little by little we rear some shrine
That shall hold all we reckon as most divine;
But the storm shall shatter it, lightning burn,
Till but ashes is left in its funeral urn.

Little by little, so endeth my song.
Little by little might make it too long.
Little by little death creeps on apace,
Little by little, so endeth the race!

𝕶𝔂𝔯𝔦𝔞𝔠.*

SHE sitteth quiet, and pale, and still;
　　A woman frail and poor.
Only in her eyes shines the living will, —
　　The power to wait and endure.

Her limbs are fettered by weakness down;
　　She hath no strength to stir;
But the goal that shall be of her life the crown
　　Is shining afar, to her.

Heavy the road she must travel o'er, —
　　A weary way to go;
And though life is so near to the other shore,
　　Her purpose ripens full slow.

Never she falters; no turning back
　　For her can written be;
Onward she presses in the same old track;
　　Changeless of purpose is she.

In her hand — that hand so white, yet so strong —
　　She holdeth the keys of heaven;
And all issues that unto her life belong,
　　To her keeping have been given.

Patient she sits, in the old carved chair
　　For a royal queen most meet;
With the Cross on her breast, — for no Crown is there, —
　　And the anchor 'neath her feet.

White are the robes she loveth to wear
　　As the righteousness of saints;
For her heart knows nothing of dark despair,
　　And she wearies not, nor faints.

Lonely, and chained to that old carved chair
　　How can her will be done?
Ask of the clouds and the darkened air
　　If ceaseth to shine the sun!

* Ye Saxon for ye Church.

Over the length and the breadth of the earth,
    Her heralds they wander forth;
To the kingly palace, the peasant's hearth,
    To the utmost South and North.

No seas so grand to be traversed o'er,
    And never a gulf so wide,
But her messengers cross unto either shore,
    And there stand side by side.

Little she cares for dividing seas;
    She can bridge them with a " WORD,"
And crush out the forms of old tyrannies
    Though never she wields a sword.

Meekly this woman beareth her lot, —
    It hath pain and agony, —
Since she knoweth she is not of GOD forgot,
    Being his for eternity.

And the bitter trials her faith must bear,
    She counteth gain, not loss;
And never she yieldeth to grim despair,
    For her shoulders bear the Cross.

By the rivers deep, by the sounding sea,
    By the little forest rills,
She will bear that cross; forever to be
    As an ensign to the hills.

The Cross, despised and scorned of men,—
    The once accursèd tree,—
Shall be lifted up, a holy thing, when
    The gods of the heathen flee.

Behold! the days come, when this woman meek
    Shall be clothed with terrible grace;
When the gods of this world shall be poor and weak,
    And as dust before her face.

When the powers of hell shall be overthrown,
    And the Prince of the air cast down;
When might shall be in the Cross alone,
    And unto it cometh the Crown!

Our Little Brother.

The wind it bloweth o'er the grass,
The summer cloudlets lightly pass
 From out the dark blue heaven;
For far away the shadows are;
All with the night and with the star
 Unto a new earth given;
But, underneath the grassy sod,
Our little brother sleeps with God.

The days they glide as heretofore;
As swift to pass and be no more;
 In the morrow dying.
Silent all they come and go;
Like to a river's icy flow,
 No ripple o'er it flying;
For, underneath the grassy sod,
Our little brother sleeps with God.

The childish laugh, that was so sweet,
Hath died away, as waters fleet,
 That never know returning.
The echo of some little feet,
That gladdened all the quiet street,
 Is hushed with their inurning;
For, underneath the grassy sod,
Our little brother sleeps with God.

O mother! in your patient eyes,
What untold depth of sorrow lies,
 Insatiate of weeping!
Eyes turning still with longing gaze
Where, underneath the summer rays,
 The little one lies sleeping..
Smile, mother, smile, above that sod!
Sleeps not our brother with his God?

Alone.

Under the clover, so fresh, so fragrant,
 Lieth the little one, sleeping sound;
Idly murmuring, wandering, vagrant,
 Breezes are blowing above the mound;

Tearful and sad, by the empty cradle,
  Sitteth the mother, alone — alone!

Never beneath the old oaken rafter
  Soundeth the patter of little feet;
Never the echo of childish laughter
  In music that waiting ear shall greet.
Tearful and sad, by the empty cradle,
  Sitteth the mother, alone — alone!

Under the stars a river floweth,
  In the fair Southern land, far away;
But a stain of blood with the pure wave goeth, —
  Blood that was warm at the close of day,
Up in the North, by an empty cradle,
  Sitteth the fond wife, alone — alone!

Alas, poor heart! She had thought, in her sorrow,
  That never the father should see his child!
That fear shall be dead with the coming morrow,
  And so, poor heart, be thou reconciled,
Content to watch by an empty cradle.
  God will not leave thee alone — alone!

Under the clover, so fresh, so fragrant,
  Lieth the little one, sleeping sound;
Under the stars, by the river vagrant,
  Lieth the father whom death hath found;
Tearful and sad, by the empty cradle,
  Sitteth wife and mother, alone — alone!

———•••———

Weary.

God loveth the little children.
  Would I were a child again;
Or lying where summer daisies
  Might shut out these years of pain!
Oh! to be quietly lying
  Where the sun shines on the hill;
Where the pulses of earth might be throbbing,
  But my heart forever still!

I know I am slowly dying
  Of a thirst that is agony,
For the clasp of some loving fingers,
  For the smile of a loving eye.

I hear the laugh of the waters,
  But they never flow to me.
Ever and always receding,
  How they mock mine agony!

I am so weary of waiting;
  So burdened with hopeless years;
So bowed to the earth by long watching;
  So wasted by futile tears;
That my soul were a bird out of prison,
  Rejoicing at its release,
Were it freed from its earthly bondage,
  And so evermore at peace!

Oh! to be quietly lying
  Where the daisies and buttercups grow;
Where its shadow, the old mossy steeple,
  At even, may over me throw;
So never to feel one wild pulsing
  Of the heart that throbbed in vain;
So to know no more the old bitterness, —
  The old, old throb and pain!

The Last Greeting.

ONLY a hand-clasp, Agatha,
  And you will give nothing more?
See, the breeze yon white sails filling,
  While my boat waits by the shore.

Waits; — and I *must* go, Agatha,
  It may be for evermore;
For the sea so fair is as pitiless,
  And the deep may not restore.

Only a hand-clasp, Agatha?
  Think; I have loved you so long;
And the heart of a man may be broken,
  Though it seemeth so brave and strong.

Hark! 'tis the signal for parting;
  And were I to dally now,
Not even your hand's lily whiteness
  Could wipe the stain from my brow.

Only a hand-clasp, Agatha,
  And my prayer hath been in vain.

God send his sun ou your path to shine;
   'Twill not smile on miue again!

Untold Love.

                It is true;
We women all too oft let our hearts go
From out our own true keepiug; kuowing not
Unto what heritage of wasted love
We give them in their fresh and golden spring.
Until some sharp dividing blow shall come, —
Unknown, unfeared, — severing the sweet bond;
And all our life is dust, red with heart's blood;
And yet we do not die!   We fold our hands
Above the gaping wound, and so shut out
All mocking eyes; all ken of careless hearts;
And iu the silence of a life we keep
Our dead most sacredly.
             But life seems long;
Made longer by the lack of that sweet boud
Whose tender clasp, whose true and steadfast shield
We may not have forever!   Yet we yearn
O'er sweet child-voices, kuowing, all the while,
No child shall call us "mother!"
              It is hard
To have our life, as woman, wrecked aud lost,
For that the bark wherein we lauuched our all
Was only drifting from us.   Never cry
Rang out across the waters, from the lips
That did but whiten in their agony;
For all our woman's pride pressed deep the seal
Upon the ashen lips and bleeding heart;
And so the tide swept on that never brought
Our hearts' belovĕd back.   God only grant
They were no readers of the human heart,
So our life-secret iu our own still hearts
Find unrevealing grave!
            We little know
How many graves of wasted love lie low
With the poor hearts that covered them!   So low,
That no material eye may fathom them.
God keepeth all such love; nor wasted so.
Back to the one immortal Fount of Love
Each tiny riplet flows.   Henceforth to be
For aye a part of that eternal sea
O'er which no *wreck* may go!

𝔄 Child's Sorrow.

THREE lives the less upon GOD's earth, — and yet
The child was smiling in the telling of it!
I questioned how they died.   A drownèd man
The one; the third, of grievous battle-wounds;
At home the other lingered long, then died
Of some disease, — she knew not what it was;
And yet they were her brothers, lately dead,
And she, a girl of thirteen years or more!
Certes, she had not grieved o'ermuch; and so
The passing sadness was a thing of nought.
Ah! children keep no reckoning with death;
And dust, once given to its kindred dust,
Is only dust to them!   They will not keep
Graves dewy green through the long lapse of years.

Poet and Reaper.

THE song of a poet was ringing
 Down the silence of the years,
What time the reapers were binding
 The last of the golden ears.

But little it matters who sang it,
 Or what hands bound up the sheaves;
(The shadow of death was falling
 On the falling summer leaves.)

For know, the work of the poet
 In that song was fully wrought;
Yet it scarce holds a place in the Present;
 To Time leaves its germs of thought;

But those germs shall have freshness and beauty,
 When the writers of to-day,
With their sparkle and froth of the wine-cup,
 Shall have utterly passed away.

And what if the reaper keep not
 One ear of the golden grain?
What if *his* work be to gather in,
 And *another* reap the grain?

Let him rest!   It was his to gather
  The harvest some other had sown.
On a thousand shores may be scattered
  The seed from that harvest grown.

On the tops of the westering hedgerows
  Shineth the setting sun;
And the poet's song is ended,
  And the reaper's work is done!

If is Nought.

ONE little word,
  Sharper than any sword,
And at my feet my world was lying,
  Shattered, — dying, —
So never earthly skill,
  Nor strength of human will,
Could mould the fragments into form again.
  A life of tears were vain!

Oh! softly tread,
Nor with light finger touch my dead.
  It passed in such despair,
The thing that yesterday was so fair!

O Sun! withdraw thy mocking light;
  A yet unburied form is here;
Fitter for darkness and the night,
  And dying of the year.

Glide by, O Day! in silentness.
No tender moaning, no caress,
  May this still shadow have.
I dare not keep its memory.
So, shrouded in mine agony,
  Unto its nameless grave
Let the poor wreck go down.
The coming years must bear the loss,
All life take up the thornëd cross
  And wear it patiently.
Who knoweth, but some after day
May put the bitter cross away,
  And hail the coming crown?

Graves.

OVER how many graves our feet are treading!
  Behold! the very dust they scatter light
Was once instinct with life.   Some brave soul, leading
  An armèd host to battle for the right,
Dwelt in this clay.   Or bard, who sang his glory,
  Forgotten now, as he had never been;
Or, nearer home, the old familiar story
  Of love, o'er which the grass is growing green.

But other "graves" there are; uncounted, only
  Because the heart doth keep them, still and low,
Sad graves, and silent; all apart and lonely,
  O'er which no breath of coming spring may blow.
We keep them darkly, as a miser keepeth
  His hidden treasures from all envious eyes;
As, 'neath the laughing river, darkly sleepeth
  Some unknown corse whereon no sunshine lies.

Green are the "graves" where our beloved lie sleeping!
  On their round sod the summer sun smiles down.
Memorial-stones their faithful watch are keeping,
  And winter robes them with its snowy crown;
But "graves" o'er which the heart is daily closing,
  Are buried all too deep for sun or snow;
No resurrection breaks their cold reposing;
  No breath of life o'er their "dry bones" may blow.

"Women are such Hypocrites!"

TRUE, we *are* hypocrites. We women wear
Light, mocking smiles, to veil the heart's despair.
Nay, our own anguish we will most deride
With angry scorn, in bitterness of pride.
With lightest laughter, most fantastic jest,
We shroud the death that warreth in our breast;
And bear us bravely, so no other know
The secret of our irremediable woe.

I have known women, in the very hour
That saw their love mown down like any flower,
Break out in sportive jest, or gayer song,
And be the centre of a brilliant throng,

While smiling lip, and cheek of rose concealed
The secret pang that never was revealed;
Who made it still their pride's incessant task
To wear on lip and brow a lifelong mask.

But all have not this panoply of pride;
And some live on in shadow; some have died;
While others strive with hand and brain's best art
To calm the pulses of a bleeding heart,
O'ermastering the pain.   And they grow cold,
So shutting out the pleasant thoughts of old,
And walk through life as if it had no joy,
And pain and sorrow were its sole alloy.

But some pure souls there are, to whom there clings
The unseen vesture of an angel's wings;
And meekly, with bowed hearts, they kiss the rod,
And own it as a message sent from GOD.
They dwell on earth, contented and resigned;
The cloud for them is with pale silver lined;
They take their lonely lot, as reconciled,
With the meek spirit of a patient child.

These make earth beautiful to other eyes;
These steal the shadow from the darkest skies;
And with souls, patient, holy, pure, and meek,
They aid the erring, and uphold the weak.
Some day, a place is vacant at the hearth,
A voice of music has died from the earth,
A silence lieth on the path they trod, —
The pure and patient have gone up to GOD.

Hymn.

HOLY Father, Source of Light!
   Humbly do thy saints adore thee;
Heaven and earth, and day and night,
   As thy creatures bow before thee;
And we, also, things of clay,
Sing thy glorious praise alway.

For the blessing of the light,
   Daily to our labor leading;
For the darkness and the night,

Giving rest that we are needing;
Hear our ceaseless songs of praise,
Sounding till the end of days.

For the Gift above all price,
  From thy right hand once descending,
For the stainless Sacrifice,
  Offered once, yet never-ending;
Lo! our morning song shall rise!
Lo! our evening sacrifice!

Christe Eleison.

By Thy many sorrows keep
Loving watch o'er all who weep,
Giving thy belovĕd sleep;
        Christe eleison.
By thine agony of tears,
Swelled by human griefs and fears,
And the sin of all the years;
        Christe eleison.
By thy cross, so meekly borne,
By thy mocking crown of thorn,
On thee pressed by hands of scorn;
        Christe eleison.
By thy life, so full of sighs,
Yielded up in agonies,
By thine awful sacrifice;
        Christe eleison.
By thy Love, that all could give,
By thy Death that we might live,
In thy rising to revive;
        Christe eleison.

"I go the Way of all the Earth."

THE golden day is past; the night hath come.
Still on the western hills the soft light shines
Caught from the sinking sun; but in the east
The shadows gather, and the stars come out
To light the earth.   There is no moon to-night.
The day is past; and I, with lingering feet,

And slow, must "go the way of all the earth."
I shall not see the morning sun arise
O'er the blue hills that I have loved so long!
No more the ripple of the sunny wave,
Nor plash of waters on a rock-strewn shore,
Shall break in music on the calm and hush
Of some fair eve of summer. Ears of dust
Hear nothing of all this. Are deaf, alsō,
Unto the sweetest music of all life;
The voice of our beloved. I shall not hear
That music any more. Until the day
When earth and sea shall render up their dead
I shall not see his face. Between us lies
A gulf so wide, that even when I die
He cannot come to me!
How the stars shine!
So will they shine, some night, upon my grave;
And I, in my dark home, shall nothing see
Of all their beauty! In that quiet grave
There shall be peace, unutterable peace,
O'er which those shining stars, as sentinels,
Keep holy watch and ward. These wasted hands,
Their work all done, lie still and folded there,
Clasping so close the cross. These weary feet,
Through all my life led o'er so many graves,
End all their toiling there. This throbbing heart,
Grown cold, and very still, shall beat no more
In pleasure or in pain; yea, know no more
The dreary void, the want unsatisfied,
That touched its pulses to such bitter pain
In the old days of earth.
I go the way
That all of earth must go. The waters rise
Above my footsteps; and the icy wave
Mounts upward to my heart. I pass alone,
Yet not alone, across the river dark;
Upheld by *One* who beareth me above
The else engulfing stream. He treads the wave
Conquering, and to conquer. I but lean
Reliant on the Hand so strong to save.
I know that underneath me are the "Arms,"
The "Everlasting Arms." I know that he
Will never leave, nor yet forsake his own;
"I KNOW THAT MY REDEEMER LIVETH!"

"At Eventide it shall be Light."

O mourner by a vacant hearth,
  Whereon the shadow lieth yet;
Thou that hast given unto earth
  The shape that haunts thee in regret,
Look up and smile. Beyond the skies,
  Beyond the darkness and the night,
The home of thy belovëd lies.
  "At eventide it shall be light."

O weary, worn, and breaking heart,
  That seest all thy hopes go down
Quick unto death, and so depart,
  Know thou skies will not alway frown.
Though dark and dreary dawns the day,
  A pallid phantom of the night,
And all the sunshine hides away;
  "At eventide it shall be light."

O thou that journeyest through the vale,
  Where shadows gather, deep and long;
Where feet must falter, high heart fail, —
  Look up and onward! Be thou strong!
Those shadows all shall pass away,
  Forgotten in the glory bright
Of God's own everlasting day.
  "At eventide it shall be light."

"Let not the Sun go down upon your Wrath."

Quarrels are bitter things. They take the bloom
From off our lives. They brush the tender dew
With all its sparkling freshness from our path,
And in its stead waters of Marah flow.
We cannot heal that stream! Our mortal hands
Are not so stainless, nor our hearts so pure,
As with a touch to sweeten the dark wave,
And it flows on, to color all our lives
With saddest memories. Perchance, to change
The very current of our heart's best blood
Into most bitter gall.
                    We often hear
"Let not the sun go down upon your wrath."

Who heedeth? For daily it doth go down,
To rise and set again, and yet it finds
Our anger burning still! Alas! the spark
A little word hath kindled, flames and burns,
A fierce, unquenchable fire. We have lit,
With thoughtless fingers as unthinking heart,
The torch that may not die until that heart
Hath burnēd into dust, or ashes lie
Upon the folded hands!
              Perchance the years,
That still all human pulses unto peace,
May quench the anger that once burned therein;
But the dead flame hath left its ashes there;
And life hath bitterness at its very source,
Tainting the stream itself, till wrath and life
Alike have passed away.
              Have passed away?
Oh! never! never! That poor *life* may fade
And perish from the earth. The *wrath* remains;
The bitter heritage of an evil hour
Left to our children, on whose lives it lies
A cloud forever; and *our* sin hath left
Its fatal impress on the young, pure hearts
We should have led to heaven!
              We are weak;
Too prone to quarrel with our brother's words;
Too quick to take offence was never meant;
Too hasty in our wrath. And what are we,
Who dare to entertain an evil guest,
Shutting the angel out? Are we so pure,
That with unwashen hands we may touch pitch
And yet be undefiled? So sinless, too,
That never need of GOD's forgiveness
Makes us forgive our brother? It is well,
If laying hands upon a quiet heart,
We plead "not guilty," and our conscience smiles;
But doth it smile, when on our puny wrath
The evening sun goes down?
              O Father, hear!
O thou most holy, keep us free from sin.
Guard thou our lips from wrath; and guide our souls
Into the way of peace. The lowly path
Trodden of old by Him who took our lot
So meekly on him — who was ever found
The pure and undefiled — the Prince of Peace —
The Holy One of Israel, and our God!

Weary.

I am weary of this toil!
It is wearing heart and brain;
And I long for childhood's frolic mirth,
And its old sweet laugh again.
But I know they cannot come,
For I lost them long ago;
With the merry days, and the dear old home,
That are cold beneath the snow.

I am weary of this toil!
And I long for rest and peace;
But I may not hope for such blessings sweet,
Till life's bitter strugglings cease.
Rest for the weary, rest!
But the boon may not be given
Till hands lie folded on the breast,
And the soul hath gone to heaven.

Rest.

Why do we toil for that which bringeth care
And little pleasure, and which doth but wear
Our very life away?   Why do we toil —
Amid such stirring strife, such endless moil —
For shadows, fading when we deem them ours,
And fleeting with the evanescent hours?
O idle questioning!   As if souls bent
On gaining some one goal could rest content
With folded hands, and see the world rush on,
While others win the prize they might have won!
Rather the toil, the rack of brain and mind,
Than in the world's race to be left behind!
Onward! the restless soul's incessant cry, —
Onward! and silenced only when we die!

We dream of rest.   We picture some fair scene
Bright with the wealth of summer's golden sheen.
A lake, serene, doth glass the glorious sky;
O'er bluest hill-tops, rosy cloudlets fly;
And we, our days of toil all passed away,
Lie idly watching the departing day.
A sense of pleasure stealeth through our veins,
Unknown amid our former cares and pains.

A gentle languor seems to float from out
The ambient air, and curtain us about;
And we lie down on roses fresh and sweet,
With but one thought: " This is most exquisite ! "

We dream, and wake.   Ah! life doth seem so bare;
Its frosts seem chilling all the summer air.
Clouds gather darkly o'er the enchanting scene,
And we are moaning o'er what might have been!
.   .   .   .

We *dream* of rest; but we are deaf, the while,
Unto the voice from out eternity,
Whispering to the soul, " Come unto Me,
All ye that labor and are heavy laden,
And *I* will refresh you; *I* will give rest
Unto your souls."   And for this promised rest
None ever seek in vain.   It is GOD's rest;
For "so he giveth his belovëd sleep."

" Remember thy Creator in the Days of thy Youth."

Now in thy youth remember Him
  Who "holdeth thy soul in life;"
Who stayeth thy feet from wandering
  In paths that with death are rife;
And GOD will hear thee; be thy stay
  Through all thine earthly way.

Life's spring is dawning.   Summer waits
  With wealth of flowers, rich and fair;
And autumn opes its golden gates,
  And shows its fruitage, ripe and rare, —
For all these blessings, give thou praise
  To Him who guards thy ways.

Spring — summer — autumn — winter, too,
  May crown thy little term of years.
GOD will lead thee thy journey through,
  Guard all thy joys, keep all thy tears,
If only thou give him thy heart,
  Choosing the better part.

And, if in youth thou pass away,
  Or in 'mid age lie down to rest,
Fear not the darkness of that day

When hands lie folded on the breast.
The GOD thou servest will give light
    That shineth through the night.

Fear not the trials life may bring;
  GOD sends them but to prove thy trust!
Fear not life's sorrows. Thou shalt sing
  The triumphs of the good and just.
Who walketh in GOD's ways shall see
    Life in Eternity.

Tired!

TIRED! It is but a little word,
    A sound of daily life;
But under it floweth a current deep,
    With a thousand meanings rife.

Tired! Ay; weary of toil and care,
    That will not let us rest;
Thinking how sweet the long sleep must be,
    Under the earth's green breast.

Tired! It may be of waiting long, —
    Of having hopes deferred;
Of feeling aye how all of life
    Was blighted by a word.

Tired! Under that curtain may lie
    A pain too deep for words:
A torture, straining sharp and fierce,
    On all the poor heart's chords.

Tired! Utter it soft and low,
    It holds its secrets well;
For few would dream what a tale of pain
    That little word might tell.

The Crown-Seekers.

BEHOLD! we seek a crown,
    Not worn by brows of earth;
Not fading with our dying selves,
    But of immortal worth.

No gems from Eastern mines shall deck
  The crown of glory we would have;
But from it stream rays, burning, bright,
  That light the darkness of the grave.

Behold! we seek a crown,
  Now, in our morn of life;
With God's dew lying on our brows,
  We enter on the strife.
The way lies straight before us now;
  We tread it with unweary feet;
A crown awaits us, and we know
  That after labor, rest is sweet.

Behold we seek a crown!
  And, though the way be long,
We are armëd as God's children are,
  And in his strength are strong.
Though life bring to us thorn and cross,
  And its wild strife be hard and dure;
Who bears the cross shall find no loss,
  But win a golden crown and pure.

Cross and Crown.

    The Cross is ours;
Through all our life its shadow lies on us.
Through *all* our life? Nay; scarcely so. Methinks,
The baby brows, whereon God's signet shines,
Know nothing of the shadow. In their hearts,
The seeds of evil, yet ungerminate,
May never spring to life; for God may take
The little children home, and they may wear
The golden crown, the thorny cross unfelt.
But we, who linger out a longer life,
Shall know, for certain, where the shadow lies.
Nay, more; may see it lengthen to our feet,
As further from th' uplifted cross we rove.
The evil seeds within our hearts shall find
A bitter time to germ. And evil thoughts
Shall throng all avenues of inner life,
As infusoria fill each tiny drop
Of the sweet, sparkling fount we thought so pure.
Unto the last we wander from the road;
And still the shadow of the distant Cross
Creeps to our straying feet, as though to lead

The rebel soldiers back. 'Tis but to turn
Our wandering feet into that shadow's path,
And, taking up the Cross, shut from our lives
Its shadow evermore. GOD's love is strong,
Enduring, and most patient; but the grave,
That shutteth us from earth, shuts out the Hand
That mighty is to save.
                          Who bear the Cross
Shall wear the Crown. GOD shall give unto them
A crown of beauty, — an immortal crown,
Whereon the rust and tarnish of this world
Shall never more be lying. Bright and pure
Shall be the circlet ringing holy brows;
So not unmeet, in adoration deep,
At GOD's own feet to lie!

----••----

"Good Gracious!"—L. C. G.

A LITTLE child was listening, open-eyed,
While I, for her sweet pleasure, read a tale
From some old story-book. I mind it well.
It told of lassies twain who went, one day,
Wandering, side by side, beyond the stream.
The one the miller's daughter; the other, —
I do forget, — but they were closest friends,
And ever mated at their sports and school.
They had free license wheresoe'er they would
To wander in their walks; only the bridge
Below the mill was interdicted them.
They might not cross at peril of their lives.

Slowly the children wandered to and fro,
Plucking the flowers on either side the path
That led adown the stream. They came, at last,
To where the old bridge trembled o'er the roar
Of falling waters; for the mill-stream now
Was at its time of flood. On the far shore
The miller's lass espied some crimson bells,
And eagerly set foot upon the bridge.
The other spake: "You know we must not cross."—
"But I will go," the miller's lass replied,
And went unto her death. The old plank broke,
Splintered in the midst, and the poor child fell
On the rough rocks below.
                          So sad a death
Sore grieved her parents; but they wept the more,

Because their child had disobedient been,
And in her sin had perished.
      "Good gracious!"
Broke sudden forth from little Lily's lips,
Sole commentary on the tale I'd told;
And the child's eyes grew rounder and more bright.
 . . . . . .

 I thought not then that she would never hear
That old-time tale again! How could I know
That but the passing of some briefest days,
And "dust to dust" was spoken o'er her grave,
And mine the voice that spake!

"The Night is far Spent; the Day is at Hand."—
Rom. xiii. 12.

 WHAT! dallying yet? Life is, at its best,
A shadow passing by. A wreath of foam,
Swept downward to the sea that buries all;
We cannot stay its course. Our puny hand,
Though armed as that which trained the lightning flash
As man's obedient slave, cannot arrest
The deathward flow of life; nor chain one soul
A willing prisoner in its walls of flesh.
To master these our skill is powerless;
And yet we dally, most unwise in heart,
O'er time that will not tarry for the prayer
Breaking from dying lips, all answerless;
And dally with our duty to our GOD!

 Awake! awake! put we our armor on!
Why do we sleep, when all sin's armëd hosts
Are thundering at our gates? Or while, more dread,
Its slow, insidious coils around our hearts
Are winding deathfully?
      Still dallying?
Know we, that he who slumbers at his post
Is playing 'gainst his soul such fearful odds,
That Satan smiles triumphant on the game
He feeleth sure to win!
      The past is past.
The present hour is ours, so guard we it,
And early consecrate our every power
Unto the GOD that made us what we are.
His yoke is easy, and his burden light;
And with a strong and everlasting Love
He keepeth all his own. From cradle-sleep,

Until the last of earth, his care shall be
About our daily paths ; and through the night,
The Builder of the everlasting hills
Doth watch above us keep.   No human love —
Though living through neglect and daily scorn,
Made stronger by the grave — but fades and dies,
If but within the shadow of his Love
Its feeble light dare shine !   No child of dust
Hath yet redeemed his brother at the cost
Of life or soul ; nor of himself hath wrought
His own salvation out.   We, born of earth,
Can frame no scheme to save the soul that dies
Beneath the curse of sin.   Only God's grace
Could shape the glorious plan !   Only God's love
Endure the Cross to save !
                     We know all this ;
Are taught the lesson while upon our brows
Baptismal dews are lying fresh and cool.
Yet all too oft the lesson is forgot ;
And blind, and deaf, we turn us from the Love
That fain would shield and save.   Alas ! the world
Hath snares too ready for unwary feet ;
And we are wooed, from out the narrow path,
By shapes of beauty that allure to sin.
Too easily we yield to earth's delights ;
And, swift of foot, press onward in the race
Whose goal we dream not may be only hell !

" Fading."

           WE have sweet dreams,
Some sunny hopes, some bright and smiling joys,
That we set up as idols in our hearts ;
But Father Time — that great iconoclast —
Hath never sparing hand, and at his touch
All earthly shapes do crumble into dust.
What careth he for beauty, or for pride ?
The first is but a flower, fragile, fair,
Blooming to perish when the first frosts fall.
The other, as some stately forest-tree
Struck down by lightning in its hour of noon,
Withered and blasted quite, shall be itself
The only monument of what hath been, —
The " whited sepulchre."

                    As that Locust,* known
In Trans-Atlantic wilds, with wings of rose
And thigh of emerald, eludes the eye, —
Seen for a moment on the bending leaf;
But, would you grasp it, straight evanishes,
And, lost in space, no more may greet your search, —
So, joys of earth, that, untouched, seem so fair,
Are shadows in our grasp.   Locust-like, also,
For that the beauty wedded unto life
Is seen not in the brown and dusty death
Tinting the insect like the withered leaves
Of golden autumn.

The Coming of the Spring.

Out in the sunshine, warm and sweet,
Soundeth the patter of little feet;
Merriest voices of childhood greet
            The coming of the Spring.

To and fro, in the balmy breeze,
Swing the tassel-blooms of the alder-trees;
And the maple flings its ensigns out,
Crimson and gold, to hail, no doubt,
            The coming of the Spring.

Under the eaves of the rocks so old,
The fern-leaves burst from their coiling fold,
To crown the stone with their soft caress,
Clothing it with beauty and gracefulness;
While down in the valley, and under the hill,
The brook it is singing, with right good will,
            The coming of the Spring.

Through the dead leaves on the island-shore,
The squirrel-cups raise their heads once more;
And, down by the brookside, the crocus pale
To the sparkling water is telling its tale
            Of the coming of the Spring.

Down in the valley and under the hill,
The violets gather, so softly and still;
Blue, and purple, and yellow, and white;
Smiling to greet, in the sun's warm light,
            The coming of the Spring.

* Locusto Transulto; found near the Rocky Mountains.

Under our footsteps, as onward we pass,
Lies the fragrant green of the vernal grass;
While over our heads shines the sky so blue;
Shining down, as to greet with its own bright hue
   The coming of the Spring.

A Souvenir of Easter-Eve, 1865.

The Dying Missionary.

YEARS ago I crossed the ocean, —
 Years ago I left my home;
Summer sunshine was upon it, —
 Sunshine, too, on ocean's foam.
Light and free the heart whose throbbings
 Were not then akin to pain;
Lighter still the joyous footsteps,
 Ne'er to be so light again.

Years ago! Ah! Time hath gathered
 All my life into his store;
Nought is left me but the record
 I shall need not any more.
Dust is lying on the pages
 Once so white and fair to see;
And, to-morrow, dust and ashes
 Will be all that's left of me.

What have I to carry with me
 To the far and Silent Land?
There's no wealth of lifelong earning,
 There's no treasure in my hand.
Naked on this world I entered, —
 Naked from it I must go;
But the grace of GOD hath clothed me, —
 Clothed me even here below.

Years ago I crossed the ocean
 To a wild and heathen shore;
Went, as priest, unto a people
 I had never known before.
How I strove and how I labored,
 This I care not now to tell;
But I made my people love me, —
 Made my people love me well.

Ah! the old familiar landscape, —
 Miles on miles of ocean-waves,

Seen through palm-trees gently waving
  O'er a few cross-bannered graves.
Far away the blue hills slumbered
  In the golden blaze of day.
At my feet the people gathered,
  Eager all to learn the Way.

Ah! I see the dusky faces,
  In the sunlight all aglow,
As I told the old, sweet story,
  Old a thousand years ago!
Mothers pressed their children closer, —
  Fathers, turning, smiled on them,
As they listened to the story
  Of the Child of Bethlehem.

Years ago! Ah! all who listened
  Then, have passed from earth away;
Gone before me through the portals
  Of the Everlasting Day.
Others sit where they were sitting, —
  Others sing the same sweet song;
But the old familiar faces
  Are not seen the new among.

Children, on whose brows I scattered
  Holy dews so pure and sweet,
Sleep beneath the waving palm-trees,
  Where the light and shadow meet.
They went from us in their promise
  Of a morning fair to see;
Went — to be forever children,
  Through the long eternity!

When the light of earth departeth,
  And returneth nevermore,
I shall see them — I shall meet them,
  On the bright and golden shore.
Hush! I see the palm-trees waving, —
  Hear the ripple on the shore;
And the voices of the children
  Singing, — singing, — "Evermore!"

The Days that Were.

Ah! they thought I had long forgotten
  Every haunt of my childhood's day;
Thought that remembrance of all things olden
  Had, with my youth-time, passed away.
But, clearer and sharper than later mornings,
  Rises the shape of the days that were.
Warm and sunny, — all sparkling and golden,
  Shine the days that are ever fair.

Down by the shore of the grand old river, —
  Rocks and beach are before me now,
Where I have played with the shining pebbles,
  And bathed in the water my heated brow.
O'er the old rocks, so slimy and slippery,
  Black and bare, when the tide was low,
Oft I have bounded with feet so fearless.
  I would not dare to tread them now!

Out in the woods there are quiet corners, —
  Stilly haunts where I loved to go;
Gathering flowers with busiest fingers,
  Keeping time with the brooklet's flow.
Purple violets out of the grasses,
  Crocus pale from the streamlet's side,
And basket, full of the varied mosses,
  Brought I home at the eventide.

Many a time have I curled into ringlets
  The dandelion's hollow stem;
Or blown its seeds into airy vagrance,
  And laughed in my glee, as I followed them;
Racing to keep the poor things from falling,
  Or wafting them hastily up in some tree.
Bubbles that burst in their rainbow splendor,
  Were not so bright nor so fair to me!

Oft in the heighth and the heat of summer
  Have I laid me down in the grasses deep;
Watching the butterflies float above me,
  Peering into some ant's sand-heap;
Wondering much, in my childish fancy,
  How these same ants got the sand-grains up.
I could tumble them down so easily;
  I could gather them in a cup.

All through June I had plenty of rambling;
 Strawberries waited in valley, on hill;
And little fingers were plying eagerly,
 Keeping pace with the feet that never were still.
Soon rosy-red were the busy fingers;
 Lips and cheeks were not unlike them;
And frock and pinafore, each were telling
 What fruit did grow on the pale green stem.

Many a time hath my frock been tattered,
 Many a time have my feet been wet,
Seeking for black-caps by crooked fences,
 Seeking the blackberry's balls of jet.
Little I cared for the old sun-bonnet,
 More often seen on shoulders than head;
Sometimes forgotten for days together.
 Nobody scolded, and nothing was said.

Later still in the autumn breezes,
 I was out in the woods to seek
Chestnuts guarded by wounding prickles,
 Butternuts browner than was my cheek.
Little I heeded the wounding prickles,
 And less the brown stains on my hands.
Happier I in my careless freedom,
 Than had I been lady o'er many lands!

Later years have brought other fancies, —
 Later years have brought higher dreams;
Yet I cling to my childhood's pastimes,
 And they are not forgotten themes.
Ah! but my heart must have ceased its throbbing,
 Have done with weariness and with pain,
Ere I can turn me from memory's glamour,
 And *not* dream the old time o'er again!

———◆———

"Love that Waiteth."

Love that waiteth, — who shall count its tears?
Or call the number of the weary years,
That, haunted by a sense of coming ill,
Did find it waiting, — left it waiting still?
I saw a picture once. It had no name.
The artist hand that traced it left to fame
No record of itself, and yet its touch
Had given life to thought. There was not much

To please a passing eye. Not very fair
The pictured face, but soul was written there.
A brow, nor high, nor low, where faintly, through
The smooth white skin, were shadowed lines of blue.
Dark braids of hair, full carelessly entwined,
That like a crown her shapely head did bind;
And lips that smiled, — a wan and patient smile,
That did mine eyes of some sad tears beguile;
But any careless gaze might note these things
And, passing on, forget them. Memory brings
Unto *my* heart, the meaning of the eyes
That, lighted by still patience, to the skies
Were looking evermore. I read that look
As if it had been written in a book.
Its tender trust, and, more than this, — the deep
And holy calm of patience that could keep
Its lonely vigil through a life of years,
Yet faint not, weary not, through hopes and fears,
That, as they were of daily life a part,
Did wrestle ever in that faithful heart.
Daily she stilled their turmoil, daily swept
All thoughts away, save one she ever kept
Shrined in her heart of hearts. A quiet thought
Of one beloved, who in far countries wrought
A bitter labor that she could not see
As a captive of the moor. Destiny
Of which she did not dream. As in an urn
Her heart did keep his words: "I shall return;"
And, with a quiet trust time made more strong,
She waited; and the years passed, weary, long,
Till, at the last, word came of him she loved.
How he had suffered much; how he had proved
The bitterness of bondage, and, set free,
Did seek again his old home by the sea.
He came. So faint and weary, sick and worn.
Could this be he, who left her that bright morn
Of the old time when both were young and fair,
And yet stood pale, and bent, and withered there?
Could this be he, so changed? Yet her true heart
Throbbed to his footfall, as, no more to part,
The loving met. Ay! for he, too, had kept
Her image sacred, and oft tears had wept
(Such tears as man may weep) o'er her sad lot, —
To wait, and wait, or deem her love forgot.
Their night hath caught its shadows all away;
The morning splendors shine upon their day.
The tale is told; the picture passed away.

" Nothing."

"NOTHING,"— only a little word,
  Falling like blight on a woman's heart;
"Nothing,"— only a shattered chord,
  Whence all the music must depart.

"Nothing,"— spoken in idleness,
  Or breathed through lips that are whitening fast;
"Nothing,"— a shadow more or less,
  But it darkeneth into night at last.

"Nothing,"— echoes of childish feet
  Die into silence before that word;
"Nothing,"— memories pure and sweet
  Are from the grave of long years stirred.

"Nothing,"— only a laugh of scorn,
  Stealing the love from some human soul;
"Nothing,"— yet wrath from a moment born,
  Shapeth clouds o'er a century's life to roll.

"Nothing,"— only a light word said,
  Tainting the faith GOD gave to the soul;
"Nothing,"— yet hopeless die the dead,
  And that soul hath wandered from its goal.

"Nothing,"— lightly we breathe the word,
  Idly we hear it, and let it go;
But a thousand streams are rudely stirred,
  Though only a passing zephyr blow.

"Nothing,"— hereafter we give account
  Of each idle word, each careless jest,
To meet us then as a poisoned fount,
  Or as arrow lodged in some loving breast.

"Nothing,"— GOD will not count it so;
  Since our poor heart may have power to bring
Nearer the day when our tears shall not flow,—
  Nearer the everlasting spring!

"Kept them in her Heart."

WE all do keep within our hearts
  A something valued most :
A look, a tone, a treasured word, —
  Thoughts of the loved and lost.

And highest dreams, and holiest hopes,
  The world nor recks, nor knows,
Find in the heart's own silentness
  A resting and repose.

Close sheltered from the outer world
  We keep that hidden shrine ;
A little less than worshipping,
  A thing not all divine.

Would we could keep that altar pure,
  Safe guarded from all sin,
So never shape with evil fraught
  Might fatal entrance win !

But ah ! the avenues of life
  Are full of deadly foes ;
Each waiting patient ; for the gate
  Once open, in it goes.

And, like a stream whose slimy tide
  O'er some fair garden flows,
Tainting the lily's whitest bloom,
  The glory of the rose, —

So to the heart's most secret shrine
  Each little sin doth go,
Polluting all its holiness,
  Laying its blossoms low ;

Till in the stead of pleasantness
  There's nought but hollow show ;
An outside fair indeed to view,
  But rottenness below.

Alas ! for all the goodly things
  That were the soul's delight !
A moment's slumbering at our post
  Hath spoiled their beauty quite.

We were not watching when the foe
    The fatal entrance found;
Our eyes were closed in careless sleep;
    Our banners on the ground.

Yet struggle on, beleaguered heart,
    There may be gain, not loss;
Death, only, closes all thy strife,
    O soldier of the Cross!

And not unaided, not alone,
    Shalt thou in battle be;
For He is ever on thy side,
    Who died on Calvary.

"The Quiet Life."

So they talk of my quiet life!
    I say, in an underbreath,
That they nothing know of the care and strife,
    And the agony beneath.
Quiet? As pools in the forest are, —
    Dark, and sluggish, and slow;
Whose waters, perchance, reflect a star,
    But a dead man sleeps below!

What do these people know of me?
    Only the outward show.
How can they read the mystery
    Of the heart that beats below?
They only look on the smiling brow,
    And the busy little hand;
And they think that the one hath work eno',
    And the other smiles at command.

They never dream that the work is done
    As a rest for the heart and brain;
That the smile on the patient forehead worn
    Is a mask to shut in the pain;
A mask that is worn throughout the day,
    To be flung aside at night,
When the watchful eyes are all away,
    And the shadows conquer light.

Ah! then the pain I have quelled so long
    Findeth its time of flood,

And rises sudden, and swift, and strong,
  No longer to be withstood.
And I bow my head to the bitter tide;
  And I suffer — ah! such pain!
I marvel oft that I have not died
  Ere the morning shone again.

Still they talk of my quiet life,
  And I give for answer back,
That men have slept 'mid the battle strife,
  And martyrs on the rack.
And what if exhaustion follow pain,
  And the days go silently?
I know that the night will bring again
  That deathless agony.

So they may talk of my quiet life, —
  I say, in an underbreath,
That they nothing know of the care and strife,
  And the agony beneath.
Quiet? As pools in the forests are, —
  Dark, and sluggish, and slow;
Whose waters, perchance, reflect a star,
  But a dead man sleeps below!

A Hope.

On what frail threads we mortals hang our hopes!
No spider's web half so attenuate.
And yet, how very fair these same hopes are;
Outshining far the tiny drops of dew
That on the spider's web suspended hang,
To sparkle diamonded by the morning sun!
Ah! hopes so fair, what mocking imps ye are!
No ignis fatuus lurking in the swamps
Doth lead th' unwary traveller such a race,
Ending perchance in death, as ye do us.
Wooed by the rainbow splendor of your light,
We follow where you lead, unheeding where;
Until the darkness swallows you, and we
Are left unto the loneliness and night.

Years since — I dare not count how many times
The summer roses followed winter's snow —
A hope dawned sweet within my quiet heart.

It was a thing of April's changeful mood;
Too near the earth to 'scape the lot of earth, —
Half shadow and half sunshine, — yet it made
Itself the world to me, and all my life
Resolved into itself.   Variableness
Did seem its essence; and, Proteus-like,
It made all shapes its own; endowed all thoughts
With something of itself, until my life
Was but a reflex of that one fair hope.

This hope did reign most royally; kept rare state;
All other hopes its loving subjects were;
While every thought and feeling owned its sway,
Its "lawful rule and right supremacy."
Its reign was absolute by day and night;
Each hour did render its sweet homage up,
And all my world was lying at its feet.

This hope did grow a giant, brave and strong,
That let no meaner shadow creep within
The compass of its own, but filled all space.
No other hope, that sought in hardihood
To hold its own, but rued its rashness soon
In dull annihilation, or was wrapt
Into that kingly hope, and lost itself
Amid commingling atoms.   All thoughts bent,
By rare attraction driven, unto it;
And little things grew mighty when they came
Within the circle of its broad domain.

This hope was fair.   More fair than any dream
The poets ever fabled.   Summer gave
Its glory of the morning unto it;
All phases of the seasons cherished it;
The gleaming waters and the changing sky
Did glass its beauty.   Yea, all nature seemed
The lovelier for the hope that brightened it.

This hope was patient; for the long years went,
And brought it nothing for the wealth it gave.
Yet burned it on, as yonder planet burns;
Its light unquenched, though cloud and tempest shut
The shining glory out!
              This hope so sweet
Had borne the brunt of many a fierce fight,
And walked the battle-field victorious.
Yea; it had looked on tears that, when they fell,
Seemed blood-drops from the heart; and heard such moans

As seem a part of death, they torture so.
This hope so fair, so changeless, and so true,
Hath died a thousand deaths, yea; lain in graves
O'er which methought no resurrection dawned;
Yet ere that thought could shape itself in words,
The living hope smiled on me as of old —
As now — as ever!
     Only when I die
This one hope dieth too.   Let " dust to dust "
Be spoken over me, and in my heart,
Its home no more, this hope shall find its grave.
I dare not say that in the other world
It hath a resurrection!

The Bluebird.

HEARD ye the bluebird sing?
There's promise of the spring
  In every song she singeth.
Clear, sweet, and musical,
Upon mine ear they fall,
  And memories glad each bringeth.

The winter's snow lies still
On every slope and hill,
  Pure in its virgin whiteness;
While on the river's breast
The waves enchainēd rest,
  Gleaming in noonday brightness.

Yet doth the bluebird sing,
As though it knew the spring
  Over the earth was stealing.
Its song doth tell the earth
Of the flowers' coming birth
  In shadowy revealing.

Ere the uprisen sun
Our day hath yet begun,
  I hear the bluebird singing.
It seemeth unto me,
Herald of what must be
  When the woods with songs are ringing.

The coming of the spring,
What joyance it doth bring
  Unto the happy-hearted!

As if all grief, and pain,
And tears that fall like rain,
   With winter had departed.

And spring, with footsteps light,
Brought sunshine warm and bright,
   To fill the golden hours;
While fast on every slope,
Like harbingers of hope,
   Shoot up the little flowers.

O merry hearts and free!
The spring-time is to ye
   As the sweet flow of a story
Upon whose waves we glide
By some beloved one's side,
   From glory unto glory.

Heard ye the bluebird sing?
Its glad song yet doth ring
   Across the winter morning;
And in my heart and eyes,
An answering gladness lies.
   I see the spring-time dawning!

"Be not Weary."—2 Thess. iii. 13.

WHAT! must we falter — turn half back —
For that the way we tread is not so smooth,
But steep and rough, and seemeth very long
Unto our weary feet? Life is no day
That, bright with sunshine and unclouded skies,
Shall only close, when death, a quiet sleep,
Shall take us hence away; no dream of bliss,
That lulling heart and soul in all delights,
Shall float us gently on our earthly course;
To find, when heaven's shores are reached and won,
Its sole awakening. Not thus, nor so,
Must our probation be.
           Since that dark day
When man, by sinning, lost the Eden bowers,
The watchful Angel of the Flaming Sword
Doth stand between him and the happy groves
Wherein GOD walked of old. No feet of earth,
Sin-stained, and erring, e'er have pressed the sod

Of that fair garden; and no human eyes
Have looked upon its beauty, or beheld
The bloom of Paradise.
      Was not the earth
Cursed for the sin of man? Therefore we toil
To win our daily bread. Therefore we find
Our daily paths so hedged about with thorns;
While snares, and pitfalls manifold, are there
To catch the unwary feet. Therefore our lives
Are as a burden that we must take up
And carry to our graves. It must be borne.
We cannot lay it down, as of ourselves,
But at such fearful cost as a soul lost
Through all the hereafter. It *must* be borne, —
This burden that grows heavier, day by day;
And this stern "must" is written on our lives.
We see it, feel it; yet our eager hands
Are ever seeking how to change the load
The shoulders weary of, — how to fling it off, —
If their poor skill might serve to compass that, —
Or else, to lighten it. Of what avail?

I know a secret, worth the hearing, here.

What if a man should lift the burden up,
And bear it cheerfully, as one might bear
A flower in the hand; and, smiling, tread
The thorny path that lies before his feet?
What if his steadfast eyes, securely fixed
Upon the certain goal, should never see
The weary roughness of the path he treads,
Or, seeing, heed it not? What if his feet,
(No stumbling on the mountains dark for them)
Upheld by secret strength, should falter not,
But press on nobly to the Land so fair
Faith gives him sight to see? What if his lips
Go softly singing all the weary way
A hymn of praise to GOD? What if his heart —
Though not unconscious of life's bitterness,
And suffering keenly every pang life gives —
Have yet within itself a balm for all;
And will not dash away the Marah-cup,
But drain it to the dregs; nor turn aside
From the rough path? Have not some holiest feet
(The feet a sinful woman washed with tears)
Left sacred traces on the path he treads?
And shall he fear to follow where those feet,
Those wounded feet, have been? What if the soul,

With prescient eye, doth look beyond the earth,
And sees, far-shining, the eternal crown
Awaiting aye the victor in the strife?
And victor in the strife he still must be
Who owns himself a soldier of the Cross,
A follower of the Lamb!

----•----

The Tress of Hair.

ONLY a tress of nut-brown hair,
Yet it told of some distant hills,
Where out in the sunshine, close by the rills,
  A little grave was made
    Some twenty years ago.
Summer's breezes, soft and low,
O'er that grassy hillock blow;
  Winter winds above the snow
  With a bitter moaning go;
    But the little maid,
Whose dust is lying all below,
  Heeds neither wind nor cold.
  Underneath that senseless mould,
    Sounds of earth reach not to her;
    Summer breezes cannot stir
The wavings of that nut-brown hair;
    All that now is left of her,
Save the dust that was so fair
    Twenty years ago!

Winter sunsets glow and shine
On the hills dark-clothed with pine,
    Where her dust is lying;
    But waters of an Eastern sea
That lave the Australasian Isles,
    Shall chant his requiem;
    And wealth of nature's empirie,
And lavish splendor of her smiles,
    Crown, as a diadem,
The little valley where he lies,
Beneath the light of golden skies
    That flame when day is dying.
      So far apart are they
Who in the old familiar days
Stood hand in hand, beneath the rays
    Of one bright summer day.
It saw them part. No more—no more—

To meet on sea, or meet on shore;
And severed wide, by all the space
O'er which the sun hath run his race
While half a day is flying.
The dust of each must rest in sleep;
And neither knew when *one* must weep
Above the *other*, dying!

Shadows.

Ah! between us a shadow lies,
Not to be seen by human eyes,
But I feel it at my heart's core,
Something intangible, dark, and cold,
That up from the depths of distrust hath rolled
And it darkeneth evermore.

Ah between us a shadow lies;
And never light of summer skies
Can shut that crescent shadow out.
Slowly it groweth, of darkest hue,
And all that was fairest, and all most true,
Doth seem as o'erladen with doubt.

Ah! between us a shadow lies.
I miss the love-light in your eyes;
The warmth and sunshine of your smile;
And my bark of hope that sailed so far,
On-guided by a treacherous star,
Is wrecked upon a barren isle.

" Parted."

Parted! the world goes on the same.
Suns rise and set, days come and go;
And yet through all this ebb and flow
Of evening's dusk, and morning's flame,
A something from my life hath gone;
And all the years that come to me,
Each fraught with its own mystery,
Will find me in the dark alone.

Parted! never to meet again!
  The darkness fadeth with the night;
  Ever the morning bringeth light;
And sunshine cometh after rain;
But never morrow brings to me
  The tender clasp of *one* true hand.
  Alone upon my hearth I stand;
No loving eyes look down on me.

Parted! a short and bitter word,
  That falls like frost on life's young spring,
  Till all its flowers are withering.
It pierceth me like any sword;
And yet I cannot heal the pain.
  All throbs of joy most exquisite,
  All loving passionate and sweet,
Will never come to me again!

Parted! and I am lonely now.
  The years to be may come and go;
  And I may live till age's snow
Lies heavy on my weary brow.
May live, and in still patience wait
  (Learning from ashes and from dust,
  In Whom my soul should put its trust)
Till openeth the Golden Gate.

Barbara.

Ah! but I love him, dearly, dearly;
  All my world in his presence lies;
Thrilleth my heart to the touch of his fingers,
  And owneth its sunshine in his eyes.
Only the sound of his voice to be hearing;
  Only the smile on his face to see;
A little thing this, save unto the loving,
  But it contenteth me.
Ah! but I love him, dearly, dearly;
  Better, I think, than he loves me;
Only my lips are so slow to utter
  What his say so tenderly.

"Once there lived a King in Thulé."

"ONCE there lived a king in Thulé,"
  Near a thousand years ago,
But his name hath been forgotten;
  On his grave the tall trees grow.
Stones that were framed in his palace
  Have been ground into the clay;
All of him, save one brief story,
  Long ago did pass away.

"Once there lived a king in Thulé"
  (Peasant lips the story tell),
Who, despite his royal splendor,
  Loved a peasant-maiden well;
And he would have had her crownëd,
  Crownëd, queenëd, in a breath;
But for One who came between them.
  No light wooer is King Death.

Dawned a fair and golden morning
  (Meet are such for bridal-day),
But no bride was there to greet it, —
  In her shroud the maiden lay.
And unto the king they bore her,
  With a slow, unequal pace;
Brought her near that he might gather
  All the silence in her face.

Peace unto the broken-hearted!
  Words are empty, — words are vain.
Never on that kingly gazer
  Will that sweet face smile again!
Hush! they go from out his presence, —
  They, the bearers, one by one;
And the stricken king of Thulé
  By that hushed heart stands alone!

"Once there lived a king in Thulé,'
  Faithful was he unto death;
Never wooed he other maidens, —
  So the olden story saith.
But he framed with loving fingers
  As a true heart might devise,
A gold cup in her sweet memory,
  And he made it on this wise.

For the stand two hands were claspĕd,
　And they held a lily up.
Only this, — but through a long life
　Used the king no other cup.
And when life was slowly passing,
　In his weak and trembling hands,
Held the king the lily-goblet.
　What says he of "other lands?"

Nay, we know not.　All is over;
　And the heart so faithful lies
Still and cold within the palace,
　For the king of Thulé dies.
And, through all the ages after
　(Nothing known of lineage, name),
Floats the old familiar story,
　All of him that's left to Fame.

———◦◇◦———

"Too Late."

NAY; I am dying.　All too late
　Your proffered love doth come.
Had it been given years ago,
Death had not mocked the offering so.
　Now I am going home!

Nay; I am dying.　See you not
　How vain all love must be?
It could not steal one hour from death, —
It could not give one added breath
　Of this poor life to me.

Nay; I am dying.　Better so;
　You will not miss me long.
The love through all these years forgot,
Is but a thing that was — is not —
　And lieth graves among.

And I am dying! Even now
　I go to my last sleep;
And earth shall have, by morning shine
(The sole thing left of all was mine),
　A little dust to keep.

June.

Waiting under the apple-boughs,
  Sat a maiden, young and fair,
Heaven's own blue was in her eyes,
  Its sunshine on her waving hair.

Breezes balmy, fresh and sweet,
  Were idly blowing everywhere;
While o'er her head the apple-blooms
  Did fill with fragrance all the air.

Low at her feet a brooklet ran
  With silvery singing to the sea;
And peeping from their grassy couch
  The purple violets decked the lea.

A few light clouds did fleck the sky, —
  White snow-drifts on a field of blue;
And in the meadows, far and near,
  Daisies and clover-blossoms grew.

Sitting under the apple-boughs,
  Through all the summer afternoon,
The maiden waited; lips and heart
  Were singing softly one sweet tune.

And fast the happy hours flew;
  Love touched them with his rosy wing;
For Hope, and Joy, and Life also,
  With her were only in their spring.

"Spero Meliora."

A Scutcheon, bearing this device, was found on the Sable Island
sole record of some noble vessel lost.

Tossed on the shore of the Sable Isle,
  A waif from the stormy sea,
Was a blazed scutcheon, carvëd fair
  With device of heraldry.
And out from the shore so rough and bare,
  From the sands so drenched and cold,
"Spero meliora" flashed and flamed,
  With its letters of burning gold.

Far, far away on a bonny knowe,
  The Calder-House standeth yet;
And over its porch, and over its hearth,
  Is that golden motto set;
Long centuries since, it was carvëd there;
  It hath storm and time defied.
How came its semblance on this far shore,
  Tossed by the rising tide?

A haughty race were the Sandilands all,
  And proud of their ancient fame;
For they traced to the days of David Bruce
  The record of their name.
A Stuart maiden had wedded one;
  For dower, her noble blood;
And another had wooed and won a wife
  From the haughty Douglas brood.

And Calder-House hath its own romance,
  And its tales of the days of eld;
And much it boasts that it was here John Knox
  His first communion held.
Blood hath been red on the oaken stairs,
  But the stains have been washed away;
And the silence of years lieth like a pall
  On the tale of that olden fray.

  .   .   .   .   .   .

Under the blue of a summer sky,
  The birds were singing on every tree;
And glad of the sunshine, warm and sweet,
  Laugheth the little burn merrily.
Over the sward, 'neath the birchen trees,
  Slowly pacing, two lovers were:
One was the heir of the Calder-House;
  One but a peasant maiden fair.

Tall and stately, and fair of face,
  As well his father's son might be;
Loving and courteous, brave and free,
  True, and gentle, and leal was he.
Proud he might be of his ancient name
  (Pride was the Sandilands' dower),
But he would not stoop so to stain its white
  By spoiling a simple flower.

And she? no flower in all the land
  Was half so sweet and fair;
And he loved the touch of that little hand,
  And the glint on her waving hair.

Well he knew that in all the world
　　Was no other love so dear
As the love throbbing sweet in that little heart,
　　Shining out from those eyes so clear.

And more he knew, — that he could not bring
　　That little nameless flower
Through the dark porch of the Calder-House,
　　Into its Lady's Bower.
But down in his heart of hearts he had vowed
　　That the flower should be his bride,
Though he left the home and the lands of old
　　To roam through the world so wide.

He wrote the vow in a sealëd book,
　　And she never saw the page ;
Else the heir of the Sandilands had gone forth
　　Alone on his pilgrimage.
This woman-heart, so loving and true,
　　Would have lived and died alone,
Had she known his thought, — but she never knew it ;
　　And together they have gone !

Many a summer came and went,
　　Bringing sunshine to the burn ;
But for the two who once wandered there,
　　Was never the word " return."
And year after year swept wearily on,
　　O'er the same old beaten track ;
But never a year of all that went by
　　Did bring the lost heir back.

The lord of the Calder-House mourned full long
　　For his first-born and his last,
Till silence fell, like a mantle, o'er
　　The story of the past,
And rarely now, save in cottage old,
　　(And then with secret dread),
Was the sad tale told of the vanished heir, —
　　Was he living ? was he dead ?

Tossed on the shore of the Sable Isle,
　　A waif from the stormy sea,
Was a blazoned scutcheon, carvëd fair
　　With device of heraldry.
And out from the shore so rough and bare,
　　From the sands so drenched and cold,
" Spero meliora " flashed and flamed,
　　With its letters of burning gold !

" Jacob Moor, Ob. 2 June, 1758. æt. 44."

Inscription on a coffin found on the shore of Spitzbergen.

ALONE he sleeps, amid eternal snows.
A coffin rude doth cradle the repose
That hath no waking; and the moveless eyes
Look alway upward to the changeful skies.
The sailor rests on bleak Spitzbergen's shore,
And there hath lain a hundred years or more;
No lines effaced; no human features lost;
Touched into marble by the eternal frost.

A hundred years! they could a story tell
Of some poor hearts, that, loving long and well,
Did patient wait upon a sunnier shore
For the pale sleeper who returned no more.
Alas! for weariness of waiting hours
That stole some beauty from the fairest flowers;
While unseen shadows from the far away
Crept o'er the sunshine of the summer-day!
A thousand voices came on every breeze
That stirred the leaves of the familiar trees
Around the cottage growing, — voices low
That floated, wind-borne, from the untrodden snow,
To tell their story of the frozen slope
Where *he* was lying, and to crush out hope.
But loving ears are deaf; they do not heed
The tale the winds have told. Hope plants such seed
In human hearts, that when the germ takes root
'Tis ineradicable, — bearing fruit
Both sweet and bitter. It but *seems* to die;
But in the passion of its agony
Hath evermore new birth; doth upward rise,
When the freed soul is hasting to the skies;
And in the world beyond, secure from strife,
It hath its rest; it hath eternal life.
Not tempest-tossed as here, — rocked to and fro
By every billow, — flung from sun to snow, —
But safely anchored on the further shore,
And in sure haven guarded evermore.

So we believe they waited, — those who wore
No mourning garments for poor Jacob Moor.
Not unto them came tidings of the fate
That left their quiet home all desolate;
And so they waited; until hope grew dim

As faithful unto death they watched for him.
The years went, slowly; but ere fifty sped
Each patient heart was resting with the dead,
And crumbling into dust; while, far away,
Beneath the eternal stars or glare of day,
His form was lying; changeless, as if death,
Who hushed the witness of the sleeper's breath,
Had taught unto himself a strange device,
And given, not dust to dust, but ice to ice.

It matters not, unto what burial
We give the dead.   Beneath the royal pall
The dust that lieth is but only dust;
And wave-tossed bodies (that may have a crust
Of cold wet sand above them, some fair day)
Are on the self-same journey, — the same way.
Severed as wide as pole from pole, on earth,
Are kings on thrones, and peasants by their hearth;
But one doom comes to all: death, and the grave,
Alike inevitable.   No strength can save;
No human art avail; and end all must,
With hearts to silence, and with dust to dust.
Rest we content, where'er our dust may be,
In earth's safe bosom, or beneath the sea,
Since GOD will give it immortality.

———•◦•———

A Dream of Youth, and the End thereof.

"Oh! but this world is a rare sweet world,
   It hath neither cloud nor storm;
And never a touch of Decay's cold hand
   Doth its beauty fair deform.

"Sweet in its valleys the flowerets bloom,
   To be gathered by gentlest hands;
And the sunlight, evermore soft and warm,
   Shineth golden on the lands.

"Quietness dwelleth above this world —
   There is never turmoil nor jar;
And the warring clang of embattled hosts
   Is heard not 'neath sun nor star.

"Peace, as a dove, broodeth in all haunts
   Where the human hearts may be;
And the freest hands and the truest souls
   Are found over land and sea.

"Clamor and wrath are as things unknown,
    And envy hath never room
In the simple hearts where a doubt comes not
    With its shadow and its gloom.

"Oh! but this world is a rare sweet world!
    We will make its beauty ours,
And sleep and wake, as the days go on,
    'Mid its sunshine and its flowers."

So dreameth Youth, while the morning light
    Falleth rosy on his way;
But a change o'er his dream cometh slow and sure
    With the fading of the day.

He hath gathered the flowers, or passed them by,
    For that fairer bloomed before;
He hath thrown them aside; yet none so sweet
    Will the future have in store.

He thinketh not so.   What his hand doth hold
    Is a thing of little worth;
What the future bringeth — ah! there shall be
    The whole glory of the earth!

The noon burned down on the morning's bloom,
    And the flowers are faded — dead —
And the evening heareth, far-off and slow,
    Over desert sands, his tread.

The night stealeth soft, with a stealthy pace,
    O'er the world he had thought so fair;
And its shadows are folding him unto sleep;
    And the sands of Death lie bare!

Night, with no shining of moon or star
    To light the way for him,
Closeth dark o'er his path, so lone — so cold —
    The very heavens are dim!

The world, so fair in his dew of youth,
    Lieth cold, and bleak, and bare;
And dark at his feet yawns an open grave,
    And the dust and the worm are there!

Where now are the blossoms so fresh and sweet?
    Where now are the golden skies?
Their beauty, their glory, have vanished all,
    And blackness over them lies.

Long since came Doubt with its poison-cup,
　　And the youth drank deep and long;
For the wine was sparkling, the foam-drops clear,
　　But the poison beneath was strong.

It dulled the beat of his throbbing heart
　　To a measure calm and cold;
Till up from their den came the shadows of hell,
　　And its mists about him rolled.

Swiftly, as fogs o'er the moorland creep,
　　Came those shadows around his path;
But he braved them all in his pride of youth;
　　He felt so strong in his wrath.

They wasted away, as the pale moon dies
　　When a cloud obscures its light;
But they gathered their forces as they went;
　　They fought as the Parthians fight.

He thought he was victor; but in his veins
　　The poison was flowing still;
And they mocked with a laughter low, not sweet,
　　At the boast of that human will.

So the years went on; and the world grew dark
　　That had been so bright and fair;
And Truth was not Truth, and over all Hope
　　Had fallen a cold Despair.

What hath this soul of its old self retained,
　　So to keep beyond the years?
What hath it garnered of precious things,
　　From the world of hopes and fears?

I have read, in a parable old, yet new,
　　Of a chamber garnished, swept,
Whence a devil had gone out; but the place
　　For his sure return was kept.

And he came again with sevenfold strength
　　To the place that was his of yore;
And finding it ready, he entered in,
　　So entering for evermore.

Thus the soul, that had fought in its day of youth
　　With the gathered hosts of hell,
Had left open its gates, and its foes had found
　　A place wherein to dwell.

Doubt's poisoned cup had well wrought its work,
    For a shuddering soul was lost;
And a fearful price, and a bitter fee,
    Had the sparkling poison cost.

Yea, the wealth of a soul that GOD had made
    Had been flung upon the dice;
And hell had well earned the bitter fee,
    And the youth, he paid it twice!

Once, when the pureness of earth was but held
    As a thing to be bought and sold;
Till the dark had been light to the night of that soul
    Which had bartered its wealth for gold.

And again — when the soul that the Father had given
    To be kept so clean from sin,
Had made broad the path — had set wide the gate —
    For the devils to enter in.

And they entered in — and the soul possessed —
    Was it accursed of GOD?
Its cry unheard at the Mercy Seat?
    Unfelt GOD's chastening rod?

No judges are we of our brother's life;
    There is no omniscience in man;
Nor can we aright, with our erring eyes
    The ways of the Deity scan.

Above the dust that once held this soul
    We spread the funeral pall;
And over it, solemnly, echo such words
    As one readeth at burial.

But it seemeth a strange and a horrible thing,
    Said in mockery of all bliss,
To give unto dust, " in the sure hope of heaven,"
    Such a sinful life as this.

We know that our lives are in shadow here, —
    That GOD seeth not as we;
And the souls *we* may shrink from as all unclean,
    May *His* chiefest angels be.

Yet still it seemeth a mockery
    Of all holy words and true,
To breathe them o'er dust that in human eyes
    Had guilt of the blackest hue.

We know " we see darkly, as through a glass,"
    But no clearer sight is given :
And if, in our blindness, we judge all wrong,
    Shall we be forbidden heaven?

What if the church forbade funeral rites,
    Unto all persistent sin ;
And found not, in any her holy ground,
    A place for its dust to rest in?

It might chance, that at resurrection-day,
    Some dust, unhallowed by prayer,
Might arise from its slumber *without the gate*,
    And stand at Christ's right hand there!

What if it were so?   *Our* eyes cannot see
    Through the dark veil of the flesh ;
But GOD. *he* knoweth, if through soiling and stain,
    The soul remain pure and fresh.

So it may be well that our mother, the church,
    Hath a larger heart than we,
And veils, with her love, all the sin of the dead,
    If only for charity.

And charity covereth a thousand sins,
    And veileth unwearyingly
All the sin-stained clay that is lying low
    Where the dust and silence be.

Whither?

OUR life is but a span ; a shadow brought
From other worlds, and into being wrought
By the one breath of GOD ; and at his will
He taketh back the life ; or good — or ill —
To wait the judgment-day.   Our race is run ;
Our course is ended, and our work all done.
Men fling above the cold and lifeless shell,
Within whose walls the human soul did dwell,
The dust of earth ; or shut in marble tomb
The shape that had been glorious in bloom ;
Or strong in strength ; or crownëd with such fire
As doth the artist-hand, or poet-pen inspire.

We give dust unto dust; but where doth go
The never-dying soul?   We do not know:
Save that the Father to himself hath taken
The spirit home; so not of him forsaken
Who holdeth it in life.   And more than this,
We dare not say we *know*.   If unto bliss, —
The glory GOD reserveth for his own, —
Or unto darkness, the freed soul hath gone,
We cannot *know;* but far and high above
All clouds of doubt, doth shine the sun of love;
And in its shining is a promise sweet,
That bids all fear and deathly darkness fleet
Before its glory; transfiguring all,
That else were only dust beneath the pall.

Upon life's ocean doth a Presence ride;
And on the rising and the falling tide,
We see the Shadow of the Crucified, —
The Shape of One, who for us lived and died.
And through the years there floats a wondrous song,
Fresh from the lips of an unnumbered throng,
That alway, day and night, are praising GOD!
Yea; unto us, in this, our earth-abode,
Doth sound forever, from immortal lips,
The glorious chant of the Apocalypse.

"Now, unto Him, that hath redeemëd us
From out all nations, sanctifying thus
A people unto him, be glory, power,
Praise and blessing, dominion every hour!
For he hath redeemëd us by his blood,
And made us kings and priests unto GOD;
And we shall reign on the earth!" and again —
We hear the wording of the glad refrain:
" Blessing and honor, and glory and power,
Be unto Him that sitteth on the throne,
And to the Lamb forever and ever! " —
"And the four beasts said, Amen!"

"The wind bloweth where it listeth, and thou hearest the sound thereof, but canst not tell whence it cometh, or whither it goeth." * — St. John iii. 8.

YEA; even so,
We cannot tell, nor do *we* know,
How to this shell,
Wherein the living soul doth dwell,
That soul did come;
Making its earthly home,
'Mid these poor walls of clay.
We do not know from whence it came,
Nor through what gate, nor by what way;
Yet let us bid it welcome, in GOD'S name.
For I have thought,
When looking on some child's sweet face,
That I could therein trace,
The loving Hand that wrought,
The beauty there;
And I have read, in silent awe,
Within the pure, clear eyes,
A shadow of GOD'S law;
As if the soul,
· So lately come from out GOD'S hand,
All innocent of sin,
Bore yet his impress fair.
And when he gathers in,
As oft he doth, the wee lambs of the fold,
It seemeth unto me,
That in the falling of their sweet life's sand,
They come and go;
And so,
We only see
Them passing from GOD'S hand that gives,
Unto GOD'S hand that takes.
Each little one forsakes
The fold for earthly shelter given,
And lives
For evermore in heaven;
So going home unto its native land!

But when in strength and fulness of all years,
And having gained the stature of a man,
And lived out its alloted span,

* As applied here, this quotation has no reference to its context.

The soul doth leave its shell,
And journeys on elsewhere to dwell,
Forever done with hopes and fears;
Where doth the spirit go?
We know,
When from the mountain's brow the torrent leaps,
That some day soon its downward flow
In the far ocean sleeps.
Our eyes can trace its long and devious way;
Follow its turnings and its course attend;
But when the soul
Upon its outward course doth wend,
We cannot say
Unto what heighths or depths its flight shall tend;
We see no certain goal!

We know that GOD will keep our dust;
And in this trust
We give the forms of our belovĕd unto earth;
And in no dearth
Of hope so give them; but the soul
That made that dust so fair,
Is no more there;
Hath passed beyond our ken;
Is known no more amid the haunts of men.
Ere death did ope the door,   .
Its dwelling was with rich or poor;
It once informed the clay,
And looked from out its windows of the eyes;
But darkness lies
On those closed windows, and the day
No more is mirrored in them; far away,
The soul that gave them light is journeying
Unto another world — another spring, —
We know not where!
Perchance in Paradise
It resteth from its labor, waiting there
The resurrection-morning!
GOD grant that in the sunburst of its dawning
It bring us life that passeth not away;
That hath no closing day!
Not with a fitful fire burning,
And soon to ashes turning,
But glorious as the everlasting Light
That needeth not the sun;
For we shall dwell where never cometh night,
Where the day is never done;
For the LORD the Light thereof shall be,

And there is no star nor moon,
But an eternal noon;
A glory inapproachable,
Wherein the soul shall dwell.

There is neither hunger nor thirst;
There, the last shall be the first;
There, sorrow and death are all forgot
And tears are not;
There, Time shall be no more;
And, o'er and o'er,
Is heard the song that none may know
Save the thousands — "one hundred and forty-four" —
Redeemĕd from the earth
As the first fruits of the Lamb.
There, robed in white,
And aureola-crowned, shall stand
The holy martyr band;
Whose souls, through torture and the burning flame,
Went up to GOD.
There, they who "through much tribulation came,"
And thorny pathways trod;
And who flung down
The world and life as things of little worth,
As shadows of this earth,
Being found faithful unto death,
Shall wear the crown.
He that is Faithful, saith,
" Behold, I give unto them a crown of life,
And they shall reign with me
And share my glory everlastingly."

Not to the grave,
Where beauty, strength and weakness must
Be all resolved to dust;
Where pomp and power,
Strength of oak and fragileness of flower,
Alike shall pass away;
Not to the grave look we to find the soul,
That, gone from out the clay,
Hath no more lodging there;
But, free as air,
Doth wander through illimitable space,
Where,
If our spirit eyes could see
Through veiling flesh, we might discern
Each sweet familiar face;
And know

How very near each franchised soul might be,
And haply learn
How alway watch and ward they keep
Alike o'er hours of waking, hours of sleep.
How round about our paths they stand,
And with their loving and yet unseen hand
Do wipe away our tears;
And unto hearts with anguish riven
Do whisper low, through all the years,
Of coming joy and heaven.

Behold! a cloud lies darkly on our way;
We see no glory of the far-off sky;
The gladness hath departed from our day;
Our lips are moaning in wild agony,
And in our hearts some grave doth open lie.
Then comes a sense of something standing near,
A presence that doth cause no fear,
A shape we cannot see;
And yet it brings
Soft on its viewless wings,
A comfort rare and sweet,
That we cannot live without.
We feel, close folding us about
The clasp of unseen arms;
And oft,
A kiss pressed soft
Upon the quivering lip or aching brow.
I say not this is so;
And yet the thought hath charms.
Nay, it hath a spell of might
That shutteth out the night,
For the clouds are breaking.   Fast and fleet
The olden glory fills the sky again;
(The sun it shineth after the rain)
And o'er the grave that was of joy the tomb,
The grass grows greenly, and the flowers bloom!

I say not this is so;
But I believe it, and the thought
Is with rare comfort fraught;
And when I go,
Across the river that doth flow
Between two worlds, and leaving, as I must,
"Ashes to ashes, dust to dust,"
I shall return again;
To light the fire that hath gone out
Upon some stone-cold hearth,

Leaving no spark,
To bring back sunshine to the earth
That sorrow hath made dark;
To give of water the "one cup"
That bears the fainting spirit up
Until it reach the further shore;
To whisper hope when hope seems dead;
To strengthen Faith; to tread down Doubt,
And crush it evermore;
To watch o'er my beloved, and, if I may,
To keep them pure from stain
And soiling of the clay;
To make more smooth the thorny paths they tread;
Counting it no loss
To help them bear their cross,
That else so low might weigh them down
That in their weariness they faint,
Take up no more that burden of the saint,
And so should miss the crown!

It were a holy thing,
With deep joy fraught,
If but my soul, with quietness, should bring
Unto some dying and beleaguered soul,
Fast wandering from its goal,
A saving thought!
If but my soul in other souls could sow
Some precious seed, and know
The golden grain
Should one day soon be waving o'er that plain
Where shines God's sun to keep out rust, —
Where God's rain falleth, as it must,
In silence through the world's loud din;
Where the harvests ripen evermore
Into such rare and goodly store,
As the angels gather in; —
If but my soul could do all this,
It were a foretaste of that bliss,
Which the angels in heaven know,
When the sinner turneth from his lust
And repenteth of his sin.
If but my soul —
I find no "but" herein.
I trust
That all this shall be so.
I will forego
Not one iota of this coming bliss.
A joy it is —

Ere yet the shadow of the heavy pall
    Shall o'er me fall —
        To know
That, in the dark, yet glorious day
When all the earth-stains fall away
And the hereafter dawneth, that I may
    A ministering spirit be!

What though this problem of the soul's employ
        To some may seem
    A solemn and unsolvëd mystery
        Not to be idly broken, —
A high and holy truth, though yet unspoken,
    Whereof men only dream,
And err much in their dreaming? — I have joy
And strong, deep faith in this my theory.

        We do not see
The shadows of our dead about us moving,
        With care so loving.
The veil of flesh shuts all that vision out;
    Yet shall we therefore doubt?
The why and wherefore of our very life
    Is all a mystery, and yet we live!
(Some doubting minds have doubted even that,
    So leaving not one airy pinnacle
As treacherous rest for their uncertain feet.)
The child's first cry doth witness give
        Of breathing life
That doth within the little body dwell;
And yet, whence came that life, or how?
    And whither doth it fleet?
    We have not yet
Solved that grand problem; still we do believe,
    And that with little strife,
That the child liveth. This we think we know;
But more than this doth lie beyond our ken;
And all the long and deep research of men,
    Hath never yet resolved what spot
In all the curious mechanism of the form,
    Holds life, or holds it not.
    It hath been thought
That life did dwell within the busy brain;
    A dream with error fraught;
Since many a hideous wound lets out
The oozing brain, yet life remains,
    And puts this fancy all to rout.
The lightning of some summer-storm

Hath brought swift death;
And bleeding veins
Have stifled breath;
But how did the warm life go?
And where?
We do not know!

A poisoned cup, a venomed sting, —
Nay, the prick of a pin,
Or any slighter thing,
May break the enchanted ring
That shuts life in;
And the bright angel vanishes like a dream
When one from sleep is waking.
Do we know
Where goes the dream the brain forsaking,
Or whence it came?
So with the spark of flame
Which we call life.
It enters this our frame with pain and strife,
To fill the world with sorrow or with mirth,
As our swift hours flow.
It leaves the teeming bosom of the earth;
And from the tiny seeds low buried there,
The flowers spring;
And bring
Unto our human hearts, so weary, sore,
A freshness and a glory evermore.
Or, diverse still, some little germ shoots up
From piny cones, or acorn's fretted cup,
In coming years to be
The spreading marvel of a stately tree,
And gloriously fair!
And so,
Through all the earth,
In kingly palace, and by lowly hearth,
This life leaps up exultingly,
So glad and free!
The world is full of it;
And throned and crownèd, it doth sit
On the apex of the earth!
It laugheth out
In the clear, ringing shout
Of childhood's frolic play;
It silent goes
Through quietness and gloom, unto repose,
As streams that flow through woods of pine,
With little of sunshine;

It moves in pride,
As with some river-tide.
Unto the mighty and resounding main;
It bears the quickening brain
Through boundless fields of thought,
Where a mighty work is wrought,
Into the unfathomable deeps
Where the tide of being sleeps;
It doth inurn the soul!

But — it dies!
The glory of its morning lieth low;
The silent waves above it go;
And o'er it lies
The shadow of an earthly nevermore;
A closèd door!

The little flowers creep
Unto a silent and a sunless sleep;
The giant trees
So brave and strong,
That spread broad branches to the sun and breeze,
Ere long
Shall have the worm Decay
Gnawing at their hearts until they fall,
Making their ruin no concealing pall;
And so they pass away;
The little child,
Whose laughter, sweet and wild,
Was dearest music to its mother's heart,
Shall from its home depart;
And the light, that there hath shone,
Shall be dim for that childish presence gone;
And the mother's life be darkenèd
For the little baby, dead!
The quiet life that onward goes
Through summer's sunshine, through the winter-snows,
And maketh no sign,
Shall silently decline,
And fleet,
As do creations fair and sweet;
And so go down
Unto the ending, upward to the crown.
The head uplift,
That seems to scorn the rack and rift,
And ride
In stubbornness of pride,
At length

Shall from its tower of might and strength
Stoop low, and bow
Stiff neck and haughty brow,
With bated breath
Unto the Smiter, Death.
The teeming brain
That seemed to hold a world within his grasp,
Shall know all tenure of the earth is vain;
And loose its clasp,
And die, and be resolved to nothingness;
Though what it wrought
Amid the fields of thought
May live long after it to curse or bless;
And when the light
Of life goes out in silentness of night,
The *soul* doth also take its flight,
Or swift, or slow.
But whither doth it go?

Flowers and tree
Alike their work have done;
Have bloomed, matured their seed, and gone
To their appointed ending;
Blending
Their dust with dust that in GOD's time shall bring
A fresh, sweet birth
Of beauty to the earth;
A brightness and a glory to a coming spring!
The little one that slept,
While the poor mother wailed and wept
Above the dust that did not stir,
Some day,
Not far away,
Shall be of her
Found waiting on the other shore!
The quiet life
(Most human lives are quiet; come, and go,
And nothing heard of them),
That by still waters sowed its seed,
Shall have a glorious meed;
And purple robe and royal diadem,
Shall be made ready for the meek,
The lowly-hearted,
Who from the world so silently departed,
And went to seek
The Better Land they knew awaited them.
The Land so fair!
The Blessèd Country trod

By saints who have attained the glory there,
And dwell with GOD!
The brain that caught
The falling mantle of divinest thought,
And clothed its work with spirit; made it fair
By daily breathings of no earthly air,
Shall reach the full fruition of its dreams;
Shall see how far
Beyond all glory of the sun or star,
The light of Heaven must be;
And know
How near their soul
Was unto that most certain goal
Which all true life is hasting on to gain;
And which it shall attain,
Not here, nor now,
But in that coming day
When heaven and earth shall pass away
As a wreath of vap'rous air;
And a new-born world shall come
From the Hand of GOD, its home, —
And be,
Through all eternity,
Beyond all dreaming, fair!

We do not know,
The while we tread this earth,
Whither the life or soul doth go,
Nor whence it came;
But we *shall* know, some day!
This flame,
Inhabiting the shell
We call our body, hath no mortal birth,
And doth not go with it
Unto the dust.
Each silently doth flit
Unto its own,
And with its own shall dwell.
All that is known
Doth rest in fewest words:
" Dust unto dust," as ever it must,
And the spirit to GOD that gave it;
And this not our will, but the LORD'S.
So would we have it!

"To Be, or not To Be."

WHAT if beyond the grave there were no waking?
  No dawn of resurrection for the dead?
Would not all hope, the weary heart forsaking,
  Die into nothingness before that dread?

Who entered hell, as in old Dante's vision,
  Left hope behind them, and without the gate;
So shut from earth were that sweet shape Elysian
  If at Death's door no after-life did wait.

What if the doom of dark annihilation
  Were meted out to every child of earth,
And never hope nor tidings of salvation
  Had shut the shadow from each human hearth?

Dost feel how empty of all joy or pleasure
  The myriad homes of this our world would be?
How vain were laying up of any treasure,
  That bore not stamp of immortality?

What if the hearts that unto us are nearest
  Gave but such love as soulless dust can give?
What if the treasures we hold best and dearest
  Should be resolved to dust, no more to live?

I see, as in a vision dark and dreary,
  A city rising from the desert-land;
No voices sweet, — no footsteps swift or weary, —
  Are heard amid the silence of the sand.

Three thousand years, or more, that sand hath drifted
  Around that giant city of the plain;
Still through the lapse of years its head is lifted;
  But none may dwell within its walls again.

Fair are its homes, as in the ages olden,
  When man first reared them 'mid the bloom of earth;
Still shine the colors, rainbow-hued and golden,
  Soft tracëd there for temple, or for hearth;

But they who built have passed away forever,
  Leaving no record of their race or fame.
The massive stones, though proof of strong endeavor,
  Are stones of death that never kept a name.

And like this city, of its own forsaken,
  Hopeless and lonely, 'mid its death-in-life,
Meseemeth were this world, if from it taken
  Were the sweet hope that stilleth all its strife.

"Up in the Morning Early."

Up in the morning early,
  Ere the golden sun-rays peep,
Riseth a little maiden
  From her quiet and dreamless sleep;
While in at her open window
  With the first breath of the morn,
Floateth the song of the bluebird,—
  A song that of joy is born.
Blithely the maiden she singeth,
  She hath neither care nor grief.
The rose is no rose yet,—the lily
  Lies folded within the leaf.

Up in the morning early,—
  But it is no longer May;
The flush and the glory of summer
  Are filling the long, bright day;
And up from a dreaming olden,
  A dreaming forever new,
Riseth the maid,— her eyes sweetest
  When the love-light is shining through;
And softly the maiden singeth
  A song without reason or rhyme;
But a sweetness is flowing through it,
  And it hath a musical chime.

Up in the morning early,—
  Though the breeze is blowing cool,
And the blossoms are faded and fallen
  In the Garden Beautiful,—
Riseth the little maiden;
  But her brow is weary, pale,
As she flingeth wide the casement
  To let in the autumn gale.
She singeth a song that is saddest,
  But she singeth unconsciously;
And a wail through it all is going
  Like the moaning of the sea.

Up in the morning early, —
  Never more these words may be,
For the little maiden lieth
  Where the snow falls on the lea.
And never more from the window
  Shall gaze those sealèd eyes;
And never song of the bluebird
  Heareth she where low she lies.
Quietly still she is sleeping,
  And she may not rise, nor stir;
And she singeth no more at day-dawn;
  But the wind, it singeth for her.

"Ashes to Ashes, Dust to Dust."

Soft glides the Spring upon the frozen earth,
  With fairy footsteps wandering to and fro.
The freed streams greet her with renewèd mirth,
  As lightly onward the glad waters go.
Her eyes are blue; soft, tender, as the sky
  That smiles above her; eyes that have no tears
Save April showers, and they pass quickly by,
  Leaving no shadow on her youth of years.
        From the dim distance crieth
        A voice that never dieth:
  "Ashes to ashes, dust to dust," it saith.

Fair laughs the Summer in the golden light
  Of tropic suns that crown her with their rays.
She moveth, like a queen, so calm and bright,
  With full, dark eyes, betokening length of days.
Yet is she passionate; and oft her wreath
  Of crimson roses, and of golden wheat,
In angry scorn she flingeth underneath
  The storm-wind's chariot-wheels, or iron feet.
        From the dim distance crieth
        A voice that never dieth:
  "Ashes to ashes, dust to dust," it saith.

With dusky cheeks, and brows with vine-leaves twined,
  Sweeps by the richly-dowered and the strong,
The many-gifted Autumn! Free the wind,
  In the deep pauses of its swelling song,
Lifts the long tresses of her waving hair;
  Revealing eyes, that wheresoever bent,

Have but one language; deeply graven there,
We trace the very fulness of content.
From the dim distance crieth
A voice that never dieth:
" Ashes to ashes, dust to dust," it saith.

All robed in white, and motionless, and still,
As statue hewn from stone, pale Winter stood.
The air so keen, so bitter, and so chill,
Had frozen the very current of her blood
To utter silence.   On her brow there shone
A halo, for she was Aurora-crowned;
Her eyes were closed, as she to sleep had gone,
And from her sealëd lips there came no sound.
From the dim distance crieth
A voice that never dieth:
" Ashes to ashes, dust to dust," it saith.

Year after year, the seasons come and go,
And ring their various changes as they pass.
Spring-flowers bloom, and Summer-fountains flow,
Till Autumn-shadows gather o'er the grass
And Winter shroudeth all things with its pall.
But year unto year telleth the same tale.
Forever and forever through them all
Soundeth the echo of a ceaseless wail.
From the dim distance crieth
A voice that never dieth:
" Ashes to ashes, dust to dust," it saith.

A Fancy.

FAR away in the dim recesses
Of the forest's solitude,
Where the shadows lie most darkly
On the old rocks stern and rude;
Where the winds go singing ever
And the brooding echoes dwell, —
Gushed a sweet and sparkling fountain
Down in a mossy dell.

There was store of golden lilies
That fountain fair around,
And the white and purple violets,
They covered all the ground.

There were tall and slender grass-blades
  That near the water grew,
And ever were they glittering
  With its still, falling dew.

Oh, the clear and limpid water,
  How it gushed and bubbled up
From the sand so white and shining
  That lined its moss-brimmed cup!
How it sang, in silvery singing,
  To the quickly passing hours,
That went by, light and trippingly,
  As gliding over flowers.

From its birthplace in the forest,
  Its green and mossy nest,
Ever onward flows the water
  With a feeling of unrest;
And slowly and dimly finding
  Through the underwood its way,
Till it shows a silver gleaming
  To some wandering solar ray.

And onward, and ever onward,
  Goeth that silver gleam,
Gathering strength and volume slowly
  From every mingling stream;
Till the fountain and the brooklet
  Go, laughing in their glee,
A free and mighty river
  Sweeping downward to the sea.

As the silver fountain, darkly
  In the forest has its birth,
And flows all dimly, silently,
  Amid the groves of earth;
As it groweth to a river,
  Strong, rushing, deep, and free,
So the rise of Love's true passion
  In the human heart may be.

The Lady Anne.

ARGUMENT.

Ye Rector goes back to ye days of his youth, to tell of
ye Ladye Anne — her birth, childhood, girlhood. He
telleth of his uncle, ye first Rector of Morven; what
manner of man he was; and of ye work that he did;
which work shall live after him; and of his death. Of
ye Aunt and Cousins (two sisters and a brother) of ye
Ladye Anne. Of Richard Leigh, — what manner of man
he was; and how he sped in his wooing. How he went
abroad for years and came not back again. Of ye Ladye
Anne and her son. How this son grew to be a man,
and went to battle, and was not. Of ye death of ye
Ladye Anne.

Exeunt Omnes.

WHAT time the year was in its youth, and Earth
Did wear her virgin livery of white,
A child was given unto Morven Hall;
A little helpless thing — a fragile girl —
The last of that proud race. Ere she was born
Her father slept in death, slain by the foe
On a well-stricken field. Her mother died
In the hour that gave an heir to Morven,—
Another soul to earth; and, side by side,
The earl and his fair lady rest forever.
Above their dust the chapel-arches rise
In stately beauty, and through stainëd glass
The outer day steals, mellowed into light
Of all prismatic hues; so falling on
The marble cenotaph that guards the dead,—
Giving and taking beauty! Quietly,
Within the shelter of the groinëd roof,
The noble dead are sleeping; but, without, —
'Neath greenest sward all spangled o'er with flowers,

Where shadows of the grand old trees are lying, —
The poor have made their rest; safe-guarded, too,
Since GOD doth keep sure ward!
                          The days went by.
Old things had been forgotten, and each hour
Was ripening the new. Summer's roses
Bloomed and died. Winter's snows had come and gone,
And Earth was older by some twenty years;
Swift years, and full of change! Thrones had been won,
And lost, and won again in that brief time;
And War had swept o'er Europe like a scourge,
With decimating sword thinning the nations.
One man had filled the earth with anarchy;
And made himself a greater than a king
In that his power rose out of broken rule,
Cemented deep by blood, sustained by swords.
Yet — strangest paradox! — he was beloved
Even to idolatry! But — he fell!
Down toppling from his height, as some huge cliff
Falls sudden in the sea; and to the sea,
The ocean dashing on Helena's shore,
We must leave his requiem!
                          Twenty years —
Whose written page, a record sad and dark,
Is blotted o'er with blood, and dank with graves —
Had passed o'er Morven's stately towers and groves,
And left not one defacing impress there.
The same old trees still bent their branches hoar
Above the old chapelle, and flung their shade
Upon the lowly tombstones of the poor;
The while their tops did point unto the sky
With a mute eloquence; as if to say,
"Not to the dust that mouldereth at our feet
Look ye, O mortals, for the loved who went
From out your world forever when they died!
For though ye gave them, dust unto the dust,
Their souls have passëd upward unto GOD,
The GOD ' who giveth his belovëd sleep!'"

    Twenty years! that came and went forever.
In the world's ages but a grain of sand,
Or less than any atom. In man's life
That grain of sand might be the whole of earth;
As full of deeds, and mingled with all change,
As is the history of this our world
'Mid all its countless periods of time.
These twenty years were pregnant with world-changes,
That from Time's womb came hydra-headed all,

And History's page was written o'er with blood.
But in far hamlets, by love-lighted homes,
Only the old sweet changes rang their chimes;
Save when the Angel Death breathed on some flowers,
Or touched with other frost than that of years
Some old and honored brow; and dust took back
The dust that had been given unto life.

Twenty years! and Morven's baby-heiress
Was a woman grown.   Fair, gentle, loving;
But as proud withal, as if the current,
Through those blue veins coursing, had come to her
From a long line of kings, who each had worn
A kingdom's coronet right royally.
I said that she was gentle, this fair girl, —
Within the covert of her stately home,
The sweetest mistress ever servants had, —
A Saxon lady, pitiful and kind.
So the poor found her ever; but her foot
Crossed never threshold save her own or theirs.
The poor did bless her with unsteady voice,
And eyes that knew swift tears in looking on her.
Rough men grew mannerly if they but met
The full, sweet gaze of those serenest eyes;
And children?   You had thought the Lady Anne
Some angel stooping from its native heaven,
Had you but seen her 'mid the little ones!
Dearly they loved her, and their hands so small,
Though brown from labor and the burning sun,
Would nestle in her white hand's loving fold
As the brown fingers knew themselves at home!

There was no beauty in sweet Lady Anne.
She had a fairy figure, and a face
Most like an angel's; but no roses there
Vied with the lily.   Never tint of bloom
Had dyed those palest cheeks; nor warmer glow
Flushed o'er the pure white brow.   A little child,
She had been quiet ever.   Ringing laugh
And merry burst of song were never hers;
And, spirit-like, she wandered through the halls
Of her ancestral towers; or roamed at will
'Neath the dusk shadows of the ancient trees.
There were none to care for her, none to watch,
And none to understand.   So the young heart
Grew heavy with its untold fantasies,
Yet bore the burthen silently; and the face,
So pale and still, was older than the years

19

The child's brief life had counted.   Soft and sad,
The large brown eyes gazed wistfully at you,
As though they wanted something; but they had
No child-look in them.   Golden-brown her hair
Shone in the sun; but evermore there fell
A darker shadow on it, as if caught
From deeper shade; a reflex of the cloud
That on the heart was lying dark and cold.
A cloud, engendered by the lonely life
And solitary musings of the child, —
A cloud, which, breaking in the after years,
Shall bring forth tears, with agony and death,
The bitterest heritage of human life.
And these were garnered by a little child, —
A child whose fingers should have plucked the roses,
Not gathered Dead Sea Fruits!
                              O childhood fair!
True Happy Valley of the Arabian Tale;
Sole Eden left to earth; unguarded all,
When adamantiné walls should shut it in;
And at its gate, for evermore should stand,
The watchful Angel of the Flaming Sword,
To keep its Way of Life!   O time so brief,
That should be tended as a sacred thing;
Kept pure from all defilement of the dust;
Made holy unto GOD! — how lightly we
Regard its innocence, letting it see
The sin that lieth nearest to our hearts,
Daily, hourly, till its common use
Veils o'er deformity, and makes that fair,
Whose native shape were one most fitting hell!
Well spake the Sage of a long passéd day, —
" Reverence to children as to GOD is due;" *
Yet we neglect the precept, heed it not,
And with light words and jests, ourselves do steal
GOD's holy signet from our children's brows;
And, in their hearts, sow seed whose germ is Sin,
Whose certain fruit is Death; yet think the while,
With self-approving smile, that we do love
Most tenderly our children.
                              Well we know
That childhood is a field whose virgin soil
Our hands make ready for the harvesting.
The soil is fresh, and waiting for the seed;
And we are servants working for our GOD;
What shall the harvest be?   A sure account

* Juvenal.

Have we to render when the reckoning comes,
And not one plea can put the hour off.
What shall the harvest be?

The Lady Anne
Had glided into womanhood alone.
The times were troublous ones, and sorrow sat
At every hearthstone; dark suspense held sway
O'er every woman's heart, and none had thought,
Or time to think, of the lone orphan girl.
And so she had become a woman grown,
With only such brief schooling as she won
From the old rector, very poor and blind,
Yet rich, as he thought, in her tender love.
She learned to read, she scarce could tell you how,
And, day by day, sat poring o'er old books
That proved rare food for her, and stirred some pulses
To a strange, throbbing life that could not last;
So faded to a longing, scarce defined,
For that which was beyond the bounded scope
Of her short vision.   This, unsatisfied,
A something intangible that no sense
Made present to her, was a haunting nothing
That filled all pauses of her daily life,
Until she grew heart-weary.   Then there came
Into her eyes the same old, wistful look
That marked her childhood, and her spirit burned
With the wild fever-thirst that comes to all,
And must be quenchèd soon, or else we die.
The cool, sweet rippling of the far-off fount
Mocking us to the last.

The Lady Anne —
She was a lady, gentle and beloved —
Had grown into the hearts of all who dwelt
Within her broad domain; learning the way
A little from the rector, who had made
His fairy pupil eyes unto himself.
I said that he was blind; and well she learned
The simple truths he taught her, giving back
Such meed of love as made his quiet life
Bright as the sunshine he could feel, not see!
So the old man was happy, and his past
Was unto him a closed and sealèd book
That might no more be opened; as a grave,
O'er which the flowers growing, veiled all sight
Of what beneath was mouldering to dust.
The present *was* the grave of all the past,

But it *had* flowers.   There was nothing more;
No haunting memory of the old time came
To cloud its sunshine, or shut out its day.
So the old man was happy!

                                        Far away,
Beneath the shadow of Ben-Nevis, lies
A little grave, grown over now with grass
And mountain heather.   Fifty years ago
That sod was broken, and a young man gave
The bride of one sweet month unto the dust
And went upon his way.   That little mound
Held all he ever loved; so the man's heart
Was homeless evermore!   And fifty years,
So pregnant with all changes, came and went,
And found him changeless; all his earnest life
In the same even current flowing, filled
With daily rounds of duty, made most sweet
By the dear love of children.   But not his.
The little grave upon the far-off hills
Had guarded him from loving woman more.
So the old rectory knew not one sweet sound
Of wife or children; yet the days went by,
And not unhappily.   No vain regrets
O'er the irrevocable, no wild dreams
Of that which might have been, moved that calm heart
To stir the ashes of the olden time.
So o'er his past, that fifty years ago,
The silence of a life had fallen.   A shroud
Not to be lifted, till the far-off dawn
Of the resurrection-morning!

                                        Lost years!
And yet, not so! nothing GOD giveth is;
And all these years, so lonely, were not lost.
The quiet heart, shut out from household joys,
Was open wide to all the friendless poor,
And had large room for all humanities;
The loving words and deeds that make life sweet
To every suffering heart.   And this true soul,
So grand in its forgetfulness of self,
Did wield a sceptre greater than a king's;
More potent far its sway.

                                        Within the sweep
Of rugged hills that bound the fair domain
Of ancient Morven, dwelt a Celtic race,
Uncared for, and untended, wild and fierce,

With little love for earth, and less for heaven.
Their native soil was sterile; scarce sufficed,
'Neath their rude culture, for the scanty meal
That made their daily sustenance; and life
Was one long day of labor unto all
Dawning in cradle, — closing in the grave!
They were a hardy race; in their rough way
Were gentle-hearted too; but life had been
An endless struggle and a weary task
For many centuries, and they could see
No sweetness in it, save the dreamless sleep
That follows after toil.   The little ones —
You scarce could call them *children* — seemed to be
As men and women dwarfed, so old they were
In face and bearing.   Never clearest laugh
Of *careless* childhood woke an echo sweet
Amid the green old woods.   The only sounds
That stirred the silence of the stony hills
Were such as tell of dull and patient toil
That nothing knew of joy.   Men *always* worked;
They did not dare be idle, lest the morn
Should find them starving.   Women's tender hands
Were brown and rough, and on their patient brows
Was set the sign of those who have no youth,
And so grow old before the appointed time.
I said there were no *children*.   It was so.
Those wizen faces, prematurely old,
Had nought of childhood's freshness or its bloom;
And were sad types most smileless, and most still,
Of all the after years must bring to them.
The slow, slow life, and age that had no youth!

    Unto these hills, — amid this Celtic race, —
Our simple rector came.   Brave heart! true soul!
That saw the work before it, hard and dure,
Yet touched the plough; and never turned away
For pleasure, pain, or rest!   And fifty years —
Did I miscall them *lost?* — had told their tale;
Had ripened to such sweet and blessèd fruit,
Angels might stoop to gather it, nor dim
Their wings in stooping.
                          A Sabbath morn
Is breaking o'er the hilltops.   Swift and clear
A little river flows adown the vale
With a low singing.   Scattered here and there,
By river-shore, on sunny meads and slopes,
A hundred cottage-homes are sending forth
Their inmates all to worship.   Clean and neat,

They gather round the porch of the old chapelle,
And wait the summons of the soft, low chimes,
Calling to early prayer. There are no forms
Amid that peaceful throng ground down to earth
By over-working. No pale faces there,
Sharp with the hunger-pain, or the keen pang
Of watching, when they could not *see* the dying.
None had grown old too soon! Stout, stalwart men,
With forms erect, not bowed, and limbs that told
Of healthful labor giving fullest strength;
Old men, and youths who lifted manly brows
And honest hearts to heaven; gentle women,
On whose sweet faces writ in loving smiles
The heart's contentment shone; light-hearted girls,
Whose laughter rippled ever, like a brook
In the glad summer-time; little children,
With questioning eyes that followed you alway,
And simple trust in other lovingness
Unshadowed by a doubt, — all these were there,
Soon drawn within the sacred walls of stone
By the clear ring of bells.
                 Sweet were the sounds
Of murmured chant and solemn litany
Through the old arches stealing soft and clear.
Then came the sermon. No belabored theme
(Half-quoted from the ancient fathers too),
Wherein the doctrines of the Church alone
Were text and sermon; but a simple tale,
That suited well the needs of those who heard;
For " unto the poor the gospel is preached."
On this brief text the blind old pastor spake.
No ornate periods crowded his discourse;
Nor show of empty learning, veiling o'er
The gospel truths with flowers. Clear and plain,
Yet with most touching earnestness, he told
The simple tale of Bethlehem. No more;
Save some few words of exhortation, meet
From one who spake as unto dying men.
Then came the low-breathed blessing. Silently,
As those who have some solemn need of thought,
All parted to their homes, — throughout the week,
Kept purer by that quiet Sabbath day,
And a little nearer heaven!
                    Fifty years
Of one man's lonely life had, under GOD,
Made all these rough paths smooth. Yet were there some
Who dared to call this life a wasted one,
For that the *world* knew nothing of its work,

Nor then, nor ever!   What did it matter?
He gave no heed to the world's praise or blame.
It never reached him!   All too far above
Such idle murmurs was the work he gave
With a pure heart to Heaven.   But the *angels* saw,
And GOD was very near!
                      This life of work
Had its rare sweetnesses; redeeming hours
That with their burthen of the purest joy
Shed a long brightness o'er the days to come
That had been cheerless else; and gave to toil
A foretaste of fruition, in itself
Outweighing far the lives of many men.
Such men as in their generation die,
And leave earth nothing but a rounded grave
And a little dust to keep!   Worthless dust,
Not clay made sweeter by the rose's breath,
And so embalmed for heaven!   A life of work
Had been our blind old rector's; slow and sure
As is the labor of the coral worm,
Rearing 'mid ocean depths its palace-halls,
Counting its work by slowest centuries,
Each grain a grave!—yet binding at the last
The once exultant waters with a band
Of all-enduring stone; till in the face
Of the proud day, a little isle doth rise
As Venus, from the sea;—in time to be
An emerald on the waters, and a home
For the wild sons of earth;—in GOD's own hour
Made holy by the hallowing voice of prayer!
Work like to this our rector's hand had wrought.
So, grain by grain, cemented fast by faith,
Made glorious by death when souls had passed
"In the sure hope of heaven," he builded up
A little church within those arid hills,
And made life sweet, and needful labor light;
Until the valley blossomed as the rose,
And the hills were green with beauty; the earth
Was never more a desert, and the land
Might be callèd Beulah!
                    Earth hath some names
That in its records fill a world-wide place;
Whose old renown comes to us through the years
We count by centuries.   Historic shapes,
The world's great conquerors, who trod the Past
With still, relentless footsteps, and through blood
Went up red steps to thrones!   Earth claimeth, too,
The nobler heritage of her gifted ones.

Bright shadows looming through a night of years;
Their pale brows wreathed with cypress and with bay;
Old days made eloquent by their burning words
That sounded onward to the days to come,
Bringing them nearer. Sons of genius, these
Crownëd kings of the highest realms of thought;
Made kinglier by the years that only bring
Fresh homage and allegiance unto them!
And other shapes there are, — with lambent brows,
Not throned of earth; but purified by fire
From taint of sin, — the holy martyr-band,
The aureola crowned of Heaven!
But, better worth than these — more holy far —
Are lives of good men who make ready here
The pathways of our Lord, and lead one soul
From earth's dark mazes to the Better Land.
True kings are they, and wide the realm they rule;
For o'er the human heart and erring soul,
Their loving hand doth hold the mastery
With a most winning sway. Yet, meekly, they
Do walk the earth; and our poor blinded eyes,
That mark the stainëd robe and marrëd brow,
See not the real whiteness of that robe;
See not the glory ringing the pure brow,
Which sealeth each, while yet they are of earth,
As the crownëd ones of heaven! They came,
Silently, as the snow. It makes no stir;
Flake after flake sinks softly through the air
By day or night, and the swift hours count them
In starry myriads, covering the earth
As with a bridal veil; and yet a shroud;
Since in its downward sweep it buries all
Impurities of earth, and in its fall
Makes fresh and pure the atom-laden air.
As falls the snow, so the earth's holy ones
Come unto earth; with their so loving hands
Making its rough places smooth for other feet,
The while their own do tread unfalteringly
The sharp and rugged flints that leave deep wounds
By none but angels tended! In our lives
Pale ministers of joy, their shapes do stand,
Holding to our keen lips the cup made sweet,
We never ask them *how;* though it may be
The heart's still sacrifice hath bought the boon,
And our poor selfish thirst hath been allayed
In the heart's blood of one who lovëd us!

If we could read the faces, pale and still,
Of some who bear us company on our way,
So learning how the poor heart burns beneath
With its unanswered longings; would we give
The love they prayed for once, but never now?
We know not; but the Past replieth "No!"
They gave us all! We did not scorn the gift,
But took it as our right; gave nothing back;
Though all life's sunshine came from their true hands
And we bask in it; seeing not the night
They clasp so closely lest its shadow fall
Upon our pathway. But they *die*, some day.
God taketh back his angels, and our lives
Have lost their sunshine; yet we think not why,
And only moan o'er our own misery.
Or it may be — we know such things have been —
Their life's deep silence was a mask of stone
Which death hath broken, and the quiet face,
We never looked on lovingly, shall wear
The likeness of an angel! All too late
We learn what we were scorning. All too late
We press vain kisses on the poor white lips
That now are dumb forever! All too late,
We clasp the cold, cold hands in loving fold,
We never touched when living! All too late
We dower the dead with love! A wasted gift,
That winneth nothing from the silent heart;
A vain oblation poured upon the grave
That hath no voice to answer our wild prayer;
Though some sad echo, caught from other graves,
May whisper low, "Too late!"
                              Too late! too late!
The old sad strain, the moan which human hearts
Must utter evermore, — how through our lives
That wail goes sounding, shutting out sweet hope
As we had buried it, and set the seal
Of an eternal silence on its grave!
We hear that wail, but we forget it ever,
And go on dreaming; weaving webs so bright,
We know that Fancy must have stained the threads
With tintings caught from the rich sunset glow
Of an autumnal evening, — beautiful
As evanescent. We see the glory,
And hold it to our hearts, forgetting still
That all the beauty of the passing day
But veileth o'er its dying; that the night,
With its dusk shadows, falleth, as a pall
Above the dead, and we are left in darkness.

Darkness, wherein the stars may dimly shine
To guide our footsteps, but their light is not
The radiant glory of the dying day.
And to our vainly longing sight they seem
But as the lamps which lone and cold do burn
In some old sepulchre, lighting up the dead,
And making some pale horror visible
Unto our shrinking sight.
        Too late! too late!
O vanity of Hope! since that dread knell
Strikes sudden on our hearts, and all their dreams
Are scattered to the winds, laid low in dust, —
The dust, perchance, of some forgotten grave!
A ship was sailing on a summer sea,
With pennants flying over sails as white
As the sea-gull's wing. Treasures rich and rare,
Brought from all climes, were gathered in her hold.
More costly freightage did she bear alsō, —
A hundred human souls! The land was near;
Another day must bring them into port;
And some were dreaming of the joy to come,
The sweet reunion. Others count the gold
Their three years' toil shall reap. The night came down,
A night of storm, and when the morning broke,
The gallant ship was gone with all her freight;
And the sea tells no tale! There had been strife
Between old friends; some sharp and bitter words,
Spoken in anger, severing old ties
That never should be broken. But the one
Thought in his heart, "This quarrel must not be;
We will be friends to-morrow!" and the morn
Heard but the tolling of the passing-bell
Low knelling out "Too late!" There had been love
Equal and responsive. But parting came,
And the long lapse of years that had no meeting, —
Sad years, whose tale was told by dying hopes,
By wild and passionate tears, whose hot drops fell
A withering blight on all life's sweetest flowers,
And by the deadly agony of doubt
Wearing the life away. Time will not lose
One shade of down from off his mighty wings
For all earth's breaking hearts! So the long years
Crept on apace. Out in the busy world
Men toil and strive, and in the eager rush
And endless stir of traffic or of fame,
Forget *who* waiteth by a lonely hearth,
Watching through many years! The years go on.
World-weary at the last, men turn their steps

To the old familiar paths, and hope to find
The same sweet face smile on them as of yore.
Too late! too late!   Another guest they find,
Who hath played wooer all these many years,
And will not now be cheated.   Death is there,
And waiting for his bride!   Could they bring back
The years they now know wasted!—silent years
That came, and went, and found their love grown cold.
Long years to one who waited! now they bring
Unto their hearts a vengeance swift and sure
For all their tarrying.   They *have* returned.
Too late! too late!   Life's tide is running out,—
The sands of Death lie bare!
                                        Poor human love,
That fain would have life linger when too late,
And sees the boon so coveted for years
Eluding its warm grasp; plucked thence in haste
By the swift doom that dallied heretofore,
But will not now delay, though life hath grown
So strangely dear to us.   Too late! too late!
And so the tale is ended; for the grave
Reveals no secrets.   All our love is dumb
Before that silence which no sound shall break
Until the trump of Judgment; when a voice
Shall say to earth, and sea, and utmost hell
"Give up your dead!"   Heaven grant that in that day
Our shuddering souls hear not for final doom
THE ALL TOO LATE OF GOD!
                                        As one who roams
Hither and thither, turning at his will
Down every diverse path; for that it seems
Fair in his eyes, or leadeth to some spot
In the old time most dear to him; so I
Turn ever from the straight course of this tale,
Wandering in fields of thought.   Pardon, dear friends,
An old man's lingering.   Not many days
Looks he to find in the coming future.
So the Past makes stronger its enchantments;
He cannot break their spell.   And then, you know,
Old age is garrulous, must have its say,
And take its own time in the telling of it.
But the end cometh soon enough!   Old days
Are haunting me; pale memories of joys
That would not tarry; and the old man's heart
Is sadly weary, pining for the rest
Earth cannot bring to him.
                                        There came a day
When Morven's lady wept most blinding tears

O'er the old rector's grave. The only friend
The Past had given to her quiet life
Had been taken home by GOD; and she was left
Alone amid her people. Though they shared
In her deep grief, and sought in their rude way
To comfort her, she could but give them thanks.
They did not know, and could not understand,
How very lonely was the Lady Anne
In the old halls they thought so beautiful.
Perchance they envied her; not dreaming once
That they so rich in all sweet household ties
Could be the envied of the Lady Anne.
Yet so it was. Poor child! she was so young
To strive with vain tears, and with loneliness,
Most bitter pang of all! And in her pain
She almost prayed for death. His coming then
Had been most welcome.
                              We moan o'er changes;
We do not fancy they can bring us joy;
The very word seems ringing out a knell.
Yet in whatever shape or guise they come
GOD sendeth them as blessings. They may seem
As giant-shadows looming dark and stern
In the far horizon, presaging ill;
A thunder-cloud of fate, that yet shall break
A summer-shower on our path of life
Bidding the flowers bloom! Perchance they wear
The aspect of an angel, and our hearts
Go forth to meet a visitant so fair,
And bring it home with triumph and with song
As the reapers bring their sheaves! But our guest
Flings off the smiling mask, and in its stead
A face looks out upon us, terrible,
Turning our hearts to stone. Or else the change
May be, of all earth-changes, holiest.
A pure heart passing from this world of sin, —
A soul returning to its native heaven;
And then the GOD who taketh, giveth too;
Since for the loss of earth, we have a friend
Awaiting us in heaven. O happy friend!
Whose chains are broken, and for whom the earth,
Our prison yet, hath never more a place.
We should not weep, but rather, bless our GOD
Who taketh *home* his own, and giveth us
A blessing in the stead of that we've lost;
And giveth upbraiding not!
                              So a change
Came o'er the dreaming of sweet Lady Anne;

And Morven's halls were all astir with life.
Fair forms, and stately, with most queenly grace
Swept through the corridors, adown the steps
Of the long, silent house; which echoed now
To low laughs musical, and silvery tones
Of young, fresh voices. or the light, firm tread
Of youth's swift footsteps; feet that knew not yet
The slow, dull measure of a heavy heart
Like beat of muffled drums.   I, too, was there;
Won from the lone and quiet rectory
By the still glamour of some soft, brown eyes
That ever smiled upon me; greeting thus
The only nephew of her oldest friend, —
The friend whose dust was lying far away
On the green hill-side by some other dust, —
The dust that he had given unto earth
Full fifty years ago.
                  I spoke of changes.
Lady Anne was changed; and the lonely heart
Basked in the sunshine of its loving self,
Made wide its doors, and gave large space and room
Unto the aunt and cousins, but just come
From far-off London.   They were all her own
(I mean the little lady fancied so),
And with sweet lavishness she gave to them
The love which had lain dormant all these years.
What gave they in return?   Some empty words
That had no meaning, but they sounded sweet
To that poor, thirsting heart; and Anne gave back
No stinted measure from her own full love;
Its tide was at the flood.   Their hearts had none.
I scanned them all; yea, read them through and through,
And saw but stagnant pools, where other eyes
Found only fairest flowers.
                  I would the gift
Of reading hearts had never come to me!
For it brought bitterness and vain regret;
And a wild, passionate longing but to save
When I was powerless.   Nay, could not lift
One warning finger to avert the blow
I saw must fall too soon.   And when it fell,
My prescient soul knew what must follow too.
The dim hereafter was not dim to me.
Would God I had been blind!
                  These cousins came
From out a world most unlike to our own, —
The world of London; bringing thence false smiles
And falser souls; their very life a lie

Made up of borrowed virtues. Hear them talk
And you had thought the angels scarce could be
So pure in heart. And they were beautiful.
Men called them so. A college friend of mine
Trod one brief measure with the stateliest;
Went mad for her pale beauty, and so died.
I never met her, but his shadow seemed
To come between her and the light of day;
The pale, sweet face that only woke her scorn,
The true, pure heart she only trampled on;
And, knowing this, I never looked on her
But he was there. Her sister had a laugh
That charmed your senses like a siren's song;
But on her brow I saw the leprous taint, —
Her mother's legacy of sin and shame, —
And over me the siren-spell fell harmless.
They knew that they had beauty, and they made
Men's hearts their playthings; in such torturing wise
As I have seen Grimalkin with a mouse,
Tossing it to and fro with velvet paws,
But never letting it go! Richard Leigh
Was brother unto these. Not over-young,
But handsome; with a low, musical voice,
Might wile your heart away before you knew
The little thing was gone. He won not mine;
I knew him all too well. There had been days
In the old cottage life, when we *had* met,
And not as brothers. In that boyish strife
I had been victor. When we met again,
I saw within his eyes the treasured hate,
A snake in act to spring! Not yet had come
The destined hour, but from the serpent's coil
The watchful eyes were gleaming evermore.
I marked the gleam, but soon forgot it quite;
For I was dreaming such a blissful dream.
The awakening was not yet.
                              And these —
A fitting trio — were the friends beloved
Of gentle Lady Anne. She did not know
What hollow masks those smiling faces were,
And I had never right to tear them off.
I was the parish rector, poor and plain,
And they were rich and courtly, — cousins, too,
And more, she loved them! I knew this too well,
So could not dim her trust with one dark fear
That kept me on the rack. I was a man,
And strong and patient. I could better bear
The torturing doubts that would have made her life

The shadow of an hour!   So I kept
That cold suspense, that agony of dread,
With a strong hand, silent.   It mattered not
That in so doing I had bound myself,
Prometheus-like, unto a slow, sure doom
That made life terrible.   It was to be;
I saw that long ago.   And when I stood
Within the church's porch, a priest of GOD,
I knew I had laid down, and evermore,
The sweetnesses of life, and taken up
An unseen cross, shrining it in my heart.
It did not make me sorrowful and stern.
Life spread before me as a furrowed field,
And in that field I had some work to do.
Was I not a laborer in the vineyard?
The spirit that burned in me was made glad
In the pure temple-service; but my heart
Throbbed with a fever caught from earth not heaven;
And I — it matters not.   A little time, —
A few more days of earth and earthly pain, —
And I shall fold my hands in sleep, and be
At rest forever.
              O Anne! little Anne!
When your soft fingers nestled in my hand
With such a quiet trust, filling my heart
With wild dreams, wilder hopes, you little thought
That I might love you other than a friend.
You called me " brother " once, and in that name
Gave me a corner of your loving heart,
But nothing more.   I should have been content;
And might have been, but for the stinging pain
That stabbed me through and through, when Richard
      Leigh
Stole shadowy to your side.   You were not used
To such soft wooing, and your guileless heart
Took such shy, trembling pleasure in it all,
You did not know that all those low-breathed words
Were worse than nothing, — only meant to win
The hand that brought wealth with it.   For the heart, —
" It was a thing not reckoned in his world,
So counted out; and love was but a word
That had no meaning; only met in books,
Or in low parlance of rude country swains,
That nothing knew of *life*."   This Richard Leigh —
I read him like a book — was not a man
Of true impulses, or of earnest faith.
No credo trembled on his full-curved lips
When others spoke of woman or of heaven.

He mocked at both, yet summoned evermore
Their whole vocabulary at his will;
And talked so finely, with such fitting phrase
(A saint had never done it half so well),
I marvel not he won the Lady Anne.
Poor, simple dove! what should she know of guile?
The serpent eyes looked lovingly on her.
She never saw their gleam when they met mine;
Nor marked the secret venom of the words
That unto her were music.   Well I knew
What veiled their poison with such wealth of flowers.
She loved him! and her love did wrap him round
As with a mantle goodly to behold,
Transforming the deformed, till, in her eyes,
He grew unto the stature of a man,
The likeness of an angel!
　　　　　　　　　　　　O young Love!
They did not err who pictured thee as blind;
Yea, bound thine eyes so no one ray of light —
And truth is light — could reach the heart through them.
O Love so sweet! how in thy world of spring
The flowers bloom eternal, and the sun
Knoweth no clouding!   Only in the *dreams*
Of later years doth such rare sunshine smile,
A golden mockery; but in thy world
Its glory is a thing of every day,
And hath no fading.   In thy summer-land
There are no shadows of a coming winter,
No tokens of decay.   Leaves do not fall,
Nor flowers wither.   Once, only, in our lives,
May our poor feet tread that enchanted ground!
And then — and then — ourselves do break the spell.
We weary of its sameness, launch our bark
Upon the waters that do guard its shores,
And with one breath of *change* do fill the sails.
Away! Away! Life's ocean bears us on,
And the wild storms gather!   We must brave them now,
And meet and conquer, or be conquered there!
The world of sunshine we have left was left
Forever!   Life hath no returning tide,
And but one haven, — Death!
　　　　　　　　　　　　O Richard Leigh,
If in the old sweet time when we were boys,
Ere envy did breed strife, and strife wild hate,
Your bark had started on that unknown sea,
And sailed unto that haven; there would be
Some broken hearts the less upon GOD's earth;
Less wealth of cursing too; and you had gone

With a whiter soul to heaven.   But now? — now?
One year ago I saw a queenly form
Within a coffin lying, shrouded, pale,
The heart at rest forever, and I knew
That your false tongue had spoken falser words,
Winning love " only for something to say."
It was a most rare jest, — a pleasant theme
For mockery and sport, — how you had won
A thing you cared not for, — the guarded heart
Of one so proud and cold.   You told it, too,
Amid your boon companions, with light scorn
Of woman's loving.   Oh! it was well done!
And she?   She heard of it, but gave no sign.
A month or so did bring her marriage-morn,
But never bridal night.   When the stars shone
They left her lying, in her bridal robes,
In a dimly-lighted chamber.   Close beside
Were the watchers of the dead!   She had been
Struck down by death at the very altar.
Some heart-disease, they said; but clearer eyes
Laid that swift doom at your door, Richard Leigh!

I mind me too, of one night, cold and drear.
I was in London.   All the streets were white
With a new-fallen snow, whereon the moon
Was shining pale through clouds.   Slow, at my feet,
The sluggish river swept unrestingly;
Moaning beneath the arches, massive, dark,
That spanned the darker stream.   A shadow passed;
A light shape flashed upon the parapet;
A plash of sullen waters, closing slow
Above a woman's form.   Then came a stir,
A rush of eager footsteps, and the sound
Of oars upon the water, swift to save,
But all too late for life.   They brought to shore
A slight form drooping strangely, limp and wan,
And sought to bring back life, but all in vain.
Some red drops oozing through the white, white lips,
Were the sole record of a broken heart
Save some few lines clenched in the little hand.
You were the writer, Richard Leigh!
                                        Poor child!
I see her now as I did see her then,
The white face turnèd upward unto heaven, —
The heaven that late did seem as brass to her, —
The long, wet hair low trailing in the dust;
And, while I gazed, a voice amid the crowd
Called loudly " Alice Hurst!"   How the name thrilled

20

On every ear! for the dead answer not,
And none replied, save in the making room
For a man to pass.　With swift foot he came,
And paused beside the dead; a cold, strange dread,
A vague, dark horror curdling in his eyes,
And whitening his lips, while through it all
A hope seemed lingering uncertainly.
It fled at once, when at his feet he saw
The pale, cold features of the drownèd girl.
"O Alice Hurst!" he said, "sweet Alice Hurst!
Thou liest there, poor lass, and I have sought
For thee through all this cruel London-town.
I would the daisies had been growing white
Above thee long ago, when thou wert yet
A little sinless child.　A *sinless* child!
Ay, *there's* the sting!　O Alice, Alice Hurst!
What shall I say to thy poor mother, lass?
She was so proud of thee!" —
　　　　　　　　　　　With clenchèd hands,
And many a wild oath, he looked to heaven,
And cursed you, Richard Leigh!　A deeper curse
Was in the silence of the poor, weak heart
That you had spoiled and broken in your lust.

GOD pardon her, poor child; for she went mad,
When all her sin did look her in the face,
So sought a hiding in the cold deep stream,
And found in it the grave.　GOD pardon *her!*
I trust he will; but I, a priest of GOD,
Stretch no absolving hands o'er Richard Leigh.
For in mine eyes, wrong-doing like to his
Is a swift road to hell; and I believe
In everlasting death!　GOD's power is great,
And infinite his goodness; but he hates
And will not look upon iniquity.
And, falter as we may with life's great truths,
There comes a day that giveth dust to dust,
"And after death the judgment."
　　　　　　　　　　　In the eyes
Of the hard world such sin as Richard Leigh's
Is but a very little thing at most,
And leaves no stigma.　But the woman, stained
By his *light* sin, is dowered with a curse;
Flung out to scorn and all contumely;
Henceforth the lost Pariah of her race.
Men crown the tempter; but the tempted, fallen,
Doth lie too low for aught save trampling feet.
A woman's soul should be as white as snow,

Her hand should bear the lily; and I hold
A man should be as pure ere he can take
That white soul unto his in marriage-bonds.
But is it so? How speaks the social law?
The sin that bows a woman to the dust
Is venial in a man; no sin at all!
Strange contradiction! In mine eyes there lies
Night's added blackness on the guilt of man,
No *self-forgetting* love redeems his sin;
No bitter shame brings pale repentance home;
For jibe and jest are sequence of *his* crime.
But GOD sees otherwise. One broken law
Dishonors all the ten. In the old time
GOD said, — "The soul that sinneth, it shall die."
Is the law obsolete? HE hath said it,
"With whom there is no variableness,
Neither shadow of turning." — Penitence
May open wide, closed doors. Persistent sin
May not so much as *see* the golden gates,
It dwells so far away. And for such sin
"There is no more remission."
                        Daisies grow
Above the broken heart of Alice Hurst;
And wild birds sing, where by the river-side
They left her lying in her nameless grave.
But a man's wrung heart still crieth "Vengeance"
For the sharp wrong that made life dark to him
And very terrible. While, far away
Two hearts that tremble on life's utmost verge
Are slowly breaking o'er the sin and shame
Of her o'er whom the daisy-blooms are white;
And yet *they* do not curse you, Richard Leigh!
The old man readeth from the Holy Book
The words of Him who died upon the Cross,
And learns the lesson of forgiveness.
The gentle wife, with her meek woman-heart
Forgiveth the deep wrong, low praying GOD
For mercy on her Alice, dead and gone.
And so they do not curse you, Richard Leigh!
But, when they die, their quiet graves shall be
Accusing spirits in the eye of heaven.
How will you meet them, Richard Leigh?
                                 I know
The world speaks lightly of the sin that gave
Poor Alice Hurst an early, self-sought doom.
But this same world forgetteth evermore
How vast a circle one small pebble makes!
They mark the pebble's fall, but never pause

To trace the ring that widens from its grave.
A rumor tells the crime.　Unto the world
It lives and dies, the ephemera of an hour.
But the sad sequence is a thing untold,
Though it be written on all after years
Of some poor hearts of earth; deep stencilled there
By such sharp agony of bitter shame
As ages more than years.　The heedless world
Recks nothing of all this, and doth not care.
But unto our GOD belongeth vengeance.
He keepeth all our tears!

　　　　　　　Too much of this.
Since life hath nobler themes for woven words
Than such a shadow as was Richard Leigh.
But in my life he was the fatal woof
That darkened o'er the else so shining web.
What if my love did never win return?
I knew it must be so, and was content.
But, little Anne, if by a life of pain
I could have shielded you from aught of ill,
My heart had borne the burthen smilingly.
It was not so to be!
　　　　　　　A friend was ill,
And willed me to be near when he should pass
Through the dark vale.　I could not say him nay.
We had been friends when life's long vista spread
Before our eyes untravelled; when its morn
Smiled fair and radiant, and its golden light
Fell fresh and glorous on the far To Be.
School-mates at first, then college-friends were we.
All life had known of early sweetnesses;
Its careless smiles, and charm of laughter clear;
The boy's dear triumphs, and the scholar's joy, —
Had still been shared between us.　Never time
That left a shadow twixt his heart and mine.
I could not fail him now!　And so I went,
No shadow of the future following me.
I buried, for the time, all thoughts of self;
I shut out memories of sweet Lady Anne;
Relived the past; and all to pleasure one
Whose life was fading like a gathered flower;
And I had my reward.　He passed away
Calmly as an infant to the Better Land;
And the Dark Valley was not dark to him!

　　Time is no laggard in his onward flight,
Nor stays his wings for moan of dying men.

The summons came in the month of roses;
But the harvest-moon shone white on Morven
When next I stood within mine own old home.
I knew not why; it did not seem the same.
There was a sorrow brooding by the hearth;
A phantom of a voice that seemed to say
"No more, forever!" but I scarcely heard.
I slept that night as sinless children sleep;
Yet woke upon the morrow with a sense
Of something gone from me; I knew not what.
The morning brought the revelation home.
Why do I linger? since it must be told.
For, wooed and won in that brief summer-time,
The Lady Anne was wife to Richard Leigh!
And I, GOD help me! — but I wished the earth,
That yesterday was heaped on Alleyne's grave,
Had covered me from sight and memory.

A spirit of unrest did haunt me long,
A weary wandering to each spot beloved
Where she had lingered, in the olden time,
That was so fair to me. The old, sweet time
When I was dreaming a wild, foolish dream
Of clear brown eyes that never turned away,
Nor looked on me in anger. All earth grew
Transfigured at her presence, as if she
Were some immortal of the days of eld
Descended from the skies. Nevermore
That quiet presence may my coming wait;
He standeth us between. O foolish heart!
Too like some heedless mariner who goes forth
With favoring breezes on an unknown sea.
Gladly he saileth o'er the waters wide,
But, in mid course arrested, finds his bark
Is wrecked and broken on some hidden rock.
So I, — what doth it matter? Life is long,
And the sharp pang endures not. Time doth steep
All human agony in its Lethean stream;
Whence it ariseth, calm and very still;
Transformed, transfigured, till the changëd shape
Of our life-passion weareth Duty's mould.
A changëd shape, indeed; of gravest mien
And pale cold features; but it seemeth still
A darkened reflex of the face beloved;
A shadow of the shape forever gone.
So the pale Duty takes the place of Love,
And life is not so lonely as we thought,
Nor its full cup so bitter. GOD is good,

And trieth not our weakness overmuch;
Since with the burthen comes the strength also.
And if the harvest that our hands must reap,
And if the work GOD giveth us to do,
Be other than we hoped, so let it be.
Why should we murmur, when he knoweth best
What kind of work is nearest to our needs;
What field most fitting for his hosts to reap?
And in our blindness we can only say,
"His will be done!"
     Not in a moment's space
Came this full truth to me, nor yet in months;
But it was mine — a holy, living truth —
Long ere I saw the Lady Anne again.
Morven was orphaned of its gentle liege
Ere "earth to earth" was spoken o'er the grave
Of Everard Alleyne. Years had gone by —
Some half a score or more — when next she came
To the old happy home, bereft so long.
The years that intervened had brought me peace.
I dared not ask how they had gone with her;
I feared the answering. On her pure brow
So white, so smooth, a shadow lingered dark;
And on her lips a trouble trembled aye.
I questioned nought, for I could read her face
More clearly than my own unquiet heart.
Poor child! poor child! I knew how all these years
Her heart's love had been dying, — wounded, worn,
Until but phantoms of its old self came
To haunt her lonely heart, — a mockery
Of that bright morn, when, as a bride, she gave
Its untouched wealth of love to Richard Leigh,
In fullest trust, — no reservation there!
How had he worn the gift? As a light toy,
The cared-for of an hour, but flung aside
With that hour's fading; as a gathered flower,
Plucked for its beauty and its fragrance once,
Then cast away, with no thought following it,
And left unto forgetfulness and the Past,
With never resurrection!
     Little Anne,
You came to me as in the days long past;
And brought your only child to greet the friend
You had not buried with those weary years.
He was a noble boy, with sunny eyes
Unshadowed and serene. A fair, broad brow,
Most like his mother's; but no sorrow there
Had set its pallid seal, or pressèd lines

With stencil deep; and on the arching lips
A pride sat crescent; shown in boyish scorn
Of little meannesses. Not one line there
Betrayed the father, for the child was heir
Of Morven's stately race and stainless name.
How proud she was of him! and loving too;
As her whole life were garnered in her boy,
And she had nothing else.
                         Too true! too true!
For she *had* nothing else. Dark Richard Leigh
Had been struck down in some wild midnight fray, —
A private vengeance (and my thought went back
Unto dead Alice Hurst); and Anne had been
For some brief months a widow. She came home
No more to leave fair Morven; but its halls
Were strangely desolate. The old-time mirth
Was gone forever, and the Lady Anne
Found never one familiar face among
The servants of to-day. Death had gathered
That household to himself. They were at rest
Beneath the shadows of the ancient trees
Around the old chapelle, and every heart
That watched above her childhood lovingly
Had throbbed its last of earth. She missed, also,
The quiet greeting of some humble friends
Whom God had taken home, ere yet her feet
Were treading England's earth. Those weary years,
That found and left her on a foreign shore,
Had been most changeful, and her painèd heart
Found no old pleasure in the coming home.
She had been gone too long. The years that turned
Her wifely love to dry and bitter dust
Had been as busy round her childhood's home;
And graves were growing green, where not one sod
Had broken been the morn she was a bride.
And the still sleepers, — were they not the same
Whose hands flung flowers on her wedding-day?
Whose lips breathed blessings, and whose loving hearts
Had followed her alway? Could this be so?
She had forgotten how life's sands run out,
And that its stream hath no returning tide,
And looked to find no change, — at least in *home.*
How could it change to her?
                         O change! change! change!
The sweetest and the bitterest thing in life.
A very Proteus in thy thousand forms,
Mocking the lights and shadows of this earth.
Now, robed in sunshine, harbinger of joy, —

Now, trailing garments of the deepest night,
The sure avatar of impending doom.
As fickle and unstable as the breeze;
Only the same in — change!
                           No question here
Of why or wherefore, since GOD wills it so;
And what hath been must be until the end.
The very pulses of Time's mighty heart
Throb only unto changes! not a seed,
Flung broadcast by the winds, or sport of waves,
But finds its place, and through mysterious *change*
Springs up, germ, leaf, and bud, to perfect flower;
Then back again to earth, till from its dust
A Phœnix-birth shall rise, once more to be
The waif of winds and waves! So, evermore,
From life to death, from death to later life,
The Protean change doth work; and so shall work,
Until the coming of that better time
When all shall rest in GOD, — "the SAME to-day,
Yesterday, and forever!"
                       Richard Leigh
Had fallen, they said, in some rude midnight fray.
This rumor told me. Lady Anne said nought
Of him who was her husband. From her lips
There came no word revealing the sad truth
Of what her life in Florence fair had been.
She was his *wife;* as such, she might not speak
Aught evil of her husband. But I knew
What all her silence could not hide from me.
A tone, a sigh, — a something less than sound, —
Were each a revelation. All those years
Had never seal for me. O little Anne!
Your loving heart had broken long ago
But for the child whom GOD had given you.
Its tiny hands did hold you back from death;
Its twining arms made life seem of some worth;
And so you did not die when Richard Leigh
Did tear the mask from off his smiling face,
And mocked at all your dreams of love and faith.
Alas, poor child! GOD, only, speaks these words, —
" I will never leave thee, nor forsake thee!"
And what HE saith we know shall be a rock
Whereon our souls may build, fearing no flood.
But human lips, though uttering such words,
Are all unstable, may deny them too;
And we, who trusted in their promise sweet,
Shall be as ships, that, battered by the storm,
With rudder lost, can find no anchorage,

So drift out helpless to the hungry sea
That roareth for its prey.   Alas for love
That putteth hope, yea, overweening trust,
In aught this side of heaven!   All too soon
The lorn hope dieth, and the simple trust,
That formed an idol from the plastic clay,
Robed it with beauty, shrined it in the heart
With many a low credo, unto which
Itself did say Amen, shall find, some day,
The poor shrine broken, and the idol gone!
Or it may find (a thing of every day)
Its golden idol but a lump of clay
Ground into dust by some most scornful feet
Trampling the shape once worshipped.   While the shrine,
Intact and perfect, hath no dent to show
What eager hands had flung the idol off;
Yet at its base a crimson mantle lies,
Flung there in haste.   Gather it up again,
And put it by.   It will not show the stain
Of some red drops its folds have blotted out.
And life goes on, with labor and with song,
With daily duties finished or begun,
With tears and laughter; ever ringing out
The same old changes; but it nothing tells
Of the grave it treadeth on!
      Poor little Anne!
You thought to bury in that foreign grave
All darker memories, so your life might be
As summer-sunshine, and as summer-dews
Unto your only child.   But, who may say
Unto the stern and irrevocable Past,
"I will have nought of thee."   It clingeth close, —
A very Nestus-robe unto our lives;
And all our future, bright though it may be,
Shuts never out the phantoms of dead joys
That haunt our hearts forever.   As a stream —
Beneath whose waters some unburied corse
Is slowly floating with the ebbing tide —
Doth tell no story to the sunny day
Of what it hideth, though that foulest shape
Doth lie so close below; so in our hearts
The things which have been find still burial,
And smiles and laughter round their silent grave.
But to that grave swift retrospection comes,
And, at her voice, it giveth up its dead.
The river *hath* its secret; but, some day,
Its depths shall render up the thing they held;

To haunt its sunshine with a memory
As an everlasting cloud.
　　　　　　　　　　　　O human life!
So long, and yet so brief!　So loud, so still;
So full of strife; so full of quietness;
Yet never bringest us one brimming cup
Of Lethe's tideless stream!　Some drops, perchance,
May mingle in thy chalice, taking place
Of Memory's frothing wine; so that a day,
A month, a year, may see no phantoms rise
From out the silent Past.　But Memory,
Asserting sway, doth take its full revenge;
And, throned again, doth rule our shrinking souls
As with a rod of iron.　Thus it is
That Earth no waters of oblivion hath,
Nor now, nor ever; and the Grave is not
What some have fabled it.　Nay, Time itself,
That so-called Lethe, doth but charm our pain
With ether-breathings.　We *cannot* forget.
No after joyance may efface the print
Life's saddest hours pressed deep upon the soul;
And shadows of what hath been follow still
The path of sunshine we are treading now;
As night moves onward where the day fades out;
A very Indian in its self-same steps,
As stealthy and as still!
　　　　　　　　　　　　In this our world,
Nor sound, nor breath, nor echo of a sigh,
Falls stillborn from our lips.　It hath its work,
And does it too, though we may never know
Unto what end it grew.　An acorn, once,
Fell from its high estate, and hid itself
Beneath the darksome ground.　A hundred years,
And from its grave a giant oak had reared
Its far-out-reaching boughs.　So little things —
A look, a tone, perchance some heedless word,
That we think blotted from our book of life —
May fall on fitting soil, and grow to be
A mighty thought, o'ershadowing the land
As stately palm, or deadly upas-tree.
In humble earnestness, then, let us pray
That God will set upon our lips a guard,
Since words, once uttered, are our own no more;
We cannot call them back.　For weal, for woe,
Those airy messengers have sallied forth,
Throughout all time their devious course to run;
And we, who let them go, must answer too,
For the wild work they do.　And, if our words,

So lightly spoken, and so lightly sped,
Go sounding ever through the coming time;
Each *act* of ours must be a thunder-peal,
Stirring the universe!   We hear it not.
Our souls are deaf; for that their house of clay
Doth dull their finer sense.   But when they stand
Without the earthen walls — alone with GOD! —
Shall the deaf adder hear!

——————

        " Hast ever watched
The earliest tracery of the coming Spring?
The soft, faint touches of her gentle hand?
Seen first on Earth's brown bosom when the grass
Sends up its tiny blades to greet the sun.
Shown next in sheltered and retired nooks,
Where through the pervious sod the hidden spring
Wells upward silently, and feedeth so
The fairy veinings of each starting leaf.
Then from its nest of darkly shining leaves,
First-born of Spring, the blue-eyed myrtle peeps;
While alder-blooms are swaying in the breeze,
Scattering their golden dust.   Along the brook,
By thousands numbered, grows the violet;
And, on the hill-side, 'mid the piny woods,
The pale arbutus trails its blossoms sweet.
Soon, from their downy, brown, empurpled leaves,
The squirrel-cup lifts up its modest head;
And tender crocus, graceful hyacinth, •
Clothe the brown earth with beauty." —
          So a friend,
From o'er the ocean, writeth me of Spring, —
The Spring that greets him on Mohegan's shores.
Not so it greeteth us.   Our fields are green
Alike in sunshine, 'neath a cloudy sky,
And when the snow is lying, cold and white,
As a virgin's pall, above them.   Silently
Spring grows on Winter, as an ivy folds
The stately ruin of some ancient oak;
And it is here, with beauty and with song,
Ere we mark its coming, or have taken note
Of the dying Winter.   We little heed
The changing seasons; but my foreign friend
Was something of a poet; and he kept
His yearly calendar, his dial too,
By the sweet signs of flowers.   If he spake
Of any hour, " 'twas when the primrose closed;"
" When morning-glories oped their azure eyes;"
Or " when the dew was fresh on violets."

And were the talk of seasons, straight he'd say,
"I mind me well, 'twas when the apple-blooms
Were thick in orchards;" — "When the golden corn
Was ripe for harvesting." Or, were he sad,
With mournful cadence, he would murmur low,
"When leaves are falling;" — "When the roses die."

I've thought, at times, how passing sweet it was
To reckon time by flowers; not by pulses,
Whose throb too often is an added pain.
But ah! not so keep we our count of time.
We reckon it by changes; by the days
When we were young; by manhood's stately prime;
By the white hairs of age, and evermore
Think what hath been more fair than that we have.
As if, in journeying to the glowing East,
The setting sun sank sudden from our sight;
And, looking backward, to the hills o'erpast,
We see them shining in the golden rays
That light our way no more. We know the morn
May bring a day more gloriously fair;
It is the Future; but, uncertain all,
Of which we say not "being," but "to be."
And count we on earth's future as we may,
It is but leaning on a broken reed.
Nor yet to-morrow may we call our own;
Since even now the word may have gone forth:
"This night thy soul shall be required of thee."

How reckon then our days? By good deeds done,
That yet were nothing but for simple Faith.
By true words, spoken with a low heart-prayer
That our poor seed may fall on goodly ground,
And to GOD's harvest grow. And by "small things,"
That seem to perish in their hour of birth;
But meet us after, full and stately grown,
GOD's chiefest blessings; as if we had cast
"Our bread upon the waters," and had found ·
"It after many days."
      What though true words
And noble deeds, linked unto Faith and Love,
Be truest data whence to reckon time?
Men count not so. Some brief success in life, —
One forward step in the world's beaten path,
Whereto it matters not, — a gain, a loss,
A fate accomplished, or a granted fame,
Stand out as sign-posts on their road of life;
And each doth tell the distance travelled o'er

In months, or years.   A woman's quiet life
Is told by heart-beats.   Joys and sorrows lie
Thick strewn upon the pages of the book
She keepeth unto Time.   A broken hope
That finds still burial, a joy intense
Through all her pulses thrilling, or a grave,
Whose silence falleth on her after life, —
Are all the data of a woman's heart.
She keepeth record of a thousand things
That in man's world are nothing.   Looks, and tones,
And utterings of words, fill her still days
Up to the very brim with happiness;
And little things are all the world to her:
And all the more, when love doth crown her life
With the o'erflowing fulness of content.
And woman's heart, too prescient evermore,
Glooms to the shadow of a nameless fear,
Hears its death-warrant in a careless tone,
And breaks in silence.   So the Spartan boy
Spake never word, the while the stolen fox
Was gnawing at his vitals.   So that boy
Of later times stood up erect and still,
The while his monarch spake sweet words of praise,
"But you are wounded!"   "Sire, it is *death!*" —
And, saying so, looked *smiling* up, and died!

So little Anne, though but a woman weak,
Wore smiles, nay, jests, upon the arching lips
Whose red curve told no tales; and yet I knew
How still a grave they veilèd from the day.

And years moved on, all unrevealingly.
The years that stole no smiles, yet left their frosts
Upon some brownest tresses: though they still
Gleamed golden in the sun.   And he, her child,
Fair Morven's bonny heir, had seen the dawn
Of early childhood fade into the light
Of youth's serenest morning, with no cloud
To dull its beauty, or its glory dim.
A childhood, pure as maiden-dreamings are,
A stainless youth, had rounded to a man
Who dared look heavenward.
                                        Dark days were coming.
Days of fierce strife; the deadly Crimean War;
And England's hope must share that revelling.
So forth they went, the gallant ones, the true,
Bearing high hearts to battle.   With no thought
That Death might meet them, deadly and most sure,

On other than battle-field.   And *he* went, —
Her boy, — she could not keep him back.   *Would* not
Had been more fitting word.   His eager soul
Burning in his eyes, he came to tell her, —
"Come life or death, he must go with the host
That England sent to battle;" so he went.

Hast ever read of that poor guest of old
Who, seated at the banquet, saw the sword
Suspended o'er him by a single thread,
So slight, a breath of air might sever it?
So one sharp fear hung heavy on the word
"News from the East" might bring.
                                        It came at last, —
The day of fate; and ushered wildly in
By the dark tale of Balaklava's charge, —
That fatal charge.   All England rang with it;
Nay, the world.   But few gave even one poor thought
To those whose best and dearest had gone down
In that wild charge to death!   What cared the world
For wealth of woman's tears, for hearts that bled
To death, o'er their belovëd lying low
On that dark field of blood?   Blood poured like rain,
And wasted as a shower on desert sands.
Blood, winning nothing, save the bitter fame
That sitteth mocking on unnumbered tombs;
Yet saying low, "Only the good are great;
Only they accounted so, when at the bar
God sits in judgment."
                                Ay, *he* was dead!
And England mourned no nobler son than he.
No truer heart, no purer soul than his
Did beat among her thousands; and the dust
Of that so crimson Crimea lies above
The last of Morven's race.   But none know where
The fair, young earl is sleeping his last sleep.
He shared that fearful charge, but came not back
Nor then, nor ever, — living nor yet dead.
And so the tale came home.
                                A little thing
It seems, perhaps, unto some careless eye,
When "*missing*," endeth low some battle-roll,
But, for the loving ones of hearth and home,
Unto whose yearning hearts that one brief word
Is all the battle bringeth, 'tis a sword,
Whose point, envenomed, makes no ghastly wound
Whence the warm life flows out; but with a scratch
Doth taint the very fountain of the blood

With intermingling of death's darker tide.
The doom, though slow, is not one whit less sure.
And, at the last, o'er all life's crimson flow
The dark wave rides triumphant. But *one word*,
One little word, hath set the death-tide free;
And over all their little isle of life
The storm-waves thunder; while their bark of hope,
Storm-driven, wanders from the port of home,
May never come to shore! But *they* have hope.
The Lady Anne had none.

It matters little where the dead may lie,
Since GOD doth keep our dust. The spirit hath
Its home on other shores; and thither we
Must all be wending. Whether to the earth,
Or to the keeping of the soundless deep,
Or unto freest winds, we give the dead,
Doth nothing trouble me; since in my heart
There resteth warm the sweet, immortal words:
"I AM THE RESURRECTION AND THE LIFE!"

I feel — yea, know — that in the far-off Land
Which we call Heaven, — where some coming day
Shall give us back to the belovèd there, —
I know that those who have gone from us here,
Seeking a better country and a home,
Shall greet us once again on that blessed shore,
With all the old familiar voices sweet,
And faces changeless in their dear old shape.
For in fond eyes, and unto loving hearts,
Sameness is beauty! How should we be known
By those most dear, if other mien we wear
In the Eternal Land? What though the form
May have a beauty passing earthly dream,
And on each brow no olden shadows lie;
Yet something of the shape that once was ours,
Though glorified, purified, shall remain
Answering the old love still. Or else what hope
For the lone hearts of earth that quiet live
Because they feel that after death shall come
Reunion? And — if in the other world
No recognition be; if those whom death
Hath early severed, do but part to meet
As strangers meet and part on this our earth;
No deathless love o'ermastering time and space
And waiting for us on the farther shore —
How bitter cold the waves of death would rise
Round our reluctant feet! How would our hearts

Recoil in shuddering from the fatal stream
That shuts all knowledge of our loved ones out;
So shutting out forever!
                              Pause, and think.
Are there no eyes, no tender, shining eyes,
That our poor hands have lidded from the sun
They look not on again?   Are there no hands
Whose gentle clasp did seem to bring fresh trust
In earthly lovingness, that we have seen
Quietly folded on a pulseless breast,
So folded that they meet our own no more?
Are there no voices whose soft echo still
Floats through our memory, waking there
Such wealth of yearning, — voices that have long
Been silent in the grave?   Are there not forms,
Once full of life and all life's lovingness,
That we have given to the dust to keep
"In the sure hope of Heaven"?   And shall all these
Take not a shadow of their olden selves
Into the other Land?   No one sweet clue
Bearing us through the labyrinthine Past
Into the presence of the souls beloved,
That went before us to the Better Land?
Nay, never so.   GOD loveth us too well!
And he — the Christ — who dwelt awhile in flesh,
Taking our mortal nature on himself,
Suffering as we, — loving as we cannot love, —
Will surely give us something of this earth,
All purer hopes and loves, to keep alway
Deepening the joy of Heaven!

———

                              Who taketh note
How the swift hours go?   We let them pass
As flowers idly gathered, and as idly flung
Aside in our soon mood of weariness.
We heed them not.   What does it matter, then,
That irrevocably the days have gone,
Dying from out our lives as blossoms die
From off the summer earth?   Their work is done;
GOD, only, knoweth *how;* and never prayer
From human lips can bring them back again.
But let them go; so in the other world
They rise not up with their accusing voice
As witness 'gainst our soul!
                              One quiet morn —
'Tis scarce a twelvemonth since — a poor man stood
Without the church's door, and paused, as one
Who dared not tread within the courts of GOD.

I marked his brow, deep graven with such lines
As passion stencils in her darkest mood.
I marked the quivering of the thin white lips,
The trembling of the frame. I questioned not
Of what his past had been, but oped the door,
And bade him enter. "God's house was not barred
To any human soul." In lowly guise
The gray head bent before me. From the lips
A thankful murmur came. Within the porch
The stranger stood, shaking in every limb
That in their weakness seemed to chain his feet.
A moment's pause, — one backward glance he gave
Unto the graves that in the morning light
Looked green and very still. Then prone he fell
Across the threshold, with a low, faint cry :
"Have mercy, God, on me!"
                        I raised him up;
But laid him down again, as faint and sick
The white lips turned more white. No need of aid.
My simple skill availed to call life back;
But when it came, I knew 'twas as a guest
Who tarrieth but a night.
                        Above our heads
The early bells pealed out their matin-song,
And through the glistening dew the people came
Unto the morning prayer. I gave the man
Into the sexton's charge, and bade him see
Him cared for tenderly. To his own home
Did Griffith bear the sick and dying man.
And, after service, there I found him, laid
In the best chamber, curtained in from light,
Whose glare was painful to the dimming eyes.
There was a trembling of the nerveless hands,
A recognition in the sickly smile
Wherewith he greeted me.
                     — "I saw you once —
In London — on the bridge — the night *she* died.
My little Alice Hurst! I was avenged.
I followed him for long; found him at last,
And stabbed him to the heart that was so false!
Life for a life. I heard a sermon once
Which preached that doctrine. I have lived it out!"

This much — no more — uttered with gasping breath,
And pauses long between. Then came the end.

We little know what tales the inner life,
With all its solemn mysteries, could reveal!
21

How, like a ghost, some buried sin doth flit
Through the heart's silent chambers, resting not;
And only laid, when we ourselves lie low
Within the grave; or when the voice of GOD
Brings peace to haunted heart and troubled soul.
But ere his love doth lay all phantoms low,
And from old griefs draw all the bitter out,
We stagger blindly up the rugged hill
Ourselves have made of straws, and daily press
Into our shrinking flesh some sharpest cross
Christ never laid on us.　Yea, think the while,
We may win heaven by the heavy load
Ourselves have shouldered; by the deathly shape
That walks so like a skeleton in the house,
Within the secret chambers of the soul,
Making life hideous.　Yet we keep it there,
As though it were a treasure past all price.
GOD send it go not to the other world, —
A fearful witness of the hidden sin
We garnered from man's knowledge, — there to be
Bound to the shrinking soul, as was the dead
Unto the living in that doom of old!

　　This wandering soul had gone to judgment.
All its sins lay heavy on it.
　　　　　　　　Death comes,
And finds us unrepentant.　With stern hand
He shuts the door of reconciliation,
No more to open to our erring souls
In the hereafter.　For the other world, —
Whereof we know but darkly — hath no time
To wear away the stains of earthly sin;
And in the world beyond the sea of death
Doth dwell no virtue purging us of sin.
The only hope, whereto our souls can cling,
Is in this present life; and yet too oft
Its holy refuge is a thing despised, —
An ark we neither seek, nor enter in.
We see no shadow of the awful Cross
Whereon GOD's Son did hang.　The Sacred Blood,
From tortured veins poured forth on Calvary,
A stream to heal the nations, flows in vain
For those who will not trust its saving flood.
And yet it floweth to our very feet;
We need but stoop, and drink!　Oh blind, blind, blind!
We will not see, that aye within our reach
That stream of life is flowing evermore;
We will not taste the sweet and precious wave

Proffered so freely.   "Whosoever will "
May come, and drink, and gain eternal life.
We will not hear the Voice that bids us "come."
Though we "labor and are heavy-laden,"
We will not seek the promised rest to find;
We will not trust our GOD!   We dare not say
" His arm is shortened that it cannot save;"
And yet we act the lie!   Our lives show forth
The sin we dare not utter with our lips;
We have no faith in GOD!   Lost sheep are we,
That wander guideless on the mountains dark,
And will not seek the fold secure to gain.
Its door stands ever open, for our Lord,
The Shepherd, knows his own.   None enter there
Who bear not in with them the Master's name,
The mark that he hath set.   Without are wolves,
That ravening seek their prey.   Without are storms,
That beat all pitiless upon the sheep
That wander from the fold.   Without are snares,
That catch the unwary feet; and pitfalls, too,
That make full many captive.   But, within,
No wolf may enter, tempest breaketh not,
And snare and pitfall are as things unknown.
Without are flowers, fair and sweet to view,
But whoso gathereth shall take poison home!
Without are fruits, most tempting to the eye,
But, plucked and tasted, they are ashes all!
Within we gather grapes of vintage rare,
Whose wine gives life eternal to the soul;
And there, the flowers of true and heavenly type
Do shadow forth our immortality!

  Within the fold of Christ!   Within the Church!
The Church he builded up by Life and Death,
From Cross and Sepulchre!   How few of us
Are living members of the Church of GOD, —
Are in the fold of Christ!   On some of us
Baptismal waters lie like holy dew, —
Pure drops that keep life's sweetest flowers fresh,
And ripen all unto the golden fruits
GOD's angels gather in.   Others brush off
The saving drops by contact with the world;
The world that hath nor part nor lot with GOD;
And so the life they should have nourished most, —
GOD's life within the soul, — is dwarfed and dies,
Unless GOD's breath shall bid the "dry bones live," —
His love redeem the captive from foul sin,
  And wash the leper clean.

                              Unto this GOD,
Whose love outreacheth far our widest ken,
We leave the soul that sated its revenge
With nothing less than blood.   I judge it not.
How know I but this soul, crimsoned with blood,
May be found whiter in the judgment-day
Than mine or thine?   It is a fearful thing
Daring to set the seal of "lost," or "saved,"
On any human soul!
                              As in the years
Of Egypt's palmy splendor men did sit
In judgment on the dead, so in these days,
Transmitted down through all the centuries,
Men keep the old rite still; but not as then.
No solemn court is held; no judges sit;
But, in their stead, each maketh of himself
Both court and judge; and with unseemly haste
Doth speak the sentence.   If, as we are taught,
The words we utter shall recoil on us,
The doom we render others is our own.
And yet, how lightly spoken are the words
That some day soon shall sound unto our souls
A thunder-peal forever, dying not!
Verily, there is a GOD that judgeth!

It seemeth strange, how on the shore of Time
The wrecks of old and former things are cast;
Recalling the forgotten, — bringing back
The dead things of the Past, as if our life
Did move in circles.   For this man who died
Did seem to end the circle was begun
That night I stood upon old London Bridge,
And saw, but could not save, poor Alice Hurst.

Do all things move in circles?   Seasons, years,
The rise and fall of kingdoms, changes, time,
Creations and entombings, — all these seem
To end where they began; and, ending so,
Do rise like Phœnix from its funeral pyre
To live another life.   Unlike the old
Perchance in phases, but alike in this:
Beginning and the ending are the same.
The tiny seed, a breath of wind doth shake
From out its cell upon the dewy earth,
Shall feel the quickening sun, and wake to life.
Two wings of green have burst their prison-cell;
Leaves grow, and the delicate stem is seen
To rear aloft its crown of golden flowers.

The petals fall, the seed-germs grow apace,
Until, full-ripe, the shaking of the wind
Shall scatter them again, to spring anew
From out the earth, to blossom, and to die.
So their brief circles run. The seasons come,
And go, and come again. Suns set and rise.
The moon fulfils her month, and wanes, and grows,
A circle in itself. Tides ebb and flow
Obedient to her changes. And the year
Is alway changing from the old to new.
No chimes so ancient as the chimes that ring
For the Old Year out, and the New Year in.
The planets have their courses. This our Earth
Keeps on her path through all the circling years.
Each planet knows its own appointed way
And doth not swerve aside, but faithful is
E'en in its retrogression. Man is made
Of the dust of the earth; and when he dies
Returns to dust again. Death treads on Life.
Life springs from Death; and so the circles run.
So shall they run, unless GOD shatter them,
Through all the cycles of eternity.

———

The day hath not yet dawned. I hear the waits
Sweet singing carols 'neath their rector's porch.
And down the vale, heard through the rustling pines
The bells are ringing out the Christmas-song:
"Glad tidings of great joy." How softly clear
The sounds come floating on the winter air
Unto my study-window! All the night
Have I been keeping vigil. Sleep came not
Unto my weary eyelids; so I sat,
Outwatching the pale stars, and counting o'er
How many years the Christmas-bells had rung
Since first they sounded on mine infant ears
From the old church far away. The dear old bells!
I hear them now as when in other days
They chiméd out at earliest Christmas dawn
"Gloria in excelsis." Dear old bells!
Your chimes ring out above some quiet graves, —
Some graves I have not seen for fifty years, —
Shall never see again!
                        How very near
Lies this our world unto that other world
Where Death, who owneth here a kingly realm,
Can never enter! All its gates are barred
Unto the King of Shadows. Never shape,
Like unto his, can win an entrance there!

I lay my fingers on this throbbing vein,
And count the pulses. Well I know that Death
Doth lurk between each throb. It rests with GOD
To bid the pulse go on, or stop forever!
A breath is all that lies twixt us and death,
So insecure is our poor hold on life,
And yet we think not of it. I have heard
Men planning schemes that only long, full years
Could crown with ripeness; yet they never gave
A passing thought unto the Shape that stands
Betwixt two worlds,—the Shape that laughs to scorn
The vain imaginings of foolish men;
And, with a touch, doth make them and their dreams
As the poor dust they daily trample on,—
The dust that once was all instinct with life;
The dust that now is nothing but the dust,
Yet some day soon may wear another shape,—
Spring up as vernal grasses fresh and green,
Or, clothed with beauty, as the flowers fair,
Or else, put on some higher, nobler form,
And walk, a man, where once was only dust.

The bells are chiming still; and o'er the snow
I see the figures of the singers glide
Each to some cottage home; ere long to meet
Beneath the arches of the old chapelle.
The blessèd little ones! Who loves not them
Is less than man, and worse than any brute.
I have lived lonely all these many years:
I had nor wife nor children,—yet my days
Have flowed on calmly, tended by the love
I know I won from all the little ones.
They came to me with such unfearing trust;
They laid in mine, soft fingers lovingly;
Their arms have oft been twined around my neck;
Their little heads have lain upon my breast;
Their kisses sweet been pressed on lips and brow,
As I had been their father. Joyous shouts
Would greet the coming of their rector's feet;
And none so welcome at each cottage porch
As he who poured upon each infant brow
The healing waters from the holy font.
Should I not be content? And so, to-day,
The Christmas chimes sound sweeter than of yore;
My heart seems singing such a joyous song,
As if it, too, would feign keep holy day.

Sick unto death!   My darling, whom I love!
Love better now than in that earlier day
When I was young, and she so fair, so fair!
Sick unto death, and I am powerless.
My little Anne!
                    Through all those saddest days
The tenderness of old had flushed my heart
As with the fire of my ardent youth.
I felt again, in every throbbing pulse,
The old, old pain; the one love unreturned,
That made my manhood lonely, and my hair
White long before its time. . . . . .

They left me there, to pray beside the dead;
But, GOD forgive me!   I had only tears,
And passionate moaning that would have its way,
I had been calm so long for her dear sake;
O'ermastering the pain with iron hand.
The hand was useless now, and the pent flood
Broke up the fountain at my heart.   I felt
The surging torrent bursting from my lips,
And knew no more.   They found me lying there,
As pale and cold as was the Lady Anne;
The red blood, staining all the snowy couch.
It could not pain her now.   They bore me home.

.   .   .   .

She is at rest.   From out this world of care
Her gentle soul hath gone unto its GOD.
It suffered, struggled, but the strife is o'er.
Death laid his hand upon the throbbing heart,
And stilled its pulses.   GOD took home the soul
That through its long probation won the rest
He "giveth his beloved."   And in that home —
It lies beyond the confines of this earth —
Are no more tears and pain.   Nor Sin, nor Death,
Are in that City.   All its gates are Peace.
No night is there.   No sun nor moon do shine.
GOD is the glory thereof, and the Lord
Its everlasting Light!

She is at rest; and all is well with her.
Thanks be to GOD for this!   In the sure hope
No man can take away, they gave to earth
Our darling Lady Anne; and "Dust to dust,
Ashes to ashes," hath been said above
Another Morven.   But the last, the last!
The name hath died with her.   No heir remains;

And so a stranger shall own lordship here.
It matters not.   Ere comes the Lenten tide
I shall have passed away.
      Behold, O GOD!
The people thou hast given to my care.
Keep them from wandering in forbidden paths;
And bring them home to thee.   My work is done,
And, with the folding of my feeble hands,
I shall lie down to rest; but these remain,
My people whom I love.   Keep them, O GOD,
Beneath thy shadowing wings; and, in the day
When thou dost count thy jewels, grant that none
Of these thy children be found wanting there!

On the River.

SOFTLY down on the rippling river
 Shineth the light of departing day;
Arrows of flame from the day-god's quiver
 Blaze on the cloudlets far away.
Blue are the hills in their dusky shading,
 Eastward looking with waiting eyes;
From westerly summits the light is fading,
 Purple and gold are the evening skies.
Slowly down on the beautiful river
 Floats our boat as the tide goes out.

Grand old trees with their branches waving,
 See themselves in the waters clear;
Little flowers their petals are laving
 In the cool ripple, so sweet, so near!
The river its evening song is singing
 Unto the pebbles upon the beach;
And the leafy aisles of the wood are ringing
 Where sing the bird-minstrels, high out of reach
Slowly down on the beautiful river
 Floats our boat as the tide goes out.

Over the waters the winds breathe slowly
 Perfumed breath from the locust-flowers;
Singing now high, and singing now lowly,
 Lullaby-songs from the forest-bowers.
Murmuring waves, with a slumberous seeming,
 Mingle their music with songs of air;

Soothing our senses, as we were dreaming,
  A dream wherein all things were rarely fair.
Slowly down on the beautiful river,
  Floats our boat as the tide goes out.

Olive and Violet.

I.

A CHIME of bells at midnight. Bells that rang
The Old Year sadly out — the New Year in.
The snow was falling softly. Thick and white
It lay upon the pavement. Not a foot
Had left its impress on the stainless snow;
And so the street wore, for an hour's space,
The cold, pure aspect of some northern hills.
No sound of revelling awoke the night
From peace and slumber. Only through the air —
The starry flakes just trembled to the sound —
Flowed, soft and sweet, the chiming of the bells.

As the Old Year was dying, children two
Were born into the world. As far apart
In their belongings as the day and night.
Alike in this: their souls must fight their way
From earthly bondage unto Heaven's gate,
Or sink them downward to the utmost hell.

One entered life, a feeble baby-girl,
'Mid fetid air, and odors damp and sour;
Beside a hearth whereon the fire was cold.
No loving ones did greet this little guest —
This stranger in the house. Yet was the house
But rarely tenantless. All had gone forth
Unto some revelling of New Year's Eve,
When, wandering through the storm, a woman came,
Unto the broken door-way (door was none),
And, blind and staggering, half-crazed with pain,
Had fallen by the cold and desolate hearth.
And there she lay, from eve till midnight came,
In one long strife with pain. As chimed the bells
From out the old church-tower, her moanings ceased.
A baby's feeble wail recalled to earth
The soul that was departing; and she drew
The baby to her breast, and wrapped it round
With her own garments, softly, tenderly.

For it was hers, — this child she could not see, —
The only thing was hers in all the world.
And then — no more. Ere yet the chiming bells
Had ceased to sound the child was motherless.

II.

Not far away, a stately palace-home
Was draped with silence. To and fro,
With muffled footsteps, went the servant train;
And, in a chamber, richly decked by art,
The lord of all this splendor sat alone.
There was a shadow on his smooth, broad brow;
A restless tremble of the upper lip;
A sense of some inquietude within;
A watching of the door. There came a sound
Of slow, descending footsteps, and he rose,
Half turning as he rose. A man came in;
And after him a woman with a child, —
A little babe just born into the world;
Thus early brought unto its father's arms.
He took his baby-daughter gently up,
Just touched its little cheek, and then, — "My wife?"
"She resteth well," the doctor grave replied,
"And hath all tendance. I return to her." —
"And I will bring my daughter." Carefully
The father held his child; and so went up
Unto the darkened chamber, where the wife,
So lately made a mother, waited him.
The child laid softly by the mother's side;
A kiss, pressed light upon pale, smiling lips;
A few low words of manly tenderness;
And then she slept. But never waking came.
And when the morning broke, the child was named
By its dead mother's name.
                    So Death had come,
And by his touch made equal these two souls.
The palace-home, the cold and ruined hearth,
Are on a level now. Each holds the dust
Of that which was a woman, and is not.
Each doth contain a little helpless thing
That, long years hence, if life be granted it,
Will be a woman. But how far apart,
Their paths in life shall be!
                    Unto our eyes —
Half blinded by the dust of worldly things —
These children's lots do most unequal seem;
And none would choose the ruined hearth for home
Before the rich man's palace. Be it so, —

God seeth not as we.   And, in the day
When he shall count his jewels, brightest there
Will be some souls, that out of darkness fought
Their way unto the light; that were long tried,
Yea, sorely tempted; yet rose out of all,
God's truest servants, worthy to obtain
The crown they never thought awaited them!

III.

Back from their New-Year's feast the revellers came,
To find the old house tenanted by the dead,
Made purer by the presence of a child
Fresh from its Maker's hand.   Rough were they all,
And foul with sin, — the very scum and froth
Society casts forth without its pale;
The dregs that lie at every city's heart,
And seethe and fester there.   Yet was there still
A touch of soundness in these outcast souls;
A something of the angel left within,
Called forth by that sad sight.   With gentle hands
They took the child from off its mother's breast,
And laid the dead out for its burial.
They thought the dead face seemed to smile on them,
So fair and sweet it was!   All lines of care
Pressed smooth by Death; all marks of pain effaced,
As if the soul had smiling gone to Heaven!

Her life was hid.   Her very name unknown;
And her last resting-place the Potter's Field.
The child could never know its mother's name!

This waif of Death — this poor and broken thing,
Cast up upon the dark and slimy shore
Of the old city — hath well done its work;
Hath left the impress of some better things
On brows all stained with crime; and given up,
Unto the keeping of these sinful hearts,
The little dove that shall bring peace to all.

We rarely think how very near a child
Is unto God; from out whose hand, so late
The little spirit came to make its home
In those weak walls of flesh.   Alas! the sin,
That with our dust is coexistent found,
Shall try the spirit sorely; and the strife
Begun in cradle will not cease on earth
Until Death end it with his still, cold hand, —
The hand whose touch brings peace unto the heart

Whose pulses throb no more forever. Peace,
As given to the soul, doth come from GOD,
And hath *its* home beyond the shores of Death.
It dies not with the dust. Oh! fair and sweet,
Past all our dreaming, is the little child
On whose pure brow the dews of heaven lie
Fresh from the holy font! The little one,
That knows no soiling of the dust as yet;
A precious lamb out of the fold of GOD,
Upon whose brow the Master's mark is set;
The little child that Jesus calls to him
With so sweet words: "Forbid them not
To come unto me; for of such as these
Is the kingdom. Their angels ever stand
Before the face of my Father in heaven."
Is it not written that he took them up
Into his arms, and blessed them? He, the GOD,
The mighty Lord of Hosts, — the Virgin-Born;
Who shall be called Wonderful, Counsellor,
The Everlasting Father, Prince of Peace!
And "He that was, and is, and is to come," —
Yet so loved us that from his throne on high
He stooped to earth, and clothed himself in flesh;
And veiled his Godhead in a woman's womb;
And was obedient even unto death:
The death accursed, — the Death upon the Cross!
That agony endured was never finite pain,
As ours is, but infinite as a GOD's.
That shame despised was gathered from all years
And poured in fire on his sacred head;
And there was never sorrow like to his!
Through all the years to come this shame is borne;
O'er all the future doth this sorrow fall;
And for all time, this deathless agony
Shall he, the Saviour, bear until the end;
When the full work, of man's redemption wrought,
Shall hail Christ conqueror; and all the earth,
With all its kingdoms, shall become the Lord's;
And time shall be no more!
      Our puny thought
Cannot attain the glorious heights of pain
Wherewith our GOD doth battle. All our lore
Could never reckon o'er the years of shame
That in the Future's womb lie darkening;
And all our woe, from Adam until now,
Were light as dust, before that awful grief
That rests, as night, upon the brow of Christ!

Yet he, the Holy One, keeps watch and ward,
And careth for his own. He heareth still
The cry of the poor and desolate ones;
And in our sickness maketh all our bed.
He leadeth home the lost and wandering sheep,
And makes them to lie down in pastures green,
Where living waters flow. And when we tread
The Valley Dark, he doth uphold our feet;
His rod and staff do comfort us alway.
And in the desert and the wilderness,
He is as "the Shadow of a great Rock
In a weary land." With a Brother's love
He careth for the children.
                Silently,
As flowers grow, the little waiflet won
A place in every corner of the house
She sweetened by her coming. Not a hearth,
Though bare and cold, but seemed to gain a glow
If she but came to it; and the old house
Was slowly putting on a cleaner garb;
"Because the child would soon be creeping round."
Men, old in crime, whose careworn, restless hearts
Had known no sunshine all these many years,
Did feel its warmth when in their arms they took
The little Olive. So they called the child,
As though some shadow of her life-work looked
From out the sweet, blue eyes. Hands, large and rough,
And sinewy arms, did learn a tender use,
That made their strength seem nought, "holding baby."
And the fierce brows grew soft, as little arms
Were stretched to meet them, and they heard the child's
Sweet crow of triumph, as it pulled the hair
That once was not so smooth. No oaths were heard.
Their very voices had a gentle ring
Answering the child's low cooing. Sullen lips
Arched into smiles, or else they dared not kiss
The baby's little mouth, but stood aloof;
With such dark fire burning in their eyes
As blazes forth from the despairing orbs
Of fallen angels, coveting the heaven
They have forever lost!
                And women, sunk
In such foul depths that never human hand
Might draw them thence, did reverence the child
That, pure as snow, brought some pale shadow back
Of their lost womanhood. A shuddering thought
Of days when they were children like to this, —
Of happy homes they left so long ago

Darkened forever by their Death in Life.
They had no tears, these women. That sweet fount
Was dried up long years since; no more to flow
Unless God's hand should smite the stony heart
And bid the waters rise to heal and save.

    Despair not, O ye fallen! Even yet
Ye may find refuge from the bitter storm,—
An ark of safety 'mid the fearful sea
That surges o'er ye. And, though ye be "dead
In trespasses and sin," ye yet may live.
Through all the noise of eighteen hundred years
The voice of Jesus comes: "Go, sin no more!"
Behold! ye took the little stranger in;
Ye clothed it with your best; ye gave it all
Was fitting for its needs,—food, raiment, time,—
Not knowing that ye took an angel home;
Not knowing, or forgetting words like these:
"Inasmuch as ye did it unto one
The least of these my brethen, know that ye
Have done it unto me."
               These women's hearts
Had long been dead within them. Sin had killed
All blossoms fair of childhood's innocence;
And in their stead grew noisome, pestilent weeds,
That drained the blood of sweetness; made more sure
The deadly poison of the life they lived;
Made nothing fair save the swift road to hell
They never thought to leave. They saw no path
Unto a purer air. They knew no way
Save that they walked in, and its end was death.
The former years were nothing to them now;
They could not bring them back, nor yet return
Unto the sunshine of the olden days.
They were too far away,— shut out by years
Of bitterness and sin. They saw no hand
Outstretched to save, across the darkening gulf;
And so they went down quick into the grave
Of the great city, and were seen no more!

    Unto these women came this new-born child,
This little Olive, as a light that shines
In a dark place, stirring some pulses there
That had not beat for many a long year.
This ray of sunshine fell, all warm and soft,
Upon these ice-bound hearts, just touching them
To a more gentle mood; winning its way
Where storm and tempest might have beat in vain.

Verily, the child was as an angel
Sent to redeem and save! Foul tongues were mute;
The awful jesting of the fallen hushed
In presence of her purity. A sense
Of inward shame, that would not brook control,
Abased their spirits, when they touched the hands
So white, as theirs can never be again;
And yet they were ashamed of feeling shame!
They did not know whose Spirit was at work,
And that the thing they strove to drive away
Was the faint embryo of a better life
Yet cold and dead; but " the breath of the Lord,
Like a stream of fire, shall kindle it! "

   And so the years passed on. The child grew fast.
Soon little feet went pattering on the floor;
Soon little hands were busy all the day;
And little eyes of looking never weary.
For them the world was gathered in small space.
A few old rooms, a narrow, narrow street,
With one small bit of sky, but never sun.
The house was small. Shut in by warerooms huge
That coveted the sunlight; let no ray
Of all its golden many, smile upon
The old house in the alley. No bad type
Were they, of some who fain would shut God's light
From out a world they love not overmuch.
Only they cannot do it. So, in this.
The over-topping warerooms shut out sun,
But never sunlight. And when sunlight went
The silent stars were shining all the night, —
Were shining down — on what? We will but say
On the old house in the alley. Weather-stained
Were walls and roof; but darker stains, they said,
Had once been seen upon the oaken floor;
Traced through the passage, down the shaking stairs,
Where'er the red drops fell, as slow they bore
A murdered man into the open air.
But this was long ago. Time had effaced
All tokens of that crime; and they who dwelt
Beneath the roof-tree of the old house now,
Knew nothing of its Past, nor cared to know.
It gave them shelter in the burning heat,
It shut out something of the bitter cold,
And gave them each a refuge for the night.
They liked the old house well. Since Olive came
It wore a brighter aspect. Doors unhung,
Went back to their old use. The few whole panes

That graced the windows were kept somewhat clean;
And for the rest (a whim to please the child),
They were as many-colored as the light
That shone but dimly through them. Pictures strange,
Torn down from some old fence (for Olive's sake),
Were pasted on the walls. Grotesque and grim,
It may be, in themselves, but something worth
For the kind thoughtfulness that placed them there.
A chair or two, both old and rickety,
Helped furnish forth each room; and for all else,
Each did the least they could, till Olive came,
And then their wants grew many. She had brought
Unto these women some old memories back
Of quiet country homes, where neatness reigned.
And all, though plain, was clean. So the old house
Began to show the changes of the time,
And wore its novel honors daintily.
It was not used to much; so made the most
Of clean-swept chambers, and of mended doors.
Perhaps it dreamed that in some coming day,
The warm, bright sun it had not seen for years
Would peep above the warerooms, just to see
If still the little house were standing there!

One room was empty, — had been vacant long, —
But when our Olive was just three years old
It had a tenant found. An agèd man
Who once had been a sailor, but the sea
Would never greet him more! Decrepit, old,
Worn out in heavy service, all his strength
Did scarce suffice to bear him on his rounds.
He was a gatherer of paper, — rags, —
But nothing ever came amiss to him.
No thing so small but had its proper use,
And should be put to it. So argued he,
And soon his room a small museum grew,
Of such rare things as sometimes find their way
Into the ash-box; or had gathered been
In some old voyage, made when he was young,
And some one waited for his coming home.
That day is passed and dead. Once he brought back
Some rare rich shells of wondrous hues and shapes,
Some carvèd trifles cut by Chinese hands,
And found a grave, not yet with grass grown o'er,
Was all that waited him. He had them still,
The curious tinted shells, and carvèd toys,
And, when he was at home, would play with them
As any child might do. Poor, simple heart!

So young — so true — so near the other world —
And yet it nothing knew of that sweet lore
Which opes the door of Heaven to the soul!
He had no key to unlock that mystery.
The hope that makes all earthly burdens light
Had not yet come to him.   But he had lived
Up to the light he had.   Had kept him pure,
As it were unconsciously, by the love
He bore the early dead.   How came he here?
The men and women round him were not like
The men — the woman — he knew long ago.
What brought him to this house?   A child's sweet face,—
The very image of that other face
Above whose rest the sea-winds swept at night.

   One day, — it was a day of summer-time, —
He had a heavy load to bear away
(Some refuse paper, and odd scraps and ends,
Thrown from the ware-rooms) ; and a storm came on.
Shelter was there none, save the dark portal
Of that old house; and thitherward he sped;
His burthen growing heavier as he went.
There Olive found him, weary, well-nigh spent,
And made him enter, prattling all the while,
As children wont to do.   And so it chanced
That he came here to live.
                              He had not kept
His pretty shells and curious toys for long,
But that the child did love them.   So all talk
Of stealing them from him did end in talk.
The child kept royal state, and had her way, —
Most queens have not, — and no one came between
Her subjects and herself.   Her little feet
Were free to wander in and out of rooms,
That else had been close shut, and she had made
Room for herself in every heart also.
They could not keep her out; did never try.
What had they been, if Olive had not come,
A ray of sunshine to their wintry hearts?
As sweet, as welcome, as to parchèd lips
Are fountains springing in the wilderness!
If such she were unto these arid souls
That, dry as dust, were withering away
For lack of Heaven's dew, we dare not say
What place she held in that old sailor's heart.
He all but worshipped her.   She used to sit
Upon the steps, when summer days were long,
And wait his coming.   No more welcome sight

Is land to weary mariner from the sea,
Than was the little figure sitting there
To that old sailor's eyes. His step grew light,
That was so heavy late; and all the heat
And burden of the day did drop away
From off his shoulders, as a cloak might fall.
All was forgotten, when he took his place
Beside her on the steps, and sang to her
Some quaint old ballad of the olden time
She dearly loved to hear. What though the voice
Were partly cracked, and somewhat quavering?
There had been music in it, and was still,
To little Olive's ear. For no one else
Had ever sung to her. For no one else,
In all that house, had ever heart to sing!

It may be — in the dead, forgotten years,
When these poor shadows were all young and fair—
There had been singing on the withered lips
That had no memory of music now.
It may have been; but sin had long since dulled
All finer senses, and those yet retained
Were little more than base and animal.
Their souls seemed buried in so dark a grave,
That you had thought for them could never be
A resurrection morning! Wait, and hope!
Since, in GOD's time, his gracious hand may sow
Some precious seed upon this sterile soil, —
A seed that, nourished by his quickening grace,
May germ and leaf, bring forth both bud and flower;
May ripen yet, and to his harvest grow
For the ingathering of the angels.
So wait and hope! On this side of the grave
We may have hope. Who sails beyond that shore
Leaves hope behind. We know "there is no work,
Nor knowledge, nor device," nor time, nor yet
Repentance in the grave. But, ere the wave
Of Death flows o'er us never to recede, —
While yet the heart with busy throb doth keep
The curious mechanism of our frame
Complete in all its parts, instinct with life,
And all Life's attributes, — ere yet the wheel
Is broken at the cistern, there is hope!
The laborer hired at the eleventh hour
Received likewise a penny.
                         Days went on;
And little Olive's lips were learning fast
The need of questioning. The time had come

When all the old man's lore, enough till now,
Was insufficient found. He had been wont
To stay at home one day in every week, —
"One day in seven," — and she oft had asked
The why and wherefore. Still unsatisfied,
Because he did not tell her *all* the truth.
And so, one day — he went not out that day —
She came to him, with sober, quiet face :
"I want to know," she said, "why you stay here."
"I have no work to do. None work to-day."
"What do they then?" "They stay at home, as I,
Or go to church." Then sharp she questioned him :
"What is a church, and why do people go?"
And sorely puzzled was the man to give
The fitting answer. "Come, show me a church!"
And, hand in hand, the old man and the child
Went forth together. Nor had far to go;
Just round the corner stood an old-time church;
Past which, through all the week, the roar of trade
Was loudly sounding. Now the streets were still;
And through its archèd windows floated tones
The child had never heard. An organ's swell,
And voices many singing an old psalm.
Awe-struck, she listened. "May we not go in?"
And, yielding to her touch, the old man went
Within the open door, and pausèd there.
He did not dare to enter; but the child,
Who had no fears, went wandering up the aisle.
A gentle hand did stay her, else her feet
Had borne her on upon the chancel-floor,
To see the stainèd window that she thought
So bright and beautiful, — a gentle hand,
That touched her own, and softly drew her back,
And gave her place beside him. Still she sat —
Her wonder kept her silent — till the church,
And all she saw and heard, were graven deep
On heart and memory. But, at the last,
She turned to look up at the grave, sad face
Of him who held her hand, and conned it o'er
With such a sober seriousness of mien
As suited well the task. Not long she looked.
The little eyes grew heavy, and the head
Went nodding at the sermon; till it fell
Against the arm was nearest unto her,
And she was fast asleep. The arm was drawn
Around her quietly, and the earnest eyes
Just dwelt a moment on the sweet, pale face,
Brown, waving hair, and softly-parted lips,

Then looked upon the preacher. Sweet and low
The organ sounded forth an interlude
That woke the child; and from the patient arms,
That were well pleased such burden sweet to bear,
She started up, half-frightened not to see
The old man's face. Then slowly turned her round,
To see, still waiting at the open door,
The one familiar form; and with light foot
She trotted down the aisle, and, hand in hand,
They twain went home.
                No dearth of questions *now,*
Questions that made the old man sad at heart;
Until he talked to Olive, as if she
Were not a child, but woman. All the tale
She had not heard before was told her then.
How he was once a little child, like her,
And had a home beside the soundless sea,
A father and a mother. (These were words
Most strange to Olive, and she questioned him
What they might mean. He made it plain to her
As best he could, then went on with his tale.)
" But they were poor; had suffered hunger, want,
Gone through much trouble; and yet were content.
They never murmured; and when I was born
My mother's heart did sing for very joy;
As if I was not to those busy hands
An added burthen. But she only worked
A little harder when her strength came back.
I learned this afterward. My father was
A fisher on the sea. I went with him,
It may be, once or twice, and then, one morn,
He went alone, and never came to shore.
I mind me well, how all that weary night
We waited his return, till morning broke
And brought no tidings. So for many days
We watched and waited; but hope faded soon.
He never came, and my poor mother's face
Was growing paler, paler every day;
Till at the last she died, and I went forth,
A sailor-boy to sea."
                " And was there, then,
No little girl like me in that old house,
To wait and watch for you? "
                    " Not then, nor there.
But, little one, the day is long past noon,
And I am weary." So he left her, perched
Upon the topmost step, and slowly went
Up to his own still chamber; there to dream

The old days back when one *did* wait and watch
Through three long years for him. The fourth year brought
The sailor back, but only to a grave! —
A grave that GOD did set before him then
To keep him from much evil.   And it kept
The man's soul purer by its memory.

Who saith the grave is but a charnel-house,
" Full of dead men's bones, and all uncleanness"?
We do not say that this may not be so;
But graves have higher uses.   It is true
Corruption is therein; and gases foul
Are there engendered.   These are things of time
And have their ending; but this dust shall rise;
" This mortal put on immortality."
And then, " Where is thy victory, O Grave?
And where, O Death, thy sting?"
                          Some graves there are
That through long ages have been sacred held,
And bear deep traces of the pilgrim's feet.
The Moslem braves the Simoon's deadly blast,
And drifting desert-sands, to say his prayers
At Mecca's holy shrine; and, in some lands,
Honors divine are paid to dust of saints.
Nations fought against nations, for the tomb
That once held Christ our King; and all earth's years
Shall bear the mighty impress of that strife.
In those old days, when immaterial things
Did take material shapes, men fought and died
Beneath the sacred banner of the Cross,
That so Jerusalem the Holy might
Be freed from Paynim rule.   In these our days
The same old strife is waged; but human hearts
Are now the battle-grounds.
                          Some graves there are,
Unnoted and unknown, which yet have kept
A soul from death by their strong memory.
The dust within them hath a charmèd spell,
And true the hearts that own its mastery.
We knew a man, who died while yet the dew
Of youth was fresh upon him.   All his life
He moved among us meekly, lovingly,
As one who walketh humbly with his GOD,
And when he died, his lowly grave did seem
An open portal leading unto Heaven.
That grave, so quiet 'mid the city's roar,
Had precious influences, hath them still;
And some who walk as GOD's own children now

Do know that grave was as a door of life
To their unthinking souls. So, evermore,
GOD grant that from the dust of graves may spring
The buds and blossoms that bear fruit for Heaven!

IV.

'Tis strange to stand beside a form we know,
And hear no breathing, feel no throbbing pulse.
All is so calm, so still, so motionless;
So like to sleep, and yet so all unlike.
No sleeper's brow hath such a changeless calm.
No sleeper's hands lie folded on a breast
That hath forgotten motion, and no lips
Of any sleeper are so cold as these.
This sleep hath never waking; and these lips
Have lost their music; hushed and pale, but sweet,
And faintly smiling still. Death hath set here
The seal of silence, not to be broken
Until the resurrection of the dead.

All dead, there is no life! All dust, no soul!
'Tis but the shadow of the one we knew;
And all our grief is dumb before the cold
And awful stillness of that silent form.
With what vain longing, with what useless love
We kneel beside the dead, and wildly pray
That GOD will yet bring back the parted soul,
And give our treasure to our arms again!
So knelt the rich man by the royal couch
That held his pride, the wife of one sweet year;
So wildly prayed. Hush! such words are not meet
For that still presence, and the soft rebuke
Of that dear face hath hushed the words that came
From the strong man's agony. To and fro
He paced the quiet chamber. To and fro,
Through all the weary day, and through the night
That followed after; till his ceaseless tread
Was all that broke the stillness of the house
That Death had entered with so swift a step,
And left all joyless.
                    O'er the city-streets,
Already full of life, the day dawned bright;
Bathing in crimson all the snow-touched roofs,
The far-off mountains, and the frozen stream.
The air was full of frost; was bracing, crisp;
And here and there, sleigh-bells were ringing out
A carol unto Winter joyously!
This death stilled not their music. It crossed not

The myriad circles that make up the sum
Of the great city's life; and scarce was known
Beyond the home that was *her* home no more.
So, to the home that hath distinctive rank,
"The home for all the living," she was borne.
They broke untrodden snow to make her grave,
And left her lying where the sun shone cold
On the City of the Silent.   There, in spring,
Pale snow-drops grew, and fragrant violets
That named her when they bloomed.   And so his hand
Had set the flowers there.   Within his home,
The little baby she had given him,
A tiny bud, another Violet,
Was waiting him.   Something to tend and love,
And be most dear to him in after years;
But nothing now.   And so the little one
Did never see her father, and was left
To give her first caress, — her first sweet love, —
Unto the gentle nurse, who loved the child
As it had been her very flesh and blood,
And not another's.   So the days went on.

    The rich man prospered.   Wealth flowed unto him
As a river to the sea.   Far and wide
His name was honored, and his worth confessed;
But he cared little for the praise of men.
Strong in his own integrity he stood,
And stooped not servilely for gold nor power.
He had enough of both.   But at his heart
A shadow sat; and in his cup of life
One bitter drop was mingled, dulling all
The sparkle of the wine.   The little grave,
Where he had laid his darling down to rest,
Rose evermore between him and all joy, —
Yea, made it agony to look upon
His baby-daughter's face.
                        He went abroad
To find oblivion, but there followed him
A haunting shape, "to startle and waylay."
He trod the Old World with unresting feet.
The sands, that for two thousand years have swept
Above the giant cities of the Past,
Low-burying all their pride, did know his tread;
And ancient Nile, upon its waters, bore
The New World's restless child.   He crossed the plains,
Where for full forty years ("when Israel
Came out of Egypt") Moses led their tribes;
Till every man who through the Red Sea came

Had perished in the wilderness. He saw
Far-off, and near, the Mount that burned with fire;
And Pisgah rose before him, sad and still,
Whence Moses looked upon the Promised Land
His feet might never tread! The Holy Land
Made bare its ruins; gave him food for thought;
And brought back memories of the sacred lore
Learned at his mother's knee. He knew it well, —
The story sweet of old; but from his heart
The world had shut its holy teachings out;
They came not home to him. Yea, even now,
When he was passing o'er Judea's plains,
By Jordan's stream, then at its time of flood,
Or rested on the Mount of Olivet,
He did not read its meaning all aright.
Verily, this man had no ears to hear,
No eyes to see, the things which are of God;
And sacred places were not so to him.
Else he had never trod on Olivet,
Nor walked the Garden of Gethsemane,
In merely curious mood!
                              "God is strong,
And very patient!" What adds the Psalmist?
"Yet God is provokéd every day!"

This rich man wandered long, yet found no rest.
Where'er he went, there followed him alway
The haunting shadow of the fair, young wife
Whose dust was lying 'neath a sunny slope,
A thousand miles away. A fevered thought —
A longing wish that he could only look
Once more on her, and die — came to his heart;
And then all speed was slow, and worse than slow,
To his wild wish for home.
                              And home he came.
He seemed to feel no change. He did not ask
To see his child, the little Violet,
But went alone unto that chamber, where
We saw him last; the room wherein *she* died.
And so the evening and the long night passed
Of his first day at home. The morning brought
Another mood, another life to him.

Light tripping down the stairs, into the room
Where he was sitting, lonely, sad, and stern,
There came a tiny shape. "Papa! papa!"
(Through all his after life that glad, sweet cry
Was ringing on his ears) and round his neck

The little arms were thrown.   He held her close,
This fairy form, so like to his dead wife,
Low murmuring o'er and o'er, "My Violet!"
"That is *my* name," she said; "it was mamma's."
She did not heed the sudden start he gave,
But laid her head against his shoulder broad,
And smiled, as if content.   Her soft, warm hands
Played hide-and-seek in his.   Her rich, brown hair
Fell curling o'er his arm.   The snowy dress,
The tiny, crimson shoes,—soft lips as red,—
And eyes of brown, sweet smiling up at him,
All made a picture that the father's heart
Kept tenderly alway.
                 She was not shy,—
This little Violet,—nor yet too bold.
But free as children are who have not known
What 'tis to fear a blow, nor yet a frown.
Her life had had no cloud.   She had not missed
A mother's loving care, since Janet sought
With all her heart to fill that mother's place.
She taught the baby-lips that sweetest prayer,
Which calleth GOD "Our Father," and she spoke
Full often of the father far away
Who would come home some day; and so the child,
In her sweet, prattling mood, would softly talk
Of the two fathers she had never seen,
But yet, should see, some day.
                    And so it chanced
That when her earthly father home returned,
The little one was glad.   She told him so;
And asked him "if *he* knew when she should see
The Father up in heaven?   Janet says
I must be very good to go to him.
That some time soon, or not for many years,
He may come for me; and then I shall see
My own mamma.   Will you go, too, papa?"
A simple question, but it tortured him.
The strong heart was not strong before the gaze
Of those inquiring eyes.   The strong frame shook;
But there was no reply.   He did not dare
To answer "yes," and would not answer "no."

This man was skilled in science, and the lore
Of many ages was not hid from him.
He knew most languages, had seen all lands,
Yet had not learned the grandest truth of all.
The truth, which lies within a child's soft grasp,
That is at home amid the poor and weak,

Was not yet found of him!   He did not know
That he whose mind would seek that highest truth
Must doff all earthly learning, lay aside
The pride of manhood, bend the haughty brow,
And, as a child, with child-like trust receive
The gift GOD giveth through Repentance, — Faith!
Then shall the man find in his treasure-house,
Which he had filled with knowledge and much lore,
A thousand things he had not seen before.
All forms of Science, and all realms of Thought,
Shall have one common Centre, whereunto
Their diverse streams shall flow; which, in Itself,
Doth make the crowning glory of them all!
Without this Centre, and without this Crown,
All human learning is an empty show;
All human theories are based on sand;
And human schemes are void and formless all.

'Tis not so hard to win this precious gift;
This " one pearl of great price."   A little child
Can win and wear it; and no sophist tongue
Can shake its perfect and undoubting faith.
The child doth never reason.   That cold steel,
So often turned by Satan to foul use
Against itself, the child's brain cannot grasp.
But, deep within its soul, an anchor strong
On which to lean, Faith hath so firm a hold,
That, but to shake it, you must tear it up.

They know not what they do, who first implant
The seeds of doubt within a child's pure heart.
They know not what they do.   As the one hour,
At morning lost is found not through the day,
Not then, nor ever; so this perfect faith,
Once dimmed and darkened, may no more resume
Its early glory.   Manhood's later faith
Doth come through trials sore, temptations strong;
Hath faltered, failed.   Man's mind is full of doubts.
Now this, now that, must all be cleared away,
Before he owns that anything is truth;
Before his lips confess " One Faith, One Lord."
His reason — broken reed on which he leans —
Doth lead him still astray.   And when at last,
Convinced against his will, he meekly bows
Low saying, " I believe," his faith is not,
As is the child's, a pure, unquestioning faith;
Is not, and cannot be!
                         Beware, light hearts!

Lest in your careless speech, unthinking mirth,
Ye brush the bloom from off a child's pure soul;
By doubt of earthly goodness, earthly love,
Shaping the doubt that reacheth up to GOD!
This early faith is strong as any oak.
A very little wedge, in time, will split
The tree from end to end. So one light word,
Forgotten by the speaker, may strike deep
At the root of faith, till all its glory lie
Cast down to earth, like some old forest tree
All rotten at its heart. And this the work—
The bitter work whose deadly fruit is death—
Of one poor thoughtless word!
     Who doubts, should be
Stern warder of himself, keep closest guard
About the open portal of his lips,
Lest aught of that his fatal treasure scape
To darken other souls. Who values doubt,
Let him be jealous of it; keep it safe
From eyes of other men, so that their hands
May not reach out and pluck the fatal fruit
To the losing of their souls.

V.

Amid the ruin and the poisonous slime
That festered slowly at the city's heart,
Some loving human souls had built a school,
And then a chapel. Free it was to all;
None were shut out; but chiefly children came.
The little ones, brought here by kindly words,—
By tender care they found not in their homes,—
Soon learnt more fitting use of their quick tongues
Than foul words, fouler oaths. Rough hair, unkempt,
Did learn a smoother wave; and grimy hands,
That little knew of water, soon grew white;
And garments, foul with all uncleanness, were
Made clean and neat. These seem but little things;
And five long years had passed in doing this,
Yet were not counted lost. Those who worked here,
Had in the morning sown the precious seed;
When evening came, would not withhold the hand;
And knew that, though they might wait many years,
Yet, in the end, they should come home with joy,
Bringing with them the harvest's golden sheaves!
Faithful is He that promised.
     One bright day,
In early summer little Olive came,
The old man at her side, unto this place,

With simple childish speech: "I come to school."
They made her welcome; gave a quiet seat
Where still the old man might sit next to her,
If so he willed to stay. He rarely stayed;
His work was otherwhere; but Olive kept
The corner-seat for him, and when he came,
As sometimes he would do, to see her home,
She made him take his place, and stay to hear
The children singing, — singing some old hymns
That told of Christmas and of Easter Day;
Of bitter Cross and Death, and how the Lord
Did alway love the children!
                    The old house
Grew strangely musical. Bird-like, the child
Went singing everywhere the sweet old hymns
The Church hath gathered in her Book of Prayer.
Strange sounds were these through those old rooms to ring!
They made the air grow purer; gave a tone
That made all other sounds seem healthier;
And had strong glamour from the long-dead Past
To throw upon the shapes that knew not now
What shape their Past did wear. Their sin had laid
All olden memories in a grave more deep
Than that we give the dust. Their lives had raised
So strong a barrier 'twixt them and Hope,
That it was all shut out; and for their Faith,
It died in childhood; had not seen since then
The sweet light of the day. Yet unto these —
These souls forlorn and lost — the child's song came,
As some stray ray of light that doth stream in,
From viewless cranny, on a dungeon dark.
It comes — it goes; but leaves its record there
As something looked for, hoped for evermore!
They scarcely knew how it had come to pass;
But Sin was growing hideous, foul, unclean,
And strong frames trembled, as the child's voice sang
Of cruel scourging, and of Calvary,
Of Cross and Crown; or rang out, clear and high,
Some grand old hymn would stir the coolest pulse:
It may be that which Martin Luther wrote
("*Ein feste Burg*"),or, later yet, the song
That hailed the Bridegroom's coming. Each and all
Had their own spell, when Olive sang them there;
Each their own work to do. But slow the work,
As though one gathered sand upon the shore,
And gathered grain by grain!
                    Easy the road,
And smooth and swift, the long descent to hell.

But they who would retrace their downward steps,
Have heavy labor, fearful work to do.*
Sin will not let her chosen votaries go.
Their vows are hers.   Their bodies and their souls
She holdeth in stern bondage, with such chains
That all the senses seem close bound to her.
She eateth, like a canker, in the flesh,
And makes that foul, which was most fair and sweet.
Her touch, defacing, blots all beauty out;
Yet she can make things hideous, beautiful;
That bright, which is most dark; and Death seem Life!
She hath a cup, wherein the wine is red, —
The grapes were poison, and the vintage hell.
But whoso drinks hath fever in his blood,
And thirst insatiable.   No stream can quench
The fire it doth kindle, till the flame
Hath burnt to ashes in the crucible
That is " repentance " called.   This wine so red
Doth stain as scarlet, and no human hand
Can wash the staining out.   No Circe cup
Did ever make such monstrous shapes as this;
Yet thousands take it daily; drain it deep;
Ay! to the dregs!   Aud then they long for more.
They have not far to seek.   It ready stands, —
Close to their very lips; they need not stoop;
Sin holds it up.   She hath a royal robe, —
A robe to deck her faithful slaves withal.
'Tis fair enough, and fitteth each full wel!;
But, would they fling it off, it hath become
A portion of themselves, part of their flesh;
A thing they cannot at their present will
Put off, or on; but clinging unto them
Through life, through death; unless One strong to **save**
Shall tear it off, and nail it to his cross;
Then pour in wine and oil to heal the wound,
And send the broken spirit on its way
Unto a better country.   Nothing less
Than He who suffered on the atoning Cross
Can break the yoke of sin, and free the soul.
Behold!   He standeth at the door, and knocks.
Arise, and let him in !

VI.

With what quaint earnestness a child begins
To study its first lesson !   Mark the brow

---

* — " Facilis descensus
Avernum.   Sed revocare gradum
Hic labor, hoc opus est."

That doth put on such wrinkles and such frowns,
As better fit a man who poreth o'er
Some problem hard to solve, or knotty point
That much disturbs his brain; but for a child
Not yet such lines should be.   Thought traceth them,
With stencil sharp, on older, graver brows,
And many years make deeper still the lines.
But this smooth brow is an unwritten page,
A fair, blank book that hath no lines as yet;
Though every day may leave some shadowing
The after-time shall fill up, clear and true.
Perchance these mimic wrinkles and these frowns,
So out of place upon the child's white brow,
Are only heralds of what shall be soon;
Are only types that shadow forth the man
When life is at flood-tide.
                      The sun was up
Above the summit of the eastern hills.
Long shadows from the trees lay on the ground;
Shadows that stole away with silent feet
Before the rising of the summer sun.
They did not like the sunlight overmuch;
Nay, not at all; and ever fled from it
Unto some favored and secluded spot
Where leaves were thickest, and where Dusk was queen
Of inner woodland and remotest dells.
Full in the sunlight, no dusk shadows there,
A fairy palace wooed the morning breeze.
A palace made for summer, — cool, and white
As marble's self could make it.   On the porch,
Just in the sunshine, sat a little girl;
A book upon her knee.   Close at her feet,
A royal dog, of good St. Bernard's breed,
Was idly lying, watching the sweet face.
It may be, wondering in his head canine
What phase of mood the sunny brow put on
With all those frowns and wrinkles.   Far away,
A lake's clear waters glimmered in the sun.

A little boat was moored beside the shore,
Slow moving up and down before the wind
That blew so freshly from the western hills.
A man sat in the stern, dipping his hand
In the cool water, as in idleness,
But watching, all the while, the little girl;
Who, on her book intent, had never heard
Her father call to her.   Eager, at last,
To know what meant this unaccustomed mood,

He raised an oar, and splashing let it fall.
The spell was broken, — book was flung aside;
And dog and Violet came running down
The green slope to the lake.   She won the race;
Was lifted o'er the gunwale in the boat,
And in her own especial corner placed.
The dog sedately took the other side
As one was used to keep the boat in trim.
With such grave nicety did he balance it,
That you might know, the dog, by strong instinct,
Was something of a sailor.   Violet
Sat strangely silent for a little space,
While from the shore the boat was drifting fast,
Then softly and mysteriously spoke:
" Do you think, papa, that I can *ever* learn
To read a *book?*   I — do — not — think — I — can."
And thereupon the little face grew sad.

No answer then; for, even as she spoke,
Her father laid within her tiny hand
A water-lily; first of all its tribe
To greet the summer, with its petals white;
The wind, with breathings of its perfumed breath.
She held it up, and looked it o'er and o'er,
Eying it curiously.   " Janet says
These water-lilies rise from out the lake
As in GOD's time our bodies from the grave.
She says they spring from out the mud that lies
Below the pure, sweet water; that the lake
Is their baptismal font.   This long, soft thread,
Which bears the lily upward through the wave.
She said was like GOD's love, that leadeth us
Through all the ways of life.   And when, at last,
Wide-open, sweet, the flower greets the sun,
She said it was like heaven to the soul
Which GOD had taken home to be with him."

So spake Violet, half in undertone,
As one repeateth o'er a lesson learnt,
And yet her father did hear every word;
And somewhat he did wonder how the child
So well remembered all that Janet said.
He had forgotten that there never was
A teacher like to Love!
                              The child talked on:
" Papa, if you and I should die to-day,
We would be like this flower, and rise, some time,
From out the dust; I, as a little child,

And you, a grown-up man.   So Janet says.
I hope she will die too.   I would not like
To leave her here alone."
                              For sole reply
The father gathered lilies, one by one,
And laid them on her lap.   Then with light touch
He brought the little boat back to the shore;
And, bearing lilies in her tiny hands,
Violet went up the green slope to her home.

If grains of wheat, that for two thousand years
In Egypt's sepulchres have buried been,
Retain their little modicum of life;
And, given to the bosom of the earth,
Spring up again, blade, ear, and perfect grain;
Seems it so hard to thee, O doubting man,
That this poor dust of ours shall rise again;
"This mortal put on immortality"?
The Hand that made the grain, and out of dust
Did form the creature, man, is strong in might;
It keeps the life within a buried seed
Through two long cycles of a thousand years;
And will not fail to gather up our dust,
Particle to particle, in the day
When the Lord shall come in the clouds of heaven,
And the dust shall meet its Maker, face to face,
No veil of earth between!   Of old, Job said,
"Though after my skin worms destroy this body,
Yet in my flesh shall I see GOD; whom I
Shall see for myself, and mine eyes shall behold,
And not another!"   And JESUS said, "He
That believeth on me, though he were dead,
Yet shall he live!"   What needeth more than this?
"The one thing needful."   The untarnished Faith,
The simple trust of childhood, the one Creed
Whereon no doubt hath fallen!
                              If, beyond
The Silent Valley, there were nothingness,—
No hope, no future, verily, "we are
Of all men most miserable."   But the Lord
In whom we trust hath never arm of flesh;
And we may rest, securely, on the Love
That wrought out our redemption by the Cross
And the first Easter-Day.   His arm did bring
Salvation to his people!

VII.

There was a shadow darkly brooding o'er
The old house in the alley.   Olive lay
Upon a bed of sickness.   Her young life
Seemed slowly passing, as a dream, away,
And all the house was eloquent of grief.
These men, these women, dared not leave the place,
Lest when they did return, 'twould be to find
Their sunshine buried in the night of Death.
Sorely they missed the child, whose little feet
Did come no more to meet them; whose sweet voice,
That ever had made music in the house,
Was hushed from very weakness.   Faint and low
Her breath came softly, as she seemed to sleep
A sleep that was exhaustion.   There had been
Hot fever burning in the little veins,
Flushed cheeks and glittering eyes.   This had all passed,
And left the child in a strange stupor sunk,
With close-shut eyelids, whose faint quivering
Just showed that Death had not yet set his seal
On the blue eyes beneath.
                The sailor watched
Beside her, night and day.   Watching, as they
Who, wrecked at sea, do see the passing ship
They hoped would save them, slowly drifting past;
As slowly, sinking 'neath the horizon.
The old man's life seemed bound up in the child's.
And, if she died, it needed no keen eye
To know he would not linger long behind.
He never seemed to weary.   All the day
Was spent beside her, and the long, long night
Did never find him absent.   At the last,
When hope seemed dying, and o'er all the house
The solemn stillness of a coming fate
Was sadly falling, he rose up in haste,
And blindly staggering, went forth on the street
That mocked him with its wealth of human life.

He stayed not long; but came not back alone.
A young man quietly did follow him
Into the silence of the chamber old
Where Olive lay a-dying.   On her pulse
The young man laid his finger.   Faint the throb
That answered to his touch; but it sufficed
To give a hope of life; and he knelt down
Amid those men, those women, as if he
Saw nothing of the stains that dark and deep

23

Were burning out their souls, as if no taint,
All foul and leprous in their blood, could bring
Defilement unto him.
                As with one heart
All bowed the head, or knelt; and, as he prayed
That GOD would spare the child, and save from pain,
And grant her length of days, days to be spent
In doing good, and serving GOD alway;
Or else, that he would graciously receive
The little one, and take her to himself
To be for evermore with Christ in Heaven; *
A shuddering sense of all that they had lost
Stole o'er these sinful souls; as unto men,
When drowning, comes the record of their lives,
No one thing blotted out!
               A moment's pause,
And the clear voice went on. — " O GOD, whose days
Are never-ending, and whose mercies are
Untold and numberless, make us to know
How very brief is this our human life,
And how uncertain all; and let thy grace
And Holy Spirit lead us through this vale,
In holiness, righteousness, all the days
That thou hast given us; that when we all
Have, in our generation, servëd thee,
We may be gathered unto our fathers;
Having the testimony, changeless, true,
Of a good conscience; in the communion
Of the Catholic Church; in the sure trust
Of a certain faith; in the comfort sweet
Of a most holy and religious hope!
In favor with thee our GOD, and at peace
With all the world. And this we ask
Through Jesus Christ our Lord." †
             None said Amen;
And yet that prayer came home to every heart
With such deep sense of all unworthiness;
"It was not meant — could not be said — for them."
No testimony did their conscience bear
That could be callëd good; they had no part
In the Church Catholic; no certain faith
Had they to trust in; and no holy hope
To comfort their poor souls. And well they knew
They could not be in favor with their GOD,
And they were not in charity with men.

---

* Paraphrase of part of the " Prayer for a Sick Child."
Paraphrase of a prayer in " The Order for the Visitation of the Sick."

What was that prayer to them?   As a boat, sent
For men close clinging to a broken wreck
O'er which the angry billows foam and sweep;
As the first draught of water to the lips
Of one who pineth 'mid the desert sands
For the life-saving stream.
                        The little one, —
Who came unto these sin-polluted souls,
As did the angel to Bethesda's pool,
Stirring the stagnant waters unto life, —
Had wrought a work that could not be undone;
Made ready these foul places for the feet
Of one who brought " glad tidings " unto them.
Her little hands by tender clasp had taught
Forgotten softness to these hardened hearts;
And opened scalèd doors.   Her clear, sweet voice
Had stirred some pulses that had long been dead;
And a strange reverence for holy names
Came to these men and women sin-defiled.
They seemed so pure and holy on the lips
Of little Olive.   All unconsciously
The child had done her work; yet none the less
Was it her work.   And now the little waif
That came, an angel, to the old, old house,
Was going home.
                        The young physician's face
Told better than all words: " There is no hope."
He did but pause to question " if the child
Had been baptized or no; " and then he stayed
To hear the story they did tell to him;
And when he went, he spake of swift return.

A long, long hour passed.   Death, hovering, came
Yet nearer to the child, but still delayed
To claim her as his own.   Then back in haste
The good physician sped, and with him brought
A laborer in God's vineyard, — a young priest, —
That so the child, ere she went home, should be
Named with the name of Christ.   Brief was the rite,
And brief the time allowed; for, as the priest
Did sprinkle water on the little brow,
The blue eyes opened once, the white lips smiled,
A hand was lifted from the tiny wrist;
And soft and clear — all solemnly and slow —
Came the voice of the young priest: " The Lord gave
And the Lord hath taken away.   Blessed be
The name of the Lord! "

                              Olive's work was done.
And yet, not so.   As year following year
Did bear some inmate of that house away
On that long journey whence is no return,
They went, as those who, reconciled to GOD,
Have lost all fear; who, at the feet of Christ,
Have laid that burthen of a sinful life
They take not up again.
                              And far away —
Beyond the city's din — beyond the strife
Of toil and traffic — they all silent sleep,
'Mid quiet valleys and on sloping hills;
Where earthly sounds are heard not; and the dead
Have their last resting-place, alone with GOD!

VIII.

How joyously the Summer doth put on
Her robe of beauty and her crown of flowers.
With what a royal step she treads the earth;
The earth, that yields her fitting reverence!
We saw her once, enthroned upon the hills;
Queenly and glorious in her golden prime.
Sunlight was burning in her tresses fair;
And full and passionate were lips and eyes.
Low at her feet were flowers, bearded wheat,
And store of fruits, — red, golden, purple, white.
Above her head, a sky of darkest blue,
Wherein did float some light and fleecy clouds;
While far away, o'er distant meadows fell
The raindrops thick and fast; and lightning flash
And loud reverberating thunder-peal
Told of the passing storm.   Against the clouds,
The many-colored Iris shaped its bow, —
Seal opaline of GOD's first covenant.

A morning — noon — had quickly come and gone.
The sun was drooping to the western hills;
And on the lake the shadows lengthened fast,
But trenched not on the lilies yet.   The day
Was dying royally.   The eastern slopes
Were all aglow with light; and shades of gold
Were streaming past a knoll of forest-trees,
Through graceful beech, and stately elm, upon
The marble palace by the lake's green shore.
A world of sweetness floated in the air,
From honeysuckle, rose, and eglantine.
A sense of pleasure and rare harmony
Did fill the rich man's soul, as silently

He waited for the dying of the day.
But — where was Violet?
                            As in reply,
A dog's low howl rose sudden from the lake.
What needeth more?   The father's prescient heart
Did cease its beating for a little space;
And then — the eager rush, the flying feet,
That only brought more near the fatal truth.

    She lay upon the shore: the long, brown curls,
All tangled with the water-lily leaves,
As from the lake the dog had drawn her out;
His strength had failed him then.   Within her hand
Was clasped a half-closed flower, that all too well
Did tell its tale, of how the child had bent
Above the water just to grasp the stem;
And then, the little soul — one moment *here*,
And in the next, beyond the earth — the stars —
Beyond illimitable space!

No more — no more — shall those soft clasping fingers
  Lead the poor father on the way to home;
But on his hand their gentle touch still lingers;
  And it shall linger through the years to come.

No more — no more — that little form shall meet him,
  Crossing the lawn with light and bounding feet.
No more the brown and shining eyes shall greet him,
  With tender love, all passionate and sweet.

No more — no more!   O death to sweet hope ever!
  O passionate wail that will not be repressed!
That hast no answer but that sad word "never,"
  Unto our mournful and beseeching quest.

No more — no more — and yet the lips seem speaking,
  As in that day when he first heard his child.
So the poor father prayeth, humbly seeking
  If yet with GOD he may be reconciled.

No more — no more — will there be earthly greeting;
  Bridgeless the gulf that aye between doth lie;
But, in the world beyond, there may be meeting
  Or parting, lasting as eternity!

A Vision of the Night.

METHOUGHT we drove,
O'er snowy roads, unto a quiet lake,
Low nestling in the bosom of gray hills,
That, when we reached, were green with vernal grass,
And flush with summer beauty. Calm and clear
The waters glittered in the noontide sun;
And, here and there, a water-lily showed
The snowy petals that the breezes kissed,
Stealing their fragrance. All the lake was shaped
Most like a lunar bow. The inner curve
Did woo us with its beauty of fair trees
And soft green turf. We wandered slowly on,
Until we came where granite rocks did rear
A barrier to our steps. All huge the pile,
And fashioned to the semblance of a church,
With chancel open to the winds of heaven.
We stood before that altar, you and I, —
My head just leaning on your breast, the while,
For I was strangely weary, — and we talked,
Or, rather, I did listen, as you talked
Of that strange pile; and much we wondered both,
If only Nature were the architect.
Those rocks did bear no trace of human hand;
No mortal chisel shaped those blocks of stone.
So huge were they, not e'en the men of old,
The giants of those days, could change their place,
Though but a hair's-breadth. And it stood there,
A mighty church of stone; untouched by Time;
And grand and solitary. Slowly down,
Around us and about us, fell the dusk;
And we stood silent, watching that old fane,
Until the morning woke me from my dream.

Lillie.

SHE sitteth alone, and she sigheth,
   And her wan lips tremble so;
And the heart of the maiden it dieth
   For a hope that is lying low.
The years of life's spring-time she numbereth,
   But their beauty and glory are gone;
And she thinks that the earth she but cumbereth,
   As she sitteth and sigheth alone.

She sitteth alone, and she weepeth,
  And her tears fall wearily,
As she remembereth one who sleepeth
  Where the dust and silence be.
See the breaking heart, how it throbbeth,
  With a faint pulse, to and fro;
And the poor, weak breath, how it sobbeth
  O'er the way that *lone* life must go.

She kneeleth alone, and she prayeth,
  And the dear GOD heareth her prayer;
And the faltering words she sayeth
  Will not all be lost in air.
She riseth from prayer, and she goeth
  Where'er there is work to do;
And she walketh alone, but she knoweth
  Whither her footsteps go.

She sitteth alone, but not often,
  And her brow is serene, though pale;
And her mission is grief to soften,
  And her coming stilleth the wail.
Soft in her soul sorrow sleepeth,
  And she pitieth all who mourn;
While her heart its lone vigil keepeth
  For him who may never return.

She sitteth alone, and she thinketh
  How softly the waters go
That bear her away, while she shrinketh
  No more from their icy flow.
For she watcheth the river flowing
  With a swift tide far away;
And she knoweth whither 'tis going,
  And she looketh beyond to the day.

To the day, that e'en now is dawning
  On the hill-tops, far and blue;
To the clear and cloudless morning,
  That knoweth no earthly dew!
She beareth a loving spirit
  To that home beyond the sky,
For she is of those who inherit
  GOD's immortality.

To S. P. H.

So thou wouldst be a poet.   Verily,
The moth doth seek the flame that is its death,
And will not be withheld. The sailor-boy
Leaves the green fields and pleasant haunts of home
With scarce a tear; since dearer to his heart
The fearful splendor of a storm-swept sea,
And moan of waves that never are at rest.
And yet, long ere that trumpet-music dies
Into brief silence, or that moan be hushed,
The sailor-boy shall find a quiet grave
Beneath the ocean that he loves so well!
In days of old, long centuries ago,
When from the crucible men sought to win
The yellow dross called gold, a student pale
Bent, day by day, and through the silent night,
Above the living flame, and fed its life
With fuel from his own, and so grew old
Before his time.   He had a pleasant home,
For all fair things did wait on him. Soft hands,
That sought to smooth his pathway, loving eyes
That rested on him ever, and one heart
That gave to him its all, and was content.
He left all this with never one regret,
And in the fiery crucible did pour
His years of youth; and, for this lavished wealth,
What did the flame give back? Apples of Sodom,
Golden-hued without, bitter dust within.
One eve, a friend, not yet estranged, stole soft
Unto the turret-chamber; in her hand
A few pale flowers from his mother's grave;
That with these mournful tokens she might win
His heart to earth again.   Her feet fell light
Upon the pavèd floor, but woke an echo,
And yet he never stirred!   The setting sun
Shed o'er his palest brow its golden light,
And from the idle crucible caught up
A gleam of gold.   The treasure sought so long
Was found at last; but the fire had gone out
Alike in crucible and human heart!

And thou wouldst be a poet!   Ask the Past
What record it doth keep of gifted ones
Who in all time have walked upon the earth,
Yet were not of it.   Ask it how they lived;

Those souls of fire that sometime trod the dust,
And made the world rich with their hearts' best blood?
They dwelt among us, living their full life
Ere meaner clay had touched maturity.
They suffered, not as common natures do, —
For every nerve was strung to agony;
And loving, they made their love immortal!
They passed away, like all things loveliest,
Leaving the world so costly legacies
It knows not half their worth; and knows still less
What price was given for them.   It is well,
This dearth of knowledge.   Did the cold world know
How every child of Genius lived and died;
Could it but read the story of their lives,
And count the quivering pulses, and the drops
Forced from the bleeding heart, as 'twere to be
The ink wherein to dip inspired pens;
And feel, the while, that every burning word
Was so much life, wrung from the poet's heart,
And given, broadcast, to the restless winds
That bear it where they will, — knew the world this,
Not *one* of all its children would resign
The calm content of home and happiness,
To win the empty mockery of a name,
For the world to gaze at wonderingly,
When that which made it is a thing of dust!

Yet thou wouldst be a poet! HOMER, blind,
And old, and homeless; TASSO, with his fate
To love above his station, and to waste
Life's chiefest years within a prison cell,
And after *death* to win the crown which *life*
Gave never to his keeping; MILTON, sad,
Yet fair to look upon; with sealèd eyes,
Portraying love so well, himself unloved;
SAVAGE, disowned, and worse than motherless;
Pillowing his head upon the flinty stones
Of pitiless London streets; and he, the boy
Who "perished in his pride," pale CHATTERTON.
POPE, mis-shapen, and loving but too well
(Until his love to bitter hatred turned)
The woman fair who mocked him evermore;
"CHILDE HAROLD," with the curse upon his brow
Of "homeless and unresting;" perishing
Of some wan sickness, not stricken by the foe,
'Neath Missolonghi's walls.   KEATS, dying young,
And leaving on his tomb "Here lieth one
Whose name was writ in water;" yet he wrote

"A thing of beauty is a joy forever!"
COLERIDGE, who lost himself with opium,
And left but shadows of his soul to earth, —
Shadows, but gloriously beautiful!
Are *these* the names whereto thou'dst link thine own,
And all to be a poet?
                    Methinks the fate
Of all these gifted ones might well deter
A bolder soul than thine, from pressing on
The race that they have run, — the weary race,
Wherein the fevered heart, and fevered brain
Have wrought alike a labor unto death,
And rested — in the grave!
                    Yet, O my friend!
If in thy heart the sacred fire burns,
I bid thee not to quench it.   Let it burn;
But feed the flame with fuel not of earth.
GOD gave the gift.   Then render unto him
That which is his; and let thine offering be,
Not as death unto death, but life to life;
And he that reigneth will not cast thee off
When the dark hour cometh; neither turn
His face away from thee.   His rod and staff
Shall comfort thee; and through the vale of death
Thou shalt not pass alone.   Thy GOD shall be
As a tower of strength to thee!

———•◦•———

"For that she Sleepeth."

AROUND the hearth-stones of a thousand homes
    Poor human hearts are weeping;
But never sounding of wild sorrow comes
    Where I lie sleeping.

Gay voices echo through the haunts of 'earth
    True time with gladness keeping;
There cometh not one tone of ringing mirth
    Where I lie sleeping.

Light feet are tripping on the grassy sod
    Out in the sunshine leaping;
But make no music on the rounded clod
    Where I lie sleeping.

The waters sparkle in the noon-day sun,
    With restless wave on-sweeping;

But silently still the rivers run
    Where I lie sleeping.

Soft eyes and loving, meet the gaze of eyes
    That with full joy are weeping;
But a seal of darkness over them lies
    Where I lie sleeping.

Silent and cold, and very dark and lone,
    With never joy nor weeping,
Is the last home whereto the dust hath gone,
    Where I lie sleeping.

No sounds of earth may ever enter there;
    For death the dust is keeping,
And love is changèd to a wan despair
    Where I lie sleeping.

Never clasping hands, nor a throbbing heart,
    Its faithful vigil keeping,
But are unclasped, or find no more a part
    Where I lie sleeping.

Only the dust to dust o'er folded hands,
    And death its harvest reaping,
Lie side by side beneath the silent sands
    Where I lie sleeping.

The ear is closed unto all earthly sounds,
    And eyes no more are weeping;
And hearts beat never in the quiet bounds
    Where I lie sleeping.

Roses Red and White.

O LITTLE one! thy questionings are sharp.
Dost think that I have never been a child?
Yet though that time was buried long ago,
I can relive it all to pleasure thee.
This faded face was smooth as is thine own,
And in my mother's eyes it was most fair.
These braids, whereon white threads are lying thick,
Were soft, and brown, and golden in the sun,
In the far days when my poor father's hand
On the wild curls with tender pressure lay.
These trembling hands — your little fingers lie

So lovingly within them — were as keen
To pluck the blossoms growing in the way,
As ever thine are now.   And the poor feet,
That scarcely bear my weak and feeble frame
Into the sunshine that I love so well,
Were once the lightest on the grassy lawn,
And ever swift to mischief.   Time hath laid
His heavy hand upon me; and the years,
Each with its burden laden, came to me,
Taming my heart's wild throb, yet chilling not
Its living fount of love.

The year was in its noon-day,
    All the flowers were in bloom;
But a shadow deep was lying
    Over one close-curtained room.
They had denied me entrance.   "Hush," they said,
    "You may not enter there," —
And I thought my mother sleeping;
    My own mother, young and fair.

Out into the garden alleys
    With a light, free step I ran;
And to pull the many roses
    My idle hands began.
The white and crimson roses,
    That blossomed all a-row,
Down by the old stone-terrace
    Where most I loved to go.

But, weary soon of such pastime,
    I flung me down to rest
Beneath the shelter of an elm,—
    My mother loved it best.
And I watched the broad, deep blaze of light
    That on each casement shone,
And saw the golden gleam flashed back
    From every pane, save one.

It fell upon the honeysuckle,
    On the roses in their bloom;
But I marvelled why the light was shut
    Out from my mother's room.
I watched till the gold-gleam faded,
    And the long shadows lay
Upon the old gray roof-tree.
    I marked it all that day.

Softly the twilight descended,
　　The stars came out, one by one,
And I thought no more of the gray house,
　　So brightly the star-wreaths shone.
But I pondered upon the lesson
　　My father had taught to me,
Of God as our Maker and Saviour,
　　The Incarnate Deity.

Swift steps moved over the greensward,
　　Steps that were moving fast;
And I heard the murmur of voices,
　　Speaking low, yet speaking fast.
"Where hath the poor child wandered?"
　　The passing voices said.
"For her father waiteth for her;
　　Her mother lieth dead."

"Dead!"　Well I knew the meaning
　　Of that bitter, bitter word,
And a cry of anguish rang across
　　The green and flowery sward.
What did it matter then to me,
　　The comforting words they said,
When I stood within that darkened room,
　　And looked on my mother, dead!

O little one! thou hast not known
　　As yet that agony;
Father and mother are all thine own,
　　God hath left them unto thee.
But I? a father's arms alone
　　Were thrown around me then,
And they bore me away.　I never looked
　　On my mother's face again!

Only in my dreams I see it,
　　Fair and gentle, sweet and mild;
Only in my dreams I see her
　　Smiling down upon her child.
Only then her arms are twining,
　　As they twined around me of yore;
But I wake to weep; such dreaming
　　Must be dreaming evermore.

The year was in its noon-day,
　　All the roses were in bloom,

When they laid my mother down to rest
    Within the cold, cold tomb;
But the year was waning to its night,
    Was drawing to its close,
When they bore my father away from me
    Unto his last repose.

Life hath brought me dreary hours,
    But the dreariest of all
Was when the only one that loved me
    Was lying beneath the pall;
When my father, tender and loving,
    Was taken away from me;
And the wide world lay before me,
    And I could no refuge see.

Life's sorrow came upon me early,
    And I bore it as I might,
All alone, with none to soothe me,
    None to show the blessëd light
That beyond the cloud was shining;
    None to lighten my despair
With soft speech of an hereafter,
    Of the Saviour waiting there!

Ere the grass was growing greenly
    Upon that rounded sod,
My little feet the tarry deck
    Of an ocean-vessel trod.
I, that had grown amid the flowers,
    A nature-loving child,
Heard nought but the sailor-boy's carol,
    Saw nought but the waters wild.

Alas for my home in the valley!
    For the roses white and red;
For the old stone-terrace that never
    Might echo to my tread!
They had passed from my life forever.
    Another's own to be;
And I? the vessel that bore me
    Was a thousand miles at sea!

Days upon days glided from us,
    In spite of the lagging breeze:
Days upon days glided from us,
    Still our Sea-Bird swept the seas.

But I little recked of Time's passing,
    Pleased and content was I
Could I listen unto some sailor's yarn
    And watch the waves go by.

Many a story they told me,
    Most marvellous and true;
High deeds of daring done upon
    The ocean waters blue.
But most I loved to listen
    To a tale they often told
Of a gallant, gallant seaman,
    Of my sailor-uncle Rold.

How once he lived by the sea-shore, —
    A sea-shore wild and rough;
Though if the sun were shining
    It was pleasant and fair enough.
But a storm from the north was fearful,
    On that coast it seemëd such.
E'en the landsman knew its terror,
    The sailor dreaded it much.

One night, when darkness was over all,
    A tempest in its glee
Burst over the rocky headland,
    Sweeping shoreward from the sea;
Till the torn and hissing waters
    Broke shuddering on the strand;
All the sky so dense and black the while,
    You knew not sea from land.

Hark to the boom of a cannon
    Sounding shoreward from the sea!
A minute-gun from yon vessel,
    Drifting on the rocks to lee, —
Drifting on the rocks to leeward,
    Spurning at man's control;
Yet a costly freight that vessel held, —
    So many a living soul.

A costly freight, — a hundred souls, —
    Yet who shall rescue them?
No boat could live in such a sea;
    No arm those waves could stem.
But still the boom of the cannon
    Is heard across the sea,

And the gallant vessel rushes on
    The rocky shore to lee.

No boat?   What rideth the waters
    As a hope that will not die,
Bringing cheer to the weary sailors
    As safety draweth nigh?
No arm?   Yet a stripling bendeth
    His to the dripping oar.
And the life-boat struggles slowly
    The foaming billows o'er.

All this they told me, and further, —
    How, when morning dawned at last,
The ship whose fate had seemed meted out
    Was anchored safe and fast.
Saved was the storm-tossed vessel,
    Saved, a hundred souls, all told;
And the stripling whose daring had saved them,
    Was my sailor-uncle Rold.

I know not the manner of it, —
    Their sea-phrases puzzled me;
But it was no common danger,
    That long strife with the sea;
And mine eyes filled fast, and my heart beat loud
    With an eager thrill of pride,
When next I stood on the quarter-deck,
    And that brave heart by my side.

Softly I laid my fingers small
    Within his own rough hand,
And it closed over mine so tenderly,
    And he looked so all unmann'd.
"Darling!" he whispered over me,
    And he said it o'er and o'er;
And he took me unto his good, true heart
    Then, and evermore.

Days upon days glided from us,
    As a dream they came and passed;
And I knew by the glee of the sailors,
    We were nearing home at last.
And they told me once, — they had wiled me
    Away from my uncle's side, —
That a fair girl was waiting for him:
    He was going home to a bride.

A morning came when a glory
    Seemed resting on the sea;
When the sun in the east was shining
    So bright and goldenly;
And its light on the human faces,
    That smilèd down on me
So kind and warm in their gladness,
    Was beautiful to see.

A glad man, that day, was my Uncle Rold,
    And he took me on his knee.
"Only one night," he whispered,
    "Only one night of sea;
And my darling shall live with her uncle,
    Never more to leave his side."
And there came such a soft light in his eyes;
    He was thinking of his bride!

Only one night of ocean!
    I was dreaming all that night
Of my own fair home in the valley,
    Of the roses red and white;
And, mingling with this dreaming,
    A vision came to me,
Of a gentle maiden waiting
    In an old house by the sea.

My dream was broken, and I awoke
    From those visions fair and sweet,
To hear, 'mid the roaring of the sea,
    The tramp of hurrying feet.
A storm had burst upon us, —
    As the lightning it had come;
And our Sea-Bird lay with broken wings,
    To sink in the sight of home!

We had sprung a leak, — it was gaining fast, —
    Man's skill was all in vain.
And we knew that our gallant Sea-bird
    Would never rise again.
Yet calmly the sailors manned the pumps,
    No lagging hand was there;
But they worked, as men whose doom is sealed,
    In calmness of despair.

They had taken me from my narrow berth,
    To a sheltered place on deck,
24

And I sat, half wondering, to see
    Our Sea-Bird such a wreck,
When an arm was folded round me,
    And I lay upon the breast
Of my Uncle Rold, and his cold lips
    Upon my brow were pressed.

" Darling, I never dreamed of this
    When they gave you unto me ;
I but thought of the joy I was bearing
    To my home beside the sea.
A joy to outlive the sorrow,
    A child to be all mine own ;
But God hath ordered it otherwise, —
    His holy will be done ! "

And he turned away., and left me ;
    He had other work to do ;
And I watched him as he moved among
    The worn and weary crew.
Watched him, with weary longing
    For the morn that would not come ;
And thinking how bitter a thing it was
    To perish in sight of home !

They had left the pumps, they had lowered the boats,
    They were rowing fast to lee ;
And I sat in the stern with my head bent down
    Upon my uncle's knee.
I felt him shudder, I heard him moan,
    I knew what it must be ;
But I did not speak ; I only kissed
    The hand that guarded me.

The morning dawned, but brought no hope with it ;
    For in the rear, far out to sea,
We saw the white line of the coming squall ;
    Vain all our strength must be.
Before us, some three miles, the lee-shore frowned,
    Fierce with its bristling rock ;
But we dared not hope to out-speed the gale, —
    We could not outlive its shock.

Wearily the sailors bent to their oars,
    Sadly they looked before ;
For they knew the tempest would burst o'er them
    Long ere they could reach the shore.

Close in my uncle's arms I lay,
    Weary, and faint, and chill;
But the weariness folded me to sleep,
    And I slept and dreamëd still.

I was dreaming of skies all pure and bright,
    Where never a cloud could be;
Of summer winds, and summer flowers,
    But never of the sea.
Was that the breath of summer winds?
    A hissing and a roar,
From the startled billows torn and dashed
    Upon the groaning shore?

A moment — and the tightened grasp
    Around my little form,
The water dashing o'er us, told we were
    At the mercy of the storm.
A moment — and the boat that bore us,
    Striking some hidden rock,
Was sinking, sinking from beneath us,
    Shattered by the shock.

A cry, that rang o'er the pitiless sea
    As if for aid, and then
A prayer of "God have mercy on us!"
    A cry of drowning men.
A flash across the darkness, lighting up
    The skies that seemed to frown, —
One look upon the pale face close to mine,
    And we went down — down — down.

Once more I breathed the sweet breath of the day,
    Once more I looked on the sun;
But its light was shining through honeysuckle;
    The day had but begun.
I was lying on a white, white couch,
    And roses, white and red,
Their soft bloom meeting mine eyes, were strewed
    On the pillow near my head.

I sought to rise, but I had no strength;
    So I lay all silently
Watching the sun-rays streaming in;
    How bright they seemed to me!

Slowly mine eyes turned from their glory,
   Gazing the chamber o'er,
But they fell on no familiar things,
   Waking memories of yore.

Each thing was strange that I looked upon,
   Save the roses red and white.
And they?   I thought their beauty must be
   A vision of the night.
Slowly I lifted my wasted hand
   To touch them; they were no dream;
And my thin, white fingers lingered there,
   In the warmth of a stray sunbeam.

Had I been dreaming a fearful dream?
   But no! I heard the roar
Of the mighty sea, its strong pulse beating
   Upon the rock-bound shore.
And in at the open window,
   On the sweet breath of the morn,
The sound that must haunt me evermore —
   The moan of the sea — was borne.

I closed mine eyes with a shudder;
   All the horror came over me
Of that long, long strife with the waters,
   Of that sinking in the sea.
I thought of the arms that had held me;
   My hands grew white and cold;
And through my wan lips, all quivering,
   Broke a wild cry, — "Uncle Rold!"

"Darling," a low voice murmured,
   "He cannot come to you;
The dust of the valley is lying
   On that heart so good and true.
He saved your life, but he gave his own;
   Yet not all pitiless the sea,
Since it left one hour of life to him, —
   One hour, but all to me.

"Darling, he gave you unto me
   To be my very own;
Something to keep as a memory,
   To love when he was gone,
He loved you well," — the sweet lips quivered,
   The head sank down by my side.

I drew it close.   I knew all now;
    She would have been his bride!

She had been watching through all that night.
    How could the maiden sleep,
When the storm was abroad on the ocean,
    And *he* upon the deep?
She had watched all night, till the morning,
    Till, in the pale, gray light,
Up the narrow path from the sea-shore,
    There came a man in sight.

A man who staggered blindly,
    Yet kept the path from the shore;
Whose form swayed ever to and fro;
    Whose arms a burden bore.
Could her loving eyes deceive her?
    Could it be other than him?
Swiftly the true heart bore her on,
    Out into the morning dim.

Swiftly she crossed the narrow lawn,
    And the shape fell at her feet
With a face like Death's.   O God! O God!
    Had they parted thus to meet?
Her cry brought help, and they bore us in,
    My Uncle Rold and I.
Their care brought back the throb to my heart;
    He only came home to die.

To die on that tender, faithful heart;
    But it was passing sweet
To look once more in the loving eyes
    He had thought no more to meet.
To feel the clasp of that little hand;
    It was much to be so blest.
But life was fleeting; those arms beloved
    But cradled him to his rest.

Calmly, patiently, she let him go,
    She had no power to save;
Meekly and sadly, a broken flower,
    She followed him to his grave,
Then sought her silent home again,
    And nursed me back to life;
But the fever-spot on her own cheek told
    Of the ceaseless inward strife.

Slowly the spring had vanished,
    And the days came, long and sweet,
When wandering through the wild woods brought
    No weariness to my feet.
I was strong again; but a whisper,
    If fraught with names I loved,
Was pain to my spirit, and my heart
To passionate anguish moved.

But I woke from my grief o'er the past,
    To a grief that was not old;
For I saw how a cheek was growing pale,
    And a white hand icy-cold.
I saw the light in some dark eyes shining
    Too gloriously for earth,
And I felt the coming shadow stealing
    Dark on our quiet hearth.

Dearly I loved the dying,
    But I knew that she must go
To the land where *he* was waiting, —
    That it was better so.
And I schooled my heart to patience
    That I might not give her pain;
And I gathered her roses daily;
    They would not bloom for her again.

I would bring them to her pillow,
    Morning, noon, and night;
For their sweetness gave her pleasure;
    Their beauty was delight.
She seemed to live on their perfume,
    But they withered in her hand.
Alas, she, too, was fading,
    Passing to the Better Land.

She lingered on through the summer;
    Ere the autumn she was gone,
And I, in that old house by the sea,
    Was left to live alone, —
Alone with the crowding fancies,
    That teemed within my brain;
Alone with my bitter sorrow,
    Alone with its gnawing pain.

Slowly the years went from me,
    No memories to them cling;

And I grew up into womanhood,
    A quiet little thing.
As a child, I had known no children, —
    I was older than my years;
As a woman, there was not one to care
    For my smiling or my tears.

Yet once there was other dreaming,
    A passionate dream and sweet;
But its fair and golden palace
    Was soon shattered at my feet.
It rose, as if built by magic,
    Stately, and grand, and fair;
But it fell, — the ruin lies on my heart, —
    As a castle in the air.

It was but a dream of loving,
    A thought that I was beloved.
Ere my heart had learned all its glory,
    Its gossamer strength was proved,
And it perished in an hour.
    Only my heart was strong,
And its veiling folds were drawn tight and close
    Over that ruin, long.

I scarce remember how we met,
    Some every-day event,
Nor where my heart first burst the bonds
    That its outward flow had pent.
But the day of full awakening
    Was dark, and deadly, and cold;
And my soul sunk deep in the bitter flood
    Where despair's wild waters rolled.

Well I remember the morning, —
    A morning of sweet June;
When gladness seemed radiant on all things,
    And all with my heart in tune.
He came to me, mournful and silent,
    A shadow upon his face,
Flung there by a feeling I dreamed not of,
    And knew not how to trace.

Long he sat, 'neath the roses
    That blossomed overhead,
Mournful, and pale, and silent,
    As if a hope were dead.

Then he spoke of his love for *another*,
  But her father said him nay;
And this other was young and loving,
  And beautiful as day!

But I was never beautiful, —
  Quiet, and seeming cold,
He looked upon the outside mould,
  And thought not of the gold
Deep buried beneath that surface rough.
  Perchance 'twas better so.
Had he known how the heart was throbbing
  He might have guessed its woe.

But he looked on my face; — the moment's pain
  Might well have been written there;
Yet it told no tale of the hidden love
  Crushed in its own despair.
And he turned away, with perhaps a thought
  That some olden memory
Had burst from its grave, and brought to me
  A passing agony.

A passing pang, — it could be no more, —
  And he lightly turned to greet
A fairy form that came dancing in
  On small and fairy feet.
Why did my fingers tremble so?
  What made mine eyes so dim?
But I *smiled* when I met her soft brown eyes;
  I loved her for loving him.

I thought "he shall be happy,"
  And I did it as I planned;
Working silently and secretly;
  And he never knew whose hand
Had shattered all the barriers
  That rose athwart his path;
Had given him his fairy bride
  And soothed her father's wrath.

For a little time there was darkness,
  Where shone not even a star;
When life was bitter and deadly,
  And Heaven seemed very far.

But the shadow passed; I was strong again,
    And my days went by the same
As in the olden quiet time
    Before the wild dream came.

Slowly the years went from me;
    I know not how they went;
With my silent life and its duties
    I had made myself content.
I had dreams, but they scarcely wandered,
    I could hold them in my hand.
I had dreams but of those who were at rest
    At home in the Better Land!

I had wealth, but I cared not for it,
    Save for books it brought to me;
And I never thought of wandering
    From my home beside the sea.
I had neighbors, and they sought me,
    But we were not closest friends.
Still the heart must cling to something;
    It breaketh, or it bends.

And I cared for the children;
    Ever they came to me,
And my silent home grew cheerful
    Amid their noise and glee.
I taught them many a lesson
    Of life's sweet charities,
And they paid me back in golden coin;
    What had I been but for these?

God bless the little children,
    For the joy they brought to me;
For the life made sweet by their lovingness,
    The heart made glad by their glee!
The earth had brought sorrow unto me,
    Dark were its teachings all;
But their twining fingers, unconsciously,
    Had lifted the heavy pall.

God bless the little children,
    And love them evermore!
For they taught me life's hardest lesson,
    Not doubting to adore.

They made me see that a Father's hand
  Had been with me all the way
I had travelled o'er; and I looked beyond
  To the slowly dawning day.

God bless the little children!
  They came from him to me,
Bringing peace to my weary spirit
  And hope for eternity.
I have lived out threescore years and ten,
  But my heart hath not grown old;
And I shall love the little children
  Till my life is a tale that's told.

THE END.

NEW BOOKS

And New Editions Recently Published by
CARLETON, Publisher,
NEW YORK.

Victor Hugo.

LES MISÉRABLES.—The celebrated novel. One large 8vo volume, paper covers, $2.00 ; . . . cloth bound, $2.50

LES MISÉRABLES.—In the Spanish language. Fine 8vo. edition, two vols., paper covers, $4.00 ; . . cloth bound, $5.00

JARGAL.—A new novel. Illustrated. . 12mo cloth, $1.75

THE LIFE OF VICTOR HUGO.—By himself. . 8vo. cloth, $1.75

Miss Muloch.

JOHN HALIFAX.—A novel. With illustration. 12mo. cloth, $1.75

A LIFE FOR A LIFE.— . do. do. $1.75

Charlotte Bronte (Currer Bell).

JANE EYRE.—A novel. With illustration. 12mo cloth, $1.75

THE PROFESSOR.— do. . . do. . do. $1.75

SHIRLEY.— . do. . do. . do. $1.75

VILLETTE.— . do. . do. . do. $1.75

Hand-Books of Society.

THE HABITS OF GOOD SOCIETY; with thoughts, hints, and anecdotes, concerning nice points of taste, good manners, and the art of making oneself agreeable. The most entertaining work of the kind. . . . 12mo. cloth, $1.75

THE ART OF CONVERSATION.—With directions for self-culture. A sensible and instructive work, that ought to be in the hands of every one who wishes to be either an agreeable talker or listener. . . . . 12mo. cloth, $1.50

ARTS OF WRITING, READING, AND SPEAKING.—An excellent book for self-instruction and improvement . . 12mo, cloth, $1.50

THE ART OF AMUSING.—With 150 illustrations. 12mo, cloth, $2.00

FRIENDLY COUNSEL FOR GIRLS.—A charming book. $1.50

Robinson Crusoe.

A handsome illustrated edition, complete. 12mo, cloth, $1.50

Mrs. Mary J. Holmes' Works.

'LENA RIVERS.—	A novel.	12mo. cloth,	$1.50
DARKNESS AND DAYLIGHT.—	do.	do.	$1.50
TEMPEST AND SUNSHINE.—	do.	do.	$1.50
MARIAN GREY.—	do.	do.	$1.50
MEADOW BROOK.—	do.	do.	$1.50
ENGLISH ORPHANS.—	do.	do.	$1.50
DORA DEANE.—	do.	do.	$1.50
COUSIN MAUDE.—	do.	do.	$1.50
HOMESTEAD ON THE HILLSIDE.—	do.	do.	$1.50
HUGH WORTHINGTON.—	do.	do.	$1.50
THE CAMERON PRIDE.—	do.	do.	$1.50
ROSE MATHER.—*Just Published.*	do.	do.	$1.50

Miss Augusta J. Evans.

BEULAH.—A novel of great power.		12mo. cloth,	$1.75
MACARIA.—	do.	do.	do.	$1.75
ST. ELMO.—	do.	do. *Just Published.*	do.	$2.00

By the Author of "Rutledge."

RUTLEDGE.—A deeply interesting novel.		12mo. cloth,	$1.75
THE SUTHERLANDS.—	do.	do.	$1.75
FRANK WARRINGTON.—	do.	do.	$1.75
ST. PHILIP'S.—	do.	do.	$1.75
LOUIE'S LAST TERM AT ST. MARY'S.—		do.	$1.75
ROUNDHEARTS AND OTHER STORIES.—For children.	do.	$1.75
A ROSARY FOR LENT.—Devotional Readings.	do.	$1.75

Captain Mayne Reid's Works—Illustrated.

THE SCALP HUNTERS.—	A romance.	12mo. cloth,	$1.75
THE RIFLE RANGERS.—	do.	do.	$1.75
THE TIGER HUNTER.—	do.	do.	$1.75
OSCEOLA, THE SEMINOLE.—	do.	do.	$1.75
THE WAR TRAIL.—	do.	do	$1.75
THE HUNTER'S FEAST.—	do.	do.	$1.75
RANGERS AND REGULATORS.—	do.	do.	$1.75
THE WHITE CHIEF.—	do.	do.	$1.75
THE QUADROON.—	do.	do.	$1.75
THE WILD HUNTRESS.—	do.	do.	$1.75
THE WOOD RANGERS.—	do.	do.	$1.75
WILD LIFE.—	do.	do.	$1.75
THE MAROON.—	do.	do.	$1.75
LOST LEONORE.—	do.	do.	$1.75
THE HEADLESS HORSEMAN.—	do.	do.	$1.75
THE WHITE GAUNTLET.— *Just Published.*	do.	$1.75

A. S. Roe's Works.

A LONG LOOK AHEAD.— A novel.	12mo. cloth,	$1.50
TO LOVE AND TO BE LOVED.— do. . .	do.	$1.50
TIME AND TIDE.— do. . .	do.	$1.50
I'VE BEEN THINKING. — do. . .	do.	$1.50
THE STAR AND THE CLOUD.— do. . .	do.	$1.50
TRUE TO THE LAST.— do. . .	do.	$1.50
HOW COULD HE HELP IT ?— do. . .	do.	$1.50
LIKE AND UNLIKE.— do. . .	do.	$1.50
LOOKING AROUND.— do. . .	do.	$1.50
WOMAN OUR ANGEL.— do. . .	do.	$1.50
THE CLOUD ON THE HEART.—*In Press.* .	do.	$1.50

Orpheus C. Kerr.

THE ORPHEUS C. KERR PAPERS.—Three vols.	12mo. cloth,	$1.50
SMOKED GLASS.—New comic book. Illustrated.	do.	$1.50
AVERY GLIBUN.—A powerful new novel.—	8vo. cloth,	$2.00

Richard B. Kimball.

WAS HE SUCCESSFUL ?— A novel.	12mo. cloth,	$1.75
UNDERCURRENTS.— do. . .	do.	$1.75
SAINT LEGER.— do. . .	do.	$1.75
ROMANCE OF STUDENT LIFE.—do. . .	do.	$1.75
IN THE TROPICS.— do. . .	do.	$1.75
HENRY POWERS, Banker.—*Just Published.*	do.	$1.75

Comic Books—Illustrated.

ARTEMUS WARD, His Book.—Letters, etc.	12mo. cl.,	$1.50
DO. His Travels—Mormons, etc.	do.	$1.50
DO. In London.—Punch Letters.	do.	$1.50
JOSH BILLINGS ON ICE, and other things.—	do.	$1.50
DO. His Book of Proverbs, etc.	do.	$1.50
WIDOW SPRIGGINS.—By author " Widow Bedott."	do.	$1.75
FOLLY AS IT FLIES.—By Fanny Fern. . .	do.	$1.50
CORRY O'LANUS.—His views and opinions. .	do.	$1.50
VERDANT GREEN.—A racy English college story.	do.	$1.50
CONDENSED NOVELS, ETC.—By F. Bret Harte.	do.	$1.50
THE SQUIBOB PAPERS.—By John Phœnix. .	do.	$1.50
MILES O'REILLY.—His Book of Adventures. .	do.	$1.50
DO. Baked Meats, etc. .	do.	$1.75

" Brick " Pomeroy.

SENSE.—An illustrated vol. of fireside musings.	12mo. cl.,	$1.50
NONSENSE.— do. do. comic sketches.	do.	$1.50

Joseph Rodman Drake.

THE CULPRIT FAY.—A faery poem. . .	12mo. cloth,	$1.25
THE CULPRIT FAY.—An illustrated edition. 100 exquisite illus-		
trations. . . 4to., beautifully printed and bound.		$5.00

New American Novels.

TEMPLE HOUSE.—By Mrs. Elizabeth Stoddard. 12mo. cl., $1.75
THE BISHOP'S SON.—By Alice Cary. . . do. $1.75
BEAUSEINCOURT.—By Mrs. C. A. Warfield. . do. $1.75
HOUSEHOLD OF BOUVERIE. do. do. . do. $2.00
HELEN COURTENAY.—By author "Vernon Grove." do. $1.75
PECULIAR.—By Epes Sargent. . . . do. $1.75
VANQUISHED.—By Miss Agnes Leonard. . do. $1.75
FOUR OAKS.—By Kamba Thorpe. . . . do. $1.75
MALBROOK.— . . . . . . do. $1.75

M. Michelet's Remarkable Works.

LOVE (L'AMOUR).—Translated from the French. 12mo. cl., $1.50
WOMAN (LA FEMME).— . do. . . do. $1.50

Ernest Renan.

THE LIFE OF JESUS.—Translated from the French. 12mo.cl.,$1.75
THE APOSTLES.— . . do. . . do. $1.75

Popular Italian Novels.

DOCTOR ANTONIO.—A love story. By Ruffini. 12mo. cl., $1.75
BEATRICE CENCI.—By Guerrazzi, with portrait. do. $1.75

Rev. John Cumming, D.D., of London.

THE GREAT TRIBULATION.—Two series. 12mo. cloth, $1.50
THE GREAT PREPARATION.— do. . do. $1.50
THE GREAT CONSUMMATION. do. . do. $1.50
THE LAST WARNING CRY.— . . do. $1.50

Mrs. Ritchie (Anna Cora Mowatt).

FAIRY FINGERS.—A capital new novel. . 12mo. cloth, $1.75
THE MUTE SINGER.— do. . do. $1.75
THE CLERGYMAN'S WIFE—and other stories. do. $1.75

Mother Goose for Grown Folks.

HUMOROUS RHYMES for grown people. . 12mo. cloth, 1 .25

T. S. Arthur's New Works.

LIGHT ON SHADOWED PATHS.—A novel. 12mo. cloth, $1.50
OUT IN THE WORLD.— . do. . . do. $1.50
NOTHING BUT MONEY.— . do. . . do. $1.50
WHAT CAME AFTERWARDS.— do. . . do. $1.50
OUR NEIGHBORS.— . do. . . do. $1.50

New English Novels.

WOMAN'S STRATEGY.—Beautifully illustrated. 12mo. cloth, $1.50
BEYMINSTRE.—By a popular author. . do. $1.75
"RECOMMENDED TO MERCY."— do. . . do. $1.75
WYLDER'S HAND.—By Sheridan Le Fanu. do. $1.75
HOUSE BY THE CHURCHYARD.— do. . do. $1.75

Edmund Kirke.

AMONG THE PINES.—Or Life in the South.   12mo. cloth, $1.50
MY SOUTHERN FRIENDS.—   do.   .   .   do. $1.50
DOWN IN TENNESSEE.—   do.   .   .   do. $1.50
ADRIFT IN DIXIE.—   do.   .   .   do. $1.50
AMONG THE GUERILLAS. —   do.   .   .   do. $1.50

Charles Reade.

THE CLOISTER AND THE HEARTH.—A magnificent new novel—
the best this author ever wrote.   .   8vo. cloth, $2.00

The Opera.

TALES FROM THE OPERAS.—A collection of clever stories, based
upon the plots of all the famous operas.   12mo. cloth, $1.50

Robert B. Roosevelt.

THE GAME-FISH OF THE NORTH.—Illustrated.   12mo. cloth, $2.00
SUPERIOR FISHING.—   do.   do. $2.00
THE GAME-BIRDS OF THE NORTH.—   .   .   do. $2.00

Hinton Rowan Helper.

THE IMPENDING CRISIS OF THE SOUTH.—   .   12mo. cloth, $2.00
NOJOQUE.—A Question for a Continent.   .   do. $2.00

Henry Morford.

PARIS IN '67.—Sketches of travel.   .   12mo. cloth, $1.75

From the German.

WILL-O'-THE-WISP.—A beautiful child's book.   12mo. cl., $1.50

The City of Richmond.

RICHMOND DURING THE WAR.—By a lady.   12mo. cloth, $1.75

Dr. J. J. Craven.

THE PRISON-LIFE OF JEFFERSON DAVIS.—Incidents and conversa-
tions during his captivity at Fortress Monroe. 12mo.cl.,$2.00

Captain Raphael Semmes.

THE CRUISE OF THE ALABAMA AND SUMTER. —   12mo. cloth, $2.00

John S. Mosby.

HIS LIFE AND EXPLOITS IN THE WAR.—With portraits. do. $1.75

Walter Barrett, Clerk.

THE OLD MERCHANTS OF NEW YORK. — Personal incidents,
sketches, bits of biography, and events in the life of leading
merchants in New York City. Four series. 12mo. cl., $1.75

Madame Octavia Walton Le Vert.

SOUVENIRS OF TRAVEL.—New edition. Large 12mo. cloth, $2.00

H. T. Sperry.

COUNTRY LOVE *vs.* CITY FLIRTATION.—A capital new Society tale,
with 20 superb illustrations by Hoppin. 12mo. cloth, $2.00

Miscellaneous Works.

MADEMOISELLE MERQUEM.—By George Sand.   12mo. cl., $1.75
LOVE IN LETTERS.—A fascinating collection.   do. $2.00
A BOOK ABOUT LAWYERS.—From London edition. do. $2.00
LAUS VENERIS.—Poems by Algernon Swinburne. do. $1.75
OUR ARTIST IN CUBA.—By Geo. W. Carleton.   do. $1.50
OUR ARTIST IN PERU.—   do.   do.   do. $1.50
HOW TO MAKE MONEY, and How to Keep It.—   do. $1.50
FAIRFAX.—A novel. By John Esten Cooke.   do. $1.75
HILT TO HILT.—   do.   do.   do. $1.75
THE LOST CAUSE REGAINED.—By Edw. A. Pollard. do. $1.50
MARY BRANDEGEE.—A novel. By Cuyler Pine.   do. $1.75
RENSHAWE.—   do.   do.   do. $1.75
THE SHENANDOAH.—History of the Conf. steamer. do. $1.50
MEMORIALS OF JUNIUS BRUTUS BOOTH.—(The Elder.) do. $1.50
MOUNT CALVARY.—By Matthew Hale Smith.   do. $2.00
LOVE-LIFE OF DR. E. K. KANE AND MARGARET FOX.   do. $1.75
BALLADS.—By the author of "Barbara's History." do. $1.50
MAN, and the Conditions that Surround Him.   do. $1.75
PROMETHEUS IN ATLANTIS.—A prophecy.   .   do. $2.00
TITAN AGONISTES.—An American novel.   .   do. $2.00
PULPIT PUNGENCIES.—Witticisms from the Pulpit. do. $1.75
CHOLERA.—A handbook on its treatment and cure. do. $1.00
ALICE OF MONMOUTH.—By Edmund C. Stedman.   do. $1.25
NOTES ON SHAKSPEARE.—By Jas. H. Hackett.   do. $1.50
THE MONTANAS.—A novel. By Mrs. S. J. Hancock. do. $1.75
PASTIMES WITH LITTLE FRIENDS.—Martha H. Butt. do. $1.50
LIFE OF JAMES STEPHENS.—Fenian Head-Centre. do. $1.00
POEMS.—By Gay H. Naramore.   .   .   .   do. $1.50
GOMERY OF MONTGOMERY.—By C. A. Washburn.   do $2.00
POEMS.—By Mrs. Sarah T. Bolton.   .   .   do $1.50
CENTEOLA.—By author "Green Mountain Boys." do. $1.50
RED-TAPE AND PIGEON-HOLE GENERALS—   .   do. $1.50
TREATISE ON DEAFNESS.—By Dr. E. B. Lighthill. do. $1.50
AROUND THE PYRAMIDS.—By Gen. Aaron Ward.   do. $1.50
CHINA AND THE CHINESE.—By W. L. G. Smith.   do. $1.50
EDGAR POE AND HIS CRITICS.—By Mrs. Whitman. do. $1.00
MARRIED OFF.—An Illustrated Satirical Poem. do.   50 cts.
THE RUSSIAN BALL.—   do.   do.   do.   do. 50 cts.
THE SNOBLACE BALL.—   do.   do.   do.   do. 50 cts.
THE CITY'S HEART.   do.   do.   do.   do. $1.00
POEMS.—By Mrs. Virginia Quarles.   .   .   do. $1.00
AN ANSWER TO HUGH MILLER.—By T. A. Davies. do. $1.50
COSMOGONY.—By Thomas A. Davies.   .   8vo. $2.00
RURAL ARCHITECTURE.—By M. Field. Illustrated. do. $4.00

www.ingramcontent.com/pod-product-compliance
Lightning Source LLC
Chambersburg PA
CBHW021538110726
47902CB00004B/931